SPELLBINDING THRILLERS ...
TAUT SUSPENSE

Peter Abrahams

PRESSURE
DROP

AN ONYX BOOK

ONYX
Published by the Penguin Group
Penguin Books USA Inc., 375 Hudson Street,
New York, New York 10014, U.S.A.
Penguin Books Ltd, 27 Wrights Lane,
London W8 5TZ, England
Penguin Books Australia Ltd, Ringwood, Victoria, Australia
Penguin Books Canada Ltd, 2801 John Street,
Markham, Ontario, Canada L3R 1B4
Penguin Books (N.Z.) Ltd, 182–190 Wairau Road,
Auckland 10, New Zealand

Penguin Books Ltd, Registered Offices:
Harmondsworth, Middlesex, England

Published by Onyx, an imprint of New American Library, a division of Penguin Books USA Inc. Previously published in a Dutton edition.

First Onyx Printing, February 1991.
10 9 8 7 6 5 4 3 2 1

PUBLISHER'S NOTE
This is a work of fiction. Names, characters, places, and incidents either are the product of the author's imagination or are used fictiously, and any resemblance to actual persons, living or dead, events, or locales is entirely coincidental.

For my father

Thanks to Yara Cadwalader, Nika Sicotte Cohen, Dick Edwards, Herb Gilmore, Gisela Tillier and Peggy and Jeff for their help in answering various questions of fact. Any mistakes are mine.

Full fathom five thy father lies;
  Of his bones are coral made;
Those are pearls that were his eyes:
  Nothing of him that doth fade
But doth suffer a sea-change
Into something rich and strange.

—THE TEMPEST

The blue hole isn't blue. It is gray, even under a clear sky; just a quiet pond in the woods. Any of the village boys could skip a stone across it, but they never do. They don't go near the blue hole because a monster lives at the bottom. The fisherman even claims he has seen it; the fisherman who drinks a bottle of rum a day.

The villagers don't go near the blue hole, so no one observes the two men in ill-fitting rubber suits, slipping under the surface and sinking down in the clear water. Each diver uncoils a long rope as he descends, one end tied to his weight belt, the other to a tree by the pond. The ropes make them feel secure.

At 50 feet, the water smells like rotten eggs and turns red. A little deeper and it is odorless and black. The men are prepared: one has a torch. He switches it on. They swim down a yellow barrel of light.

At 122 feet, they enter a cave. They have been in it before. Their supplies are waiting by the back wall. The cave is narrow. There is room for only one man to work. The other man shines the torch.

These are smart men, but untrained in the use of underwater equipment. They make mistakes. First, they don't realize how quickly a working man can exhaust his air. Second, the man with the torch forgets to shine it on the working man's pressure gauge; he shines it on the man's hands instead. So there is no warning. The working man, already breathing hard with exertion, has not noticed the extra strain of his last few breaths. He breathes in, breathes out, breathes in: and nothing comes. He drops the rocks from his hands, turns to the other man, makes gestures in the cone of light. Frantic gestures. The man with the torch doesn't understand, backs away. The working man panics and grabs at his companion's regulator. He misses it, and knocks the torch out of his companion's hand. It falls. The light goes off. They are blind.

The man with no air clings to the man with air. They are wedged together at the back of the cave, bodies and ropes entangled. Now the man with the air panics too. He reaches for his knife, finds it, hacks at any rope he can feel. He is in such a frenzy that some time passes before he realizes he is free; in utter darkness in a cave in the blue hole that isn't blue, but free.

|HENRIK|

|1|

He knew the ceiling so well. Its soft white smoothness, a perfect screen for the unreeling of his aquatic daydreams, was marred only by a single hair pulled from a painter's brush and caught in the matte finish. The hair didn't bother him. It gave him something to focus on in all that vast bleakness. What did bother him was the spider web in the corner, directly above his head, and the fat brown spider, leaning over the curve of the gilded molding. Sometimes the spider rubbed the tips of its two front legs together, as if knowing something delightful and a little nasty was about to happen.

He was an expert on the ceiling. The problem was he didn't know what room he lay in.

A muffled footfall. His hearing, like his vision, had become acute. It picked up the tiny metallic squeak of the doorknob turning. The spider ducked back behind the molding. Then a draft touched his face, cooling it; the door had opened. Somewhere music played. He longed for music. This was Wayne Newton, singing "Viva Las Vegas." He longed for music, and when it came he got Wayne Newton. He wanted to laugh. He laughed on the inside. The door closed, cutting off the singer in mid-tremolo.

Footsteps approached. He believed he knew whose they were, but when no face came into view, he began to doubt. On the lower edge of his vision, where everything grew blurry, he thought he saw a liver-spotted hand. Then it was gone. He couldn't be sure.

Cool air curled around his body; the cover had been pulled back. Dry fingertips brushed over his stomach. They manipulated something, fingertips dry as cracked old paper. Then a long hard foreign body was drawn slowly out of him. The relief was immense, breathtaking. It was almost too much to bear.

But the manipulation hadn't ceased. The dry hand gripped him, not gently, not roughly: purposefully. It began to move in purposeful ways. The liver-spotted hand: *God, God,* he wanted to cry out at the top of his lungs. But he was silent, and his autonomous flesh responded in a fleshly manner. The pleasure came in a spasm of despair; for an instant he felt something cold and smooth, like glass. Then it was over.

Footsteps withdrew. The doorknob squeaked. The opening door sucked fresh air into the room. No music played. The door closed. He heard a single footfall. Then silence.

The spider crept out over the curve of the molding. It rubbed its two front legs together for a while. *Could no one see it? Could no one see the web, and with a flick of a broom sweep it away?*

The spider rounded the curve of the molding and started walking down the wall. It came closer. Then it passed out of his range of vision. He waited to feel its legs in his hair, on his face.

While he waited, he looked at the ceiling. It turned blue, deep-sea blue. He hated the sea and always had, how it rose and fell like a breathing thing. He dropped into it, down, down. Green eels stretched toward him, watching him with their little eyes, watching him sink. He sank. A leather suitcase tumbled slowly by until all he could see were its brass corners reflecting the occasional gleam of watery sunlight from far below, like lost coins.

|2|

All happy families suck. Unhappy families suck too."

At 6:47 on the morning of her thirty-ninth birthday, Nina Kitchener stared at those eight words. They made up the entire first paragraph of the manuscript on her breakfast table: *Living Without Men and Children . . . and Loving It*, by Lois Filer, Ph.D. A glob of no-sugar, no-fat, no-taste marmalade slid off Nina's pumpernickel bagel and onto the page. She tried to brush it off, but instead smeared an orange crescent through the second paragraph, like the mark of some far-gone editor.

Taking the manuscript, Nina went into the little room she used for an office and climbed on the Lifecycle. She turned the pages as she pedaled. Page 7: "The time has come for new modalities. If you can't have it all, what do you really want?" Page 160: "Ask yourself: are you living for others, or are you living for you? If you're living for others, then think about this: *Who is living for you?* Do you still want to be thinking about that when you finally realize the answer is no one *and it's too late?*"

In ten minutes, Nina had absorbed the gist of the manuscript; in twenty she'd cycled 7.3 miles. With a red pin, she marked her progress on a large wall map of the world. She was cycling from Paris to Rangoon. The red pin put her into the heart of the Hindu Kush. Next week she would be in Pakistan, in a month, Kashmir. Nina went into the bathroom, where she brushed her teeth with a secret formula anti-plaque paste probably not for sale in the Khyber Pass. She had the best of both worlds.

The teeth in the mirror were good teeth, not as white as the capped teeth that Dr. Pearl, her dentist with three alimonies to pay, kept touting, but white enough for real ones. The hair was good hair—dark brown, thick, healthy—and subtly cut by Sherman of Sherman's at a hundred dollars a pop, not counting tip. The face? Safe to say that it was not: aristocratic or peasant; hawk-nosed or snub-nosed; sexpot or cutesy; arrogant or submissive. And that it was: intelligent; well-proportioned; middle-class; the kind of face that might turn up in an early Manet. Would it be too much to suppose that the big dark eyes would have given him a chance to show off a little?

Nina, looking in the mirror, wasn't dwelling on all that. She was searching for signs of being thirty-nine. There were plenty of those, but none that could be called lines, except by an unfriendly viewer. Still, she could see where the lines were going to be. Enough. She splashed her face with cold water, rubbed hard with a towel, dressed, stuffed *Living Without* in her briefcase, and rode the elevator down thirty-five floors to the streets of Manhattan.

"Morning, Ms. Kitchener," said Jules, holding the door for her. He was dressed like a Swiss Guard, only a little more gaudy. "Lovely morning," he added, almost as though he meant it, which wasn't like him at all, and Nina, walking out into eighteen degrees and driving snow, remembered that it was the Monday after Thanksgiving: the start of tipping season.

Nina walked to work, sharing the sidewalks with stiff-legged masses hunched miserably into the wind, everyone's vapor breath rising in the air like cartoonists' balloons empty of dialogue. She made eye contact with nobody except a motionless man in rags at the corner of Third and Forty-ninth who suddenly swayed toward her and whispered, "Merry fucking Christmas." No one else took any note of him.

Thirty-nine. Three nine. As she walked, Nina imagined the digits tolling like village bells in a Frankenstein movie. In fact, she was still clinging to the last few hours of thirty-eight. She hadn't been born until noon. Then had come twenty happy years, a period closed by the death of her mother from breast cancer, made remote by the death of

her father a few years later from colon cancer. That was
Act One, The Nuclear Family. Then, with some overlap,
came Act Two, The Boyfriends. This wasn't the right word
to describe them—one of The Boyfriends had been fifty-
two, at least he had said he was, although he had sometimes looked older, especially on the fatal day when he
and Nina encountered his daughters on the nude beach at
the Club Med in Tahiti—but there was no right word.
"Lover" was too specific, "friend" too general, "para-
mour" too operatic, "mate" not operatic enough, "significant other" too much like something John Cleese might
have sneered at on "Fawlty Towers."

The Boyfriends: David, who left her for an ashram in
Marin County; Richard, whom she left for Lenny; Lenny,
who went back to his wife; Alvie, who took drugs; Marc,
who took her money; Zane, who came too soon; another
Richard, who never came; Ken, who talked about a mén-
age à trois whenever he had too much to drink, which
turned out to be most of the time.

Those were the ones she had been serious about. The
others were better forgotten. The Boyfriends themselves
were probably better forgotten too, but that would mean
forgetting large parts of her own history. David, Richard,
Lenny, Alvie, Marc, Zane, Richard the Second, Ken.
They defined her past in seemingly comprehensible periods, like a genealogy of the kings of some troubled state.

Now they were overthrown. Nina was out of the boyfriend game for good. The business had given her the
strength to do that. Once in a while there was a setback—
a Boyfriend might pop up, at a nearby restaurant table
perhaps, or in a bad dream. But she could handle that.
She was on her own. Living without men and children.
She wanted to find out more about the "and loving it"
part.

The office was a four-story brownstone with a little iron
railing out front, a little brass plaque that said KITCHENER
AND BEST by the door and a mortgage like the rock of
Sisyphus. A furious-looking Pekingese was defecating at
the base of the first stair. A woman in a mink coat and
fluffy pink slippers held the dog's leash. "Hurry up, you
little prick," she said, snapping the animal into line behind
her the moment it had finished.

"Jesus Christ," Nina said, stepping over a turd that

seemed grossly out of proportion to the size of its maker, and entering the building.

Jason Best was at the front desk, on the phone. Behind him, a computer was blinking a screenful of multicolored nonsense. "Please hold," Jason said, punching a button. "Please hold." Punch. "Please hold." He glanced up at Nina, giving her the kind of bemused look Cary Grant used to deliver so well. Jason resembled Cary Grant in other ways too—a little taller, perhaps, a little darker, a little more handsome. "There's a fuck-up on the L.I.R.R.," he said to Nina, covering the mouthpiece. "Amalia won't be in till noon."

"There's dog shit by the door."

"Ick," Jason said, and punched another button. "Kitchener and Best. Please hold."

The morning papers were on the desk. The *Post* said: "SEX MANIAC WOUNDS 3, SHOOTS SELF, PIT BULL." Nina took it outside and cleaned up the mess. Then she went up to her office on the top floor.

Jason hadn't mentioned that it was already occupied. That wasn't the way he worked. Two women sat on the couch by the window. They might have been about her own age, perhaps slightly older. One had long salt-and-pepper hair; the other had blond hair, cut very short, and wore glasses with oversize frames.

"Hello," the salt-and-pepper one said. "I think we're a little early."

"The snow and all," the other added. "We weren't sure how long it would take."

"womynpress?" Nina asked, wondering how to vocalize the lowercase *w* used in their cover letter.

"That's us," said salt-and-pepper. "I'm Brenda Singer-Atwell, publisher."

"M. Eliot," said the other. "Editor-in-chief. And you're Nina Kitchener, right?"

"Right."

"We've heard good things about you, Nina," said Brenda.

"From who?"

"Everybody," replied M. "Gloria, for one."

"Gloria Steinem?"

M. nodded.

"That's funny. I don't really know her."

"Well, the word is out—you're the medium to the media," said Brenda. "Did you have time to go over our manuscript?"

"Yes," Nina said, sitting at her desk. "Like some coffee?"

"Great," said Brenda. M. nodded.

Nina picked up the phone and buzzed downstairs. "Rosie called in sick," Jason said. "The NBC guy wants to make it at four instead of five, and Amalia won't be in till two." The pressure was on; Jason's voice was rising into a register Cary Grant never used, not even when helicopters were chasing him.

"Any coffee?" Nina said.

"Coffee?" asked Jason.

"In the machine."

Brenda and M. were watching her closely; at least, Brenda was—M.'s enormous glasses were reflecting the light, masking her eyes.

"I'll check."

"Thanks." Nina put down the phone.

M. turned her head slightly, revealing her eyes. Sharp ones, and they were indeed looking closely at Nina. "New coffee boy?" she asked.

"That was Jason Best," Nina said. "My partner." The sharp eyes shifted away and Nina realized her voice had gotten hard.

A few seconds passed in silence before Brenda said: "So what did you think?"

Nina took the manuscript from her briefcase, placed a yellow legal pad beside it. "Before we start, I have to explain that this initial consultation costs one hundred dollars. After, if you decide to proceed with us, it's two-fifty an hour, plus expenses. Expenses vary, but we don't do anything big—like travel, entertainment—without checking with you first."

Brenda and M. looked at each other.

"We were told," M. said, "that you had a less . . . exacting fee structure for feminist organizations."

"Who told you that?"

"Several people."

"Gloria Steinem?"

M. opened her mouth to say yes, but Brenda said, "No," before she could.

"Well, it's not true," Nina said. "Our fee structure is set." She tried to stop herself from adding, "Exacting or not," and almost did. Maybe after a few more birthdays she'd be able to.

Brenda and M. were looking at each other again. Silently and quickly they came to a decision. Nina saw how they worked: like a good lion tamer act. M. made trouble and Brenda ran the show.

"It's a deal," Brenda said.

"The clock is ticking," M. added.

Nina turned to her. "One. The manuscript is badly written. It doesn't have to be art, but it has to be better than this. That's your territory. Two. There's not enough anecdotal material, especially in the first two chapters. They're too theoretical, too boring. That's where you need the personal stuff, up front. Three. You've got to have an introduction, written by somebody who's well known and as mainstream as possible. Preferably a man."

"A man?" said M.

"Four. Tell the author to lose that Tolstoy parody or whatever the hell it is at the beginning. It's unnecessarily off-putting and it begs comparison with the big boys, comparison that reviewers won't find in her favor."

Brenda glanced at M. Faint pink patches appeared on M.'s face.

"Having said that," Nina went on, "there may be a market for this book. Demographically. There are lots of women in the boat she describes and they read books. You've got to sell them on the 'and loving it' part. That aspect of the book has to be completely rethought. Then, supposing you can make these changes, it will come down to two things—the personality of the author, that's the main one, and the package, important but secondary."

Brenda was writing rapidly in a notebook. M. was sitting very still, her jaw jutting out a little.

"Is Dr."—Nina glanced down at the manuscript—"Dr. Filer married, by any chance?"

"Of course not," M. said.

"Good. Any children?"

"No."

"What's her Ph.D. in?"

M. looked at Brenda. Brenda looked at M. M. said: "I'm not sure. Sociology, maybe. Does it matter?"

"Of course it matters," Nina said. "If it's in metallurgy you might as well bag it now."

Silence. M. looked at Brenda. Brenda said: "I understand you know people on the Donahue show."

"That's right. But they don't do me any favors, and I don't try to sell them anything that'll make Phil look like a jerk."

"Do you know him?" Brenda asked.

"I've met him. I don't know him."

M. stuck her jaw out a little farther. "But you called him Phil."

"Jesus. It would be a bit silly to call him *Mister* Donahue, wouldn't it?"

Jason came in, balancing three cups on a tray. "Coffee, tea, or me?" he said. Brenda looked at him blankly; M. with a stone face; Nina laughed.

They drank coffee. It was excellent, with a slight taste of walnut. Jason wasn't capable of making coffee like that; Nina knew he had sent out for it. Brenda and M. seemed to relax a little on the couch.

"I'd like to meet the author," Nina said.

Brenda smiled; a nice smile, not as dazzling as Jason's, but warm, and Nina sensed they could be friends. "We thought you might. She should be here any minute. I hope you don't mind."

"Not at all."

The phone buzzed. Nina picked it up. "Hello," she said.

"Mummy?" said a little boy. He was crying.

"Mummy?" said Nina.

The little boy's voice broke. "The man said my mummy was there."

"Just a minute." Nina looked up. "There's a child on the phone. Do either of you—" But Brenda was already up. She took the phone.

"It's Mummy," she said. "What's wrong, Fielding?" She listened. Nina heard more crying. M.'s foot tapped the carpet. "I'm sure she didn't mean that," Brenda said. "She's really a nice person. Don't cry, angel. I'll see you soon." Pause. "Not long. Right after work." Pause. "No, that's on Wednesdays. Today is Monday. I work the full day on Monday. Bye-bye."

She hung up. "Goddamned Gina," she said to M. And

to Nina, "We're having nanny problems. You don't know of a good one by any chance?"

"No," Nina said. "How many children have you got?"

"Two, but the older one's in school."

Nina turned to M. "What about you?"

"What about me what?"

"M. has a daughter," Brenda said.

"Who lives with her father," M. said, in a tone devoid of editorial comment. And is her name N.? Nina wanted to ask. But she didn't.

"And you?" Brenda said.

But before Nina could reply that she seemed to be the only one in the room who fit the target audience of the book they were pushing, Jason opened the door and said, "This way, please," to someone in the hall. Then the author walked in.

The author had a pleasant face, if a little too much of it. And there was much too much of the rest of the author—Nina's companion in the target audience, and candidate for television, where no one had yet invented a gizmo that stopped the camera from adding the obligatory ten pounds.

Why the hell did she have to be fat? Nina thought as they were introduced. Dr. Filer squeezed herself on the couch between her publishers. For one moment, Nina was afraid that some sort of Three Stooges–style slapstick was about to erupt. Instead Dr. Filer surprised her by saying: "I'm so glad you're able to see us. I'm here to learn." The surprise wasn't just in what she said, but in her voice, a soft Southern contralto that sent a clear message to Nina: radio.

"Fine," Nina said. "Sell me on the 'and loving it' part."

Dr. Filer smiled. She needed dental work. That could be bought. "It's simple," she said. "It's time women discovered what men have known for a long time—there's life beyond the home. Work, friends, self-fulfillment, even the life of the mind. If lots of women are going to end up alone in life, as seems certain to be the case, they might as well learn not to feel devastated about it. Women have taken some big steps in the last twenty years and the men haven't kept up. There aren't enough quality men out there, and that's not going to change very quickly."

It wasn't a bad answer, but it wasn't great, either. On

paper. But the voice was lovely, musical, soothing. The woman was handsome. They had time: time to fix the book, time to send her to a spa, time to get her teeth fixed.

"Okay," Nina said. "We've made a start. I'll send you a summarizing memo tomorrow and we can go on from there."

"Great," said Brenda.

"Wonderful," said Dr. Filer.

M. said nothing. She was looking at the marmalade smear on the first page of Nina's manuscript.

"By the way, Dr. Filer," Nina said, "I think we can do without that Tolstoy parody."

"I agree completely," Dr. Filer said sweetly. She smiled at M. "It wasn't in the original draft." The pink patches appeared again on M.'s cheeks.

They left. Nina called the Donahue show and spoke to Gordie. She and Gordie had worked together long ago in radio on "All Things Considered." Nina described the book and the author. Gordie promised to get back.

Nina worked. She had two more meetings, took phone calls, made phone calls, wrote the memo. Amalia never showed up. Rosie called to say she had a fever of a hundred and two and probably wouldn't be in tomorrow. Outside, night fell. Nina looked out the window, noticed for the first time that snow was still falling, fat flakes lit pink by the city's glow. Jason came into the room.

"Happy birthday," he said. He put a bottle of champagne on the table.

"Roederer Cristal," Nina said. "What did that cost?"

"You can't ask. It's a present. Enjoy."

"All right. Crack her open."

"I didn't mean now."

"Why not?"

"You want to drink it here? With me?"

"Who else?"

Nina brought wineglasses from the tiny third-floor kitchen. Jason poured. "Many more," he said.

"Yeah."

They drank champagne. Pink flakes fell. "Sorry about the impersonal quality of the gift," Jason said. "It's hard to know what to get you."

"Don't be silly. It's great."

They gazed out the window. Snow muffled the sounds

of the city. Nina put her feet on the desk and drained the
last of the champagne. Good champagne: it had the power
to stop time, or at least her caring about its passage. She
closed her eyes and felt warmth spread through her body.
For a moment, she was in touch with all the Ninas in her
life: little Nina, schoolgirl Nina, graduate student Nina,
career girl Nina, businesswoman Nina, and saw the essen-
tial Nina, as simple and clear as a line drawing. Or thought
she saw. The drink quickly lost its power. Nina opened
her eyes and found that Jason was watching her.

"What would you really like for your birthday?" he
asked.

"A baby," Nina said. The answer popped out on its
own: uninvited, unexpected, unnerving.

"A baby?"

Nina laughed, a strange, embarrassed laugh that didn't
sound like hers at all.

"Do you mean that?"

Nina didn't have a chance to answer. The door opened
and Jon came in. "Hi guys," he said. He gave Nina a shy
smile and Jason a kiss on the cheek. They left a few moments later.

Nina went down to the kitchen, poured herself a glass
of Scotch, and returned to her desk. She turned the pages
of Dr. Filer's manuscript. *The time has come for new modalities.*

The phone buzzed. Gordie. "Thumbs up," he said.

"Yeah?"

"They love it."

"They?"

"Everybody."

"Phil?"

"Everybody includes Phil." He lowered his voice. "And
vice versa," he added.

"My client will be ecstatic."

"And pay you appropriately, I trust. When's pub date?"

"When's your next opening?"

Gordie laughed. "I'll get back to you."

Nina sat at her desk. She finished the Scotch, poured
another, a small one. The snow stopped falling. The phone
stopped buzzing. The working day was over, even for the
diehards. Little Fielding had his mummy by now. Nina
rose, went downstairs, put on her coat and boots, locked

up, began walking home. She saw the night's TV schedule in her mind, laid out in handy boxes.

The streets were white and deserted, as though the slate had been wiped clean. Christmas plenty filled the stores, but everything was closed. Halfway home Nina paused outside an antique shop. A gleaming white rocking horse stood under a spotlight in the display window. It had a proud head with flared nostrils, a flowing jet-black mane and long jet-black tail, a fine red leather saddle and bridle. The horse even had a name, hand-tooled on the red stirrups: ACHILLES. Nina stared at it for a long time.

She heard a sound and turned. A man in rags approached, weaving through the snow. His watery eyes moved to her, to the rocking horse, back to her. Nina recognized him.

"Merry fucking Christmas," he said, and stumbled on.

3

"Top-notch cervix," said Dr. Berry when Nina had her legs together and her clothes back on. "Absolutely first-rate. No reason at all why it can't be done." Dr. Berry put on gold-rimmed reading glasses and ran his eyes down her chart. He was a wiry man with a ruddy face and pure white hair, very straight and very soft. A sign on his wall read: "Over 12,000 Delivered." He might have been a troubleshooter in Santa's workshop. "General health excellent, blood pressure excellent, no history of pelvic infection of any kind." He looked up. "Ever had pain during intercourse?"

Not physical, Nina thought. "No," she said.

Dr. Berry's eyes returned to the chart. "Abortions?" he asked.

"None."

Dr. Berry looked up and smiled. "Even if you said you had, I wouldn't believe it. Not with a cervix like that."

Nina was beginning to think it might be her best feature. "Don't you want to do any tests or anything?"

"Not necessarily, not at this stage, anyway. I'm not saying you're as fertile as you would have been at twenty-five. That would be nonsense. But who knows how fertile you would have been at twenty-five? You might have been a real queen bee. So if you're somewhat less fertile now, it really won't matter that much. It's like an aging pitcher who's lost a little off his fastball but can still get the job done. See what I mean?"

"Sure. I just have to go with the off-speed stuff. Move it in and out, up and down."

Dr. Berry put his glasses back on, blinked through them at her. "I could run some tests," he said in a cooler tone, "a uterotubogram, an endometrial biopsy. But they're not particularly pleasant and we have no reason to think that anything's broke yet. I suggest we get the ball in play first. How does that sound?"

"Good," Nina said. "But I haven't made up my mind about this. I'm just doing the research."

Dr. Berry peered at her over the rim of his glasses. Then he scanned the chart. "I see your birthday was last Monday."

"That's right."

He gazed at the chart for a long time before saying, "Forgive me, but did that set you thinking?"

"That, and other things. Even if I am a queen bee, time is running out, isn't it?"

Dr. Berry nodded.

"And aside from the whole fertility question, isn't there increasing risk to the baby?"

"That's true. But we'd do an amnio, other tests . . ." His voice trailed off. Nina thought she could follow his thinking: Down's syndrome, to abort or not to abort, months of misery, scars that lasted forever. It was a road she could easily imagine, and that he had probably been down many times. "But all that is secondary. Getting pregnant comes first. You're right to do research, right to take as much time as you need to make up your mind. But— and I'm not saying it's now or never—but . . ."

"Soon or never?"

He smiled. "That's it."

"There's one more thing," Nina said.

"What's that?"

"We'd need a father."

"I see."

"I was thinking of artificial insemination. That's why I came to you—I saw you quoted about it in the *Times*."

"They got everything wrong," Dr. Berry said.

"The picture wasn't bad."

"My wife hated it." Dr. Berry folded his hands on the desk and leaned toward her. "Do you have anyone in mind as a donor?"

There was Jason. He probably had one of the most dominant pulchritude genes ever known. But he was her partner. They already shared a business. Could they share a baby too? And did she even want a father in the picture? Besides, Jason was gay. What if there was a genetic component to gayness? Would she be just as happy with a gay child? That train of thought appalled her. It was as though it had steamed in from another mind. She had her first intimation of the magnitude of change a baby might bring.

"If you have to think that hard, the answer is probably no," Dr. Berry said.

"It's no."

"Then we'd have to get hold of some sperm." He tapped a pencil on the desk, wrote "sperm" on a notepad and drew a box around it. He added a flowerpot on top of the box and put a cactus in the pot.

"Do you make those arrangements?"

"What arrangements?"

"For the sperm?"

Dr. Berry shook his head. "But I can put you in touch with several places that do. The one I'd recommend is the Human Fertility Institute."

"Why?"

"I've had success with them in the past. They're well run, scientific and their fees are competitive."

"I have to pay for the sperm?"

"Certainly. Especially for theirs."

"Why is that?"

"All their donors—anonymous, of course—are men of accomplishment. Nobel Prize winners, successful artists, that kind of thing. It was a stipulation by the benefactor who set up the institute in the first place. Some of my patients have found that aspect off-putting, others not."

Nina found it off-putting. But why shouldn't the baby be as bright as possible? There it was again: another thought that didn't seem to originate in her own mind. "I don't know," she said. "I'll have to think."

"Take your time," he said.

"Within reason."

Dr. Berry smiled. "That's the ticket. Within reason."

He stopped smiling. "But do think about it. It's a big decision—how far you're prepared to go."

"I don't understand."

"To have a baby, I mean."

Toughness counted, Nina saw, even in Santa's workshop. "How far is too far?" she asked.

Dr. Berry sighed. "I don't know." The expression on his face changed: the M.D. mask softened a little, like wax gently heated. "But are we simply manufacturers of sperm and egg, products like any other for trade on the open market?" He waited for an answer. Nina didn't have one. "Sorry," he said. "I don't usually sermonize."

"Do you have children, Dr. Berry?"

"Four. Are you saying it's easy for me to say?"

"Not as baldly as that."

He laughed.

When Nina left Dr. Berry's office the sun was shining. She called Jason from a phone booth. "Do you need me this afternoon?"

"I need you all the time."

"But can you handle the rest of the day?"

"Sure. If the NBC guy stops bugging me. Also, those weirdos want an answer."

"What weirdos?"

"The ones pushing *Pumping Imaginary Iron: The Zen Guide to Bodybuilding*."

"Tell them yes if they can demo it, no if they can't."

"Demo?"

"If a skinny little guy in a dhoti can walk into a studio and lift a safe over his head, it's a go. Otherwise not."

"Check."

Nina started walking. She walked south for fifty blocks. Sometimes the sun shone between buildings and warmed her face; most of the time she walked in shadow. She looked at nothing except the question, which she examined from every angle. At five o'clock she was on Wooster Street, standing outside Gallery Bertie. Through the window, she could see Suze standing on a stepladder. Nina went inside.

"Hey," said Suze, adjusting a blue spotlight. "What are you doing on the loose at this hour?"

"Jason's in charge."

"Good God." Suze reached up and turned the spotlight a little.

"Isn't that skirt a bit short?" Nina asked.

"I remember things you wore that didn't even cover your ass."

"That was then."

"Tell me about it. There. How does that look?"

Nina followed the blue beam to the exhibit that ran along the far wall. It was a sculptural installation, showing three children in striped Auschwitz clothing standing behind barbed wire. Everything, the children, their clothes, the wire, a hut in the background, was made from parts of a pink 1957 Cadillac Eldorado.

"I couldn't tell you," Nina said. "Maybe the '64 Chevy would be better. More universal."

"Don't mock. The artist is brilliant. He's going to be a household name someday."

"Like Henry Ford?"

"And he's gorgeous to boot."

"Yeah?"

"But from Jason's side of the tracks."

"Of course."

Suze climbed down from the ladder. She wore lots of makeup, lots of jewelry and a coiffure that might have been her hairdresser's take on the barbed wire fence. But only partly hidden in all that were her eyes—amused, alive, sharp—eyes that a stranger might not have found comforting, but that Nina, who had known them for a long time and seen them in every possible mood, did.

"Let's eat," Nina said.

"Now?"

"Now."

They had hot and sour soup at Wang's. Suze drank Tsingtao. Nina had a glass of beaujolais, then another.

"What's up?" Suze said.

"What makes you think something's up?"

"The air is thick with clues. Must I enumerate them?"

"No."

Nina stirred her soup. "Do you ever think about having a baby, Suze?"

"You know I don't."

"I know you say you don't. But do you?"

"No."

"Never?"

"No."

"Not late at night, or when you see a baby in a stroller or something?"

"No, no, a thousand times no. What do you want from me?"

"I think about it a lot lately."

Suze's eyes narrowed. "Who's the lucky fella?"

"You know there's no lucky fella."

"Then that's that, absent immaculate conception."

"That's what I'm looking into. Now they call it artificial insemination." Nina described her visit to Dr. Berry.

Suze picked up her beer bottle and drained what was left in one swallow. Then she said: "When was the last time you got laid?"

"What has that got to do with anything?" The bartender turned to look at them.

"It has a lot to do with it. There's no man in your bed, you just turned thirty-nine, you read all this retro bullshit about biological clocks and the new conservatism, you deal with a bunch of shallow assholes every day of your life— it's no surprise that all of a sudden you're in a panic. I think you should go see Lisa's therapist. She's very good."

"I don't need a therapist." The bartender turned to look again. So did a Chinese man with green hair sitting a few tables away. "The problem's objective, not subjective."

"And a baby will fix it?"

"Why not? Is it so unnatural to want a baby?"

"It would be perverse in your case. You've worked like a slave building that business, you've got a great reputation in certain circles, you're going to be able to write your own ticket in a few years. Do you want to throw that all away for the pleasure of losing your figure and mopping up shit and puke all day?"

"I wouldn't have to give up anything."

"That's twaddle and you know it."

"I could cut back a bit. We could build a little nursery on the second floor, where Rosie's office is. She doesn't need all that space."

"Now you're going to talk nesting. You're making me sick."

"What's sick about it? I don't want to be a teenager forever."

Suze went pale. "Let's change the subject," she said.

But there was no other subject. Nina picked up the bill, Suze insisted on paying her half and they left a few minutes later, parting at Wang's door; Suze headed for the Auschwitz Cadillac, Nina for home.

She walked all the way. She'd been doing a lot of walking since Monday, but it didn't seem to tire her. Jules let her in.

"Nice night," he said. She hadn't noticed. There was liquor on his breath. She poured some for herself when she got inside her apartment.

It was a nice apartment. It had cost her two hundred thousand dollars five years ago. The furnishings and rugs were nice too, and the art was nice as well, thanks to Suze. The Lifecycle was nice. The bed was nice. She lay in it, and pulled up the covers.

Soon she was crying. She cried for a long time. She had never missed her mother more than she did that night.

|4|

The Human Fertility Institute was a marble-faced palace
on the Upper East Side. It sported excrescences from various architectural periods and a sign attesting to its status
as a national landmark. It had a leather-padded front door
which Nina could barely force open and, in the lobby, an
oil painting of a pink-cheeked man who might have been
a nineteenth-century robber baron except that his suit was
too modern and his chin too weak.

A Christmas tree stood under the portrait. The people
around it had drinks in their hands. The Chipmunks were
singing their Christmas song, the one in which Alvin hopes
for a hula hoop. It didn't sound very danceable, but a few
couples had rolled back a huge Persian rug and were dancing to it anyway. Nina approached a woman dressed in a
nurse's outfit. The woman turned from a long buffet table,
dropping ice cubes into a glass of pink zinfandel.

"I've got an appointment with Dr. Crossman," Nina
said.

The woman raised her eyebrows. "You do?" Clink.

Nina nodded. "Can you tell me where to find him?"

"Did I call you?"

"Not that I know," Nina said.

The woman sighed. "Second floor," she said, gesturing
with the wineglass. "Third door on the left." Pink zin
slopped over the rim and onto her white shoes. "Oopsie-
doo," she said.

Dr. Crossman's door said: RUSSELL R. CROSSMAN, M.D., DIRECTOR. It was half-open. Nina tapped on it, stepped inside and found herself alone in an outer office. She glanced at the VDT on the secretary's desk. "List," it said. "Mom - stockings. Benny - Prince CD? Jennifer - stockings. Joanne - stockings. Melissa - stockings?"

"Puts and calls," said a man's voice. "That was your big idea, if I remember." Nina looked through an inner doorway.

A man sat at the kind of desk a good props department might have furnished for a Mussolini biography. On the wall behind him hung a photograph of the weak-chinned man wearing a white dinner jacket and standing beside a palm tree. The man at the desk had a slightly stronger chin and a neat mustache with a faint red tinge. He wore a chalk-striped banker's suit, a silk rep tie and a green conical party hat with silver moons. "A big if," he said into the telephone. He saw Nina. His eyes flickered up and down. "All right, all right," he said. "I'll take two. Bye."

He hung up the phone and looked at her.

"Dr. Crossman?"

"That's right."

"I have an appointment." She introduced herself.

Dr. Crossman consulted an appointment book. "Not today," he said. "All appointments were cancelled for today."

"No one told me."

"Someone should have. We're really not open. It's the Christmas party."

"I thought it might be the usual state of affairs."

"The usual state of affairs?"

"At a fertility clinic," Nina explained. Dr. Crossman's brow furrowed. "It doesn't matter." The phone buzzed. Dr. Crossman took a honey-colored pastille from a tin box on the desk and stuck it in his mouth. The phone stopped buzzing. "The appointment was made last week," Nina said.

"Yes, I see it here," said Dr. Crossman, sucking on the pastille. "But it's been crossed out. The whole day is crossed out." He turned the book around so she could see. "Moreover," Dr. Crossman added, "this is not a fertility clinic. It is a research institute that takes human fertility as its subject."

"But you do perform artificial insemination."

He pointed a finger at her. "On qualified candidates," he said. His fingers were long, thin and freckled.

"Dr. Berry referred me."

"Yes, I see that too. And I have nothing but respect for Dr. Berry. But he doesn't decide if you're qualified. That is solely up to us."

"What are the criteria?"

"They're extensive. That's what the preliminary interview is all about."

"Can we get started then? Since I'm here anyway."

Dr. Crossman felt his mustache with his long forefinger. The sight of the reddish hairs brushing the freckled skin gave Nina an inexplicable queasy feeling, reminding her of a time in early childhood when she had become nauseated while eating a baloney sandwich and listening to a story about a frog on the radio.

Dr. Crossman looked at his watch, thin and gold, with no numbers. Perhaps that was why he spent such a long time studying it. "All right," he said. "All right." He went into the front office, returned with a file folder. Nina saw her name on it. He opened the file, leaned forward slightly in his chair to read it. His eyes moved back and forth. He looked every inch the careful and concerned physician, except for the party hat.

"You're thirty-nine," he said, not looking up.

"That's right. Is there an age limit?"

"Not carved in stone. It's just one of the factors." He took a pen from an inside pocket and wrote "39" on a blank sheet of paper. "Five feet eight," he read aloud. "One hundred and thirty-seven pounds. Pulse sixty-two. Blood pressure one-twenty over ninety. General health excellent. Medical record good. Any major injuries?"

"I tore ligaments in my knee once. Is that major?"

Dr. Crossman glanced at her. "How did you do that?"

"Playing field hockey."

"Did you have surgery?"

"Yes."

"Who performed it?"

"Dr. Hunneycutt."

"Walter was a good man," said Dr. Crossman, rising. "Retired now." He came around the desk. "Let me see."

"See what?"

"The knee."

Nina stared at him. "Does my knee have something to do with my ability to have children?" Dr. Crossman didn't notice her stare; he missed the edge in her tone too.

"We have to know all we can about your general health," he said. "It's routine."

He stood over her. Nina raised the hem of her skirt an inch or two. Dr. Crossman bent over, peered at her scar. "Nice work." He straightened, but before he did his gaze slid swiftly up her leg. Nina tugged her hem back down.

Dr. Crossman sat back down at the desk, stuck another honey-colored pastille in his mouth, turned the pages of her medical record. He glanced up. "Both your parents are deceased?" The information seemed to make his tone more lively.

"Yes."

"Any brothers or sisters?"

"No."

Dr. Crossman wrote, "No: P's, B's, S's." He underlined it. "Who is your closest living relative?"

"I have some cousins in California."

"First cousins?"

"Distant. I've seen only one or two of them, and that was years ago." Dr. Crossman drew a second line under "No: P's, B's, S's." "Does this have something to do with my qualifications for raising a child?" Nina asked.

"It's just part of our standard interview," Dr. Crossman replied. "Do you have a will?"

"No."

"Who would your heirs be if you did?"

"Excuse me, Dr. Crossman, but I don't see the relevance of this."

"No?" He leaned toward her across the desk; she expected to smell honey, but detected tooth decay instead. "What if something happened to you, for example. Who would be responsible for the child?"

Nina hadn't thought about that. "Is it necessary to decide now?"

"No. It's just one of the factors. Are you a college graduate?"

"Yes."

"What's your degree in?"

"I've got a B.A. in French Literature."

"From where?"

"Barnard."

"Do you remember your SAT scores?"

"Not exactly."

"Approximately?"

"They were good. I don't know the numbers."

"We can get hold of them, I suppose. Repeat the following in reverse order—five, seventeen, thirty-six, nine, twenty-three."

"Why?"

He looked severe, as severe as a man could in a pointed green hat covered with silver moons. "It's part of the interview, Ms. Kitchener."

"Twenty-three, nine, thirty-six, seventeen, five," Nina said, before she forgot. "I don't see that this applies."

He opened his desk drawer and took out a sheet of paper showing five different geometric figures. "Which one doesn't belong?" he said.

"That one. Are you testing my IQ, Dr. Crossman?"

"Not exactly, Ms. Kitchener. But perhaps Dr. Berry didn't explain to you that all HFI sperm is donated by men of exceptional accomplishment in their fields. I'm not giving away any corporate secrets when I tell you that more than a dozen of our donors are Nobel Prize winners—and not just in physics, chemistry and medicine, we're more broadminded than that. One of our donors won the Nobel Prize for literature." He paused for Nina to ask who. When she didn't, he went on. "Naturally, I'm not at liberty to reveal any names."

"It wasn't Henrik Pontoppidan, by any chance?"

"I beg your pardon?"

"The winner in 1917." That was all Nina knew about him. Henrik Pontoppidan had been one of her father's favorite names, along with Mongo Santamaria and Cotton Mather. He had invoked them to record surprise or disgust, the way other people swear.

"The technology did not exist at that time," Dr. Crossman said. "But I assure you that our man is rather more celebrated than the one you refer to. My point is that while we are not really testing you, it is one of the goals of HFI, given the caliber of our donors, that their . . ." Dr. Crossman searched for the remainder of the subordinate clause.

"That their seed not be wasted?" Nina asked.

"Precisely." Dr. Crossman's long fingers moved toward the box of pastilles, reconsidered, retreated. "It says here you're president of something called Kitchener and Best. What is that?"

"We're publishing consultants."

"Successful ones?"

"Are you thinking of employing us, Dr. Crossman?"

He gave her the stern look again, then decided she was making a joke and briefly shaped his lips in the form of a smile. The rest of his face retained the stern look. "What were your personal earnings last year?"

"No concern of yours, Dr. Crossman." Nina stood up. "I don't think this is going to work," she said.

To her surprise, Dr. Crossman rose too, anxiously brushing his hair. His hand encountered the party hat. "Christ," he said, taking it off and dropping it into a wastebasket. "Don't be hasty, Ms. Kitchener. We have to have some idea of your financial status. First, because our services are not free. Second, because we have to know that any resultant progeny will be properly raised, at least in a material sense."

Nina, on her way to the door, paused. "How much do your services cost?"

"Five hundred dollars. Seven-fifty for a laureate."

"Do they get royalties?"

"I beg your pardon?"

"Are the donors paid too?"

"That information is confidential."

"Does the cost include the birth?"

"Oh no. Our clients use their own obstetricians. Please sit down, Ms. Kitchener." Nina sat. So did Dr. Crossman. "We can refer you to an obstetrician if you wish," he said.

"I have Dr. Berry." Nina didn't want those long, freckled fingers anywhere near her.

"Jim is good." Dr. Crossman took a form from his drawer. Printed on it were rectangular boxes in the shape of an inverted pyramid. "Just one more thing," he said, writing "Nina Kitchener" in the top box and handing the sheet to her. "Fill in your family tree as far back as you can. Include maiden names, countries of origin, ethnicity, causes of death, if known."

Nina filled in the boxes. Mother: Alice Landers. Born: Syracuse, N.Y. Caucasian. Died of pneumonia. It was true: she had caught pneumonia near the end. Father: John Kitchener. Born: Chicago. Caucasian. Died of an accident. That was true too: weakened from chemotherapy, he had fallen down the stairs a few days before his death. Neither "breast cancer" nor "colon cancer" appeared in the rectangular boxes. Nina didn't want Dr. Crossman to worry about risking his prize-winning sperm on an odds-on cancer carrier.

She had fewer details for the lower boxes. Her mother's maiden name: was it Turley or Tolmey? And deeper in the past, Kitchener had been Kupstein or Kapstein or something like that: an upwardly mobile German-Jewish immigrant had picked the grandest English name beginning with K that he knew; not only a status seeker, her father had once said, but a bigamist as well, running from the law in his native land. But Nina didn't know exactly what the name had been or when the change had been made, so she omitted mention of it, simply putting question marks at the roots of her family tree.

"Dr. Crossman?" The nurse who liked pink zinfandel was at the door. Her eyes were sparkling. "Sorry to interrupt, but we're cutting the cake now."

"I'll be down in a minute." The nurse gave Nina a big, drunken smile and went away. Nina handed Dr. Crossman the form. He glanced at it. "Well then, Ms. Kitchener, is there anything more you'd like to know?"

It seemed to Nina that he'd been the one doing most of the finding out. "Would I get the donor of my choice?"

"That's not possible. All of our donors remain strictly anonymous. Beyond knowing that they are free of all hereditary disease and will be genetically matched to you regarding blood type and a few other characteristics, they will remain that way."

"What other characteristics?"

"Race, for example. Although that would be automatic, since all our donors are white."

"I wasn't aware that the Nobel was restricted."

"Oh, it's not, Ms. Kitchener. It's just that—"

"Your clientele is all white."

Dr. Crossman smiled. This time the rest of his face joined the act. "Fourteen hundred," he said.

"Fourteen hundred?"

"I'll bet that's what you scored on your SATs. You get to be a good judge of things like that, sitting on this side of the desk." He wrote "1400" beside "No: P's, B's, S's." Then he folded the sheet of paper, pocketed it and said: "Thank you for coming. We'll let you know."

"Know what?"

"If you're a suitable candidate. The committee meets on Thursday. We bend over backwards to be fair."

Nina almost said, "Don't bother." Almost.

Nina went home. She looked up her SATs: 1420.

Thursday was the twenty-fourth. Kitchener and Best had their Christmas party. Nina was the last to leave. She didn't want to go back to her apartment. On a whim, she went to Rockefeller Center, rented skates and circled the rink with many others. She skated for hours, but it didn't tire her at all. She finally quit when her knee began to hurt; it hadn't bothered her in years.

She went home. *It's a Wonderful Life* was on television. She poured herself a drink and sat down in front of the screen, the remote control in her hand. The phone rang.

"Ms. Kitchener? This is Dr. Crossman."

"Yes?"

"When was your last period?"

"Why do you want to know that?" Nina said, making no attempt to mask her annoyance.

"Because we have to set the date for your procedure, Ms. Kitchener. Congratulations. You've been chosen."

"I have?"

"You passed with flying colors, Ms. Kitchener. Merry Christmas."

|5|

"My name is Percival," said the man in the black suit, extending a plump hand that felt soft and slightly hot when Nina shook it.

"Are you in charge of the procedure?" she asked. Nina could hear the anxiety in her voice. She wasn't ready for the procedure. She still hadn't made up her mind. But if she hadn't made up her mind, what was she doing back at the Human Fertility Institute?

"Procedure?" said Percival with a laugh. He had a throaty laugh: he might have just swallowed a bowlful of thick cream. The laugh seemed to suit him: with his bald head, round, soft face and clear pink complexion, Percival could have been a country squire from the days before the discovery of cholesterol. "Goodness no," he said, handing a card across the desk.

"*Ablewhite, Godfrey, Percival & Glyde*," it read, adding a midtown address and a phone number that ended in three zeroes. "I'm just in charge of the paperwork."

"Paperwork?"

"It never ends," Percival said. "Please sit down."

Nina sat in a red leather chair. She was on the second floor of the institute, in a plush office down the hall from Dr. Crossman's. It had leaded windows, through which she could see falling snowflakes, browning fast in city air; heavy gold curtains of the type that would just fail to conceal Peter Sellers' feet in an Inspector Clouseau movie;

and a framed photograph of the weak-chinned man whose oil portrait hung in the lobby. In the photograph the weak-chinned man was shaking hands with the Duke of Windsor.

Percival opened a briefcase, took out papers and stacked them on the desk. "Here are some forms that need your signature," he said.

"What kind of forms?"

"Legal ones," he said, pushing the stack toward her, "so look them over."

Nina had a look at the papers. Percival described them as she flipped through. "That's the financial contract—straightforward exchange of payment for services rendered. That one's the malpractice waiver—you agree to absolve the institute from acccountability for any pregnancy difficulties or birth defects. That's the support form—the institute shall have no responsibility for the support, medical expenses, upbringing, room, board, education or any other expenses of or pertaining to any resulting issue. That's the anonymity form—the donor shall remain anonymous and neither you nor any resulting issue shall make any attempt to learn the donor's identity. And that's the estate rider—neither you nor any resulting issue shall make any claim on the estate of the donor after his death."

Nina looked up. Percival was picking his nose. He quickly folded his hands on the desk. "How can I sign for 'any resulting issue'?" she asked.

Percival smiled. He had big teeth, yellow as old piano keys. "Of course you don't have to," he said.

"I don't have to?"

"In the same sense that you don't have to register if you don't want to vote."

"Perhaps you've missed my point," Nina said. "How can I sign anything in the name of someone who doesn't even exist yet?"

Percival was still showing her his yellow smile. "I didn't miss it, Ms."—he glanced down at a file folder—"Kitchener. You're free to consult your attorney about this or any other question."

Nina thought about her attorneys: she had Janet for taxes and Louise for contracts; there was also Jason's friend Larry the Litigator, who had represented her successfully in the bicycle crash lawsuit, gaining a settlement

of ten thousand dollars, of which he had taken five. Nina
didn't want to consult any of them. Neither was it necessary: she knew what they would say, and she didn't think
she wanted to hear it. A thought sprang up in her mind,
grew out of proportion to all the others swirling around
there: I want to register. I want to vote.

The next moment Nina heard herself ask: "Have you
got a pen?" She felt dizzy, as though suddenly swept up
in a powerful current: baby-making had a momentum all
its own.

"Why, certainly." Percival reached into the inner pocket
of his jacket. He had two—a fat gold fountain pen and a
common blue ballpoint. He came around the desk and
handed Nina the ballpoint, politely pointing the inky end
at himself. Standing beside her, Percival sorted through
the stack of papers. His soft round fingers, graceful in their
natural element, danced through the pages. "Sign here,"
he said.

Nina signed.

"Now here."

She signed.

"And here. And here. And here. Initial this corner. And
this. And once more. Good." The pages flew by.

The phone rang. "Yes?" Percival said into it. "I'll take
it." Percival listened, his free hand caressing the stack of
signed papers on the desk. The hem of his black suit jacket
brushed Nina's shoulder, rested there. She shifted away.
"I understand," Percival said. "Yes, that's taken care of."
He laughed his creamy laugh. "That's a good one. . . . Not
at all, Mayor. Goodbye." He hung up, smiled, walked
around the desk, sat down.

"Well then," he said, his smile fading, "any questions?"

"That's it?"

"That's it. Shall I buzz the nurse?"

"Okay."

The nurse who liked pink zinfandel arrived. She smiled
at Nina, a smile half the size and brightness of her drunken
one, and said: "All set?"

"All set," Percival answered for her.

Nina rose and followed the nurse to the door. "Best of
luck," Percival called after her, locking the papers in his
briefcase.

The nurse led Nina into a tiny elevator at the end of the

hall. It had a sliding brass grille door and a suede bench along the back wall. The nurse pushed button number 5. The elevator shuddered for a moment or two and then began to rise at a stately pace. "Don't you just love this elevator?" the nurse said. "It's so romantic."

Nina, on her way to an assignation with frozen sperm, said nothing.

At the fifth floor, Nina and the nurse stepped out of the elevator and into utilitarian surroundings: uncarpeted hallway, bare green walls, fluorescent lighting. Behind them the elevator shuddered again and returned to the elegance below.

"Right in here," said the nurse, opening the door to a small room: white Formica counters and wall cabinets, a sink, a high stool, an examination table with stirrups, a blue paper dress on a hanger. "If you'll just get into this."

The nurse went into an adjoining room. Nina took off her clothes, put on the blue paper dress. It came halfway down her thighs. Through the open doorway, she saw the nurse uncovering a large metal container that looked like one of Ali Baba's urns. Puffs of liquid nitrogen vapor rose from it, reminding Nina first of genies, then of swamps that the monster rises from in drive-in horror movies. Using tongs, the nurse removed a stoppered test tube and read the label. She clamped the test tube in a centrifuge and pressed a button. The contents of the test tube whirled in a white blur.

"What's happening?" Nina asked.

"Spinning forces the strongest swimmers to the top," replied Dr. Crossman, entering by the other door. "In theory. And the strongest swimmers are the ones we want." He smoothed his red mustache. "Hi, I'm Dr. Crossman." His eyes made a furtive trip: down, up. Nina finished tying the paper ribbons behind her. "And you're"— he consulted a clipboard—"Nina. Right?"

She nodded. She had been Ms. Kitchener when they last met, but then she hadn't been wearing a paper dress that showed her legs and wouldn't close in the back.

Dr. Crossman studied the top page on the clipboard. "I just got your bloods from the lab," he said. "You're ovulating." He turned a few pages. "Let's see. Your last

ovulation was the tenth of January, according to Dr. Berry,
and I saw you . . ." He flipped through the pages.

"The day of your Christmas party."

Dr. Crossman frowned. "That doesn't sound right," he
said. He began going through the pages more carefully.
"I don't usually see anyone . . ." His voice trailed off.
"Oh, yes, here you are," he said, still sounding puzzled.
He stuck a pastille in his mouth and read for a while.
"Today's the day, then," he said, more sure of himself
now. He finished reading, removed a file folder from the
clipboard and handed her the computer printout that was
inside. "Meet the father."

Nina felt the paper dress dampening under her arms as
she read the printout:

> *VT-3(h)*
> White male/U.S. citizen
> Origins: N. Euro.
> Ht.: 6'
> Wt.: 175
> Hair: Lt. Brn.
> Eyes: Bl.
> Skin: Fair
> Blood: A
> Hered. Disease: None
> Eyesight: 20/20
> Build: Med.
> Hat sz.: 7
> Ft. Sz.: 11B
> Rng. sz.: ?
> Educ.: M.F.A. (Music)
> Athl.: Varsity soccer
> IQ: 128
> Status: Professional
> Comments: Left-handed

"So," said Dr. Crossman. "How do you like him?"

No reply came to mind. Nina was still searching for one
when the nurse came in, carrying a syringe containing a
button of milky liquid. "Here we go," said Dr. Crossman,
pulling on surgical gloves. "If you'll get up on the
table . . ."

The table was high, but there was no footstool to step on. Nina put her bare back against the side, placed her hands on top and, with a little jump, launched herself just high enough to land awkwardly on the padded table, her paper dress rising above her waist. She tugged it down as well as she could, looking up in time to see Dr. Crossman's eyes shifting away. He had caught the whole performance. What did it matter? Moments later, she was in the stirrups and he was standing between her legs, brow furrowed in thought, like an actor in *The Story of Louis Pasteur*. He switched on a bright overhead light.

The nurse rolled in a table of instruments. "Betadine, please," said Dr. Crossman.

The nurse opened a bottle of brown liquid. Dr. Crossman dipped a gauze swab into it, leaned forward and dabbed inside Nina. He didn't have a light touch, but he didn't hurt her. Perhaps she couldn't have felt it if he had: she was trying to shut off all physical sensation. She thought of the long freckled fingers under the translucent plastic, and of frogs and baloney.

"We're ready, Sal," said Dr. Crossman.

The nurse attached a clear plastic tube to the syringe and handed it to him. He glanced at the printout. "VT-three-h?" he said.

Sal read the label on the empty test tube. "Check," she said.

Dr. Crossman bent forward again, a speculum in one hand, the syringe and plastic tube in the other. Nina glimpsed the white fluid; then all the tools were out of sight, hidden by the raised hem of the paper dress.

"Wait!" she wanted to call out, but didn't. She felt the plastic tube slip into her antiseptic insides; felt the hairs on Dr. Crossman's bare forearm brush against her thigh, once, twice, high, higher; felt the pressure of his gloved hand as he slowly squeezed the syringe. It seemed to remain in her for a long time. She thought about having an abortion.

Dr. Crossman withdrew the syringe. His bare forearm brushed her again. Dr. Crossman's eyes moved up to Nina's face. "Stay like that for a few minutes," he told her. His red mustache twitched, as though it were itchy but he didn't want to scratch it with his hands in their present state. He left the room.

Sal looked down at her. "Not so bad, huh?"

"No."

"Good," said Sal. She wheeled the instruments away. "Back in a jiff." The door closed. Nina wondered if she would ever have an orgasm again.

Soon the door opened. "Oh, you didn't have to stay like that," said Sal. "Not in the stirrups. He meant on your back, that's all."

Nina felt herself blushing. "Can I get up now?"

"Sure. I'll take you down to the business office."

Nina put on her clothes, leaving the paper dress hanging on a stirrup. Sal left her in the business office on the ground floor. "Keep your fingers crossed," she said.

Nina was handed a bill for five hundred dollars. "What if it hasn't worked?" she asked.

"Didn't you read the financial contract?" the clerk replied.

"I don't remember," Nina said, making no attempt to soften her tone.

The clerk blinked. "You return at no additional cost," he said. He blinked again. "Paragraph thirteen D."

Nina wrote a check for five hundred dollars. "I guess I didn't get a laureate," she said, remembering the two-hundred-and-fifty-dollar premium.

"I wouldn't know about that," he said, taking the check. "Can I just see your driver's license?"

Nina went home with VT-3(h) inside her and her mind still not made up. She had a long shower, as hot as she could stand.

Thirty-five days later, Dr. Berry said: "Congratulations." Nina must have replied something, but she wasn't conscious of what.

She walked out of Dr. Berry's office into driving freezing rain. It was the most miserable day of the year. But the sun was shining on Nina and it was eighty degrees. None of the pained-looking sufferers on the street seemed to notice; nor did they have any idea of the secret she bore. It was the happiest moment of her life.

Not long after, soaked to the skin, Nina found herself entering the antique shop halfway between her apartment and the office. The man at the desk looked up from *Vogue*. "And how may I help you?" he asked.

"I'd like to buy Achilles."

"Achilles?"

"The rocking horse. With the red saddle."

"Oh dear," said the man. "It was sold yesterday, I'm afraid. But here's an adorable nineteenth-century doll from Bavaria."

|6|

The last day of July turned out to be a bad one for N. H. Matthias. It began badly because he had to wear his necktie. It was his only necktie, the necktie he always wore when neckties had to be worn. Matthias had paid $3.95 for it at a Woolworth's in Raleigh, North Carolina, in 1972. His necktie was maroon with a pattern of abstract figures that might have been green sunbursts; its width had been in and out of style several times. Now it seemed to be on the way out again. Matthias told himself that he hated wearing neckties only because they were uncomfortable, especially in Miami on the last day of July, when the temperature stood at ninety and the humidity was a little higher. But there was a lot more to it than that.

Ties mean business: all the men and most of the women working in the Carib-American Bank on Biscayne Boulevard were wearing them, including the tellers, the loan officers, the vice-presidents of this and that, and Dicky Dumaurier. Dicky sat behind a little plastic sign that said, MR. DICKY DUMAURIER, ASSISTANT MGR. Matthias had been dealing with him for more than ten years. It was a sporadic relationship, conducted mostly on the phone and through the mail, but they called each other by their first names and had even had drinks together once. Matthias, to appear businesslike, had worn his tie on that occasion too. Mr. Dicky Dumaurier had downed three planter's punches, two mai tais and a blue margarita; at one point, they had watched a bored-looking naked woman dance with a bored-looking naked snake; soon after, Matthias had helped Dicky into a taxi. This friendly shared history must not have made it easy for Dicky to say no to Matthias. But he wasn't an Assistant Mgr. for nothing, and rose to the challenge.

"I'm really sorry, Nate," he said. Dicky had a prominent Adam's apple; it throbbed in silent counterpoint to his words. "Really and truly very sorry. And I mean that. I want you to know I mean it. In this business, as in any business—you're in business, so you know what I'm talking about—we sometimes say things we don't really mean. This isn't one of those times. Please believe me. But . . ." Dicky sighed, a rich, breathy sigh that conveyed hopelessness, disillusion, surrender. "But, but, but. It can't be done."

Matthias should have walked out at that moment; the idea occurred to him. Instead he ignored the message of the sigh, and said: "Does that mean you can't do it, or you won't?"

"It means it can't be done. Not by Carib-American, or any other reputable institution."

Get up, Matthias thought. Go. But he said: "On what grounds?"

"Nate, let me be candid." Dicky straightened his tie—fabric: silk; width: au courant; color: yellow, with pink and lavender diagonals. It could have been the tie of a regiment that had won its stripes at the Battle of Capri, or someplace like that. "I've always been candid with you, Nate, and I don't want anything to change that, now or in the future."

Matthias thought: Future? He said: "Heaven forbid."

"Nate. Please. I'm trying to be candid. Let me tell you about this guy we had in here last week, a small businessman with six kids and a wife dying of cancer. I'm not making this up. We'd done business with him for twenty years and his father before him and his grandfather before that, and we still had to pull the plug."

Matthias waited for him to continue. When he didn't he said: "What's the moral of the story?"

"The hard decisions are hard, Nate. You wouldn't want to be in my shoes."

Matthias tried to see through the smoked lenses of Dicky

Dumaurier's glasses to the eyes behind. Dicky looked down at the papers on his desk, shifted them around. "It's black and white, Nate. Even if we forget for a moment about the judgment—"

"I plan to appeal."

"—we've still got the two mortgages and a cumulative nut of thirteen-five a month. You can't go on like that—you haven't got the capacity. You've been sinking deeper for years. So how can we talk about another note? You don't meet the guidelines."

Because, Matthias thought, without the money, there would be no appeal. No appeal, no more Zombie Bay. But that wasn't banker talk, so he said: "Bookings are picking up."

Dicky searched through the papers. "I've seen your projections for the winter. I've worked the numbers. Believe me, I've worked them. I was up till after 'Nightline' working them. It's just not in the cards, Nate. I really hope things turn around. Believe me when I say we'd hate to have to foreclose."

"Foreclose?"

"Don't get me wrong, Nate. Your place is . . . charming. Although it's unfortunate you're not a tad closer to the beaten path. It wouldn't be of much use to us at all."

"My condolences."

"Huh?" said Dicky. He licked his lips. "It would be a headache, in fact. Despite all its many, many good qualities. For us, you see. But, my goodness, I don't have to tell you about the trials and tribulations of doing business in the islands, do I? The point is, I'm pulling for you, Nate, honestly. We all are, here at Carib-American."

Matthias put his hands on Dicky's desk and leaned across it, feeling his suit jacket straining at his back and shoulders. He was aware of his size, his strength, his deep tan—acquired not because he wanted to be unfashionably dark or die of melanoma, but because he worked outdoors in a hot country—and of the Carib-American Bank, with its deathly green computer screens, its telephones that made electronic noises instead of ringing like bells, its cold air. He might as well have had a bone through his nose. "I'm glad you're pulling for me, Dicky, really and truly glad. But if I don't get the money, I can't pay the lawyer. And if I can't pay the lawyer, I lose this case by default."

Dicky shrank back in his padded chair. He bit his lips, first the top, then the bottom; he pursed them; he sighed again. "But we'll still be protected, Nate, no matter what happens. Don't you see?"

Matthias rose. He kept his fists by his sides. "Don't call me Nate," he said, and walked out of Dicky Dumaurier's office.

"But I've always called you Na— that," said Dicky, somewhere behind him. "What should I call you?"

Friends called him Matt, but why pass that on to Dicky? Matthias strode through the gleaming lobby of the bank. He wanted to do something violent. But he was forty-four years old and a responsible citizen of two countries. So he just ripped off his necktie. He considered flinging it across the lobby, but ties don't fling very well. He jammed it in his pocket instead.

Matthias walked out of the bank and into white glare. A taxi materialized, like a special effect in a film about commuters in deep space. Matthias raised his hand, feeling the sweat already dampening his armpit. The taxi stopped. Matthias got in, spoke the address he wanted to the back of the driver's head. The head nodded. The car began to move. Matthias looked out the window, saw nothing. After several blocks he realized that the driver hadn't understood him and tried again in Spanish.

"*Perdón*," said the driver, making a violent U-turn. He glanced at Matthias in the mirror. Matthias had seen that glance before; now the driver would either leave it alone or pursue him along a line of inquiry that Matthias had gotten used to. The driver glanced at him again, cleared his throat. "*Usted no me parece cubano, señor*," he said.

"*No soy*," Matthias answered.

"*Anglo?*"

"*Sí.*"

"*Pero usted habla español muy bien.*"

"*No es tan raro.*"

"*Pero habla como un cubano.*"

Matthias grunted. The driver swung into the passing lane and stepped on the gas. Traffic was heavy, but that didn't keep his eyes from shifting to the mirror from time to time.

"*Eran uno de sus padres cubanos, señor?*"

"*No.*"

The driver nodded. He had a thin neck with two prom-

inent tendons. The tendons lengthened and shortened as
he nodded, then came to rest, giving Matthias the impres-
sion that the driver's head might be fastened insecurely to
his shoulders. This image, and the driver's questions about
his past, brought back another image, recalled from long
ago: an image he hadn't wanted to see again.

The taxi had almost reached the Grove when the driver
said, *"Perdón, señor, pero ha usted vivido alla?"*

"Adónde?"

"Cuba, señor."

"Sí."

"Antes de Castro?"

"No."

The taxi stopped in front of Café Martinique. Matthias
paid the driver. The driver opened his mouth as if to try
one more time, but all he said was, *"Gracias."*

Matthias went into the restaurant. It was packed with
the lunchtime crowd, but Matthias spotted Marilyn the
moment he walked through the door. She sat at a pink-
covered table by the water, stretching her lips taut while
she applied lipstick of the same shade. Drawing nearer,
Matthias saw that Marilyn was outdoing Dorian Gray, not
just retaining her beauty, but growing better looking with
time. Her cheekbones seemed more prominent, the blond
highlights in her hair blonder, her smooth skin smoother,
her white teeth whiter. She looked like the figurative million dollars; she was probably wearing twenty thousand
real ones in clothes and jewelry, although Matthias didn't
have enough experience to know for sure. That was one
of the lesser reasons for the break-up of their marriage.

Danny was sitting beside her, wearing orange-tinted sunglasses and catapulting snowpeas with his spoon. It was a
trick Matthias had taught him long ago, in a moment of
bad parenting: a good trick, and cute at the time, when
Danny was four. But now he was almost fifteen.

They both saw Matthias coming at the same moment,
and looked up with expressions on their faces that weren't
easy to read. "Hi, Danny," said Matthias, sitting opposite
them. "Hello, Marilyn."

"Hi," said Danny. He didn't remove the orange-tinted
sunglasses and he didn't say "Dad."

"We went ahead without you," Marilyn said.

"I was delayed."

Marilyn studied her lips in a small oval mirror, snapped it shut and said, "I've got to run." She turned to Danny. "Please be at Howie's office no later than six, Daniel. We're going to the Biermeyers'." Marilyn signed the bill, picked up her Gold Card and was gone.

Matthias looked at Danny. "Had enough to eat?"

"Yeah."

"Then let's go."

"Where?"

Where. On these paternal afternoons, he and Danny had been everywhere in South Florida, from Lake Okeechobee to Marathon. "We could shoot some hoops at the Y," Matthias said.

"The Y?"

"Anything wrong with the Y?"

"I'm not into hoops."

"You used to like it."

Danny shrugged.

"We could go to a batting cage."

Danny made a face.

"Not interested in sports anymore?" Matthias asked, trying to peer through Danny's lenses, the way he had with Dicky Dumaurier. He saw only his own broad, dark face, wearing the same baffled expression Dicky must have witnessed; except now it was orange.

"Yeah, I am."

"Like what?"

"Golf."

"You like golfing?"

Danny made another face, different from the first. This was a face Matthias had seen many times before on Marilyn, but never on his son. "Not golfing," Danny said. "Playing golf."

"Is there a big difference?"

Danny said nothing. He flicked a pea off the table with his middle finger.

"All right," said Matthias. "Let's go." He smiled. "I'll golf and you play golf." It wasn't much of a joke, and Danny couldn't be blamed for not smiling too. "Do you have any course in mind?"

"I play at Turnberry Island."

"Good enough," said Matthias, rising.

Danny remained seated. "You have to be a member."

"Are you?"

"Howie is. He arranges everything." The orange lenses were directed at Matthias's face. He thought of the chain gang boss from *Cool Hand Luke*. "Maybe I'll call him and see if it's okay," Danny said.

Matthias sat down. "Who's Howie?"

"Howie? You know. Howie."

"I don't."

"He's Mom's . . ."

Matthias watched his orange face react to this information, in duplicate. "Dessert?" a waiter said.

Matthias shook his head.

They found a driving range near the airport. Matthias hadn't held a club in thirty years, not since his last summer as a caddy. Now, standing on a pad next to Danny's, Matthias felt his hands take the driver in the right grip all by themselves. He watched Danny tee up. The boy took no practice swings, stood over his ball, hit it. His swing wasn't bad, but he took the club back a little too fast, and his head came up a little too soon. The ball, topped, but not by much, whistled off on low trajectory, dove to the ground and rolled to the 100-yard marker.

"Fuck," Danny said.

He quickly teed up another ball, took less time, hooked it low and left across the range. "Fuck," he said, reaching for another ball. This time his head came up right away and he squibbed the ball a few yards to the right. "Fuck." He reached into the ball basket, teed up. Matthias saw that the ball was even with the wrong heel, his right one, and that he was standing too close to it.

"Why don't you take a few practice swings?" he said.

But Danny was already into a jerky backswing; this time he barely touched the ball. It fell off the tee, rolled to the edge of the rubber pad, hesitated for a long second, then dropped on the burnt grass. Danny rounded on him: "Don't you know enough to shut up while a golfer's addressing the ball?"

Matthias looked down on him. If this were my kid, he started to think, I'd pull him off the course. But Danny was his kid. Matthias turned away.

A few pads beyond him, a well-dressed old woman was watching. She quickly bent over her ball and stroked it smooth and straight beyond the 150-yard marker.

On the other side, Danny took another furious swing and whiffed. "Fucking shit."

"Relax, Danny, it's not—"

"Don't talk while I'm playing," the boy yelled. He swung a few more times, missed, banged the club hard on the rubber pad, kicked the ball basket and stomped away. Balls fanned out slowly across the grass.

Matthias picked one up. He set it on the tee, stood over it and took the club head back. All at once he saw the ball with great clarity: a moon with sharp-edged dimples in its northern hemisphere and shadow-filled ones in the southern. He hadn't intended to hit it very hard, but somewhere on the downswing he changed his mind. The ball landed beyond the 300-yard marker and bounced over the metal fence at the end of the driving range. He felt better for a moment.

"Bravo," said the old woman. And the moment was over.

Danny was talking on a pay phone. He hung up as Matthias approached. Sweat was running down his face, but he seemed calmer. "What would you like to do, Danny?" Matthias asked.

"When I grow up, you mean?"

"I meant right now. But when you grow up will do."

"Investment banking," Danny said. "Or maybe commercial real estate."

There was a multiscreen cinema across the highway. Alone in a little screening room, Matthias and Danny watched a comedy in which Dabney Coleman played twins separated at birth. One becomes an encyclopedia salesman, the other head of the KGB. The CIA finds out and sends Encyclopedia Dabney on a mission to Moscow. There are complications. KGB Dabney has a wife and a mistress who, et cetera et cetera. It was funny when Dabney Coleman was on the screen. The rest of the time, Matthias stole glances at Danny, who had taken off his orange glasses. By the flickering light from the screen, Danny looked much older than he had on Matthias's last visit. Perhaps it was just the way he watched the movie, and the jokes he laughed at. His childhood was almost over. Matthias tried to picture him as an investment banker and easily could.

After the movie they took a taxi downtown. "Any plans

for a visit before school?" Matthias said. "Rafer's always asking about you."

"Who's Rafer?"

"Moxie's son."

"Oh yeah." Silence. Danny's head turned to follow a big limo going the other way.

"How about it?"

"I don't know," Danny said. "We might be going to Greece for a few weeks."

"That'll be fun."

"You've been there?"

"No. But it sounds like fun."

"Yeah." The taxi stopped in front of a tall glass building. Danny opened the door. "Do you know where to go?" Matthias asked.

"The penthouse," Danny said. "I've been here lots of times." He paused with his hand on the door, about to say something. For a second Matthias let himself think that Danny was reconsidering Greece. "How's your case going?" Danny said.

"We're still in there pitching," Matthias said. "Nothing's going to happen for a while, if you were thinking of coming down."

"It's not that. It's—it's just that they say you haven't got a chance."

"Who says?"

"Mom. And Howie."

"What does Howie do?"

"He's a shrink."

Matthias wondered if Marilyn's relationship with him had begun on a professional basis. He kept the thought to himself. "I'm not sure that qualifies him as an expert on Bahamian law."

"Howie's an expert on everything. He's got a mind like a computer."

"That's nice." Danny put one foot on the ground. Matthias held out his hand. "Call me when you get back from Greece." They shook hands goodbye. For a moment, Matthias felt the man-boy hand in his. Then it was gone.

"There's his car," Danny said. A red Porsche emerged from the parking garage beside the tall building. The attendant hopped out and held the door. A man walked swiftly out of the building and got into the car. Danny ran over to it, jumped in the other side. The man didn't look at him.

Matthias stepped out of the taxi and found himself walking over to the Porsche. He heard Danny saying, "Sorry if I'm late."

" 'Sorry' won't get us there any faster," said the man in the driver's seat.

Matthias put his hands on the roof and leaned into Danny's window. "He's not late. It's five minutes to six."

The man looked at him. He wore orange glasses identical to Danny's. "Who's this?" he said.

"My father," Danny answered.

"Dr. Howie Nero," said the man. "Pleased to meet you, but we've got to run."

Matthias kept his hands off the car. He took in Dr. Howie Nero's diamond ring, tan suit, lime green open-collared shirt. He reached into his pocket, pulled out the necktie and tossed it in Howie's lap.

"What the hell is this?" Howie said.

"Let's get polluted," yelled someone in the back of the plane. The flight from Miami to Nassau lasts forty-seven minutes but it was long enough, as Matthias had often observed, for tourists to get the pollution process well under way. They were itching to check into the hotels of Paradise Island or West Bay Street, where a getaway world of booze, smoke and sex with partners whose names they didn't always get straight was waiting just for them: the sheets were being changed at that very moment. There were no raised voices on the return flights.

The plane banked between two thunderheads, descended over water that changed abruptly from deep indigo to translucent green, glided over a narrow stretch of scrubland and jack pine and landed at the airport. The door opened. Hot, moist air came in. Hot, moist four-day-three-nighters went out. They filed unknowingly past the empty corner in the terminal where Blind Blake had played his banjo for so many years and into the long lines at the immigration booths. Matthias went to the booth with no lines, marked RETURNING RESIDENTS. "Nice trip, Mr. Matthias?" asked the immigration officer, waving him through.

In the parking lot, two shirtless boys, ten or eleven, were eyeing his Yamaha 535. "You boys don't want this old thing," he said, climbing on and starting the engine. "Too slow." They giggled. Matthias drove off.

The bottom of the sun was just touching the horizon

when Matthias leaned into the turn at Love Beach and rode through the feathery shadows of the casuarinas. The sun wobbled at the impact, as though it had really been made of Jell-O all the time, and quickly slipped away. A minute later the sea, which had been a caldron of red and gold, went black. By the time Matthias reached the downtown part of Bay Street, the sky, which had been a pastel version of the sea, had blackened too, and a round white moon had risen over the low roofs of the shops and office buildings.

The shops were closed, the office workers had gone home, the street was quiet. The air felt hot and wet and thick, more like a low density ocean than a mixture of gases. Matthias parked his bike in front of Island Cameras and approached the adjoining door. There were half a dozen bronze name plaques on the wall—Island Imports, Inc., The Bank of Zurich and the Bahamas, the Nassau Panamanian Bank, RR Group, RR Investments Ltd., Ravoukian and Ravoukian, Barristers and Solicitors—but only one buzzer. As Matthias reached for it, he heard a husky whisper from the shadows: "Smoke?"

Matthias didn't reply.

The whisper came again, more insistent. "Hey, mahn. You wan' some smoke?"

"Nope," said Matthias. Soft footsteps padded away.

Matthias pressed the buzzer. A voice crackled from a speaker above the door. "Yes?"

"Matthias," Matthias said. The door clicked open.

Matthias stepped inside, closed the door behind him and climbed a worn wooden staircase. At the top were another set of name plaques and a single door, partly open. As he went inside, through the simply furnished waiting room, with its mildewing copies of *People* and *Ebony*, he smelled burning tobacco, strong and European, the same smell released on opening a book by Eric Ambler.

Ravoukian sat behind his desk in the inner office. He was writing rapidly on a legal pad; blue smoke curled slowly up from his cigarette until the ceiling fan sucked it in and whirled it away. Ravoukian looked up. He was a short, round man with big dark eyes, made bigger by the thick lenses of his glasses. "Not good?" he said.

"Not good."

Ravoukian leaned back in his chair and sighed, blowing

a smoke cone across the room. "You look tired, Mr. Matthias. Sit down."

Matthias sat. Smoke rose. The ceiling fan turned. Through the walls came the faint chordings of a guitar. The Bahamian beat: like reggae, but a little faster and less pronounced. Ravoukian stubbed out his cigarette in a styrofoam coffee cup. He peered for a while at the ashes inside as though reading tea leaves. "It's too bad," he said. "Too, too bad. I think you have—would have had—better than a fifty-fifty chance on appeal."

"On what grounds?"

Ravoukian waved his plump hand. "Various. There were procedural errors. Some of the medical evidence might be shown to have been tainted. A few other things." Somewhere behind the wall, the guitarist stopped playing. The room was silent.

Matthias said: "Do you ever work on a contingency basis?"

"What are you suggesting, Mr. Matthias?"

Matthias forced the words out; perhaps he was only able to speak them because he knew what the response would be. "Take the appeal and I'll give you half of Zombie Bay."

Ravoukian smiled. He had a mouthful of crooked teeth that he'd never bothered to fix. Ravoukian didn't have to waste money on front: his reputation was all the front he needed. "And what if we lose? What happens to my share then?"

"You said I had a better than fifty-fifty chance."

"And that is my true opinion. But I'm not a gambler, Mr. Matthias. I charge a fee, based on my experience and the amount of work invested. My retainer for any work in the Court of Appeal, as I think I mentioned, is fifty thousand, U.S."

Ravoukian already had thirty thousand dollars of his money from the first trial. Matthias rose. His body suddenly seemed very heavy and it was a great effort. The big dark eyes were watching him without expression, as though viewing a not particularly interesting movie already seen several times.

"I have had one small thought, Mr. Matthias."

"About what?"

"Taking your appeal. Sit down, please."

Matthias felt like a clinical subject in a stimulus-response experiment, but he sat down.

Ravoukian pushed the legal pad aside, cleared a neat space on the middle of his desk. He put his hands together in the attitude of prayer and rested them in the cleared space. "When you first came to me about this matter, Mr. Matthias, I knew nothing about you. I hadn't even heard of you. You'll pardon me for noting this fact. I've been practicing law from this office for thirty-five years. I thought I knew everyone in the Bahamas. Of the ownership class. But somehow you escaped my knowledge. My loss, Mr. Matthias, because I have since learned a little about you, all creditable."

"Like what?"

Ravoukian waved his plump hand again. Matthias wondered whether it was a tic that jumped in him whenever he was asked for details. "You were a Seal, for instance. I've always been an admirer of the training provided by elite military organizations. I've also heard something of your Cuban adventure. And—"

"Who have you been talking to?"

"No one special. It seems to be common knowledge, in certain circles, at least. I've also learned how Zombie Bay came into your hands—an inspirational tale, if true. It all confirms my belief that you could be a very useful man."

"To whom?"

Ravoukian showed his crooked teeth. "As a Seal, Mr. Matthias, were you trained in the use of underwater explosives?"

"Yes."

"I thought as much. I'm an admirer of the Seals, the Green Berets, all those groups. I like the philosophy they instill."

"I didn't enlist in the Navy for its philosophy," Matthias said. "I needed someone to pay my college tuition. It was that or the draft."

"Yes, yes," said Ravoukian, as if Matthias had reinforced his argument. "Of course. Precisely the attitude certain acquaintances of mine would desire."

"Are you proposing something, Mr. Ravoukian?"

Ravoukian leaned forward slightly. "These acquaintances might have a job for you. If they did, and if you were prepared to take it on, I would be prepared to handle your appeal gratis."

"What job?"

Ravoukian sat back. "That would be better described by them. Perhaps a meeting could be arranged."

"Perhaps."

"Naturally your expenses would be taken care of. Airplane tickets, hotels, meals, et cetera."

"Tickets to where, Mr. Ravoukian?"

"Paris would be a good meeting place, I think. Do you know Paris, Mr. Matthias?"

"No. Are these friends—"

"Acquaintances, Mr.—"

"—or whatever you want to call them, are they countrymen of yours?"

"Do you mean Bahamians, Mr. Matthias?"

"I mean Armenians."

"I don't think we can speak of Armenians as countrymen. Armenians have no country of their own, Mr. Matthias." Ravoukian's tone remained bland and professional, but his stubby fingers shook slightly as he reached for a cigarette.

Matthias said: "Does this job involve underwater explosives, Mr. Ravoukian?"

Ravoukian didn't reply right away. He sucked on the cigarette. Its end glowed and so did his eyes. "That's for my acquaintances to answer."

Ravoukian's last word lit up a memory in Matthias's mind: Cesarito, who had listened to Top 40 radio all the time to improve his English, singing softly from the bow on that last night: *De ansair ma fren is blown in de win.* "I'll have to think about your proposal, Mr. Ravoukian."

"By all means. But there are time constraints." Ravoukian rose and crossed the room to the file cabinets. He wore sandals. Matthias smelled leather and sweat. Ravoukian found a file and returned to the desk. He took out a letter. "This is from the plaintiff's U.S. counsel. It's a polite reminder that notice of appeal must be filed by the twelfth of December—six months from the finding of the lower court. Otherwise the judgment stands and, as it says, 'payment of said judgment, that is one million one hundred thousand dollars (U.S.), will be due on that date.' " Ravoukian laid the letter on his desk. The paper itself seemed intimidating: thick and deckle-edged. And so did the letterhead: Ablewhite, Godfrey, Percival & Glyde.

Matthias rose again. "I'll let you know," he said. This time Ravoukian didn't call him back.

Matthias rode to the East Bay marina. He parked the bike beside East Bay Divers, dropped the key in the letter slot and walked to the end of the dock. *So What*, his nineteen-foot Mako with the twin Merc nineties, floated in the last slip. Matthias climbed aboard, cast off and motored slowly west along the channel. A big cruiser was coming the other way, much too fast; its wash foamed in the moonlight. The cruiser went by with a roar of motors and music; Matthias, rocking in its wake, saw a man and a woman standing with champagne flutes in the stern. The man wore a white suit, the woman a white skirt and nothing else. She saw Matthias and waved. Her breasts gleamed like marble. The man tilted his head and drained his glass.

Matthias passed the tip of Paradise Island, rounded Silver Cay and backed off until the compass came around to two hundred and seventy-eight degrees. Then he pushed the throttles all the way down. *So What* raised its bow in the air like a rearing horse and surged forward. Matthias headed for home.

The sea was a flat sheet of silver and black. The boat skimmed along so smoothly it seemed to have levitated above the surface, gliding the way boats glide in the dreams of little boys. Nothing moved except the moon rising above, and Matthias cutting through the water below, like two bits of matter scattered by the Big Bang. There was no sound but the twin nineties, and after a while it ceased to be sound, leaving Matthias alone with his thoughts.

He thought of everyone he had mishandled during the day, of Dicky Dumaurier, Marilyn, Ravoukian—and Danny, most of all: Danny, swinging at a ball he couldn't hit; Danny pounding his club on the rubber mat. Danny was to the ball as he was to Danny: he hadn't connected. Perhaps Danny was already beyond his reach, driven away by the Big Bang of the divorce. Or was it just his own ignorance of what a father did and how he did it?

Matthias had no memories of his own father. He had
died young, leaving him a name he didn't like, a blurred
photograph and a medal. The name: Nathan Hale. Was
it chosen because his father admired the patriot or had a
premonition his son would come to a similar end? Matthias
didn't know. The photograph: a sailor in dress blues standing on a beach with a smile on his face. It had lain in the
back of a drawer in a plywood chest that had been lost on
one of the moves. The medal: the Medal of Honor in a
velvet-lined box. Matthias could still recall the feel of its
inanimate coolness in his hand: touching it was one of his
earliest memories, reaching back to a time long before he
had ever heard of Okinawa or World War II. The medal
was sold by Stepdaddy Number Two to make a monthly
payment on his Coupe de Ville.

Matthias could no longer picture the face of Stepdaddy
Number Two, but he retained a sparkling image of that
two-tone Coupe de Ville, its red-and-white bodywork polished by Stepdaddy Number Two until it glowed. One
Sunday morning an errant baseball went through its windshield while it was parked in the yard; the sound had gotten
Stepdaddy Number Two out of bed and running outside
in his undershorts, whirling his belt in the air. Matthias's
legs had frozen at the sight. He hadn't been able to run a
step. Number Two had given him the kind of beating that
was known in their neighborhood as "a good whipping."
Matthias could picture the belt as vividly as the Coupe de
Ville—snakeskin with a silver buckle. Once he'd woken
in the night and seen his mother wearing it and nothing
else.

So What glided over the Tongue of the Ocean with Matthias barely touching the wheel, never checking the compass. The boat knew the way. On the northwest horizon,
where the black of the sky met the lesser black of the sea,
Matthias saw the rounded shadows of the Berry Islands,
as clearly as he would have seen them by day. The full
moon lit the world as finely as the sun, but worked only
in black. It had been on a silent night much like this that
they had drifted in to the beach at the foot of the Sierra
Maestra. Cesarito. Rodriguez. Cruz-Romero. And the boy
Tonio.

Cesarito. *De ansair ma fren is blown in de win.*

Cesarito had sung nervously under his breath while they unloaded the crates on the beach and waited for Rodriguez's brother's men to come down out of the hills. Matthias had set the anchor and swum in to help them. He needn't have done that: he was simply the boatman, in for the money. That little swim had led to his second whipping.

Men had come out of the Sierra Maestra, but they were Fidel's men, not Rodriguez's brother's. Guns went off. Rodriguez and the boy had fallen on the spot. Tonio. A skinny boy. A burst of automatic fire had cut through his neck; Tonio's head had hit the sand with a thump Matthias heard clearly, distinct from all the noises of the fighting. Then he had turned toward the boat, seen the way blocked and run into the hills. Two days later, filthy, ragged, scratched by thorns, he had stepped out of the bush into the gunsights of a patrol. "*Yo soy turisto,*" he had said, raising his hands. They hadn't even cracked a smile.

Then came two years on the Isle of Pines: sleeping every night with a knife made from a fork in his hand. Isla de Piños, where he had done what he did for Cesarito and where they punished him for it; where Cesarito died anyway, but left him a gift: Zombie Bay, one of many things owned by the son of rich Habaneros. But no amount of money could ever have bought Cesarito's freedom: he was a class enemy. Matthias, a lower and less worthy form of antagonist, was swapped for medical supplies. Two years on the Isle of Pines. He'd survived. He'd even come back with a few funny stories to tell, at least they seemed funny in the bar at Zombie Bay. He came back with those funny stories and the scars on his back.

Now Matthias could make out a square-topped shadow due west: the Bluff. He thought he could even see a yellow light shining from its northern end. Hew had trouble sleeping. He read old copies of *Punch* until dawn. Matthias pulled back on the throttles. The sea lifted the bow into the air and let it gently down. Matthias set the throttles at neutral and switched off the engines.

True silence fell all around him. All sound was of his own making: his breathing, his pulse, the scraping of his hard shoes on the deck. His businessman shoes. He took them off. Then he took off his suit, his shirt, his socks, his undershorts. He stood behind the console, floating over the Tongue of the Ocean, the bottom a thousand fathoms beneath his feet.

Matthias climbed over the side of *So What* and slipped into the sea. The water was warm, warmer than the air. He floated on his back for a while, drifting on a slow current beside his boat.Then he rolled over, jackknifed and kicked down.

Not far. Forty feet, maybe fifty, he couldn't tell, didn't care. He saw the same thing eyes open or closed: blackness. The sea drummed and gurgled in his ears. Matthias stopped kicking, straightened, hung suspended in the water. The ocean drummed and gurgled its soft song to him. *Yo soy turisto*, he thought, almost laughing aloud. Then he realized where he was: not far from the spot where the plaintiff and his nameless partner had gone down. Matthias kicked his way back up.

So What had drifted to the north. The current was running faster than he had thought. The tide had turned. With long easy strokes, Matthias swam after it, caught the transom, pulled himself up. As he dried his body with his shirt, he sensed the day coming behind him. He turned and saw a milky spill in the eastern sky. Everything was black and white for a few moments. Then color was discovered and immediately splashed across the sky and sea without restraint. Matthias knew there was something much bigger than mankind. Not God, necessarily, just bigger. It was a something you never saw in places like the Isle of Pines.

Matthias had his answer to Ravoukian's offer. Yes, he knew how to use explosives underwater. Yes, he wanted to keep Zombie Bay; it was hard to imagine his life without it. But he wouldn't do anything that would put him on a Turkish version of Isla de Piños. He wouldn't let himself be that stupid twice. He also wouldn't be stupid enough to believe he had better than a fifty-fifty chance. The answer was no. He had until December twelfth to think of something else.

Matthias switched on the engines and headed for Andros. The blue-black water turned bottle-green; he ran south along the Bluff to Gun Point, then threaded his way through the coral heads they called The Angel Fingers and sliced a widening V in the baby-blue water of Zombie Bay.

The club lay under tall palms behind the long curved beach: the central hut with the bar, dining room and library; the office; the cottages; the equipment shed. How tiny it all looked, like a play town in a sandbox. But it was perfect.

Dawn. August 1.

|8|

August first was not a good day to be six months pregnant in the city of New York. Nina had the feeling she'd been teleported to Planet Greenhouse, with a gravity like Jupiter's and a climate like Kinshasa's. All the life forms swung back and forth between somnolence and psychosis, smelled like goats and wheezed with every breath. Everyone who could get out of town had done so. Suze was at Tanglewood with the Auschwitz Cadillac man; Jason was on the road with the West Village Croquet Team. Nina had an invitation to Nantucket, but August first was the date of her introductory childbirth class.

She staggered outside. A cab shimmied over to the curb. Nina got in and and gave the address to the driver.

"Fucking shit," he said.

Too late, Nina realized the air-conditioning wasn't working. She closed her eyes. She felt the car move, stop, move, stop. From time to time the driver said, "Fucking shit," again, but Nina didn't open her eyes to find out why. Then, in the thick of a noxious crosstown traffic jam, Nina felt something for the first time: movement in her womb. It was a little rolling movement, as though a sleeper had changed positions in the middle of a long night.

Nina placed her hand gently on her strange, round belly, hoping for more. "Are you okay, baby?" she said.

"Huh?" said the driver.

Her womb was still.

The class was held at the West Side Women's Reproductive Counseling Center. Every woman except Nina had brought a man. The men were either soft and round or long and skinny; the women had pink faces and mottled skin. They sat in a circle on blue gym mats, like Brownies and Cub Scouts at their twentieth reunion. "Who's afraid of pain?" asked the instructor, who looked slim and snappy in culottes and a tank top.

Hands went up. Various deodorants warred in the still air. "Not you?" she asked one of the soft men, whose hand had remained at his side.

"I've got a high tolerance," he replied.

The instructor smiled at him. "Imagine you had to defecate a watermelon," she said. "Think you could tolerate that?"

The man blushed and looked down at the mat. The instructor was used to whipping rogue males into line. "Today," she continued, addressing the group, "we're going to begin learning techniques for mastering pain while resorting as little as possible—preferably not at all—to potentially harmful drugs and medical procedures. We'll start by working on awareness. First let's establish the difference between discomfort and pain. I want all you labor coaches to pinch the biceps of your expectant partners. Expectant partners, close your eyes and concentrate on your physical feelings. All set? Oops. Hold on a sec." Nina found that the instructor's quick eyes were on her. "You haven't brought your coach?"

"I'm still interviewing."

The instructor didn't laugh. Neither did anyone else. "I'll do the honors," said the instructor, coming around and sitting beside her. "Ready? Go."

Then Nina felt bony fingers on her right biceps. They squeezed—until the word "squeeze" no longer applied and had to be replaced by "dug into"—Nina's flesh, causing shooting pain up and down her arm. Nina had a mad vision of punching the instructor squarely on her bobbed little nose. The vision sustained her until the bony fingers went away.

"Tweet," said the instructor, calling a halt. "Now then, what did we learn about pain?"

"That it hurts?" an exhausted-looking woman suggested tentatively.

"Very good. And what about discomfort?"

"It doesn't hurt?"

"That's right. What does it do?"

Sucks, Nina thought.

"Bothers?" said another woman.

"Excellent. Today we learn to turn pain into bother."

They turned pain into bother. This was accomplished by sniffing-and-blowing, huff-huff-huffing-and-puffing, tune-tapping and several other techniques Nina forgot immediately.

"Tune-tapping?" someone asked.

"Especially recommended for the second stage," the instructor said. "Think of a favorite tune and tap out its rhythm on the sheet. Put your whole self into that finger, into that rhythm, that favorite song. It's important to have the song selected well ahead of time, just as it's important to have a full tank of gas and a packed ditty bag."

The couples conferred.

" 'When a Man Loves a Woman'?"

" 'Last Train to Clarksville'?"

" 'The Night They Drove Old Dixie Down'?"

" 'In-a-Gadda-da-Vida'?"

They resolved to return in three weeks with their selections set and ditty bags organized. Nina left with a bruise purpling on her arm and the realization that she wouldn't be back. On the street a tall, well-dressed old man carrying shiny new garden shears passed by, glancing quickly at her belly.

The Cub Scouts and Brownies filed out behind her. "Chosen a name yet?" one asked.

"Anton," replied another. "Ophelia, if it's a girl."

Nina went home and had a cold shower. Then she lay down on her bed and thought about names. None appealed. She would call it Henrik, for now. "Kick me again, my little laureate," she said, looking down at her belly and speaking out loud for the second time to a fetus that couldn't possibly hear her. It was a Saturday. There was work to do at the office. But Nina stayed on the bed, doing nothing, thinking nothing, waiting without boredom or impatience for Henrik to kick again. After a while he did. "Good boy," she said.

A month later, the Sunday that *Living Without Men and Children . . . and Loving It* first hit *The New York Times'*

bestseller list, Nina got a call from a woman at the public
health department.

"Ms. Kitchener?"

"Yes."

"I understand you are no longer attending the West Side
Women's childbirth clinic. Are you having any problems
with your pregnancy?"

"No."

There was a pause. "I trust you understand the importance of good nutrition and health practices during pregnancy."

"Of course."

"Smoking and drinking alcohol can cause severe birth
defects."

"I know that," said Nina, who had just opened a bottle
of champagne sent over by womynpress. "What's this all
about? There's no law that you have to go to childbirth
class, is there?"

"No. This is simply routine. I'm so glad everything is
all right." The woman hung up.

Nina drank a glass of champagne and half of another.
Then, still a little annoyed, she called the West Side Center
and got the instructor's home number.

"Do you always inform on anyone who drops out of the
childbirth class?"

"What are you talking about?"

Nina described the phone call.

"We have no connection with the public health department," the instructor told her. "None at all. What was the
woman's name?"

But Nina hadn't gotten a name. Had the woman said
she was a nurse? Nina couldn't remember. She hadn't
sounded like a nurse: a little too old, perhaps, old and
upper-class. Nina pictured a grandmother, the kind of
grandmother who might have tea at the Carlyle and own
a house in the South of France. She apologized to the
instructor and said goodbye. What was happening to her?
She had learned to talk like an idiot to a fetus, but she'd
forgotten how to get the facts straight from a simple phone
call.

Nina drained the glass and poured another. Henrik
gave her a kick, the hardest one yet. She put the glass
down.

|9|

One day the white ceiling moved.

"Do you think it's all right?" asked Mother, somewhere out of sight.

"Not to worry," said the medical man, drifting into view. "He's completely stabilized. The fresh air'll do him good." The medical man looked down at him with a too-big smile. "Hello, Happy," he said. "Dr. Robert, remember? It's a beautiful day. Feel like going outside?"

All the while, the ceiling kept moving. He lost sight of the molding, the spider web, the spider. Of course the ceiling wasn't moving: he was. He could hear wheels turning beneath him as he passed under a lintel, then under a cream-colored ceiling that went on and on—he was in the first-floor hall in the old part of the house: he'd been in the nursery the whole time!—and finally under another lintel and out. Out beneath a blue sky that was beautiful, as Dr. Robert had said, beautiful beyond anything he'd ever seen. Blue itself was beautiful. Blue saturated his senses. He could feel blueness and even taste it. The taste made him thirsty. He longed for a drink, a tall blue drink with bobbing blue ice cubes. How long had it been since he had drunk anything? He had no idea.

A crow flapped slowly across the sky: Happy could see its yellow feet tucked up under the tail, and hear the beating of its heavy wings. High above, towering white clouds floated by like weightless icebergs. The whole earth was alive, a living thing. Its electromagnetic force tingled in every inch of his skin.

"Do you think he understands anything?" Mother said in a half-whisper.

Dr. Robert sighed, then spoke at normal volume. "The tests still aren't conclusive. There may have been some memory loss, but if it's true locked-in syndrome, then yes, it's possible he understands. It's even possible that he understands everything. But there is some indication of damage above the lower brain stem. We're still back-and-forthing on that. If it turns out to be the case . . ."

"Then what?" asked Mother, speaking still more softly, perhaps in an effort to get Dr. Robert to whisper too.

But he didn't take the hint. "Hard to say," he replied.

Mother spoke again. This time Happy could hardly hear her. He thought she said: "How does all this bear on the prognosis?"

"In what respect?"

Mother answered inaudibly.

"Oh, it has no effect at all," Dr. Robert said. "The chances of that are nil, I'm afraid, barring some miraculous advance in medicine."

Then he was rolling again. Trees loomed overhead. Maple, beech, elm, poplar, all crowned in autumn colors. They cut sharp-edged red and orange holes in the blue sky. He thought: Modern art isn't modern—it's been here all the time; and lost himself in the patterns. Lost himself until he had another thought: Autumn. How could it be autumn? And of what year?

Those were questions Happy would have liked to ask. But he couldn't ask, and even if he could, no one seemed to be around. Not Mother, not Dr. Robert. He was alone with the sky, the trees and a metallic clip-clipping sound that came closer and closer.

Then a rose appeared, inches from his face. A white rose of purest white, whiter than anything he had ever seen. Whiter than the clouds, whiter than snow, whiter than chalk. The petals fanned out in fleshy concentric circles, heavy, moist, sensual. A red bug no bigger than a pinpoint skittered toward the depths of the flower. And the smell: he had no words to describe the smell. It was the smell of the living planet.

Then he saw the hand holding the rose: a big, veiny

hand, the skin old and liver-spotted. He wanted time to
think about that hand, but before he could, a voice said:
"Do you like this rose?"

Fritz. The gardener. Memory loss: he had almost forgotten Fritz. Fritz's face came into view: a bony face with
eyes almost as blue as the sky, and hair almost as white
as the rose. Fritz was old. He had always been old. Now
he must be very old—eighty-five? ninety? more? But Fritz
was up and sinewy, and he was down.

"I bred it myself," Fritz said. "From an unusually white
Athena and a hybrid of my own invention." Fritz's face
came closer and Happy saw his sun-damaged skin, mottled, wrinkled. "Breeding is half the battle," Fritz said.
"The other half is weeding. Breeding and weeding. Do
you understand?"

Was he waiting for an answer? There was no answer.
Fritz produced a pair of shiny garden shears, snipped the
rose off the stem and stuck it in the lapel of his old tweed
jacket. "I know you understand," he said. "You're a smart
boy."

Boy?

Fritz was gone, and the rose-smell gone too. Happy
looked up at the sky. He almost lost himself in the sight.
Then he began to see a suitcase tumbling through it. He
felt cold and wanted to go back inside. He waited for
someone to take him.

|10|

When it drops .
Oh you gotta feel it
Know what you were doin' wrong
It is you oh yeah yeah yeah
I say pressure drop oh pressure oh yeah
Pressure gonna drop on you.

Krio, dreadlocks swinging in the candlelight, sang in his soft baritone and strummed his sun-bleached guitar. He was sitting on a bar stool, shirtless, barefoot, but still wearing his apron. Moxie stood behind the bar, holding up a pretzel and trying to get Chick to talk. "Say 'son of a bitch,' Chick. Say 'son of a bitch.' " Chick stared straight ahead and said nothing. Matthias sat at a corner table, sorting through piles of charge slips and entering figures in a ledger. All the guests—the main house was full, as were all the cottages except 6, which had the toilet problem again, and 8, where the cockroach incident had taken place—had gone to bed.

"Power be comin' on?" Moxie said.

Krio stopped playing. "It always do," he said. He struck a match and lit a fat joint. The joint moved back and forth across the bar, passed from one brown hand to another. It was offered to Matthias. He shook his head: he didn't want the numbers to start swimming across the page.

"Pressure," sang Moxie, off-key, "oh pressure."

"Pressure gonna drop on you," Krio finished the lyric, drawing out the last note like a siren fading into the distance. Then it was quiet, except for the sea, stirring restlessly on its bed.

"Say 'son of a bitch,' Chick," Moxie said. Chick did not respond.

Matthias held up a salt-stained slip. "What did the Lorings do today?"

"Loring?" said Moxie.

"The couple in Two."

"She the one who puked in the pool last night?" Krio asked.

"No," said Matthias. "The one whose husband sent the wine back."

"Oh yeah," said Moxie. "I took them to the Joulter reef." A smile tugged at the corners of his mouth. He suppressed it.

"What's so funny?" Matthias said.

The smile, liberated, spread across Moxie's face. "First ting, I give the warning. You know—I be pointing to the fire coral, waving no no."

"And?"

"The man he dive down, break off a piece and stick it in his pants."

Krio laughed, shooting a smoke ball into the air. The lights flickered and came on.

"Son of a bitch," said Chick, flapping his green wings.

"Power," said Moxie, popping the pretzel in Chick's beak.

"To the people," Krio said, leaning across the bar to blow out the candle.

Matthias totaled the dive charges for the day. The barge, *Two Drink Minimum*, had taken twelve divers to the coral heads off the Bluff. $12 \times \$40 = \$480$. Moxie had taken the Lorings in *Who Cares* to the reefs off the Joulter Cays, with picnic lunch. $2 \times \$75 = \$150 + \$25 = \$175$. The two divers from the Baltimore Dive Club, in Cottage 4, had taken four tanks and *So What* to the drop-off. $2 \times \$50 = \$100 + \$150$ (for the boat) $= \$250$. Matthias charged them $175. He liked having good divers at the club.

"Numbers okay?" Krio asked.

Matthias looked up. They were both watching him, Krio's face bony, ascetic; Moxie's fuller, more like a choirboy's: he was thirty, but he looked eighteen. Matthias knew Krio wasn't asking about the numbers: he was asking about the future.

"Good enough," Matthias said. "We'll be fine as long as the weather holds."

They all glanced outside, past the palm fronds which fringed the roof of the open bar, past the patio, the pool and the beach, and saw curls foaming on the inner reef and a sky sparkling with stars. "Nothing wrong with the weather," Krio said. He laid his guitar on a shelf behind the bar and took off his apron.

"What's tomorrow night?" Matthias asked.

"Conch fritter. Grouper, if Nottage gets me some. Guava duff."

"Sounds good."

Krio, knowing it would be good, nodded. He offered Chick a pretzel, which was ignored, and went off. They heard the engine of his old car fire, heard it clank and rumble south on the dirt road that led to his tiny house on the edge of Conchtown, clanking and rumbling down the decibel scale.

Then out of the darkness appeared Mrs. Loring; her bare feet had made no sound on the patio. Mrs. Loring was wearing a filmy top that covered her hips as long as she made no sudden movements. Chick shifted on his perch and turned his hard yellow eyes on her.

Between Mrs. Loring's eyebrows were two vertical frown lines Matthias didn't remember noticing before. "I don't suppose you've got any calamine lotion," she said.

"In the office," Matthias said, getting up. He left the bar, cut across the corner of the patio and opened the office door. Mrs. Loring followed him; he heard the soft padding of her bare feet close behind.

Matthias turned on the light, then felt around on the top shelf along the back wall, where the first-aid supplies were kept. "It's not for me," said Mrs. Loring. "It's for El Kabong. He's got himself a rash in a very peculiar place."

Plain aloe would do a better job on Mr. Loring's fire coral stings and some grew right outside the door; it would have been a simple matter to break off a piece and give it to her. But Matthias didn't want to get into the nature-boy routine with Mrs. Loring.

"He's my third," said Mrs. Loring, as Matthias's hand closed around the jar of lotion. All at once she was very close behind him; he smelled wine on her breath and as he turned her breast touched his forearm.

"Here you go," he said, handing her the lotion.

She took it. Her hand managed to make a lot of contact with his during the exchange. She looked up at him, eyes filling with hot promise, the way eyes do in boy-meets-girl movies.

"Best to keep your hands off any coral, Mrs. Loring," Matthias said, "until you're sure you know what stings."

"Sometimes I like to be stung," said Mrs. Loring. She reached for his chest and stroked it in a way that left no doubt about the contents of any movie they might make. "And call me Rhoda," she said.

Matthias backed away. "Good night, Rhoda," he told her. "I hope your husband feels better in the morning."

The temperature dropped in her eyes. "How kind," she said, and turning abruptly—a movement that raised the hem of her top, exposing her buttocks in a way that made her seem vulnerable rather than sexual to Matthias, and so made him feel bad—she walked out into the darkness. There was a gulf between men and women, all right, and he wanted to bridge it, just once. But it took more than a penis; he'd learned that in his marriage and in his early years at the club, with other Rhodas. Matthias returned to the bar.

"Drink?" said Moxie.

"Sure."

Moxie poured half a glass of Mount Gay, added ice cubes and slices of lime. Matthias crossed the room to get it; he had never overcome his aversion to being waited on by the employees, especially by Moxie, who was a diver and filled in at the bar only when they were short-staffed.

Matthias sat on a stool. "Have something, Mox."

Moxie opened a Pauli Girl and tilted it to his lips, draining the contents in two gulps. Matthias wrapped his hand around the tumbler, found himself staring into it, where capsized green boats floated on a golden sea. Feeling Moxie's eyes on him, he raised the glass, swallowed some rum, then some more. Moxie poured more. Matthias drank more. "Open another, Mox," he said. Why keep costs down now? "Don't have to ask."

Matthias waited for Moxie's laugh, a musical giggle that he never tired of. Moxie didn't laugh. He stared at the busty fraulein on the beer bottle for a while then drank the contents down. "Danny comin' soon?" Moxie said.

"No."

"Rafer he always aks me."

"How is Rafer?"

Moxie looked down at his blurred reflection on the polished bar. "Okay," Moxie said. A few moments later he added, "I guess." Moxie's boy was with his wife in Nassau. It didn't look as if she were coming back.

Matthias had another glass of Mount Gay. Moxie had another Pauli Girl. "What you say about the numbers . . ."

"Yeah?"

"It be the trut', mahn?"

"Sure."

Moxie nodded. His eyes moved toward the sea. "So what means that about the . . . accident?"

"Nothing new." That was true. What Moxie didn't know was that they had less than eight weeks to file the appeal. Matthias hadn't told him, not because he didn't want Moxie to know; he just didn't want to say it out loud. Now he hoped Moxie would talk about something else.

But once started, Moxie couldn't. "It happen just like I say," he said, as he had many times before.

"I know that."

"They come, they show the dive card, Brock say okay, I fill the tanks. Like always, with the door open."

"I know."

"Then how it happen, mahn?"

That was the question Matthias couldn't answer and Ravoukian hadn't been able to finesse.

"Give me a kiss," said Chick.

Moxie swept the room and went to bed. Matthias put the account books in the office and started up the path to the Bluff, taking the bottle of Mount Gay with him. The half-wild dogs that roamed the night heard him coming and began their savage barking; their low shadows glided through the scrub.

There were two houses on the Bluff: Hew's big one,

where a light still shone, at the top, and Matthias's little
one halfway up. Matthias climbed the stairs to the deck,
slid open the screen and went inside. Without turning on
the lights, he poured a drink and sat in the small living
room, looking east. His view was all sky and sea: two magic
cloths stitched invisibly at the horizon. Here, at its nar-
rowest point, the Tongue of the Ocean hooked south,
extending the length of the island. On the other side of
the underwater canyon, Two-Head Cay, an eroded H with
the legs cut off, was the only land in sight.

Matthias finished his drink, went into the bedroom and
lay down. He felt sand on the sheets, but didn't bother to
brush it off. He was used to it. He closed his eyes. The
image of Mrs. Loring's white buttocks was the first thing
he saw, now no longer vulnerable, but sexual. He opened
his eyes and watched the ceiling change from black to
charcoal gray.

There was no need for the fan. Sea breezes blew around
the Bluff every night. He could hear them slipping through
the louvers, hear the surf pawing at the coral cliff below.
These were the sounds that always prefaced sleep, but
tonight sleep didn't come. The wind and surf sounds just
grew louder instead, until there was nothing soporific
about them. Matthias got up.

He sat at his desk, switched on the light and removed
the file he kept in the top drawer. He took out the tran-
script. It opened by itself to Moxie's testimony.

PLAINTIFF: Describe, if you will, the events of September
2.

WITNESS: When the two men come?

PLAINTIFF: Correct.

WITNESS: They ask for air. I say I need to see a dive card.
Mr. Matthias, he say no card, no air. The man had
a kind of card, but not PADI, not NAUI. Brock
say—

PLAINTIFF: Brock?

WITNESS: Brock McGillivray. The divemaster. He say it be
a French card, so fill the tanks. I fill them that night.
Next morning, they take them.

PLAINTIFF: Is this one of the tanks in question?

WITNESS: What question?

PLAINTIFF: Is this one of the tanks you filled? The stenographer is unable to record a nod. Answer aloud. Is this one of the tanks?

WITNESS: Yeah.

PLAINTIFF: Note that the air tank, bearing the Zombie Bay Club logo—this ZB with the silhouette of a descending scuba diver—and numbered 27, is entered into evidence as Exhibit D. Now then, Mr. Wickham, can you recall the number of the other tank?

WITNESS: 28.

PLAINTIFF: And where is tank number 28?

WITNESS: I don't know.

PLAINTIFF: You don't know? Isn't it true that number 28, filled, like number 27, with poisoned air, went to the bottom of the ocean on the back of the man who showed you the French dive card? The stenographer cannot record a shrug, Mr. Wickham. Did the tank go to the bottom?

MR. RAVOUKIAN: Objection. The witness is being asked for speculation.

JUDGE: Sustained.

The judge had sustained many of Ravoukian's objections, allowing him to lop off this or that appendage of the plaintiff's case. But he hadn't been able to touch the core of the lawsuit: that tank number 27, belonging to the Zombie Bay Club and last filled on the Zombie Bay compressor, then rented to Mr. Hiram Standish, Jr., of New York for twenty-five dollars, had contained, according to laboratory analysis, a 7 percent level of carbon monoxide, which, because of the effect of submersion on the partial pressures of gases, had caused Mr. Standish to fall into a coma from which he would never emerge.

How had it happened? Ravoukian had asked that again and again. The compressor was tested and found to be working perfectly, although as plaintiff's counsel had observed, there was no proof that it hadn't been repaired between the time of the accident and the test. Moxie swore that he had followed the usual procedure—the doors and windows of the compressor room had been opened during the fill, allowing the circulation of air. But there was only Moxie's word for it. It was also possible that a car with its engine running might have been parked outside while the tank was being filled, and that the prevailing wind could have blown the exhaust gases into the compressor room. None of this mattered, according to the plaintiff's attorney—it wasn't necessary for him to show exactly how the negligence had occurred, only that it had. The judge had agreed.

One million one hundred thousand. U.S.

Matthias closed the file and replaced it in the drawer. He sat for a while looking at nothing. Then he turned off the light and looked at nothing in the dark.

Later he rose and found the bottle of Mount Gay. He took it out to the deck. A front was moving in from the east. The sea breezes blew harder, merged, became a strong wind. A solid line of thick pearly edged cloud slid over the stars. Soon the only lights left were Hew's, at the top of the Bluff, and a faint yellow flicker from the direction of Two-Head Cay. Two-Head Cay was owned by Hiram Standish's family, a fact that Matthias hadn't known until the trial, but Ravoukian had discovered that no one except the caretakers, Gene Albury and his wife, had lived there for many years, and that Standish hadn't been there before his arrival at Zombic Bay.

The wind blew. Hew's light went out. Clouds covered Two-Head Cay. Matthias threw the empty bottle into the darkness. It arced out of sight and made no splash that he could hear.

Something rustled in the sea grapes; a bent form moved unsteadily on the path up the Bluff. "Nottage?"

The shadow was still. "Don' scare me like dat," said Nottage in his deep, ragged voice. After a long pause he asked: "You got a drink?"

"All gone. Maybe you should get some sleep. Krio wants grouper tomorrow."

"I ain' sleepy. An' I got my own drink." Liquid gurgled. Nottage came closer, close enough for Matthias to distinguish his curly white Afro over the deck railing; the black face remained unseen. "Sea on fire, boss," Nottage said in a low voice. "Sea on fire."

"Everything's okay, Nottage. You can sleep on the deck if you like."

"Don' wan' no deck," Nottage said. He weaved away up the path, and out of sight.

It was still dark when Matthias walked down the Bluff to the beach. The dogs had gone to sleep, or maybe they couldn't hear him because of the wind. The compressor shed stood in a grove of palm trees at the side of the dirt track leading to the dock. Matthias went inside and switched on the light. The room remained dark. He remembered Hew's light going out. The power was off again.

He knelt in front of the compressor and felt the intake filter. It was clean, if that mattered. This was a new compressor—the old one, Exhibit A, still hadn't been returned—and the case was closed.

Matthias walked out on the dock. The beams creaked under his weight. A shadow moved at the far end. A big shadow.

"G'day, Matt," said Brock.

"It's night," Matthias said, sitting beside him.

Brock had a six-pack. They drank it and watched the dawn come up. First it lit the clouds, then the sea, then Brock's long sun-tinted hair and the gold hoop in his ear.

"Let's go to the drop," Matthias said.

"What part of the drop?"

"You know."

"You're driving yourself crazy," Brock said, but he followed Matthias to the slip where *So What* was kept, freed the lines and jumped in, landing lightly, very lightly for such a big man, as Matthias started the engines.

The wind blew harder, disrupting the surface of the ocean with sharp-edged waves that made the bottom unreadable. Matthias didn't need to read it. He turned north a few hundred yards offshore and cut the engines not far beyond the Angel Fingers. Brock tossed the anchor over the side. Line ran out. Brock tugged at it, nodded, let out some slack. Then they spat in their masks, donned fins and snorkels and slipped into the water.

Matthias felt the swells raising and lowering his body; he might have been a microbe on the chest of a giant. He looked for the anchor, saw it had hooked itself in the orange forest of elkhorn coral at the edge of the wall, forty feet below. It was the same coral head that *Who Cares* had been anchored to when Moxie came out to see why it was overdue and found Hiram Standish, Jr., floating in the water and the Frenchman gone. Matthias took his deep breaths, stilled his body, then jackknifed down.

In a moment he had left the surface turbulence behind. Matthias kicked with long slow strokes and kept his hands by his sides. The secret of deep diving was using as little oxygen as possible. That meant diving down in a straight line and getting the most power from the fins with the least effort. Matthias glided down past the coral head, out to the edge of the drop and looked into the deep blue of the Tongue of the Ocean, deep blue as far as he could see. He glanced at his depth gauge—45 feet—sensed Brock behind him and kept descending along the face of the wall. It unreeled upside down as he went by.

Sea fans, yellow and pink, grew out of the rock, and at 70 feet there were lacy branches of black coral. Fish felt the currents his body made and ducked into their holes— tiny fish like purple-headed royal grammas and big ones like Nassau groupers with their thick lips and stupid stubborn eyes. At 85 feet a green Moray stretched its head out of the wall to watch him go by and then curled back out of sight.

Now he could see the big shelf, overgrown with staghorn coral, that stuck out from the wall at 100 feet. He had seen it many times in the days following the accident, when he had put on tanks and dived the wall over and over, all the way to 300 feet, the scuba limit, looking for evidence he never found, answers to all the questions unanswered at the trial: who was the other man? where was his dive card? how had tank ZB-27 come to be filled with poisoned air?

Twenty feet below was a smaller shelf, about the size of a king-sized bed. A big brown nurse shark was resting on it now, its still body curved gracefully, like something Henry Moore might have worked on. Matthias hung at the 100-foot level, watching it. He felt a tap on his shoulder.

He swung around. Brock hovered beside him. He pointed toward the surface. Matthias nodded. Brock was an excellent free diver, especially for a man his size, but he didn't have Matthias's bottom time. Brock kicked away; the first stroke of his fins sent a surge of water around Matthias's head. Looking up he saw the surface, a circle of light far above, and Brock rising toward it, his enormous homemade spear gun hanging from his belt. Brock was an experienced ocean diver and the best divemaster Matthias had ever hired, but like a lot of divers who had learned on the Great Barrier Reef, he dove armed.

Matthias felt the cough reflex tickle the back of his

throat. He controlled it and it went away; this was the dangerous time—the time when carbon dioxide buildup would have forced most people to take in a breath. There would be no other warning, just unconsciousness. Matthias peered down into the blue-black chasm. He saw nothing that shouldn't have been there.

Matthias flicked a fin and started up. He passed a big grouper on the way. Each grouper had its hole. This one had probably lived in the same one for years. Matthias looked into its dull eyes, wondering what it had seen on that September day, wishing science could dissect its little brain in some way that would tap into its memory.

He broke the surface, blew the waste air out of his lungs and sucked in a huge breath. Gold sparkles ignited all around him. He had been down too long. He lay on the surface, inhaling long slow breaths through his snorkel. The dizziness passed.

Matthias climbed into the boat. Brock, standing behind the console, studied his watch. "Three fifty-two," he said. "That was a long pull."

"Yeah."

Brock looked at him. "One day you won't come up."

Matthias, taking off his mask, said nothing. He already knew that the sea, free diving especially, was like a drug to him. He didn't want to get into a discussion about it.

"See anything?" he asked.

"Of course not," Brock said. "What would be left to see by now?"

"The other tank."

"Right. It's five thousand feet down, Matt. And if you found it what would it prove?"

Matthias had no answer. Brock hauled in the anchor. Rain started to fall, first warm then cold. It washed the salt from their bodies, flattened the sea and leached all the color out of Zombie Bay. Matthias and his divemaster rode home in a gray silence.

|11|

Business had never been better. *Living Without Men and Children . . . and Loving It* was still on the bestseller list and bidding for the reprint rights had reached the high six figures. Dr. Lois Filer, with her new body, teeth and haircut, had been on Donahue twice, Oprah once, and local shows from coast to coast. She had even appeared, as the last guest and for only four minutes, on "The Tonight Show," but she had managed, in her sweet contralto, to get off a little joke that may or may not have invoked similarities between politics and fellatio, which brought down the house and made Johnny toss his pencil in the air. *Washington Post Book World* had run twenty-two column inches on womynpress, accompanied by a photograph of Brenda Singer-Atwell and M. brainstorming at a famous disco. Word of Nina's role in all this had spread. Now when she rode her stationary bike, which wasn't as often as before because she couldn't get her belly in a comfortable position, Nina worked at the same time, talking into a dictaphone or reading a manuscript.

Late in October, on a Saturday perfect for tailgate parties on Ivy League campuses, Nina, in the city, worked on a proposal from a small magazine publisher who wanted to start a periodical devoted to the care and feeding of exotic birds. The proposal consisted of thirty pages of enthusiastic but vague text, five-year-old data on the numbers and demography of exotic bird collectors, and color glossies of gorgeous birds. At seven she hurried downtown where she joined Suze and a few dozen other spectators in a basement theater.

"God," said Suze as Nina squeezed into her seat, "how much weight have you put on?"

"Shut up."

The house lights, already dim, dimmed a little more. A ragged curtain parted on a tiny stage. On the stage lay a stuffed, sleeping or dead pig. Big hooks hung from a wire above.

"What's this?" Nina asked.

"Le Boucher," Suze replied. "She's incredible. She's going to be the biggest—"

"Shh," hissed someone behind them.

A naked woman entered from stage right. She had bulging muscles, a shaved head, thick hair under her arms and over her vulva. She began singing the old Cream song "I'm So Glad." Then, holding one hand behind her back and not looking at the audience, she strode to the stuffed, sleeping or dead pig and squatted beside it. She drew her hand out from behind her back, revealing a long butcher knife. Still singing, she proceeded to butcher the pig. The knife rose and fell to the rhythms of the song. The pig showed no signs of resistance, so it hadn't been sleeping. On the other hand, there was a lot of blood, so it wasn't stuffed either. Le Boucher, her magnificent body splashed with red, pirouetted in a musclebound way to hang the pieces of meat on the hooks, her feet squishing audibly in the intestines that had begun to spread across the stage.

"Oh God," Nina said.

"Strong stuff, huh?" said Suze.

"It's not that," Nina replied. "I think I'm in labor."

"Oh God," Suze said. "How do you know?"

"Because I just had a cramp like I've never had before. Kind of twisting."

"Maybe it's just a bad period."

"Suze, you asshole. You don't have—" Nina stopped talking. She felt something give inside her. The next moment warm liquid gushed out between her legs. She rose. "Let's go."

Nina hurried from the theater, Suze close behind her. They didn't attract any attention. On stage the performer was winding pig intestines around her body, and lots of other people were hurrying out too.

There was a taxi parked outside but Nina was too slow and the theater critic of *The New York Times* beat her to it. Nina stood on the dark street while uterine flow dampened her legs and Suze hopped up and down beside her.

"I haven't even got my fucking ditty bag," Nina said.

"What?" said Suze.

Nina's womb churned again, a sudden, utterly involuntary movement that didn't hurt, exactly, although Nina wouldn't have wanted to make a night of it.

"Oh God," she said again, realizing that she was about to.

"What's a ditty bag?" Suze asked. "Maybe we can get one on the way."

"On the way where?"

"To the hospital. Aren't we going to the hospital?"

"I guess so." Then she remembered that she was supposed to call Dr. Berry first. She had his home number. There were two public telephones in front of a warehouse on the other side of the street. Nina walked toward them. Suze ran to the corner to find a taxi.

Someone had ripped the receiver off one of the telephones. A man was talking on the other. "I don't know," he was saying. "What do you want to do?" With his free hand he hitched up his pants, wriggling his flabby hips to assist the process. "Naw," he said, "I don't want to go there again. They're all a bunch of assholes. . . . All right, all right, not Charlie. Charlie's not an asshole. He's a douche-bag." The man laughed. "Just kidding, *paisan.* Charlie's a real *paisan.* You're a *paisan.* I'm a *paisan.* We're all a shitload of fucking *paisans*, just itching for a little you know what, right? Am I right or am I right?" The man listened to the reply. Then he said, "So, you're bored, I'm bored, what do you want to do?"

Nina tapped him on the shoulder. "I need to use the phone," she said.

The man turned very slowly and looked down on her. He had long greasy hair and needed a shave. "Unlax, Fuddsy," he said. "No, no, Zimmy, I'm not talking to you. I've got a very impatient customer here who doesn't give an apparent shit for my constitutional right to converse with you."

"I'm about to have a baby, you jerk," Nina said.

The man's eyes ran down her body. They widened. "Zimmy? I'll call you back." He hung up, ran his eyes down Nina's body again and walked rapidly away, glancing back once, but briefly—lest he be turned to a pillar of salt, or something.

Nina dialed Dr. Berry's number. A woman who might have done the voice-overs for Betty Crocker answered. "Just a minute please, dear," she said, and called, "Jim. Jim."

Opera played in the background. Dr. Berry came to the phone, humming "Salut Demeure, Chaste et Pure." "Hello," he said.

"It's Nina Kitchener, Dr. Berry. I think the baby's coming."

"When's your due date?"

"Next Thursday."

"No problem," said Dr. Berry. "How far apart are your contractions?"

"How far apart?"

"Approximately."

"In time, you mean?"

"That's right. You're not timing them?"

"I forgot. But I think my water broke. I know it did."

"Splendid," said Dr. Berry. "Get to the hospital. I'll meet you there and we'll see what's what."

Nina hung up and looked around for Suze. There was a squad car parked halfway down the block. Suze was talking to the driver, gesturing wildly. When Nina arrived Suze turned to her and said, "There are no fucking cabs. And this guy's balking at doing his sworn duty."

The cop inside peered up at Nina. He'd been shaving for maybe three months and still had adolescent pimples on his cheeks. "I'm on a stakeout," he said in a high voice. "I can't just up and leave." He regarded Nina more closely. "Maybe I can radio for an ambulance."

"Stakeout shmakeout!" Suze screamed at him. "And an ambulance could take an hour. You know it, I know it, the whole fucking town knows it. What are you, from Omaha Flats, for Christ's sake? Now open up and get us to the hospital pronto."

"But it's my first crack bust," the cop pleaded.

"Sure, sure," Suze said. "But tomorrow the paper will

say 'Mom Has Baby on Street While Rookie Cop Panics.' And then we'll sue you and the city up and down till you can't even get hired by the goddamn Sanitation Department. Your life will be over, boychick, with a capital O."

The cop unlocked the doors, let them in and sped off.

"Hit the siren," Suze commanded.

He hit the siren. They flew uptown on a wailing carpet of sound. Nina had another contraction, much stronger than the ones before. This time the line between discomfort and pain was approached. She took Suze's hand. When the contraction eased, Nina said, "You're behaving like the ditziest father in the worst screwball comedy ever made."

"Screwball," said Suze, giving Nina's hand a squeeze. She raised her voice. "Screwfuckingball. Doesn't that just say it all?"

The cop glanced back at them in the rearview mirror. Nina had never before seen naked terror in a man's eyes. She saw it now. Then her womb twisted again. "Jesus," she said. She felt sweat pop out on her brow.

"Is it on the way?" Suze asked.

"Of course."

"I mean right now."

"I don't know."

The cop put the pedal to the floor.

"Oh shit," Nina said.

"What now?"

"I forgot to look at the time."

"What difference does that make?" Suze asked. "Anything on your schedule will have to go on hold, for God's sake."

"Here comes another," Nina said. This time she kept her eyes on her watch. The contraction lasted thirty-one seconds. The next one began two minutes and forty-three seconds later.

Suze pounded on the bars that separated them from the driver. "Can't you make this shitbox move?" she yelled.

"I'm trying, I'm trying," the cop said, hunched over the wheel and almost in tears.

At the hospital there were forms to fill out. Nina sat in a chair. Suze stood behind her. "This person is going to have a baby any second," she said. "Can't the paperwork wait?"

"No," said the nurse, chewing gum. She took the forms from Nina. "Have you taken a childbirth course?" she asked.

"Yes," Nina replied, not going into detail.

"Good. Then we'll put you in a birthing room on the fourth floor. "Where's your coach?"

"Right here," said Nina.

"What?" said Suze.

The birthing room had a hospital bed, a chair and a TV. The TV was on. Julia Child was cooking *ris de veau*. The director was fond of shooting overhead closeups of the *ris de veau* hissing on the stove. "Turn it off," Nina said.

"Really?" said Suze. "I think she's mesmerizing." But she turned it off.

A nurse looked in. "Had our enema yet?" she asked.

Half an hour later, Nina had had their enema and lay on the bed, flattened by contraction after contraction. Suze stood on the other side of the room, biting her lip and occasionally looking over at the blank TV screen. Dr. Berry walked in, followed by a black nurse twice his size. He wore a red cashmere sweater and green tweed pants and was growing a snow-white beard; now he resembled not so much one of Santa's helpers as Santa himself, on his day off.

"Well well well," he said.

"Am I glad to see you," Nina replied. "This is my friend Suze."

Dr. Berry shook his head admiringly. "I can see that everything's under control. You two aren't going to need me at all."

"Oh yes we are," Suze said.

Dr. Berry laughed, but his eyes were on Nina and he said: "Got one coming on now, have you?"

Nina, crossing quickly over the discomfort line, could only nod. Dr. Berry laid his hand on her belly; his touch was calm, sure, gentle, but it didn't take the pain away. He didn't speak while the contraction lasted. Then he said: "Good, good. You're not in hard labor yet, of course, but it's a nice start."

"She's not?"

"I'm not?"

"Ha ha," said Dr. Berry, as though he were an out-of-towner come to Broadway for sophisticated repartee and getting his money's worth. He washed his hands and carefully slipped one inside Nina, cocking an ear like a hunter listening for distant game. "I remember this cervix," he said. "This is going to be a cakewalk." He turned to the nurse. "Three centimeters."

"Will you be at home or Beefsteak Charlie's?" asked the nurse.

"Home, I think," said Dr. Berry. "I had a big dinner already."

"You're leaving?" asked Nina.

Dr. Berry smiled. "You're doing great, for first stage. Three centimeters! But you don't need me hanging around till you're fully dilated."

"How much is fully?" Suze asked.

"Ten centimeters," Dr. Berry answered.

"What's that in inches?"

Dr. Berry laughed again. He was shaking his head with amusement as he went out the door.

The nurse came forward. "You can stay for now," she said to Suze, "but you'll have to leave when we get to second stage."

"Why?" Nina said.

"That's the rule. No friends in the room during delivery."

"But she's my coach."

The nurse swung slowly around to Suze. "She is?"

Suze nodded vigorously.

"Then you'll have to get gowned," the nurse said. "Down the hall, third door on the right."

Suze left. The nurse consulted a clipboard. She made a few tick marks with a pencil, then said: "Should I order up an epidural for later?"

Stick it in me now, Nina thought. From the moment she had walked out of the childbirth class she had never considered anesthetic-free labor. But she said to the nurse: "Let's see how it goes."

Then she was seized by a contraction that seemed to turn the entire force of her body against her. Nina was hardly aware of the nurse's hand on her stomach. She tried to remember sniff-and-blow, huff-huff-and-puffing. In the end she settled on drawing in deep breaths and letting them out in long, even exhalations. It might have helped a little.

"Not bad," the nurse said, withdrawing her hand. "That's the kind that does a quarter of a centimeter all by itself."

"A quarter?"

The nurse smiled a knowing smile. "Think about that epidural," she said. "Everyone ends up having it, even you natural childbirth types."

I'm not a natural childbirth type, Nina thought, but she couldn't get the words out before the next contraction hit.

Ten hours later there was a new nurse, bigger than the other one, in the room, breakfasting on a peanut butter sandwich; Suze's spiked hair was drooping over her forehead and she had purple smudges under her eyes; Dr. Berry was back, wearing a fine tweed jacket; the epidural had still not been ordered; and Nina was nine-and-a-half centimeters dilated. She had learned all there was to learn about controlling pain through breathing, which was that it didn't help much, and she had learned that birth, like any other struggle for independence, hurt. She had also learned that Suze thought she was a stubborn asshole, had thought so all these years. "Order that fucking epidural," she had said one of the times they were alone in the room, "or I'll never speak to you again."

"Let's see how it goes."

"It's going terribly, you blockhead. It couldn't be worse. Why are you doing this?"

But Nina didn't know, and she didn't have to explain at that moment because another contraction had started and they had agreed not to talk during contractions.

"Just a couple more," said Dr. Berry. "Then we'll be cooking with gas."

A couple more happened. After they passed, "epidural" was the only word in Nina's mind. Then she remembered tune tapping. The only tune she could think of was "Salut Demeure." She began tapping her finger to it, although the song seemed to have no beat at all and she didn't know the words. A contraction like a rapidly expanding beach ball struck her. "Sing fucking 'Salut Demeure,'" she screamed at Dr. Berry.

Dr. Berry blinked. "Chaste et Pure?" he said.

"Yes, yes."

Dr. Berry sang "Salut Demeure Chaste et Pure." He

had a light, trained tenor, which he reined in at half-voice. Nina was fully dilated by the end of the aria. She lay on the bed, her hospital gown in disarray, panting, drenched in sweat, chewing ice shavings that Suze kept bringing by the cupful because she had noticed a father-coach collecting some down the hall a few hours before.

"Do you like Puccini?" Dr. Berry asked. "Or is he too schmaltzy for you?" Nina, feeling the first knotting of a coming contraction, didn't answer. "I hope I'm pronouncing it properly," said Dr. Berry, sounding worried for the first time.

While Nina endured the pain, Suze said: "She's not Jewish—I am. And how else would you pronounce it? Schmaltzy, schmaltzy, schmaltzy. It couldn't be simpler. Christ."

Dr. Berry looked stricken. "I'm sorry if I've given offense," he said.

"Just sing," Suze told him.

"Puccini?"

Nina, coming out of the contraction, said, "That would be nice."

Dr. Berry reached inside her. "Positioned perfectly."

"You can feel him?" Nina said.

"Or her," Dr. Berry replied. "Lined up like a little trooper."

Dr. Berry began with "Non Piangere, Liù," then ran through Tosca: "Recondita Armonia," "E Lucevan le Stelle," "O Dolci Mani." By that time the muscles in Nina's body were wringing her apart; the nurse was holding one of her legs and Suze the other. Blood came out of her in gobbets, dribbles, gushes; enough, she thought between contractions, to impress even Le Boucher.

"I could knock them dead with this act downtown," she said, hearing how hoarse her voice sounded.

"What?" said Suze, looking up, a streak of blood on the side of her nose.

The next contraction came before Nina could reply. It dwarfed all the others. "Don't push, don't push," cried the nurse. Suze was squeezing her leg with all her strength but Nina could hardly feel it.

"The epidural," Nina said, panting. "Give me the goddamn epidural."

Dr. Berry, sailing into "Nessun Dorma," peered between her legs and broke off in mid-note. "Too late," he said. "We're crowning. See?"

Suze peered in too. "That?"

"That," said Dr. Berry.

Nina's heart rate rose to another level, something she would have thought impossible. "Is something wrong with the baby?"

"Looks just fine," said Dr. Berry. "Push on the next one. We're coming down the stretch."

Nina pushed on the next one, and the next and the next. "Push, honey, that's it," said the nurse. Nina pushed with all her might. She felt Suze stroking her leg.

"Don't stop," she said.

Suze looked at her. There were tears in Suze's eyes, and love too, as easy to read as if the four letters had lit up in her irises. "You're a horse, Nina. Just a fucking horse."

"One more time," said Dr. Berry.

Nina pushed one more time, a push that ended in a tremendous slide of relief. "Bravo!" said Dr. Berry, holding up a bloodstained baby boy.

Nina tried to sit up, and almost did. "Is he all right?"

"Perfect," said Dr. Berry.

Tears ran down Nina's face, but she was laughing at the same time. Dr. Berry handed the baby to the nurse who took him to the other side of the room.

Nina stopped laughing. "But he's not crying or anything."

"What's there to cry about?" said Dr. Berry. "He's breathing. That's what counts."

His last word triggered a thought. "Suze! Count his fingers and toes."

"Ten of each," said Suze. She leaned over and kissed Nina on the forehead.

"What a good coach," said the nurse. "You've done this before, I can see." Then she held out the baby, all cleaned up, for Nina to take. Nina was afraid. He was so small, with stick arms and legs and tiny features on his tiny face; but his eyes, blue eyes that seemed very big, were looking right at her. It was so simple. He needed to be held, and she was the holder. Nina took the baby, not with exaggerated delicacy as though he were made of Limoges, but as though she had been handling newborns all her life, and laid him on her breast. She felt the movement of his little lips, and shifted her nipple between them. He took it and tried to suck.

"Will you look at that?" said Dr. Berry. "This one's going to be a real killer-diller."

Nina held the baby. She stroked his fine hair, which was surprisingly long in the back and so blond it was almost white. The next time she became aware of her surroundings, she realized that everyone had gone.

She looked down at her baby. He was looking right at her again, with serious blue eyes that were the eyes, or so she thought, of someone who was trying to show her that he was always going to hold up his end. This was no Henrik. This was a human being who needed a serious name. But she still couldn't think of one.

"What's your name, little boy?" she asked.

Nina gazed down at him again. Now his eyes were closed. A momentary jolt of panic shook her, but before she could shout for the nurse, she felt the breath from his nostrils on her skin. Nina stroked his fine blond hair and hummed, very softly, one of the tunes that Dr. Berry had sung. He kept breathing on her breast, breaths that were tiny, but as steady as the ebb and flow of the tide. The universe shrank until it fit comfortably inside the little birthing room on the fourth floor.

|12|

Are we the most fucked-up generation the world has ever known?" Suze asked the next day.

"Of course not," Nina replied, lying on the bed in her private room on the maternity ward, with the baby sleeping beside her.

"What's the competition?"

"The last of the dinosaurs."

"Dinosaurs," said Suze. "That's an idea. How about Rex?"

"Rex?"

"Doesn't grab? What about Marley?"

"Marley? Marley Kitchener?"

"After Bob Marley. You love Bob Marley."

"I love Thelonious Monk too."

They both eyed the baby. He didn't look like a Thelonious. "Mrs. Monk must have been an interesting woman," Suze said.

A messenger entered bearing bouquets of roses, orchids and dahlias, and a bottle of Roederer Cristal. There was a card from Jason, signed by everyone at the office, with a picture of a dam bursting and the caption, "Everything copacetic in your absence. Have a great time."

Nina and Suze drank the champagne. "Guess who I'm having dinner with tonight?" Suze asked.

"Dr. Berry?"

"Very funny."

"His wife?"

"That's nasty, but a little closer. I'm dining with Le Boucher."

"That's a cheap date. She can bring her own food."

Suze showed Nina a review from the *Village Voice*. The writer called the pig show "a breathtaking tour de force of post-feminist feminism that has the balls to say what needs saying about female-male relations in these dismal days."

"I bet she's already stuck that on her meat locker," Nina said.

"I want her to do something for the gallery," Suze said. "She's going to be big, Nina."

"She's big enough already."

Suze regarded Nina out of the corner of her eye. "She's talking about doing a book. She wants to meet you."

"She's not getting through my door unless she shaves her pits," Nina said.

Suze's laughter woke the baby. Nina decided to change him. It took a long time: she tried to put the Pamper on backwards, the tabs kept getting stuck in the wrong places, it rode all the way up to his chest in the front but left him uncovered in back.

"Where did he get that tight little butt?" Suze asked.

Nina gave it a soft pat. "Takes after his mother," she said.

"Dream on," said Suze, and left for her dinner soon after.

The baby stirred and made a little squawking noise. He batted one of his stick arms in the air, the arm that wore the bracelet saying "Baby Kitchener." Nina put him to her breast. His lips searched frantically for purchase, found her nipple, sucked. Nina felt his body relax. She looked down at him; now he had a preoccupied look in his serious blue eyes. She knew with certainty that she was his whole world, but didn't know what to think about that. She stroked his hair at the back where it grew long, so fine. After a while he fell asleep, his head lolling to the side. Nina laid him in the crook of her arm. Then she touched her nipple, felt the wetness, tasted it. She had produced milk for the first time, thin but sweet. Nina smiled. She was still smiling when a nurse came into the room.

"There's a phone call for you at the nurses' station."

"Can't I take it in here?"

"We tried to transfer it, but your phone's not working. Maintenance'll be up later."

Nina, still a little unsteady, rose from the bed.

"Can't leave the baby there by himself," the nurse said.

"But I've got rooming-in."

"Only when you're here. The rest of the time he has to be in the nursery."

Nina, carrying the baby, followed the nurse to the end of the hall. Through the nursery window, Nina saw rows of bassinets, but all except three, which contained pink-wrapped bundles, were empty. The nurse held out her hands for Nina's blue-wrapped bundle.

"Can't I take him in myself?"

"No moms in the nursery."

Nina, noting that this was the first time she had been included by anyone in the mom category, surrendered her baby. She watched as the nurse went inside, laid him in a bassinet at the end of the row closest to the window and said something to a plump nurse sitting at the back of the room, a newspaper in her lap. The baby's head was turned so that she could see his face. It was their first separation, the first time, except for a few minutes after his birth, that they hadn't been in physical contact. He was sleeping quietly. Nina backed slowly away, then walked down the hall to the nurses' station.

"Is there a phone call for me?"

A nurse glanced up from a chart she was writing on. "What's your name?"

"Nina Kitchener."

"Room?"

"Four twenty-two."

The nurse went through a stack of yellow slips and handed her one: a message to call Jason at the office. "Pay phone's on the fifth floor."

Nina avoided the elevator, taking the stairs at the far end of the hall so she could pass the nursery on the way. Her little blue-wrapped boy was sleeping in the same position he had been before, except that he'd worked one of his hands free; it rested, a tiny, perfect object, on the white sheet. The plump nurse at the back was now doing the crossword. As Nina approached the door leading to the stairs, she passed a woman pushing a cart piled with magazines, newspapers and candies. The woman, who had leathery, wrinkled skin and wore a volunteer badge, said: "Candy, dear?" She had an accent, vaguely English perhaps.

"No thanks," Nina said, and passed through the door.

She made her way up the stairs, surprised that despite her bicycling—she was past Rangoon and en route to the Amur River, via Shanghai—she almost had to stop for a rest on the way. The phone was beside a door that said: CAUTION: RADIOACTIVE MATERIALS. Nina dropped in her quarter.

"Hi, Mom," said Jason. "I hear he's a little cutie pie."

"Suze said that?"

"No. It was on Rona Barrett this morning. Have you chosen a name yet?"

"No."

" 'Jason' is nice."

"It would be confusing, otherwise I wouldn't consider anything else. What's up?"

"The Birdman wants to talk to you ASAP."

"The Birdman?"

"With the magazine."

"What's so urgent?"

"He got a nibble from Condé Nast. They're thinking of putting up half the money. He says. But he's meeting with them tomorrow and wants to know what you think of the proposal."

"I'll call him," Nina said, trying to remember anything at all about the proposal. She might have read it in a past life.

Nina called the Birdman. He had a high voice and talked very fast. "Goodness, you're hard to reach," he said. "This might be the most important episode in my life."

"You've reached me," Nina said. "What do you want to know?"

"Your reaction to the proposal, of course. I'm meeting with them at nine-thirty in the A.M. Condé Nast, for God's sake."

"Who specifically?"

"A woman named Linsky. Or Lansky. Something like that."

Nina tried to imagine any good coming from a meeting between Cynthia Lansky and the Birdman and failed. "What has she said so far?"

"It's a bit worrisome, actually."

"What is?"

"She says she wants me to consider changing the concept somewhat."

"How?"

"Before I answer that, I insist on knowing what you think of the present concept."

I don't give a shit about you, your silly voice, your concept or Cynthia Lansky, Nina thought. I want to get back downstairs. "The pictures are great," Nina said. "But it seems to me that the text is too narrowly focused on ornithology to attract anyone but specialists, and therefore I'm not sure what Condé Nast's interest is."

There was a pause, so long that Nina said: "Hello. Are you still there?"

"Yes," said the Birdman, his voice momentarily dipping toward the sepulchral. "That's exactly what the Condé Nast lady said. 'Too narrowly focused.' "

"So what did she propose?"

"That I make it into a big glossy for rich birdwatchers, full of pictures of scenic birdwatching locales in fancy resort places all over the world," the Birdman said, his tone resuming its approach to hysteria. "She wants me to think, think very seriously, she said, about calling it *Oiseau*."

"And what's your reaction?"

"It's obscene," said the Birdman.

"Then say no."

"But they're willing to put up half the money. And on the strength of that I can borrow the other half."

"Then you're going to have to make a decision."

"You're right," said the Birdman. "You're right, you're right, you're right. Ms. Kitchener?"

"Yes?"

"Would you come to the meeting with me?"

Nina thought. She was due to leave the hospital at noon the next day. The Birdman's meeting was at 9:30. She could leave the baby in the nursery while she was gone, then return and take him home. This was the first test of how she would combine job and family. She hadn't expected it to come so soon.

"I'll have to call you back on that," she told the Bird-man.

"Please, Ms. Kitchener," he said. "I'll increase your fee."

"That's understood," Nina said. "I'll call you after dinner."

Going downstairs was easier. Nina returned to the fourth floor and looked in the nursery window. The little blue-wrapped bundle still lay quietly at the far end of the first row, but now he was turned the other way so she couldn't see his face. Nina tapped on the glass. The plump nurse looked up from her paper. Nina went through a series of hand signals that eventually drove home the point that the baby in the front row was hers and she wanted him back. The nurse put aside her paper, rose heavily and ambled across the nursery. She leaned forward over the bassinet at the end of the first row, her hands extended to take the baby—and suddenly stopped. She looked up at Nina with a strange expression on her face.

The sight of it detonated a fear in Nina unlike any she had ever known. She bolted through the nursery door and across the room, unaware at that moment of the stitches tearing along her episiotomy. She had heard of crib death, accidental smothering, infants who died for no apparent reason. Nina pushed past the plump nurse, who seemed stuck to the floor, and grabbed the blue-wrapped bundle.

Her baby wasn't inside the blue blanket. In his place was a Cabbage Patch Kid.

|13|

These events followed, in order:

Nina turned to the nurse and said: "Is this some kind of joke? Where is my baby?"

The nurse shook her head rapidly from side to side.

Nina said: "What's going on? Has there been an accident? Did he fall? Have they taken him for tests or something?"

The nurse kept shaking her head, faster and faster.

"What is wrong with you?" Nina said. She fell to her knees and peered under the bassinet, finding nothing.

The plump nurse stopped shaking her head. She spun around, bumping an empty bassinet and knocking it over, then examined the three pink-wrapped bundles. All contained baby girls, identification bracelets on their wrists.

Nina, on all fours, scrambled across the nursery, searching under every bassinet.

The nurse stood motionless in the middle of the room.

Nina rose and shouted: "Where is my baby?"

The nurse said: "I—I—I—I—"

Blood dripped down Nina's legs.

Nina ran up to the nurse and took her by the shoulders. "But you were here. What happened? Did someone take him? Where is my baby? Are you stoned on something?"

"I—I—I—I—"

Nina shook the nurse. The nurse, much bigger than Nina, did not resist. Her head snapped back and forth.

Nina ran down the hall. A scream rose in her chest. She forced it down. Her robe opened and slipped off her shoulders. She arrived at the nurses' station in disarray.

The head nurse looked up. She had seen all there was to see in a big city hospital. "Is there some problem?" she said.

The scream burst out. "Yes, there's some fucking problem. My baby's gone."

"Please lower your voice," the head nurse said. "What do you mean 'gone'?"

Nina swept her arm across the counter, scattering papers and charts. "I mean gone," she replied, making no attempt to lower her voice. "Gone, gone, gone."

The head nurse's face reddened. She started to rise, angry words forming on her lips.

The plump nurse appeared. She found her voice. "She's right," she said, starting to blubber. "Her baby's gone and it's my fault. It's all my fault."

The head nurse focused her anger on her colleague. "Whatever are you talking about?"

The plump nurse's mouth opened and made speaking motions, but no sound came. Tears ran down her face.

The head nurse strode down the hall to the nursery and saw what there was to see. She came back with the Cabbage Patch Kid in her hand. "What is going on?" she said to the plump nurse. "Did you leave your station?"

The plump nurse shook her head yes and began blubbering again. Blubbering turned to bawling.

The head nurse, followed by Nina, walked quickly along the hall, checking the bracelet of every baby in every room on the maternity ward.

"What's going on?" some of the mothers asked, regarding Nina with alarm.

The head nurse did not reply. She was running now. She ran to the station desk. She picked up a telephone, punched a button and called out: "Fourth floor code blue. Fourth floor code blue."

People arrived. They were running too. Jabbing her finger at them, the head nurse issued instructions. The people spun off in all directions.

Pushing past orderlies, nurses, doctors, security guards, Nina ran down the hall, back to the nursery, back to the bassinet at the far end of the first row. It was empty. She screamed a scream unlike any she had ever uttered or heard, a wordless scream that filled her head and started the pink-wrapped bundles crying. Then Nina fell sobbing on the empty bassinet.

Someone threw a blanket over her shoulders. Someone said: "Here. Drink this." Someone held out a green pill.

Nina knocked it aside. "I have to search every floor," she said. "And the basement."

Someone said: "We're already doing that, honey. There's nothing you can do right now. And we've got to sew you back up."

Nina glanced down and saw a red puddle expanding on the floor.

A man said: "We need a description. What's the name on the bracelet?"

The head nurse checked a chart. "He doesn't have a name," she answered. "Just 'Baby Kitchener.' "

"I want him to have a name," Nina cried.

Strong arms urged Nina into a wheelchair. She resisted. "I've got to search." The strong arms pushed harder. She fell into the wheelchair.

The plump nurse glanced at her chair where the newspaper lay, folded open at the crossword. She started blubbering again.

The head nurse raised her voice for the first time: "Go to the toilet and don't come out until I call you."

The plump nurse covered her mouth and hurried away. Nina rolled down the hall.

A man said: "Don't forget to check the dumpsters."

A cop said: "What the hell is this?"

A security guard said: "A Cabbage Patch Kid."

The cop said: "What are you giving it to me for?"

The security guard said: "It's evidence."

"Of what?" the cop asked.

Nina rolled into an elevator. Someone stuck a needle in her arm. She hardly felt it.

Whoosh. The door closed, boxing her in. The box rose.

"What's all that blood?" someone asked.

Whoosh. The door opened.

"Going down?"

"Nope."

Whoosh. The box rose.

"What's a code blue again?"

"Sanitation just came and picked up all the dumpsters. Twenty minutes ago."

"Then find out where they take them and go search every goddamn one."

"And wear thick gloves. There's all kinds of medical shit in those fucking things."

"Jesus Christ, what a day."

"Take me to the basement," Nina said, trying to rise. Her legs failed her. "I want my baby." The drug prevailed and her eyes closed.

| NINA |

| 14 |

Detective Delgado of the NYPD was tired. She wore a lot of makeup and her hair had been freshly frosted and permed, but nothing could hide the red veins in her eyes or the blue bruises under them. She pulled a chair up to Nina's bed and said: "How are you doing?"

"I don't know," Nina replied. "Fine. Physically." Nina tried to sit up, couldn't; she tried again and did. "Are you handling the search?"

"The investigation. The search, at least the search of the hospital, is over. We've been through it from top to bottom."

"And?"

Detective Delgado shook her head.

"What about . . . ?" Nina couldn't get the word out.

"What about what?"

"The dumpsters."

"They've all been checked, including the ones removed by Sanitation. *Nada.*" For a moment, Nina thought that Detective Delgado was suppressing a yawn. The detective covered her face with her hands and rubbed hard.

"What about the basement?" Nina asked.

"Yes. The basement." Detective Delgado leaned back in the chair and stretched her legs. Nina smelled her smell: a strong orange blossom cologne mixed with cigarette smoke. "Apparently you referred to the basement several times, Ms. Kitchener. Any reason for that?"

"Not that I can think of."

The detective nodded. "Are you aware that there are five basement levels in this building, six if you include the parking garage?"

"No."

Detective Delgado nodded again. Nina had the feeling that she had just been bested in some contest, but what kind of contest or why she didn't know.

"I'm not clear about what's happening," Nina said. She could feel the power of some drug waning inside her; its departure allowed patches of unease to blossom in her mind. They coalesced rapidly into dread—everything hit her again, like the back side of a hurricane after the eye has passed. "About what you're doing," Nina added.

"What we're doing," said Detective Delgado, "is treating this as a kidnapping." The uttering of the word made Nina's blood pound. She felt pain between her legs. Detective Delgado reached into her pocket and took out a notebook and a pack of cigarettes. "Can I smoke in here?"

"I don't think so."

Detective Delgado sighed and put the cigarettes away. She opened her notebook, moistened her finger with her tongue, a tongue that looked yellow and dry, and turned the pages. "Correct me if I go wrong," she said. The detective's tone flattened to those of a reader making no attempt to render the material interesting. "At four thirty-five P.M. yesterday, you were informed you had a phone call at the nurse's station. You gave your baby to a nurse. The nurse delivered the baby to Verna Rountree, who was in charge of the nursery. You then went to the nurse's station, received a message and proceeded to the fifth-floor pay phone to make your call. Right so far?"

"Yes."

Detective Delgado moistened her finger again and flipped a page. "At about four-forty, a hospital volunteer entered the nursery and told Verna Rountree that her husband was in the cafeteria and urgently wanted to speak to her. Verna Rountree is separated from her husband. He left her a few months ago to live with another woman. This, says Verna Rountree"— the detective turned the page—"broke my heart. Quote unquote. Verna was desperate, quote unquote, to go see him, but she couldn't leave her post and was afraid to ask the head nurse for a replacement because she knew the head nurse disapproved of personal visits during the shift and she thought, rightly, it turns out, that the head nurse didn't like her anyway."

"So the volunteer offered to stay in the nursery till she got back."

Detective Delgado glanced up sharply. "That's right." Her reddened eyes focused on Nina for a moment; she wrote a few words on a fresh page of the notebook. "Taking the stairs so she wouldn't have to go past the nurses' station," the detective continued, "Verna went as fast as she could to the cafeteria, failed to find her husband and hurried back to the fourth floor. When she reached the nursery, she found that the volunteer was gone and that the four infants in her charge were all sleeping quietly. She says. But—she didn't bother to check each one up close. What she did was amble to the middle of the nursery and look around from there. They were all wrapped up in their blankets, three pink and one blue. Then she returned to her chair at the back, where she found a Hershey Bar, which she assumed the volunteer had left for her. She checked the time—it was four-fifty—realized she'd been gone ten minutes at the most, and that no one had noticed. She ate the Hershey Bar and threw the wrapper in the wastebasket. It's been recovered and is now being checked for fingerprints.

"A few minutes later, just after she had finished with the candy bar, you returned for your baby. At that point Verna Rountree went to his bassinet and discovered what she discovered."

Nina sat up a little higher. She was beginning to feel stronger. Her mind filled with questions. For no reason that she could explain, the first one that came out was: "What's happened to Verna Rountree?"

"Suspended without pay," said Detective Delgado. "Pending investigation. Of course, if her story doesn't hold up, it'll be much worse than that."

"Why wouldn't her story hold up?"

"For one thing, no one else on the ward saw a volunteer during the relevant time period. No volunteer was scheduled to be on the ward at that time, and all the volunteers who were in the hospital have been questioned and been able to show they were elsewhere. In addition, Verna's description of the volunteer is very sketchy."

"I saw her," Nina said.

"You saw who?"

"The volunteer."

Detective Delgado leaned forward in her chair. She still had the red veins in her eyes and the puffiness under them, but she didn't look as tired. "Where? When?"

"In the hall, past the nursery on my way to the stairs. Just after I—just after I gave the—my—baby to the nurse."

"You took the stairs?"

"Yes."

"Why not the elevator?"

The reason was because she had wanted to pass by the nursery to see the baby, although, by that point, according to Detective Delgado's calculations, they had only been separated for about two minutes. So Nina toyed with saying, "Because I felt like walking," or "I don't like elevators," or "I don't know." She said: "Because I wanted to see the baby on the way by."

Detective Delgado wrote in her notebook.

"Do you have any children, Detective Delgado?" The question just popped out.

"Why do you ask?"

"No reason."

"I don't have children," Detective Delgado said. She gazed down at her notebook, but wrote nothing and didn't appear to be reading either. "I have a nephew I'm close to," she said. Fatigue struck her again; Nina could see it whiten her face. Detective Delgado pinched the bridge of her nose, hard, and asked: "Did you get a good look at the volunteer?"

"I got a look at her. I wouldn't say a good look."

"Would you recognize her if you saw her again?"

"I might."

Detective Delgado got on the phone. In a few minutes, a uniformed policeman entered the room and handed her a manila envelope. "Sergeant Shapiro wants you to call him," the policeman said. "And Ezekial made bail last night."

"Christ Almighty," Detective Delgado said. She handed Nina the envelope.

Inside were laminated ID photographs of every volunteer associated with the hospital. Nina examined them all.

"No," she said.

"Any of them close?" asked Detective Delgado.

"No."

Detective Delgado sighed. "Describe the woman you saw."

Nina closed her eyes. She saw a blurred image, a face without eyes, nose, mouth. "She was between fifty and sixty, I guess. Wispy hair."

"How do you mean, 'wispy'?"

"Thin. Not neatly combed or brushed."

"What color was the hair?"

"Grayish." The vague image she had was fading entirely. Nina opened her eyes. "I remember thinking she had spent a lot of time in the sun."

"She had a dark tan?"

"Not really."

"She was a white woman, right?"

"Yes."

"But not tanned?"

"No."

"So why did you think she had spent a lot of time in the sun?"

"Her skin, I guess. It was all wrinkled and leathery. Like a farm woman in the Depression, or something."

"Did you see her hands?"

"Not that I recall."

Detective Delgado wrote in her notebook. She filled about a page and a half. "Anything else you can remember?"

"She had a kind of accent."

"You spoke to her?"

"She spoke to me."

"What did she say?"

"I don't remember the exact words. She asked if I wanted a chocolate bar, I think. She called me 'dear.' "

" 'Dear.' "

"Yes."

"Think hard. Had you ever seen this woman before?"

"No."

"Did she seem to recognize you?"

"Not that I noticed."

"What kind of accent did she have?"

"Sort of English."

"Sort of?"

"It's hard to explain."

"Like Princess Di?"

"Nothing like that."

"The Beatles?"

"No. It was more old-fashioned. Old-fashioned and . . . genteel."

"Genteel."

"Yes."

"Double-ee-el?"

"Yes."

"So you do mean upper-class."

"No. More like Blanche Du Bois. Only English."

"Okay," said Detective Delgado, her voice suddenly more lively, as though things were starting to make sense. "Is there anyone in your life who might consider you an enemy?"

Nina thought. She had business competitors, but not many, and had been involved in some difficult negotiations where harsh words had been exchanged, but afterwards everyone made a point of saying it was nothing personal. So she answered, "No."

"You're not estranged from your husband?"

"There is no husband."

"You're divorced?"

"I've never been married."

"What is your current relationship with the father of the child?"

"There is no father," Nina said. Detective Delgado's eyes narrowed, and Nina saw the toughness, even meanness, that was in her. "I used artificial insemination," Nina explained, "and the donor was anonymous."

Detective Delgado relaxed. "So this isn't one of those custody affairs."

"It couldn't be," Nina said. "But what is it?"

Detective Delgado made a few more notes in her book, then sat back, crossing her legs, heavy legs that stretched the seams of her trousers. "It's too early to tell. But my hunch is—and I've been involved in a number of these now—that we're dealing with an unstable, very screwed-up woman who gets it into her head that she wants a baby and just walks into a hospital and takes one. There was a case at Bellevue just last month."

"And what happened?"

"There was an anonymous phone call a couple days later, probably from a neighbor of the woman, and we went in and got the baby. He was fine. Sometimes it's a psychotic episode that passes and the woman strolls back into the hospital, leaves the baby in the lobby and strolls out. We even had a case where a baby was delivered right to the nursery."

"Do you always get them back?"

Detective Delgado yawned; this time she couldn't stifle it. "There's no 'always' in my line of work."

Nina pushed back the covers; she couldn't think straight, lying there like an invalid. She sat on the edge of the bed, put her feet on the floor, took a deep breath and stood up.

"What are you doing?" asked the detective.

Nina was too busy fighting off dizziness to answer. She walked to the window and opened the curtains. Hazy daylight glared through the dirty window. "What floor am I on?"

"Twelfth. General surgery."

"What time is it?"

"Nine-oh-five."

"Tuesday?"

"Yeah."

Her baby was two days old. Nina gazed down at brightly colored dashes far below, going nowhere in heavy traffic. "Do these women you're talking about usually do a lot of planning?"

"Planning?"

"Like getting hold of a volunteer badge and a cart of magazines and candy. And finding out about Verna Rountree and her husband."

Nina turned from the window in time to see Detective Delgado shrug. "That's not much planning, really. She could have grabbed someone's badge in the volunteer supply room on the ground floor and dropped it off on the way out—that's where the cart probably came from too. As for Verna, our volunteer probably didn't know she was having trouble with her husband, but Verna wears a wedding ring, so—" Detective Delgado shrugged again. "She was improvising, role-playing. It fits—like the way she offered you chocolate. That's typical psycho behavior. She played volunteer for a while, now she's going to play mom."

Nina turned and looked down at Detective Delgado, stretched out in the chair. "But why my baby? Why did—" She cut herself off, afraid of the tears she felt building inside her. She didn't want to cry in front of Detective Delgado.

Detective Delgado rose to her feet. She was taller than Nina, and much broader. A gun butt stuck out past the lapel of her suit jacket. "That's just bad luck," she said. "And wasn't he the only boy in the nursery?" Nina nodded. "Well, there you go," said Detective Delgado. "We're checking out all the women with a history of this sort of thing. We'll keep you informed." The detective turned to go.

"But there must be more we can do."

"Like what?"

"I don't know what. You're the cop. You tell me."

Detective Delgado's eyes narrowed again. Then she said, "Aw, shit," reached into her pocket, took out the cigarettes, lit one, sucked deeply and tossed the match on the floor. She blew a cloud of smoke luxuriously through her nostrils. "The Surgeon-General says I'm an addict, like a drug addict, you know? I know what an addict is. I bust them every goddamn day of my life." She took another deep drag. "You got any money?"

"What kind of money?" Nina asked, wondering for a second if some sort of incentive beyond the detective's salary was being suggested.

"Reward money," replied the detective. "For information leading to the recovery of. Don't say arrest or apprehension or any of that shit. In fact, say no questions asked."

"How much?"

"Not too much. We don't want anyone to think you're rich. You're not, are you?"

"No. What about five thousand?"

"Make it ten if you can. People will do a lot for ten grand in this town, even something good."

After Detective Delgado left, Nina lay down again. She had to get the reward set up. She thought about the best way to do that, wishing she had asked Detective Delgado. Then she tried to recall the clinical definition of "psy-

chotic" from Psych 101, especially what it said about vio-
lence. Her eyes closed. She drifted toward a dream. It
began with a genteel voice saying: "Candy, dear?" Then
the telephone rang. Nina jerked up in the bed, grabbed
the receiver.

"Hello?"

"Where the heck are you?" said a high-pitched voice.
"It's nine twenty-three and I've been trying to reach you
for hours."

"Who is this?" said Nina, fighting to shake off her
dream, and whatever drug they had her on.

"Who is this? Who is this? Is something wrong with
you? We just talked yesterday and you said you'd get back
to me." It was the Birdman.

"Oh God."

"Oh God? What do you mean, 'Oh God'? I'm at Condé
Nast right now and the most crucial meeting of my entire
life starts in . . . four and a half minutes."

"Postpone it till next week."

"Postpone it? What do I tell them?"

"Tell them anything. Tell them your mother died."

"My mother's been dead for ten years."

"Then it won't be a lie."

"Listen, god darn it. Is this some kind of what-do-you-
call-it? Shakedown? Are you trying to get more money
out of me? Because if that's the case, I think it's highly
unethical, and what's more—"

Nina hung up. Now she was wide awake. She started to
get out of bed. The door flew open and Jason rushed in.

"Oh, Nina," he said, "I've just heard everything." He
hugged her. She began to cry. Jason cried too. She felt his
tears falling on her shoulder. She stopped crying and patted
him on the back.

"I want to get out of here," she said.

"Then goddamn it, I'll get you out," he said.

The hospital released Nina thirty minutes later. "Where
do you want to go?" Jason asked.

"Home."

In the taxi, Nina told Jason about the reward.

"Good idea," Jason said. "I'll put ads in the papers,
and maybe get some posters printed too. But we can do
more than that."

"Like what?"

"You've got some pull in this town, Nina. It's time to use it."

"What do you mean?"

"I mean that the kind of psycho—the kind of unbalanced woman—who does a thing like this maybe doesn't read the papers, or look at posters. But she watches TV."

"So?"

"So I'll call Hy Morris."

The name sounded like one Nina should know, but for some reason her mind couldn't supply the details. Nina felt weak; the alertness stimulated by her conversation with the Birdman seeped away; what remained was a slow-growing ball of dread in her stomach, and the pain between her legs. "Who is Hy Morris?"

"The NBC guy," replied Jason, sounding surprised.

"But he's in entertainment."

"He'll be able to get you on the local news. That's what we want."

"It is?" said Nina, picturing herself on television, another forty-five-second mom-face that might or might not crumple in tears before it was time to move on to a fire in the Bronx or Joe Isuzu.

"Of course," said Jason.

Was there even the smallest chance that Jason was right? "Okay," said Nina.

The taxi stopped outside Nina's building. "Hey," said Jules as he opened the door. "Had the baby yet?"

Nina couldn't answer. "Everything's going to be all right," Jason told him as they went past.

"Is something—" Jules clamped his mouth shut on the rest of the question.

In the apartment, Jason picked up the telephone in the hall and began making calls. Nina found herself being pulled toward the study, like a bit of space debris caught in the gravity of the sun. She went into the study. Of course it was no longer a study: in the past month she had changed it into a baby's bedroom. She had removed the Lifecycle, the desk, the PC, and replaced them with: a white crib, its headboard and footboard painted with apple trees heavy with big red apples; and a mobile of mirrors cut in different geometric shapes that hung between the rails.

And: a changing table, already stocked with a giant box of Pampers in the smallest size, and a giant box of Huggies in case the baby was allergic to Pampers, as well as powders, creams, lotions.

And: stuffed animals. A polar bear and a baby polar bear; a penguin; a goose with a gold-painted egg inside; a tiger; an elephant as tall as Nina; Winnie-the-Pooh. She was gazing at all of this when Jason came into the room.

"All set," he said. "I've got ads in the *News*, the *Post* and the *Times*, and a film crew'll be here in an hour."

Nina turned to him: her partner, a man she had worked with almost daily for five years, who laughed at her jokes and made her laugh at his; and she saw the determined optimism in his eyes and how hard he was trying to help.

But she said: "Where's Suze?"

Jason's eyes darkened a little. "I can't get in touch with her. She's in L.A."

"L.A.?"

"Something about a performance artist. The woman at the gallery wasn't too clear."

"Le Boucher," Nina said.

"What?"

"Nothing. I'm going to lie down."

Nina went into her bedroom and lay down. She closed her eyes and saw painted apple trees, gravid with big red apples, big and red as the apple the witch gave to Snow White. When she opened her eyes, Jason was sitting on the chair by the dressing table, watching her.

"Go back to the office, Jason. I'll be all right."

"But 'Live At Five' will be here any minute."

"I can handle them."

"You're sure?"

Nina nodded. "You've been great."

Jason waved her remark away. He came to the bed, bent down, kissed her on the cheek and just managed to keep his voice from breaking when he said: "Don't worry, Nina. We'll get him back."

Jason left. Nina rose and went to the dressing table. In the mirror she saw the face of a twin who had lived a different life from hers, a much harder one. She repaired it as well as she could, then put on a dark skirt and a blue sweater, the sort of blue that video people like.

"Live At Five" arrived. They filled the apartment: producer-director, reporter, camerawoman, soundman, lightingman, researcher, driver. They homed in on the nursery.

"It's terrible, terrible," the producer-director said.

For an instant, Nina thought he was speaking to her, but then the lightingman said, "Not to worry. I'll throw a reflector up in the corner and use the four hundred. We'll be all right."

"Live At Five" set up equipment. The reporter spent twenty minutes in the bathroom doing her face and her hair. "I look like absolute shit," she said. In a low voice, the researcher tried to fill her in on the details of the story. "Just absolute shit," the reporter said, running a brush through her hair one more time.

"Ready everybody?" said the producer-director.

First they shot the stand-up. Off camera, the researcher held up big cue cards. The reporter began. "I'm standing here in the brand new nursery in the Manhattan apartment of—hold it, hold it. Is that Neena or Nine-a?"

"Neena," replied the researcher, adding quietly, "I told you before."

"You did not," snapped the reporter.

"Let's try it again," said the producer-director.

"I'm standing here in the brand new nursery in the Manhattan apartment of Nina Kitchener. There should have been a brand new baby in this nursery right now, but as you can see"—the reporter swung around toward the crib—"the crib is empty. A first-time mother's worst nightmare has come true. Barely a day after the birth of . . ."

After the stand-up came the interview. The lightingman held his meter up to Nina's face. The soundman checked his levels. "Just talk," he said. "Say anything."

"I'm talking," Nina said into the mike. "I'm saying anything."

"You're being so brave," the researcher said. She was a plain-looking girl with thick glasses and a soft voice.

"Where did you get that sweater?" the reporter asked Nina. Then she did the interview, her tone husky, her eyes sympathetic, her questions full of long pauses: doing her best to get Nina to cry on camera.

Nina didn't cry. She answered the questions in a quiet but clear voice and concentrated on getting her message across: there was a reward, no questions would be asked, here was her phone number. She gave the number twice.

The cameraman shot the reporter's reaction shots. She nodded, looked deeply concerned, nodded, looked deeply concerned. Then the producer-director's beeper went off. The researcher's beeper went off. The driver's beeper went off. "Live At Five" packed up.

"Thanks," said the producer-director as they hurried out the door. "And good luck. Nine-hundred-and-thirty-thousand people are going to see this."

At twenty minutes after five, Nina became one of them. She saw the face of Nina Kitchener's twin who had lived a harder life; it refused to crumple. She heard her voice giving out the phone number, but only once—the editor cut the rest of it. The reporter said, "Back to you, Jed." Jed and the other anchorperson made worried faces at each other. Jed said, "Let's hope this comes to a happy and speedy resolution." The other anchorperson ad-libbed, "Let's hope." A man crashed through the wall of a muffler shop.

Nina switched off the TV, but continued to sit in front of it until Jules called up. "I'm very, very sorry to bother you," he said. "But there's a messenger with a package for you."

"What's written on it?"

"Your name. And it's from Kitchener and Best."

"Send him up."

The messenger arrived and delivered the package. Inside was an envelope. It contained a note from Jason saying, "I drew this from the current account," and one hundred one-hundred-dollar bills.

Nina sat back down in front of the blank TV screen, the unwrapped package in her lap. Her breasts felt strange. She touched one of her nipples. It was damp. She had heard about expressing milk to keep it flowing during separations of mother and baby. She squeezed her breasts. Nothing came. She called the West Side Women's Reproductive Counseling Center and got no answer. She tried squeezing her breasts again, harder and harder. No milk came. Her face finally crumpled, much too late for the people at "Live At Five."

But Nina hadn't been the only viewer. Not long after ten that night, while she was staring out the window and thinking about the bottle of Scotch in the liquor cabinet, her telephone rang. She picked it up.

"Yes?"

"Hello," said a woman who sounded very young, more like a girl. "Are you the woman who was on TV about the baby?"

"I am," Nina said, holding on to the phone with both hands.

"Is it true about the reward?"

"Yes, it's true."

"Ten thousand dollars?"

"Yes, yes, do you have something to tell me?"

All at once the woman's voice was muffled, as though she had placed her hand over the mouthpiece.

"Hello, hello?" Nina said. "Are you still there?"

"I'm still here," the woman said. "Is it in cash?"

"Yes."

"And no questions?"

"No questions. What do you know about my baby?"

The voice was muffled again.

"Hello? Hello?" Nina said.

"I'm still here, okay?" said the woman, sounding harried. "Meet me at Lumumba's Pizzeria on East Fourteenth at eleven-fifteen tonight. Bring the money. And come alone. With nobody. Or there's no deal."

"But what is it you—"

Click.

Nina's whole body began to tremble. She checked her watch: 10:23. She looked up Lumumba's Pizzeria in the phone book. From the address she guessed it would be somewhere between First and Second Avenue. There were more dangerous sections of town. "Compose yourself." Nina spoke the words aloud. She called a cab, picked up the envelope that Jason had sent and went downstairs.

A silent taxi driver drove Nina downtown. At 11:13, he let her off two doors from the corner of First Avenue in front of a building with a blinking orange sign: LUMUMBA'S PIZZERIA. Only after the taxi left did Nina notice that although the Lumumba's Pizzeria sign seemed to be working perfectly, the restaurant itself was boarded up.

Nina looked around. She became aware for the first time how cold the night was. A strong wind, baffled by the tall buildings of the city, came in biting gusts from every direction. There was no one in sight and half the streetlights were broken. Nina walked under a functioning one and checked her watch: 11:17.

"Hey," came a whisper from the shadows. A woman's voice. Or a girl's.

The sound had come from the west side of Lumumba's Pizzeria. Nina, still standing under the streetlight, peered into the darkness, seeing no one.

"You," the voice whispered again.

Nina walked along the boarded-up front of the building. At the side was a narrow alley. A pale-faced girl, fifteen or sixteen, stood at the head of the alley. She retreated as Nina came closer, but in the blinking light of the Pizzeria sign, Nina could see the girl's threadbare jacket, flabby figure, uncut greasy hair; she could also see that the girl held something in her arms.

"It's you, right?" said the girl. "The one from the TV?"

"Yes. What have you got there?"

"I—"

"Shut up," barked a man standing somewhere behind the girl. It was too dark to see him, but Nina could tell from his voice that he was much older than the girl and much rougher. "The money first," he said.

"I wasn't gonna say nuthin', Ray," the girl said.

"You just said my name, you stupid cunt. Let's have the money first." A hand, brown and hairy, came grasping out of the shadows. At the same time, the bundle in the girl's arms began to cry.

"Give me my baby," Nina said. A look of fear crossed the girl's face. She shrank back.

"The money first," the man said. "And no questions. That's the deal."

Nina put her hand on the girl's wrist and gripped it hard, so she couldn't run away. Then she dropped the envelope in the grasping hand. A match flickered. Bills riffled.

"Okay," the man said. "Sheeit."

The girl handed the baby over to Nina. Then she and the man ran off down the alley, disappearing in the darkness. Nina walked into the street, toward the light, holding the baby tight.

"Are you all right, sweetheart?" she said.

The baby cried.

The first thing Nina noticed under the streetlight was the soiled and bloody sheet wrapped around the baby. And then she looked inside and saw that the baby wasn't hers.

The baby in her arms was a newborn, like hers, but it was half black. Nina's mind raced right to the edge of craziness. Was it her imagination? She tore open the dirty sheet and discovered that the baby was also a girl.

A wild sound like the howl of an animal tore up out of Nina's throat. The baby jerked in her arms and began crying wretchedly. There was nothing for Nina to do but hold it tight. She even rocked it a few times.

|15|

"I dislike NBC," said Fritz, glancing at the TV. "If that's the one with the peacock."

Did they still have the peacock? Happy wondered. He couldn't remember.

"A very stupid bird, the peacock—and quite ugly," Fritz added. On the screen a happy black family gorged on Big Macs. Fritz frowned.

They were in Fritz's cottage late on a cool November afternoon, Happy on his roller bed in front of the fire, Fritz at the rough-hewn kitchen table. Fritz had spent the past few hours harvesting the last of the pumpkins, while Happy had lain on his bed beside the pumpkin patch and watched a strong west wind blowing clouds across the sky. The wind had grown colder and colder. Happy had begun to shiver, but Fritz hadn't noticed. He had kept bringing him pumpkins to see. "Isn't this a beauty? Have you ever seen a finer pumpkin? The garden has been good to us this year, very good. Of course, we worked hard, didn't we, and hard work brings fruit." Happy kept shivering. As the sky grew darker, Fritz finally wheeled him into the cottage.

Now Fritz was cutting the top off a pumpkin and removing the seeds. He salted them lightly, then roasted them over his fire. "Delicious," he said, tasting one. Then he looked at Happy and sighed, perhaps because he noticed the IV bag that provided all of Happy's nourishment, dangling above Happy's bed. He moved out of sight, chewing pumpkin seeds. Happy loved pumpkin seeds, lightly salted, just the way Fritz had always prepared them on Halloween years ago.

Fritz had placed Happy so he could see the fire. After a while, the flames tired his eyes and he tried to watch the TV instead. It stood in the corner of the room, at the edge of his vision. He needed to be turned a few feet to the right. Fritz returned, opened a bottle of Schloss Groenesteyn, poured himself a glass and sipped the wine. He didn't seem to realize that Happy wanted to be turned a little.

"Hi," said a woman on the screen. "I'm Bonnie Bascom."

"I'm Jed Turaine," said a man. "And this is 'Live At Five.'"

Car chase music played. Zooming, panning, trucking, upside-down shots of the city spun across the screen. Then the camera moved in on Bonnie. "Our top story tonight—new revelations in the lobster payoff scandal. But first, here's Geddy with a quick look at the weather."

"Thanks, Bonnie," Geddy said. "Folks—button up those overcoats."

On the periphery of his vision, Happy took in the weather forecast. He absorbed the lobster payoff revelations, learning something about the effects of PCBs in the ocean; he watched a story about a homeless man who had won a lottery but given the winning ticket to a woman who said her dog ate it; he watched a fire in the Bronx, and was beginning to think he might as well watch the fire in Fritz's stone fireplace instead when a beautiful woman appeared on the screen. Her dark eyes dominated it; they were full of powerful, painful emotions, barely under control, emotions Happy didn't understand but found unsettling. Off camera, a woman said: "So you're saying that your day-old baby—barely a day old, is that right?"

"Yes," said the dark-eyed woman.

"Your barely-one-day-old baby was just snatched right out of the hospital nursery?"

"That's right."

"Well, Ms. Kitchener, how does that make you feel?"

The camera moved in on Ms. Kitchener. Happy thought he saw her lower lip tremble, very slightly, but he couldn't be sure, especially from where he lay: with a head he couldn't turn and eyes he couldn't move.

"I can't really describe my feelings," the dark-eyed woman said. "I want my baby back very much, more than anything, and I want to use this opportunity to say there is a reward of ten thousand dollars for information leading to his return, a reward that will be paid with no questions asked." The woman gave her phone number. While she was doing it, the camera cut away to a shot of the reporter nodding. The reporter then said: "Thank you, Ms. Kitchener, for sharing this with us. Back to you, Jed."

Jed and Bonnie talked with concern about the kidnapping. A man crashed through the wall of a muffler shop. Fritz snapped off the TV.

"Garbage," he said. "This is a culture of garbage." Happy saw that Fritz's face, normally so pale and translucent, had turned pink. He poured himself another glass of the Rüdesheim. His hand shook a little, more than a little—the mouth of the bottle clinked several times against the rim of the glass. Fritz was a very old man.

|16|

"Up your ass with a crowbar," croaked Chick when Sergeant Cuthbertson of the CID came in.

Sergeant Cuthbertson smiled. He had a beautiful smile, the smile of a model in a toothpaste ad, except that he wasn't trying to charm anybody with it. His smile seemed brighter because of his skin; Sergeant Cuthbertson was one of those islanders without a trace of slaver's blood in him. He was in uniform: spotless short-sleeved white shirt with red trim, black pants with a straight crease down the front and a red stripe down the side, hat with a patent leather brim. "Is that a St. Lucia parrot?" he asked.

"I don't know," Matthias replied.

"Where did you get it?"

"Someone on a boat left him as a gift, years ago."

"I believe it is a St. Lucia parrot," Sergeant Cuthbertson said, studying Chick more closely. "Or possibly an Imperial, from Dominica." Chick sidestepped on his perch. "Equally rare," Sergeant Cuthbertson added.

"Yeah?" said Matthias.

"And equally endangered," said Sergeant Cuthbertson. "Export, trade and sale of such species are illegal. A lot of animal smuggling goes on, Mr. Matthias."

"And vegetable."

If Sergeant Cuthbertson got the joke he showed no sign. "I've made more than one arrest myself in this area," he continued. "We have a duty to protect our heritage and its threatened wildlife."

"I agree, Sergeant," Matthias said. "But Chick's more threatening than threatened."

Sergeant Cuthbertson wasn't smiling anymore. The smile didn't mean much anyway—Sergeant Cuthbertson, who Matthias knew only by reputation, had made more drug, armed robbery and homicide arrests than any other policeman on the force; years ago he had shocked the nation by turning in someone for attempting to bribe an officer of the law. "Exactly when did you acquire this bird, Mr. Matthias?"

"I can't remember exactly. Six or seven years ago. Did you come all this way on a parrot investigation, Sergeant?" The sergeant's seaplane, tied to the dock, was bobbing gently in Zombie Bay.

Sergeant Cuthbertson hitched up his pants and sat on a bar stool, back straight. "Given the length of time, which may place the act of acquiring the bird prior to the passage of the relevant laws, you may rest easy on this matter, Mr. Matthias."

"That's good," Matthias said, sitting himself two bar stools away. "I don't think Chick would be happy in the wilds of St. Lucia. That's not his kind of thing at all."

Sergeant Cuthbertson regarded the parrot for a moment. "Is there something unusual about his eyes?"

"Meanest eyes I've ever seen," Matthias said.

"What holds him to that perch?"

"Nothing."

"Then why doesn't he just fly away?"

"No one knows."

"Does he ever fly around the room or anything?"

"Never," Matthias said. "How about a beer?"

"Not just now, thank you."

"I'll accept payment."

That brought the smile again. There may have been some humor in it after all. "Right now," Sergeant Cuthbertson said, "I would like to speak with your divemaster." He consulted a notebook. "Would that be Mr. Wickham or Mr. McGillivray?"

"Mr. McGillivray. You'll have to wait a few minutes."

"Why?"

Matthias pointed out to sea. *Two Drink Minimum* was chugging around Gun Point with Brock at the helm. The air was so clear that Matthias could see the green bottles of beer Moxie was passing out to the divers in the bow. Moxie had painted the barge in rainbow colors the year before. Matthias and Sergeant Cuthbertson watched it come in: rainbow boat, baby-blue bay, green bottles.

"The underwater part," said Sergeant Cuthbertson. "The most beautiful aspect of our little nation, apparently."

Matthias felt the sergeant's eyes on him. "So they say," he replied. In the silence that followed, the line that was almost never crossed, the one between black and white, remained uncrossed.

Brock walked in. "G'day, mates," he said. "Looking for me?"

He stopped just inside the pool side entrance, his head almost touching the palm fronds: yellow hair, still wet, slicked back on his golden brown shoulders. He wore nothing but his Speedo and a piece of eight around his neck.

"I don't suppose you've got your work permit on you," said Sergeant Cuthbertson.

"I could make a funny joke," said Brock. He took a closer look at the sergeant and added, "But I won't. You want to see my work permit?"

"Please."

Brock left. A female guest off the barge, wearing little more than Brock, gave him a glance stripped of ambiguity. He gave her a smile that might have meant anything. Matthias reflected, not for the first time, that immersion in forty or fifty feet of warm water while sucking on a regulator was a potent aphrodisiac.

"What's up, Sergeant?" Matthias said. "There's nothing wrong with Brock's work permit."

"I'm sure you're right," said Sergeant Cuthbertson. "But I always like to begin with work permits."

"And then?"

Sergeant Cuthbertson watched a woman by the pool roll over on her back without bothering to refasten her bikini top. His eyes revealed nothing. The fan turned.

"Have you ever been to France?" Sergeant Cuthbertson asked.

"No," Matthias replied, wondering if the sergeant had been reminded of St. Tropez or some town like that.

"Nor I. I don't think I'd care for it."

"Why not?"

"Just from dealing with these Sûreté people."

"What Sûreté people?" asked Matthias.

"Their police. M'sieu Perrault, specifically. French citizens seem to be a higher form of life to him. Even when they're dead."

Hope, faint and inchoate, fluttered in Matthias's chest. "Are you saying he knows the identity of the man who went down?"

Sergeant Cuthbertson shook his head. "That's what he wants to know. He keeps sending cables. Patronizing ones." Sergeant Cuthbertson removed his hat and placed it on the bar. "I don't suppose anything's floated up?"

"After all this time?"

"Is it impossible?"

"Almost. It's five thousand feet deep out there."

"As deep as that?"

"In places."

Sergeant Cuthbertson wrote something in his notebook. He was still writing when Brock returned wearing faded shorts and a T-shirt advertising Broken Hill Lager. "Here you go," he said, handing the sergeant his work permit.

Sergeant Cuthbertson examined it. "Perfectly in order," he said, handing it back. "If a little unusual."

"How's that?" asked Brock, sticking it in his pocket.

"One doesn't come across many permits for divers these days. The government wants to encourage the development of our own diving corps."

"I got the original permit a while back," Brock said. "The summer before last, to be exact."

"I noted that," Sergeant Cuthbertson said.

"Brock's highly qualified," Matthias pointed out, trying to forestall any immigration problem. "He's brought Moxie up to instructor level and he's working with some teenagers from Conchtown."

"Fine, fine," said Sergeant Cuthbertson. "But as I explained, I haven't come about Mr. McGillivray's work permit. I'm here at the behest of the French government to learn more about the identity of the missing man."

"The Frenchman?" said Brock. "I already told the other sergeant, the one who came at the time, that—"

"Sergeant Morse?"

"I guess so. I told him I didn't remember the name on the card. See, I don't really look much at the name. It's the card itself that's important."

"And this card was a . . ." Sergeant Cuthbertson turned the pages of his notebook.

"An FFSA card," Brock said. "Fédération Française des Sports Aquatiques." The words ran together fluently.

"An FFSA card," the sergeant repeated. "And how did you recognize it as genuine?"

"I've seen lots of them. I dove out of Ajaccio for a year." Sergeant Cuthbertson regarded Brock with the same sort of look he had given Matthias. "That's in Corsica," Brock added, which Matthias would not have done. Brock was fifteen years younger and had never been to the Isle of Pines.

"Is it?" said Sergeant Cuthbertson.

"Yes. So I've had experience with French divers, you see. I also worked with Cousteau's people one summer. I've got a letter from them in my résumé, if you want to see it."

"That won't be necessary. Enough to establish that you were familiar with this particular card. Are there registration numbers on these cards, by the way?"

"I'm not sure," Brock said. "I think so."

Sergeant Cuthbertson turned to Matthias. "The number wouldn't have been recorded on the tank rental bill?"

"No. The bill just says 'Cottage Six.' But the police have already looked into all this. The bill was part of the evidence—the court still has it, as far as I know."

"This is not a criminal investigation, Mr. Matthias. The case has never been a criminal one. It was a civil suit, now concluded, barring appeal, as I understand it. I am merely cooperating with French authorities. Initial efforts to trace the missing man through relatives and friends of Mr. Standish failed. He had no French acquaintances that anyone knew of. So, whatever facts you can supply will be helpful."

Brock supplied the facts, as he had supplied them to Sergeant Morse. Fact: He had been in charge of the club the day Standish and his companion arrived; Matthias was in Miami on business. Fact: Standish and his companion flew in on a chartered plane from Nassau late in the afternoon. They arranged to go diving the next morning. The Frenchman, he recalled, was short and thin, forty or forty-five years old. Brock had no clear memory of his features. Moxie filled the tanks that night. Fact: The next morning, the two men went out before breakfast in *Who Cares*, as arranged. Fact: Noticing they were overdue, Moxie had gone out and found Standish floating face-down in the water and no sign of the other man. He had begun CPR.

Sergeant Cuthbertson wrote the facts in his notebook. "How long had you been working here at the time, Mr. McGillivray?"

"About a month. Right, Matt?"

"Yes." Brock had walked into the bar, duffel bag over his shoulder, on a hot afternoon in early August. Matthias had hired him before dinner.

Sergeant Cuthbertson wrote that down too. Then he flipped to another page, studied it and said: "And what about the luggage, Mr. McGillivray?"

"Luggage?"

"Didn't one of the maids report seeing luggage in Cottage Six when she turned down the sheets?"

Brock shrugged. "I never saw any."

Sergeant Cuthbertson closed the notebook. "Thank you, Mr. McGillivray," he said.

"That's it?"

"That's it."

Brock left to prepare the afternoon trip. Sergeant Cuthbertson watched him go. "How tall is he, Mr. Matthias?"

"Six-six, I think. How about that beer, Sergeant?"

"Not just now."

Matthias walked Sergeant Cuthbertson to the dock. Weathered seashells covered the path; the sergeant's polished black shoes crunched them as he passed, making a sound like an army on the march. "What is this wall that everyone talks about, Mr. Matthias?"

"It's just the edge of the continental shelf, really. But here it starts in shallow water and drops almost straight down. You can see a wide range of marine life without going very deep."

"So that's the attraction?"

"Yes."

The pilot of the seaplane opened the door. Sergeant Cuthbertson stepped on the pontoon and climbed into the cockpit. As he was strapping in he said: "We looked into Mr. Standish's PADI card. He qualified for it through a dive shop in Fort Lauderdale. The day before he arrived here."

"What dive shop?" Matthias said.

Sergeant Cuthbertson reached out and handed him a sheet of paper: a photocopy of Hiram Standish's card. The pilot started the engines, swung around and accelerated across Zombie Bay. The plane rose from blue up into lighter blue and soon shrank out of sight.

Matthias walked back up the path. He met Krio coming the other way, dreadlocks dangling all around his head and a bloody cleaver in his hand.

"Phone," Krio said.

The only phone at Zombie Bay was in the office. "Matthias speaking," Matthias said into it.

No one responded.

"Hello?" Matthias said. "Anyone there?" He was just about to hang up when a voice said:

"I'm not happy."

It was Danny.

Lauderdale. Dockside Dive Supply was three blocks inland from the public marina, sharing side walls with a liquor store and a used books shop, all three in need of a fresh coat of paint. Matthias parked and checked the photocopy of Hiram Standish's dive card, front and back, which Sergeant Cuthbertson had given him. The card certified that Hiram Standish had completed a basic course in skin and scuba diving which included twenty-two hours of instruction. It was signed on the back by Hiram Standish, diver, and Wendell Minns, instructor.

Matthias went inside. He'd been in a lot of dive shops. He could grade them at a glance. Dockside Dive Supply had the usual gear: tanks, regs, BCs, masks, fins, snorkels, backpacks, gauges, watches, wet suits, but not much of any of them, and nothing of the best: D. But the prices could have been higher, and a yellowed photograph of Valerie Taylor, mask pushed up on her forehead, hung on the wall: D plus.

A man came through a back door, wiping his hands on the sides of his jeans. "Hey there," he said. He went behind the counter, eyed the open cash register drawer and closed it. "Looking for something in particular?"

"Someone in particular," said Matthias. "A diving instructor named Wendell Minns."

"You in the market for a course?"

"No. I just want to talk to Wendell Minns."

"About anything special?"

"Hiram Standish, Junior."

The man's crinkly little eyes crinkled some more. "Who's he?"

"Mr. Minns will know."

"Why is that?"

"Because Sergeant Cuthbertson of the Bahamas CID discussed his case with him."

The man grunted. Then he seemed to concentrate on some mental activity. At last he said: "You a lawyer, or something?"

"Do I look like a lawyer?"

The man studied him. "Nope."

"I'm a diver on Andros. I just want to find out more about him, that's all."

More mental activity. Then the man said: "I'm Wendell Minns. But I already told that nigger all I knowed."

"Do you mean Sergeant Cuthbertson?" Matthias asked, very softly.

"Huh?"

"Nothing."

Wendell Minns was one of those instructors who proved that you didn't have to be fit to be a scuba diver. He had a flabby face, narrow shoulders, a small frame and a potbelly that looked as hard as a basketball.

"Hang on," Wendell Minns said, locking the cash register. "The compressor."

He went out the back door. Matthias followed him. Minns had an old Worthington with a couple of tanks hooked to it. He checked the pressure gauges, then shut off the machine, bled the hoses and unhooked the tanks. The tanks had a 3000 p.s.i. capacity. Matthias had been close enough to read the gauges: 2400 and 2350. Cheating his customers of air could hardly be very profitable for Wendell Minns; it might even be dangerous. Perhaps he was simply the kind of man who cheats whenever the opportunity arises.

Wendell Minns heaved the tanks out of the cooling tub, banging one of them against his knee. "Fuckin' shit," he said. He swung them into line with some other tanks along the wall, allowing them to strike the cement hard, as though he were paying them back for his knee.

"I'd hate for one of those to turn into a bomb," Matthias said.

Minns turned and squinted at him. "What'd you say you had to do with this Hiram fella?"

Matthias looked once more into the crinkly eyes; the eyes of a not-very-smart man who had spent too much time on the water, but who also cheated for the sake of cheating and might be crafty for the sake of being crafty.

"I'm from the Andros Hotel Association," Matthias said. He liked the sound of it. "They've sent me over here to find out what I can about Mr. Standish, in order to minimize any bad publicity."

"Like I said, I already told that nig—"

"Yeah, I know. But this isn't very high on his list and he just hasn't had the time to go over it with us. I was hoping you would."

Minns looked at his watch. "I'm gettin' ready to close for lunch."

Matthias searched for the magic words and tried these: "I'll buy."

"Yeah?" said Minns, withdrawing once more into some mental process. "Well, why not, huh?"

They lunched at Al's. Al's had a bartender, a prostitute and a waitress, all of whom greeted Minns without enthusiasm. Al's: nautical motif—frayed fishnets, rough wood paneling, rusting anchors, harpoons and chains, and air that smelled of the sea, or at least the way the sea smells in Lagos harbor, or somewhere like that. It was the most authentic nautical experience Matthias had ever had in a restaurant, especially if the hold of a slave ship was the specific object of simulation.

The jukebox was playing Duane Eddy's version of "Dixie" as they sat down. The menus came, nice and greasy. Minns ordered two fries, two bacon cheeseburgers and a sixteen-ounce Bud. Matthias made sure that the tuna was canned, then asked for a tuna sandwich.

"Anything to drink?" asked the waitress.

Water was what he wanted, but he guessed that Minns would feel more comfortable if he ordered a beer too, and he wanted Minns to be comfortable. "The same," Matthias told her.

The beer came first. Minns downed half of his in one gulp, then wiped his mouth on the anchor tattoo decorating his left forearm. "Andros, huh?" he said. "The armpit of the Caribbean."

First: The armpit as metaphor was a cliché Matthias despised. Second: The Bahamas are in the Atlantic, not the Caribbean. Third: He'd seen many anchor tattoos; Minns' was the worst executed, and much too grandiose for his flaccid little forearm.

Matthias said: "How so?"

"You know," said Minns. "Ugly. And the fuckin' bugs. Christ."

"They're not so bad by the water."

Minns assumed his crafty face. "What else are you gonna say, bein' with the tourist board and all?"

"Got me there."

Minns laughed graciously, as though such rhetorical coups came easy and often. He ordered another sixteen-ouncer. "Make that two," he called after the waitress. "I'm thirsty something terrible today," he confided to Matthias. "Mouth's drier'n popcorn farts."

"You'd better drink up."

Minns squinted at him. Then his eyes shifted, and he once more made contact with his interior life, but not for long—maybe beer had already spilled over that domain. "So," he said, holding the ketchup over the fries and banging the bottom of the bottle, "you want to know about this Hiram fella."

"That's right."

The mouth of the ketchup bottle spat out a red glob; then came a flood. This seemed to be what Minns had been trying to achieve. "So ask," he said, mouth widening to accept a red forkful of fries resembling some bleeding tentacled creature. "It's your dime."

"What kind of student was he?"

"Student?"

"Diving student. Theory. In the pool. Open water."

"Open water?"

"You had him for twenty-two hours. You must have gotten him into the water."

Wendell Minns, one or two mouthfuls from the bottom of his third sixteen-ouncer, failed to pause for reflection over Matthias's information, where it came from, or where it might lead. Instead, he leaned forward confidentially. "You said you're a diver, right?"

"Right."

"You teach diving?"

"I used to."

"You ever get somebody who needed a card quick, like just before a holiday or something?"

"Probably."

Minns leaned forward a little more. An overhead light mounted in a dusty glass fishing float shone on his greasy lips: glistening greenly in a way that drew a nauseating parallel between food and reptiles in Matthias's mind. "Probably, he says," said Minns. "Every instructor has it happen, sooner or later. Am I right or am I right?"

"You are."

"So what did you do?"

"What did I do?"

"When some turkey wanted a dive card quick."

"What everybody else does, I guess."

Minns laughed again, the laugh that accompanied his debating victories. "Sure as shit you did, buddy, sure as shit you did." He held out his hand. Matthias shook it: a hot wet hand pulsing with body language—suggesting, so Matthias thought, complicity, dishonesty, theft, perversion. When the handshake was over, Matthias forced himself not to wipe his hand on the napkin and ordered more beer—his second, Minns' fourth. Minns watched closely the arrival of the two big mugs on the tray. Free beer had meaning for some people far beyond the mere saving of money. It saved them from responsibility.

Minns took a sip, almost dainty. "Ah," he said, sitting back and folding his hands on his hard potbelly.

"How many hours did you give him exactly?"

"Hours?"

"The Hiram guy."

"Oh." Minns smiled. The crafty look reappeared, slightly lopsided now. "I gave him a pool checkout."

"One pool checkout?"

"Yeah. But a long one. Plenty long for him—he didn't

like the water much. I'd say an hour and a half, easy. Three hundred bills, quick and dirty. Plus a little theory in their room, after. Funny thing, he really knew the theory. Without being told, I mean. Narcosis, embolism, partial pressures, they knew it all."

"They?"

"Him and his pal. A little frog, or something. They had a room at the Tangiers. Not far from here, and they got a pool."

"Frog?"

"French dude."

"What made you think he was French?"

"I saw his passport. It was lying on the table and it said France on it. I don't miss much, Mister—what did you say your name was again?"

"Nero. Howie Nero."

"Nice to meet you, Howie." Minns stuck his hand out across the table. Matthias had to shake it again.

"Since you don't miss much," Matthias said, "did you happen to get his name?"

"Whose?"

"The Frenchman's."

Wendell Minns thought. He actually closed his eyes and scrunched up his face. "What's that cat?" he asked.

"Cat?"

Minns' eyes opened, but his brow remained furrowed. "In the cartoons. With a funny name."

"Garfield?"

Minns shook his head impatiently. "Nah. Before that. Way before that."

"Sylvester?"

"Who's Sylvester?"

"A cartoon cat. With Tweety, the bird."

"Oh, yeah. He's always trying to get into the cage. I like that one."

"So that was the name?"

"What?"

"Sylvester?"

"Nah. This cat don't look nothin' like Sylvester. Smaller, and not so hairy."

"Not so hairy?"

"Skinnier, maybe. And older."

"Older?"

"Like he came first, you know?"

"Do you mean he was a character from earlier cartoons?"

"Yeah."

"Felix? Felix the Cat?"

Wendell Minns slammed his palm on the table. "Felix! Felix the Cat! Bingo!" Minns picked up his mug and took a big pull, as though he'd earned it.

"So Hiram's friend was named Felix?"

Minns put his mug back on the table, carefully superimposing it on the previous condensation ring. "That's what I just tole you, i'n' it?"

"Felix what?"

"Huh?"

"What was Felix's last name?"

Minns blinked. "The Cat, right?"

"The other Felix. Hiram's friend."

"Fuck if I know."

"Then how do you know his first name was Felix?"

"Jesus Christ. Because that's what the other fella called him. He'd say, 'Felix, can you give me a hand with this.' And shit like that."

"A hand with what?"

"Like putting on the equipment. Beside the pool. The little guy knew something about diving. He knew the gear." Minns leaned forward again. "He had that frog passport and shit, but you know what?"

"What?"

"He looked like a kike to me. Like one of those kike lawyers down to Miami." Minns thought for a moment. "But what kind of kike got a name like Felix, right?"

"Mendelssohn, for one."

"Huh?"

"Nothing. Do you have any idea why Hiram wanted his card so quickly?"

"Sure. So's he could rent tanks on his trip. I already told you that."

"So you think it might have been a sudden trip?"

"Huh?"

"Did they talk about the trip at all?"

"Nope."

"They didn't mention where they were going?"

"Nope."

"Or talk about the kind of diving they would be doing?"

Minns, mug halfway to his mouth, paused. "I don't know about that."

"What do you mean?"

Minns brought the mug to his mouth and drained what was left. "Shit, this is good beer."

Matthias ordered another. He didn't bother ordering one for himself and Minns didn't notice. "What kind of diving were they talking about?"

"Deep diving."

"How deep?"

"Deep. The little guy kept asking me how deep you can go with scuba, what the record was, all that shit."

"What did you tell them?"

"What I tell everyone—only an asshole goes deeper than one-fifty."

"Good advice. How deep did they want to go?"

"Search me."

"But you told them that anyone with just an hour in the pool had no business going anywhere near one-fifty."

"An hour and a *half*," Minns said. His eyes were red now, and Matthias found himself wondering if Minns was armed. "An hour and a fucking half," he said, thrusting his face forward into the green light and crinkling his eyes, approaching once more the mammalian-reptilian border.

"First-rate," Matthias told him, meeting his stare.

"First-rate?"

"Instruction," Matthias explained.

Minns averted his eyes. "Gotta piss," he said. Minns pushed himself to his feet and moved carefully to the back of the restaurant and out of sight.

Matthias didn't wait for his return. He paid the bill, rose and walked to the door. That meant passing the bar, where the prostitute sat on the last stool. The Shirelles were singing "Will You Love Me Tomorrow?" The woman raked her fingernail lightly on Matthias's wrist as he went by.

"You busy this afternoon?" she asked.

"Afraid so."

"That's too bad. You're a big good-looking man. I could give you the special rate—twenty bucks."

"I'll have to pass."

She held on to his arm. "Fifteen bucks. And I'll be quick, if you're really in a rush. I'll have you up and down in two minutes. Money back if I don't."

"Sounds inviting," Matthias said. "But not today." He freed himself and went outside. He took a deep breath. He had always liked the Shirelles and he wouldn't let his lunch at Al's change that.

The Hotel Tangiers was less than a mile from the restaurant. At one time, some of the rooms might have had an ocean view: now newer, bigger hotels had squeezed themselves into the space between the Tangiers and the beach, blocking off all but the occasional narrow vertical of blue.

Matthias entered the lobby. It was small, barely accommodating the registration desk, the two old men playing gin rummy and the dead rubber plant that bent over their heads. Matthias walked up to the desk and rang the bell.

The gin players sighed. One of them got to his feet, shuffled across the room, through the waist-level swinging door and behind the registration desk. He was short, with a bald head, pink and peeling from the sun, and pale watery eyes that were almost colorless.

"You want a room, Mister?"

"No. I'm looking for somebody."

The little man raised his voice and said to the other card player, "He doesn't want a room. He's looking for somebody." But there was no answer: his partner had fallen asleep, cards splayed open on his lap.

"He's not here now," Matthias said.

"He's looking for somebody who's not here," the man called across the lobby.

"But he might have been here on September first of last year. And I'd like to check your register."

The man sniffed. "You're from the police maybe?"

"No."

"So. Mister. You don't want a room, you're not from the police and you're looking for somebody."

"You've got it."

"I've got it, he says," said the old man to the other old man, who made no response. "What somebody?"

"A man named Felix."

"Felix. I don't know any Felix. Does this Felix have a last name?"

The old man had a scrawny neck that Matthias's hands would have fit around easily. Matthias wiped that image from his mind and said: "That's the problem. He's got several. So that won't be a help. But he always uses Felix. Because he was named after Felix the Cat, see?"

The old man's eyes brightened. "He was named after Felix the Cat?"

"Right. And he likes the image. So if I could just have a peek at the register . . ."

"You would know what, exactly?"

"Whether he stayed here."

"But that was a long time ago."

"Right. But it's a crucial piece of the puzzle."

"What is this puzzle?"

"How to get him to pay the money he owes me."

The old man grinned, revealing three teeth, two on top, one on the bottom. "I thought so," he said. "That, or how to get your wife back."

"You're very shrewd." That had been Matthias's other thought too.

"So, how much are we talking about?"

"Enough."

"Six figures maybe?"

"Maybe."

"Six figures." The old man lingered over the phrase as though it were a snatch of beautiful poetry. "That's a lot of money."

"It is."

"So maybe this service I might be willing and able to provide for you . . ."

Matthias took out a ten-dollar bill.

"Twenty's better."

Matthias added a five. "So's fifteen."

"Six figures," the man called across the room, "and he makes a tsimmes over five dollars." But he accepted the money and showed Matthias the register.

Matthias turned back the pages fourteen months to the previous September 1. Only one person had checked in that day: H. Standish, Room 109.

"H isn't for Felix," said the old man, shoving the money deep in his pocket, in case their deal was going sour.

"I'd like to have a look at one-oh-nine," Matthias said.

"A look at one-oh-nine."

"To get a mental picture."

"A mental picture. I can tell it to you, a mental picture. Two double beds. Color TV. Sliding door to the pool. Got the mental picture?"

"Yeah, but it couldn't hurt to see it."

The little man shrugged. "Okay. You're a nice guy. A nice guy with a problem. You want to see? You'll see." He opened the swinging door and led Matthias down a poorly lit hall. Through a closed door, Matthias heard a TV voice say: "He was killed with an ice pick in Mexico City."

Ahead of Matthias, the old man muttered, "Who was Trotsky."

On TV, a woman said: "Who was Nanook of the North?"

"Remember," said the first TV voice, "the category is 'Reds.' "

"Feh," said the old man. He took out a key and opened 109. "One of our nicest rooms."

Room 109 was just as he had described, except for the plasticized yellow curtains covering the sliding door. Matthias pushed them aside, slid open the door and walked out to the pool. It probably could have fit inside Room 109: too small for swimming, too shallow for scuba instruction. Matthias knelt and dipped his hand in the water. It was cold. "There must have been two men in one-oh-nine."

"So? Am I the vice squad?"

"That's not what I'm suggesting. I just wonder if you remember them at all. They had a scuba diving lesson in this pool."

"Are you kidding?" the old man asked. "My memory's shot. I can't even count the cards anymore."

"You remembered Trotsky."

The old man showed his three teeth. "That was a long time ago. A long time ago I remember. It's not so long ago I have trouble with."

"Here," Matthias said, handing him a Zombie Bay Club card. "In case Felix's last name ever comes back to you."

"It wasn't there in the first place," the old man said, but he put the card in the pocket with the ten and the five.

Matthias followed him around the pool and into the lobby through another entrance. "Thanks," he said, opening the door to the street.

"Don't mention it," the old man replied, going behind the registration desk.

The door hadn't quite closed when Matthias heard the old man's partner say, "You should have held out for the twenty, putz."

Danny was waiting near one of the Bahamasair counters at the airport. He wasn't wearing his orange sunglasses; Matthias could see his troubled eyes and the dark circles under them. He also saw that the boy had grown, and not just taller: his shoulders had broadened and muscle had begun to swell his chest. Matthias felt an urge to embrace him, but he held back. Shaking hands would be stupid, so he didn't do that either, and so no physical contact was made. Thanksgiving vacation: father and son. Matthias said: "Hi, Danny. Where's your mother?"

"She got tired of waiting." Danny's voice was changing too.

They boarded the plane. They had it almost to themselves. Danny looked out the window, watching the Florida coast slip away. "Are you going to talk about it?" Matthias asked.

"About what?"

"What's bothering you."

"Everything."

"Like what?"

"Mom. Howie. Tucker."

"Who's Tucker?"

"Howie's kid."

"I didn't know Howie had a kid. How old is he?"

"A year older than me. Mr. Wonderful."

"Mr. Wonderful?"

Danny didn't reply. The plane rose. The sun set. Florida vanished in a purple glow, and then the sea. Danny started crying, silently. "What is it, Danny?" Matthias said. "Did

Howie do something to you?" He felt the awakening of a killing rage inside.

"No!" Danny said. "It's nothing like that."

Matthias regretted his question at once. "Then what is it?" He thought of putting his hand on Danny's knee. Danny's leg moved away. Matthias said nothing further.

The plane had begun its descent when Danny said: "It's like that fucking fax machine."

"What?"

"Howie's got a fax machine in his Porsche."

"What for? I thought he was a psychiatrist."

"Some land business. He does it while he's on the road. Every night the car fills up with paper and Tucker and I have to take turns cleaning it out in the morning, so Howie can look it over at breakfast. And the other day it was Tucker's turn and he didn't do it and Howie lost fifty grand he could have made. And I got blamed."

"Why?"

"Because," Danny said, turning on Matthias in anger, "he said it was my turn, and they believed him."

"What did your mother do?"

"Oh, she backed him up. He can do no wrong. He gets straight A's and Howie's already talked to someone at Harvard about him. He shot an eighty-four last week from the blue tees and he's captain of the tennis team. He's Mr. Wonderful and I'm a jerk."

"You're not a jerk."

Danny didn't speak. Matthias, aware of the weakness of his own response, remained silent too. He spent the rest of the flight formulating ideas. The wheels were down when he finally said: "Any of your friends into scuba?"

"Some."

"Well, you're good at that."

"It's not the same."

"As what?"

"Tennis. Golf."

Matthias smiled. His son saw him smiling and seemed a little taken aback. Perhaps he hadn't seen him smile enough. "That's true," Matthias said. There wasn't much bragging to be done about scuba. "But what about free diving?"

"Free diving?"

"Want to try some?"

"With you?"

"Sure. Brock and I will take you out. I'll bet you could pull forty feet right now."

"I could?"

"Yup. You've got the body for it."

"I do?"

"Yup. And you're ready."

|18|

Nina lay in her bed. The television was on. *Rosemary's Baby*. A strange choice for Thanksgiving evening, Nina thought, but she wasn't really watching it. She was thinking about the half-black baby girl, now in the hands of the child welfare people. Nina could picture the girl's face very distinctly; the image of her own baby's face appeared much less clearly. Only her fingers, as though they contained their own organs of memory, had vivid recall: she could still feel the baby's fine blond hair, so long at the back.

He didn't have a name. Henrik, she thought, and suddenly despised her frivolity so much she squirmed on the bed.

A bottle of wine sat on the end table. Nina drank from it steadily. Her thoughts turned toward Tuesday: her fortieth birthday, and the first anniversary of the day the words "a baby" had popped out of her mouth in answer to Jason's question about what she really wanted. A big decision, Dr. Berry had told her, although she hadn't understood what he meant at first. *How far are you prepared to go—to have a baby, I mean*. Nina thought about what he had said. And all at once, she really did understand it; more than that, Dr. Berry's statement seemed to come to life in her mind. The first thing it did was couple with what was happening on the TV screen. The juxtaposition shocked her. She got out of bed, her eyes fixed on John Cassavetes. Of course, these were just a bunch of good

actors getting the most out of a good story and having
some fun at the same time: she could see that in the extra
little twist of Cassavetes's lips. But, like Rosemary, she
had allowed sperm of uncertain provenance inside her
body—although in her case no one had conspired to get
her cooperation. She had done it to herself.

And now she was being punished.

But that was sick thinking. Nina could not accept the
existence of any punisher, any judge, who would harm a
baby. She had never been, would never be able to do that.
She snapped off the TV.

That left her alone with an empty screen, an empty
bottle and an empty bed. And an empty crib in the next
room. She turned off the lights and tried to sleep. She
sensed *Rosemary's Baby* still unreeling, somewhere beyond the audible and visible parts of the spectrum. Only
connect.

But with whom? Jason was in Vermont for the weekend.
Suze was still in L.A., acting as some sort of agent for Le
Boucher, who had lucked into a major role in a barbarian
movie when the leading lady had torn her hamstring on
the first day of shooting. Suze had asked if Nina wanted
her to fly back, and Nina had said no, half-hoping Suze
would anyway. But Suze hadn't, and the other, non-hoping
half didn't really care. Suze couldn't help her. Who could?

Nina dressed and went down to the street, catching Jules
in the act of stuffing a bottle in his pocket. "Happy Thanksgiving, Ms. Kitchener," he said, slurring just a little. She
saw his face too late recalling her situation as she walked
out into the night.

A cold wind blew. Nina walked. The city had a smell
the wind couldn't quite blow away, as though something
had plugged the entire sewage system, and somewhere
below things were approaching a critical mass. Nina passed
by the usual sights without really noticing: a woman with
a stack of videocassettes under her arm, a man lying in a
fast-food doorway, wrapped in a Hefty bag. Two eyes
looked out at her from his emaciated face; for a moment
Nina thought he was about to say something, but he did
not.

Nina walked. She walked herself into fatigue and beyond. Then, finally, when she had walked her mind quiet

and turned for home, "Salut Demeure" began to play in it.

Her feet took over then and walked her to the hospital instead. *Sometimes they stroll back into the hospital, leave the baby and stroll out.* Yes. Of course. Reality lights up, if only for a moment, and they try to undo what has been done. Nina walked faster and faster. She was running by the time she got there.

Random details impressed themselves on Nina's brain: the hiss of the sliding doors; the too-bright lobby; crushed coffee cups and a blob of pink gum on the stairs. Then she was on the fourth floor, outside the nursery window.

There had been a population explosion since her last visit. Almost every bassinet was filled, including the one at the far end of the first row, where a blue-wrapped bundle now lay. A blue-wrapped bundle with a blond tuft of hair sticking out of the blanket.

The next thing she knew, Nina was inside the nursery, standing over the bassinet. There was a blond baby boy in it, but he wasn't hers. One glance at his features brought back the nearly lost image of her own son's face. But doubt stirred in her mind anyway; was there just a remote chance she could be wrong? Very gently, Nina began unwrapping a corner of the blue blanket, to see the identification bracelet on the baby's wrist. She was careful not to disturb the baby, so she had still not seen the bracelet when strong arms seized her from behind.

"Help! Help!" someone cried, right by her ear.

Nina struggled, twisted, saw she was being held by a tall nurse, not Verna Rountree, but a nurse she hadn't seen before.

"Help!" the nurse shouted. Babies began to cry. People came running. "I caught her red-handed, I caught her red-handed," the nurse told them, gradually lowering her voice. "She was just about to snatch another one."

They surrounded Nina. They knocked her to the floor, perhaps not deliberately. They stared down at her, yelling and questioning; the babies cried. Nina lay on her back, unhurt but unable to make a sound. Then one face came closer, separating itself from the crowd. It was the head nurse.

"Oh, for Christ's sake," she said.

* * *

The head nurse took Nina down to the lobby and called a taxi. "I can walk," Nina told her.

"You've done enough walking. But you'd better think about getting some therapy."

"Therapy?"

"To get you through this."

"I don't need therapy. I need my baby back." Nina was angry, but she couldn't find the strength to raise her voice.

The head nurse looked at her closely. "Are you planning to sue?"

"Sue?"

"The hospital. The administration's worried about it."

"It hadn't occurred to me."

"No? They say you're some kind of wheel downtown."

A taxi pulled up. The head nurse walked Nina to it and opened the door for her. "Anyway, I hope you do."

"Why?"

"They deserve it."

"For what happened to me?"

"No," the head nurse replied. "In general."

The door closed. The taxi pulled away. The driver was listening to a late-night call-in show on the radio. A woman said: "I hate all the holidays, but Thanksgiving is the worst. It's the pits."

"You're the pits, lady," said the host, cutting her off. "You depress me. Hello, line two? Hoboken? Hoboken, you're on the air. What's on your mind? Hoboken?"

Nina spent the rest of the night lying in bed with her eyes open. At first light she rose, walked past the closed door of the nursery and pulled the Lifecycle out of the hall closet. She sat on it and began pedaling. Almost immediately she felt weak and tired, and her mind, rather than shutting down, focused sharply on the baby. Nina got off the bike after only a few minutes.

She called Detective Delgado's office. "Delgado's not in," a man told her.

"When can I reach her?"

The man called to someone nearby: "When's Delgado back?" Then he said to Nina: "She's out of town all week."

"All week?"

"Annual vacation."

"But—"

"Got to put you on hold for a second."

Click. Nina was cut off instead, like the depressing woman who hated Thanksgiving. A sob rose in her throat. She clamped it back down. "Stop it," she said aloud. Use your brain, your fucking business brain. Someone must be handling Detective Delgado's caseload. Nina reached for the phone. It rang just as she touched it.

"Yes?" said Nina, answering it.

"Hello." It was a woman, with a quiet voice, even hesitant; not Detective Delgado, not the head nurse: no one she knew. "Is this Nina Kitchener?"

"Yes."

"I hope I haven't called too early."

"You haven't."

Silence. Fragments of another conversation buzzed softly on the line; Nina wondered if it was a long-distance call.

The thought might have carried down the wire, because the woman said: "I'm calling from Boston. My name is Laura Bain. The NBC station here showed that interview with you."

Silence.

Nina, thinking of her encounter in the alley by the pizzeria, and the girl and the man who had traded a baby for ten thousand dollars and were still on the loose, pressed the RECORD button on her answering machine. But if the woman had some scam in mind, she seemed in no hurry to begin.

It was Nina who broke the silence. "And?" she said.

"I feel very badly for you. And I'm really sorry for bothering you at a time like this. I know what you're going through."

"Do you?" Nina replied, unable to keep the bitterness out of her tone; she felt a pang of guilt about it—even over the phone and in her condition she could sense how much stronger than the other woman she was.

"Unfortunately I do," Laura Bain said in a voice that sank away to almost nothing. "My baby was kidnapped five months ago."

"Oh God."

Silence. More conversations whispered in the wire; someone laughed in one of them. Nina sensed the answer, but she asked anyway: "Have you got him back yet?"

"Her," said Laura Bain. And: "No."

"I'm sorry."

Nina heard Laura Bain take a deep breath. "The reason I'm calling is that while I was watching you on TV I had a thought and it just won't go away. I—I've got to ask you something."

"What?"

"Did you use a sperm bank?"

"Yes. Why?"

"Was it the Cambridge Reproductive Research Center?"

"No. The Human Fertility Institute. Here in New York. Why?"

"I used a sperm bank too. The Cambridge one."

Nina waited for the woman to continue. When she didn't, Nina said, "I have no idea what you're getting at. Why did you even think of asking if I'd gone to a sperm bank? I never discussed that with the news people."

"Because you remind me of me," Laura Bain said. "I think we should meet."

| 19 |

Long ago at Camp Wapameo, reading in her bunk by flashlight while the other girls slept and the counselors sat around the fire on the beach, swatting mosquitos and trying to tune in rock 'n' roll from anywhere on a cheap transistor, Nina had come upon a story about a drunken man whose hat falls into a mysterious ring and disappears. Reaching for it, the man stumbles into the ring and falls forward in time. There he meets another man, a little older than himself, whom he finds troubling. Not long after, he steps into another ring, meets a man older and more troubling than the first. And into another ring, and so on. Eventually it hits him that all the men he encounters are himself, at later stages of life. Nina remembered the story the moment she spotted the woman she took to be Laura Bain.

The woman, standing just beyond the security station for the Pan Am shuttle gates at Logan Airport, wore a finely tailored tweed coat and was biting her lower lip. She looked about forty-five years old. Her face was thinner and paler than Nina's; her hair was almost the same shade of brown, except she had a lot of white in it, and Nina still had none. Her dark, deep-set eyes were alert, even intense, as she scanned the line of arriving passengers. They lit on Nina and recognized her immediately; for a moment Nina thought something uncanny was going on. Then she recalled that the woman had seen her on TV. But she was still thinking of the time machine story when the woman stepped forward.

"Hello, Nina," she said in the same quiet, flattened tone Nina had heard on the phone, a tone that didn't match the nervous energy in the movements of her face and body. "I'm Laura Bain." The women faced each other. They might have shaken hands, might even have embraced, but their timing was off and in the end they did nothing. "Hungry?" Laura said.

"Not really."

"Me either." A smile crossed Laura Bain's face, so quickly it barely existed, like some wondrously short-lived species on "Nova." "I'm never hungry anymore," Laura said. "And I used to be such a pig."

"But it's not a weight-loss method you'd recommend."

Laura laughed, a harsh and surprisingly loud laugh. She gave Nina's hand a little squeeze: Laura's skin felt hot, as though she were fighting a disease.

Laura unlocked her car, a Jaguar with a cellular phone inside, and drove toward the city. Nina waited for Laura to begin. Laura bit her lip and said nothing, until the phone buzzed and she picked it up. "Hello." She listened for a few moments. Then, still in the same flat voice, but without indecisiveness, she said: "It's too early. Tell him to hold on till I'm back from Accra." She hung up and entered the tunnel under Boston Harbor. Her hands gripped the wheel tightly, as if it might try to do something on its own at any moment.

"What do you do, Laura?"

"For a living? I'm a commodity investment analyst." She handed Nina a card. "Strictly cocoa, actually. But I'm thinking of taking on coffee as well. More work. Less time to think about Clea."

"Clea?"

"The—my baby. My daughter. What's your baby's name?"

Nina began to regret her trip to Boston. "He doesn't have one," she answered. Unless, she thought, the woman with the leathery skin had given him one. She'd had plenty of time by now.

"Oh," said Laura. They climbed out of the tunnel into hard, cold sunlight. Nina saw that Laura was crying. She looked away, but not before Laura noticed. "That wasn't true about the coffee," she said. "How can I take on coffee? I can barely handle the cocoa anymore."

Nina tried to think of something to say but couldn't. She didn't want to spend the afternoon locked in a Jules Feiffer dance to self-pity with this woman. As if volleying that thought back at her, Laura stuck a cassette into the player. Laura's sound system was first-rate, to Nina's ear perfectly reproducing the lifelessness of the New Age instrumental she had chosen. The music made the minutes spent in stop-and-go traffic long and gloomy.

Laura parked in front of the Beacon Hill Bistro. "Don't mind me," she said, no longer crying, her voice even brightening a little. "I have two states of mind—basketcase and robot. I'm safely back in robot now."

The waiter knew Laura. He led her and Nina to a quiet table in the back corner. "We've got a lovely fresh salmon today, served en brochette with a raspberry basil sauce and a little goat cheese salad on the side."

"That sounds nice," Laura said. But when it came she didn't touch it. She did drink all but one glass of a bottle of Bourgogne Aligoté. Nina had the rest.

"Well," said Laura, rubbing her hands together as though kindling something positive. "Down to business."

"I'm not sure what our business is, exactly," Nina said.

Laura stopped rubbing her hands. She laid them on the mauve tablecloth. The nails, polished and manicured, were bitten to the quick. "Maybe it is silly," Laura said. "Calling you. Sperm bank. Kidnapping. Ergo—what?" And maybe had the waiter not been passing at that moment she wouldn't have ordered another bottle. But he was and she did. Then she caught Nina looking at her and lost herself in thought.

"But—" she was beginning when the waiter returned. He drew the cork. "Just pour," she told him. He raised his eyebrows the way David Niven might have if he'd ever accepted a waiter role. "I'm sure it's fine," Laura told him. He poured and went away. "But," Laura said, "it's been five months of doing less and less and finally almost nothing. To get Clea back. I call Detective This or Detective That once a week, as though it were any other item on my schedule. What else can I do? I've tried everything." The robot broke down and tears came silently again. "I don't even walk the streets anymore looking for her." She dabbed her cheeks with a thick mauve napkin. "And then I saw you. And I just thought—okay, here's a chance to do something."

Nina didn't want to bring on the tears again, but she did want to understand what Laura Bain had in mind. "Like what, though?"

Laura's voice, which had risen slightly, fell again. "I don't know." She stared into her wineglass.

Nina soon found herself staring into hers too, as though performing some ritual. She made herself look up. "What made you go to a sperm bank in the first place?"

Laura raised her head, slowly, like someone emerging from a trance. "Biological clock, et cetera. And I haven't had a serious man in my life since I was twenty-eight."

"How old are you now?"

"Thirty-five." Laura saw a reaction in Nina's face and misinterpreted it. "A little older than you, I guess."

Laura paused, perhaps for Nina to give her age. But Nina, shocked that she was five years older than Laura, was thinking of the time machine, and how fast it could move when something happened like what had happened to Laura and to her. She had stepped into the ring; in the next five months was it going to line her face and whiten her hair and flatten her voice and leave her with wary eyes like Laura Bain's? Would that defeated face soon be her own? Nina pushed the thought away and tried to pursue whatever half-formed idea Laura had in mind: "It wasn't someone in a volunteer's uniform, was it?"

"What?"

"Who took your baby, I mean."

"Oh, no. My—Clea—wasn't taken from the hospital. We'd already been home for two days. It was after lunch on a Saturday. The last Saturday in June. The nanny was arriving from Ireland on Monday and I was going back full time the following week. It was a nice warm day and I took Clea out in the backyard in her carriage. I've got a house in Dedham—bought for Clea, really. I sat in a chaise longue, fooling with some figures. Clea went to sleep." Laura's eyes were drawn back to the wineglass, almost as if she were reading her story in the calm surface of the liquid. She sighed. "Then I guess I fell asleep too. I don't know why. I never need more than six hours. But I was still very tired from the birth, and Clea hadn't been

sleeping much at night. I just—fell asleep." She dabbed
with the mauve napkin again, then continued. "A barking
dog woke me up. It was late in the afternoon by then—
I'd slept for hours. I went over to the carriage, thinking
Clea had slept too—I remember feeling happy because I
was beginning to worry she might be a colicky baby or
even sick or something—and I pulled back the insect
screen and Clea was gone." She continued staring into the
glass. Nina waited for more. But there was no more. Laur-
a's head bobbed up suddenly and she said: "That's it."

"That's it?"

"Nothing's happened since. Nothing good. The police
came. They took fingerprints on the carriage. They questioned the neighbors. They questioned a woman who once
snatched a baby at the Dedham Mall. They told me to
offer a reward, which I did. They told me to hang on. I
hung on. Then I saw you on TV. And there was no mention
of a husband or father or anything, and I just thought—
sperm bank."

"And you were right. But where does that take us?"

"I don't know. Let's say we were divorced, or in the
middle of a bad separation or something and our children
disappeared like this. Where would the police go first?"

"To the father."

"Right."

"But there is no father, Laura. There's just frozen
sperm."

"I know. But it's something we have in common. And
maybe there's more."

"Even if there is, where would it lead?"

"I'm not sure. But I can't go on like this." Laura's eyes
were being drawn to her glass again.

"All right, all right," Nina said, trying to make her voice
gentle. "Let's try. But all I can see are differences. Your
baby was taken from home, mine from the hospital. The
police are pretty sure I saw the kidnapper; you saw nobody." Nina described the woman with the leathery skin
and the volunteer badge. Laura had never seen her.

"But that doesn't mean she wasn't the one," she said.
"In fact, I'm going to pass that description on to the police.
Tell me more."

Nina sensed Laura's stubbornness. Perhaps they did
have something in common, after all. She told her story,

starting with the message that there was a telephone call and ending with the Cabbage Patch Kid. As she spoke, what little light that had begun to shine in Laura's eyes faded; the woman was stubborn, but hope was almost gone. When Nina finished there was a long silence.

The waiter came to clear the table. Most of the customers had already gone. The restaurant grew quiet and a little eerie, like a theater after the play. Laura went to the bathroom. Nina checked her watch, wondering if she could catch the next shuttle. Laura returned and insisted on paying the bill. While signing the credit card slip, she said: "You didn't have a phone in your room?"

"What room?"

"At the hospital."

"It was out of order."

Laura nodded. They got back in her car and started toward the airport. New Age accompaniment played. In the pause that came while the auto-reverse reversed, Laura said: "What was your sperm donor like?"

"Why do you ask that?"

"I don't know. Clea had my features, I think, but not my coloring. She was much fairer. I hadn't requested a blond heartthrob or anything—I wanted someone healthy and reasonably intelligent, that's all. I'm just curious about him, I guess."

"Didn't they give you the information?"

"They showed me a printout. But it really didn't say much, not that I remember." She thought for a moment. "I'm not even sure I've got a copy."

"My donor's name was VT-three-H," Nina said. "Six feet tall. Blue eyes. Played soccer in college. And there was a question mark beside his ring size. That seems fitting somehow for a sperm donor."

Laura didn't smile. She was biting her lip again. "Could I ask you a big favor?" she said.

"What?"

"If you could catch a later flight."

"Why?"

"Because I'd like to go to the sperm bank in Cambridge," Laura said. "I want to have a look at that printout."

Nina didn't understand that; nor did she understand why her presence was needed. But there was no hurry to get

home and being with Laura made her feel strong for the
first time since the kidnapping; perhaps that was repre-
hensible, but it was the truth. "Okay," Nina said.

Laura drove across the river, into Cambridge, past Harvard Square and up Massachusetts Avenue. She stopped
in front of a three-story steel and glass building. They were
out of the car and walking toward the entrance when Laura
halted. She glanced around: up and down the block, across
the street. Then she stared at the steel and glass building.

"Is something wrong?" Nina asked.

"It's gone," Laura said.

"What's gone?"

"The sperm bank."

Nina looked at the sign on the building: TWENTY-FIRST
CENTURY VIDEO AND SOUND, INC. "Are you sure we're in
the right place?"

Laura nodded. They went inside. A young man wearing
a black leather tie came forward. "How can I help you
ladies?"

"Where has the Reproductive Research Institute gone?"
Laura asked.

The young man's smooth brow wrinkled. "Is that part
of MIT?"

"No. It was right here in this building. Last year."

"Gee," said the young man. "I just started in September."

He lent Laura the store's phone book. It had no number
for the Cambridge Reproductive Research Center. Neither
did the operator. Laura called her obstetrician and reached
the answering service. She left a message and hung up.
"That's funny," she said.

"The rent probably went up," Nina said.

"But where did they go?" Laura asked.

"Frankly, I don't even know what the rent is," the young
man told them. "The owner'll be back at five. In the meantime, would you ladies like to check out the new sixty-
four-inch screen?"

Laura drove Nina to the airport. "Thank you for coming," she said. "It's meant a lot to me. I'll call you when
I hear from my obstetrician. If you don't mind."

"Of course not," Nina said.

Laura walked her all the way to the security gate. She
stood there with her hollow eyes as the time machine sped

her further and further from her baby. That's what Nina was thinking as she stepped forward and embraced her, once more feeling how hot she was. Then she walked quickly through the gate and down the concourse.

"Nina!" Laura called after her.

Nina stopped and turned. "What?"

"Did they want to know your SAT scores?"

"Yes. What makes you ask that?"

"I don't know. What were they?"

"My SATs?"

"Yeah."

Nina remembered looking them up. "Fourteen-twenty, I think."

Now she saw Laura's smile for the second time. It lasted longer than before: Laura had a beautiful smile. "I beat you," she said.

| 20 |

Not long after midnight, Nina entered her apartment. She checked the message machine:

"Suze here," said Suze. "I've got a new number—it's in Palos Verdes. It's—shit, it must be in my other bag. Any news? I'll call back."

"Delgado." The line buzzed with static. The voice sounded far away. "You've been trying to reach me? There's nothing to report. We'll contact you when there is." Buzz. Click.

"Hello? Nina? It's Laura. Laura Bain. I guess you're not home yet. I had a thought after you left. I—I'll try to get back to you tomorrow."

On the kitchen counter, Nina found a basket of fruit and a sinkful of red roses. She read the note, on Kitchener and Best stationery, in the basket: "Happy Birthday from everyone here." The handwriting was Jason's but smaller than usual, subdued. No Roederer Cristal this year. Nina counted the roses: forty. The day had passed without her once thinking of it. She was a mature woman now. A mother. In some cultures she would already be a grandmother.

Merry fucking Christmas.

She remembered the bum, the wino, the homeless man, whatever he was, whose eyes had sought her out, twice: the misshapen troll in the fairy stories with a warning just for her. He might have frozen to death during the winter, but he had left an enduring memorial in her mind, if no-where else. What was his message? *This is the punishment for the woman who goes her own way*?

"Fuck that." This wasn't about punishment, or about judgment: it was about crime, and she was the victim. Nina went to the liquor cabinet, filled a glass with Scotch and was about to take her first sip when she thought of Laura.

She went to the phone, imagining Laura as she picked it up: what thoughts would fly through her mind at the moment she awoke to the ringing phone? What wild hope might start to soar? It wasn't fair, but Nina wanted to know what idea had come to Laura's mind. Crime was a violent force, but it left behind inertia, a defense mechanism to prevent its solution; Nina had heard that inertia in Detective Delgado's voice, had seen it in the ponderous gait of so many cops on the beat. A counterforce was required. It would have to come from her.

Nina took out Laura's card and found it gave only her business number. She tried Dedham information. Laura's home number was unlisted.

Nina drank the glass of Scotch and went to bed. She rose a few hours later and got on the stationary bike. She was full of counterforce but had no idea what to do with it. She pedaled. She pedaled for half an hour, an hour, an hour and a half, more. She didn't play games with wall maps. She just wore her body out. Then, dripping sweat, she lay on her bed and fell asleep.

In the morning, Nina awoke with a headache and a sore throat. She took two Tylenol and went into the nursery. She tried not to see the new books on the shelf, wrapped in their brightly colored and still pristine jackets—*Madeline*, *In the Night Kitchen*, *Goodnight Moon*, *Dr. DeSoto*, *Go Dog Go*—or the stuffed animals or the economy-sized box of Pampers or the Handiwipes or the Q-Tips or the crib with its painted apple trees. She went to the file cabinets, now jammed into one corner, and began searching for the printout with all the details about her sperm donor. She couldn't find it, couldn't remember if she'd even had a copy.

Nina went into the kitchen, started the coffee and dialed the Human Fertility Institute.

"HFI." It was Nurse Sal.

"Hello," Nina said, but the word remained unuttered. She tried again, forming "hello" and using lungs, throat, tongue, lips to turn it into sound. Nothing resulted but the faintest whisper. For the first time in her life, she had laryngitis.

"Hello? Hello?" said the woman at the institute. Click.

Nina wanted to scream. She couldn't. All she could do was pick up the unwashed glass that had held last night's whiskey—a pretty Waterford glass, Lismore pattern, part of a set Richard II had given her during the period when he liked to talk of marriage, especially on Friday nights, before their first fuck of the week—and fling it against the wall. It spoke beautifully for her. She should have done it long ago. There would be no trousseau for her, pseudo or quasi, and it didn't matter and never had. What mattered was the baby. She had to move and keep moving until she had him back. The laryngitis was part of the inertia. She had to fight it. Nina tried and failed to utter a sound.

Nina showered and brushed her hair. In the mirror she saw her first white strand. Forty: right on schedule. She plucked out the hair with much more force than necessary and took satisfaction in the accompanying twinge: as if she had struck a blow against time.

Nina dressed in business clothes, grabbed a notebook and a pen and went outside. She wrote the address of the Human Fertility Institute in the notebook, ready to show to the first cabbie who came along. But the only cabbies who came along were off duty, so Nina started walking.

The wind was blowing an invisible storm of grit through the city, it might have been a test devised to identify all the contact lens wearers on the streets. They blinked and teared as they went by. But Nina was scarcely aware of them, or of the cold, or of much else. She moved forward through a tunnel, on legs made sore by last night's Tour de Nowhere. She began to feel hot, and was sweating by the time she reached the institute.

Nina pushed open the leather-padded door and stepped into the lobby. The Persian rug was rolled up again, but the Christmas tree hadn't come yet. The portrait of the weak-chinned man had been taken down; it leaned against the wall, putting Nina eye to eye with him. At that level,

Nina could see the mediocrity of the artist: the weak-chinned man's eyes were simply smears of blue, expressing and revealing nothing.

No one was around. Nina walked up the marble staircase and along the hall to the door that said: RUSSELL R. CROSSMAN, M.D., DIRECTOR. As she knocked, she smelled Nurse Sal's perfume.

"Come in."

Nina went in. Nurse Sal sat at her desk, wearing jeans and a sweatshirt and packing some papers in a cardboard box. She looked at Nina with no sign of recognition. "Can I help you?"

Nina tried to say yes, couldn't, and nodded instead. She approached the desk, wrote *laryngitis* in the notebook and showed it to the nurse.

Nurse Sal said nothing. She motioned for the notebook and with her own pen wrote: *You've come to the wrong place.* She was about to hand back the notebook when she noticed Nina waving her hands and shaking her head, like a frustrated charades player. Nurse Sal took up her pen and added a few words. With a smile she returned the notebook to Nina.

Nina read: *We don't do ear nose and throat.* Nurse Sal had added a little smile face. Nina glared at her, pulled a chair up to the desk and wrote: *It's not about laryngitis. I want to see Crossman.* She turned the notebook so Nurse Sal could read it.

Nurse Sal circled her first sentence, *It's not about laryngitis*, drew an arrow to it and wrote at the end of the shaft: *Then why are you here?*

Nina pounded her fist on the desk; a china figurine of Goofy bounced off its surface and smashed on the floor. Nurse Sal's eyes were still widening when the inner door opened and Dr. Crossman poked his head in. "Everything all right?" he asked, looking first at the remains of Goofy, then at Nina, without recognition, last at Nurse Sal, with his reddish eyebrows raised.

"She's got laryngitis," Nurse Sal said.

"That's too bad," Dr. Crossman said. "Friend of yours? There's really not much I can do for her. Rest, aspirin—hold on." He popped back out of sight, returning in a moment with a metal tin of honey pastilles. Taking one between his freckled fingers, rather than holding out the open box, he offered it to Nina, saying, "Here. This won't do anything for the laryngitis, but it'll soothe your throat a little."

Nina waved it away, aware of, but not examining a thought that flashed through her brain: I've received sperm from this man, I don't want to take communion from him too. She took the notebook, wrote: *Don't you know me? Nina Kitchener. I was impregnated here last Feb.*

They all gathered around the notebook. Dr. Crossman fingered his red mustache. Nurse Sal watched him doing it. "Can't say I remember you," he said. "Do you, Sal?"

"When was this?"

Nina pointed out the words *last Feb*.

Like when exactly, wrote Nurse Sal on the next line.

Nina wrote: *Don't write. Talk. Feb. 8.*

Nurse Sal blushed. She had the kind of skim milk skin that blushes easily. Dr. Crossman said: "Okay. I'll take your word for it. But what can we do for you now?"

Nina wrote: *My baby was stolen from the hospital.*

"Oh, dear," said Nurse Sal.

"Stolen from the hospital?" said Dr. Crossman. "You mean kidnapped?" Nina nodded. "That's awful."

"Have you got the baby back yet?" asked Nurse Sal.

Nina shook her head. She felt hot, and a little faint.

"Oh my," said Nurse Sal. "Oh my."

"Are the police working on it?" asked Dr. Crossman. Nina nodded again. "This kind of thing happens sometimes. It's usually some kind of crazy woman. I'm sure the police have told you that they almost always get the baby back in these situations."

Nina nodded once more.

"She doesn't look too well," said Nurse Sal.

"You're right," said Dr. Crossman. He placed his cold, damp hand on Nina's forehead. "Goodness," he said. "She's burning up. Get some aspirin, Sal."

No, Nina tried to shout. She made a very weak sound.

"What was that?" asked Dr. Crossman.

"I don't think she wants aspirin," Sal told him.

"But it'll bring down that temp."

Nina banged her hand, open this time, on the desk. Nurse Sal and Dr. Crossman jumped. Nina turned the page in the notebook and wrote: *I want the sperm donor printout.*

"The donor printout?" asked Dr. Crossman. "All the data on donor background and genetics?" Nina nodded. "But you should have that. We always give it out."

Nina wrote: *I DON'T!*

"Okay, okay," said Dr. Crossman. "We can get you a printout."

Good, Nina wrote.

"But why do you want it at this particular . . . time?" asked Dr. Crossman.

Nina wrote: *Hard to explain. BUT I WANT IT.*

"Fine, fine," said Dr. Crossman. "And you shall have it."

Nina looked at Nurse Sal. Nurse Sal didn't seem to be going anywhere. Neither did Dr. Crossman. She wrote: *Will it take long?*

"Will what take long?" asked Dr. Crossman.

Getting the printout.

"Oh, you can't have it just now," said Dr. Crossman. "The computer's down and everything's . . ."

"Topsy-turvy," said Nurse Sal.

"Right. Topsy-turvy. But we'll get it out to you as soon as possible." He smiled encouragingly. So did Nurse Sal.

Nina wrote: *Don't you want my address?*

"It'll be in your file," replied Dr. Crossman. "On the disk. When the computer comes back up."

"Unless she's moved," said Sal.

"Right. Have you moved?"

Nina shook her head.

"Then not to worry," said Dr. Crossman. "We'll have it out to you this week. Make a note, Sal." Sal made a note. "Now you better get home and take care of yourself," Dr. Crossman said. "Have you got any sleeping pills?"

Nina shook her head again.

"Sal, would you get her a bottle of Seconal please? In the supply cabinet."

Sal went through the inner door. Nina held up her finger.

"Something else?" asked Dr. Crossman.

Nina nodded. She wrote: *Are you affiliated with the Cambridge Reproductive Research Center?*

Dr. Crossman bent over the desk and examined the question. "Never heard of them," he said. "We're an independent institution. Why do you ask?"

A woman who used them had her baby stolen too.

Dr. Crossman bent over again and peered at the sentence. He looked up at Nina, rubbed his mustache, looked away. "I don't know what to tell you. Where is this place?"

Cambridge, Mass.

He shrugged. Nurse Sal returned and handed him a bottle of pills. Dr. Crossman passed them on to Nina. "Go home, take two aspirin and one of these. After that, one before every bedtime. You're exhausted and feverish. Drink a lot of liquids. You don't want to catch pneumonia. And let the police handle this. That's what we pay them for." He put his hand on her shoulder. "Good luck," he said.

"Yes, good luck," said Nurse Sal. "I'm sure everything's going to be fine. Hang in there."

Clutching her notebook and sleeping pills, Nina went home. She poured a glass of water, swallowed two aspirin and one sleeping pill. She drank another glass of water. Then she went into the nursery and sat on the floor. She gazed at the crib. There was a puffy comforter inside, with a pattern of impossibly fat and friendly cumulus clouds. Nina remained like that for a long time. Then she lay down. Her eyes closed. She spent a while in a place with a lot of shouting and running about. Then she dropped down into a region of silence and stillness.

Nina awoke on the nursery floor, her arm draped over the polar bear. Daylight filled the room, but it was daylight of the next day; 10:35 A.M. precisely, the radio told her. Her fever was gone, the ache in her legs was gone, she could speak. She checked the machine. No messages.

Nina found Laura Bain's business card and dialed the number.

"Hello?" answered a woman, neither announcing the firm name nor sounding very businesslike. In fact, she sounded as if she was crying.

"Laura Bain please," said Nina.

"Lau— I—who is this, please?"

"My name's Nina Kitchener. I'm a friend of Laura's from New York."

"Oh God. I don't know what to tell you."

"What do you mean?"

"Oh God. I—"

"What is it?"

"Laura's dead."

"Laura's dead?"

"Last night. She—they, I mean the police, they say she . . ."

"What?"

"Oh God. Committed suicide."

Brock McGillivray had made a spear gun that only he could load. The rubber band was one inch thick, so you had to be strong, but first you had to be able to reach it, and the shaft was five feet long. A few divers had been able to get the clip within two inches of the notch on the spear; Matthias had come a little closer. But Brock did it every time he went spearing, and he did it with no sign of strain.

They floated in rough water on the far side of the Angel Fingers: Matthias, Danny, Brock. The Angel Fingers were a few small reefs of elkhorn coral rising from a sandy bottom thirty-five to forty feet down to within a foot or two of the surface, at low tide. They were marked on most charts, but every four or five months some yachtsman struck them, leaving fresh white scars in the coral and chunks of rocky antlers on the bottom. After that they came into the bar at Zombie Bay, got drunk and tried to figure out who could be sued. The next morning they returned and asked for help.

Matthias felt the heavy swell bobbing him up and down. A cold onshore wind herded the waves quickly by; in their rush, some toppled on themselves. Matthias kept himself steady with movements so practiced he didn't notice them; whitecaps broke all around him, but no water entered his snorkel. Without being obvious, he kept Danny between himself and Brock at all times. The boy struggled with the waves more than once, kicking hard and fast and using his arms to keep from being thrown against the reef; sometimes he sucked water into his snorkel and choked, but always it came blowing out immediately; he kept his face down and he didn't panic. That was what Matthias had wanted to see.

It was the last day of Danny's visit. On the first Matthias had placed a depth gauge on the bottom not far from the dock. It had read 42 feet. Danny had brought it up on his third try. Since then he had spent most of his time in the water, with Matthias, or Brock, or Moxie and his son Rafer, whom Matthias had flown in from Nassau. In the late afternoons, Danny and Rafer walked along the beach, wading in the tidal pools on the rocks under the Bluff, picking up shells, not appearing to say much. That didn't surprise Matthias: one boy knew about fax machines, the other had already dropped out of school.

Now Brock sliced through the surface and kicked down to the bottom: eight or nine strokes of his jetfins and a gentle glide onto the sand. He was looking at something under a coral outcrop. Danny followed him, his dive not nearly as smooth, his kicks not nearly as powerful, but he went down in a straight line and his hands remained still at his sides. Brock pointed, then pulled himself further into the reef, so that only his legs showed. Danny tried to see what it was, but couldn't stay down any longer and swam to the surface. Brock followed half a minute later, raising his index finger. He wanted to talk.

They held their heads above the waves, pulled out their mouthpieces. "Bloody great rockfish in there, Matt. Twenty, twenty-five pounds. Should we give the lad a crack at it?"

Matthias looked at Danny. He couldn't tell whether the boy wanted to or not. "With what?" he asked.

"I've got my gun in the boat," Brock said. "I'll cock it and take it down for him. It'll be all right."

"Oh, I don't think—" Matthias began, but he stopped himself. "What about it, Danny? It's up to you."

"Okay," Danny said. But his lips were blue and he was shivering.

"You don't have to, you know."

"Come on," said Brock. "He'll have a good time."

"I want to," said Danny.

Brock swam over to the boat for the gun. Matthias drifted closer to Danny. "Cold?"

"No."

He tried to think of ways to talk Danny out of it, but gave up. Instead he said: "The thing about a rockfish is it can expand its gills to make itself bigger than the hole."

A wave slapped Danny's face. He kicked hard, raising himself a little; one of his fins caught Matthias in the knee. The boy was tired. Deep inside, like most people, he feared the sea, and didn't know how to simply let it take him, while using its force at the same time. "Maybe we should come back tomorrow," Matthias said. "He'll still be there."

"I'll be gone tomorrow." Danny's teeth chattered.

"That's true," Matthias said. A wave raised him high above Danny, then moved on and raised Danny above him.

"So what about the rockfish?" Danny asked.

"It makes itself bigger than its hole if threatened or wounded. So——"

"You have to kill it on the first shot?"

Matthias smiled. "Right."

Brock swam back with his gun. "All set?" he said. Danny nodded. Then, with one hand, Brock reached for the clip on the thick rubber band and pulled it back, stretching the band until he could get both hands on it; after that, he stuck the butt of the gun against his stomach and in one motion drew the band all the way back, clicking the clip into place. A moment later he was halfway to the bottom. Danny made a hurried duck dive and followed, thrashing a little and thus using too much oxygen right from the start.

Matthias hung on the surface, torn between the desire to be with Danny and the fear that his presence might somehow spoil everything. He saw Brock lying on the bottom, kicking forward into the hole, and Danny hovering a few feet above the man's fins. Danny still had baby fat on his body, making him slightly buoyant even at that depth, forced to keep kicking to stay down. Brock backed out of the hole, motioned for Danny and laid the gun on the sand. Danny descended with a few jerky kicks, stirring up the bottom, and grasped the gun. Brock reached out and switched off the safety. Matthias started down.

Through the clouds of sand that Danny was raising, he saw the rockfish with its big protruding eyes, thick lips and massive head; a dumb, conservative creature relying on the safety of home. Danny's eyes, behind his half-fogged lens, seemed to be protruding too. He pointed the gun, briefly and unsteadily, and from much too far away squeezed the trigger.

Green liquid billowed out of the hole. Blood was green at forty feet. Matthias shot forward, grabbed the line and yanked the fish out of the hole before it could expand its gills. The spear had angled into its side, about halfway back, nowhere near a kill shot, but deep enough to hold. The rockfish struggled, convulsing on the steel spear, spewing green. Danny dropped the gun and scissored frantically toward the surface. Brock took the gun; Matthias let go of the line and followed Danny up.

Danny reached the boat ahead of him. When Matthias climbed in he saw that Danny was vomiting, partly over the side, partly on the rail. "You all right?" Matthias asked.

Danny nodded. But he vomited more when Brock came up and slapped the fish, still impaled and wriggling, on the deck. "Hell of a shot, Danny," Brock said, clapping the boy hard on the back. Then he jammed the spear all the way through the fish's body, unscrewed the tip with its barb and pulled the shaft, now free, back through. The fish, not moving anymore, still had blood to give. Now it was the right color. Danny turned away. "Twenty-five pounds if it's an ounce," Brock said. "Right, Matt?"

Twenty, tops, Matthias thought, but he said: "Right."

"Hell of a shot," Brock repeated, picking up the fish by sticking his thumb in one of its eyes and his first two fingers in the other and tossing it into the stern. Danny vomited again. Brock noticed and said, "Getting a bit rough. Want me to pull the anchor?"

"Yeah," Matthias said. But Danny wasn't seasick. It was, Matthias realized, the first time he had killed anything that couldn't be killed by stepping on it. Danny had crossed a line, into a country where he and Brock and men like them had been for a long time, and the journey had made him travel-sick. Yes, Matthias knew, he ate fish, so what difference did it make who killed them, and spearfishing on a lungful of air was more sporting than et cetera et

cetera, and picking up a fish of that size the way Brock
had done was the easiest way, but for the moment he had
seen it all through Danny's eyes, and he understood how
coarse he was compared to the boy, and what time and
the life he led had done to him.

"We'll feast tonight," Brock called from the bow as he
raised the anchor, the muscles swelling in his back. Matthias fired the engines. Danny sat, shivering and pale, on
the deck. Matthias couldn't think of anything to say to
him. He swung the boat around and headed back into
Zombie Bay.

Two hours later Matthias drove Danny to the little air-
strip. They walked across the packed dirt, Matthias carrying Danny's bag. At the foot of the stairs leading to the
plane, Danny stopped and turned to him. "Mom says
you're a dinosaur."

"Yeah?"

"And now I know what she means."

"Yeah?"

"Yeah. But I like dinosaurs." Danny smiled. He held
out his hand. Matthias shook it.

"See you."

"So long."

Danny took his bag and climbed the stairs. Matthias
drove back to Zombie Bay. A handshake was better than
nothing. Maybe it was the best he and Danny could do.
Blown in de win.

"Do I have bad breath?" asked Hew Aikenfield, baronet.

"I don't know," Matthias answered.

"That's because you've never been close enough to find
out," said Sir Hew. "A pity, my boy, a great pity. But
that's by the way. The point is, if I have bad breath it's
not my fault. I never got into the habit of brushing my
own teeth, you see."

"Someone else brushed them?"

"Exactly," said Sir Hew. "My, you are quick. It was
Lizzie, to be precise."

"Lizzie?"

"A servant girl. She had lovely teeth herself, white as
snow. Of course, teeth always show best in a black face.
In Hong Kong I once came upon a toothpaste called Dar-
kie, with a Stepin Fetchit character on the wrapper. Hor-

rible racialists, the Orientals. Almost as disgusting as we are, in that respect. Very clean though." Hew fell silent.

They sat on the terrace of Hew's house, watching the moon climb the dome of the sky and listening to scratchy Edith Piaf records. The moon was full and shone brightly on Hew's long white hair, his delicate pale skin, his washed-out eyes. Hew's house, at the top of the Bluff, had the best view on the island; it also had a name, Les Rochers; stacks of old copies of *Punch*, shelves of old Penguins—P. G. Wodehouse, Agatha Christie, Evelyn Waugh; an original portrait of a Polynesian youth reclining beneath a palm tree, signed "Gauguin"; and cases of Armagnac in wax-topped bottles that had nothing written on them except "1909."

"Care for another?" asked Hew. He was a white Bahamian, but he didn't sound like one. He had been schooled at Harrow and Cambridge, and in accent and tone his voice closely resembled the Queen of England's.

"Sure," said Matthias. "If you're having one."

"I'm always having one, dear boy," said Hew, pouring more Armagnac. Matthias had never tasted anything like Hew's Armagnac. It slid so lightly over the tongue that it seemed scarcely liquid at all, but pure aroma.

Hew cocked his ear toward the marble-floored living room, where Piaf's voice came from. "Ah," he said, briefly closing his eyes. Matthias listened to the old recording and wasn't moved. Hew's eyes opened. "Can you make out the words?" he asked.

"I don't know French."

"Really?" said Hew. He sipped from his glass. "She's singing about a couple who meet just for one afternoon in a dingy hotel." He listened again. "My God. Paris was just like that. My Paris, that is. Between the wars. Of course, it was a Paris that never was. All in the mind, you see. But the things I did! Indescribable. Not that they had the same meaning for the other participants. It wasn't in their minds, that Paris. Erections all the time. Continuously. Nonstop. Without end. Almighty God, it was lovely. Now, I needn't add, erections are few and far between." Hew smiled a wicked smile, made wickeder perhaps by the state of his teeth. "But I don't waste a single one." He laughed, a cackling laugh much like Wilfred Brambell's in *A Hard Day's Night*. "I'm referring to *le plaisir tout solitaire*, naturally. The boys don't come up here the way they used to."

"You're lucky no one's father ever arrived with a machete."

"You surprise me," said Hew. "It's not that way at all. Bahamians"—he grinned—"we Bahamians don't make such a to-do about sex. It's like trying to stop the tide. Can't be done."

A meteor shot across the sky, leaving an orange trail. Five or six more soon followed, like a posse. Edith Piaf sang about the Paris that never was. Matthias, because of his Spanish, found he could understand some of it. He couldn't help liking the song about regretting nothing. Hew refilled their glasses. "Hungry?" he asked.

"No."

"That's fortunate," said Hew. "I've got biscuits, those Ritz things, but nothing more I'm afraid. Won't have till the middle of the month, when the next bank draft comes."

"Can I help?"

"Thank you, no, dear boy," said Hew. "From what I hear, you're scarcely in a position to do that. Besides, I'm used to the life of an impecunious *rentier*. I've been living it long enough." He took a deep drink. "One day I was rich. The next I had nothing, nothing but this house and a monthly check from Barclay's. In sterling. Which wasn't much then and is less now. Don't ask me to explain how it happened. Something to do with an investment scheme and the MacMillan government. Tedious in the extreme. But I can't complain. Never worked a day in my life, y'know. Well, that's not quite true. I was an artist's model on the Riviera in the summer of '33. But that was just for fun." Hew cackled again.

"When did you move back here?"

"From Paris, d'you mean?"

"Yes."

"In '39, of course. At that time I had the Lyford Cay house too. But '39 was the end of Paris. Couldn't stomach the Nazis. Unlike some of the others."

"What others?"

"The little band of provincials that ran these islands in those days. The Bay Street Boys. This was a very backward place. Still is, but in the modern way now. That's why Churchill sent the Duke and Duchess of Windsor here for

the war. Whatever foolishness they uttered would go un-
noted. And he must have relished marooning two such
egotists in what passed for Nassau society back then."

"Did you know Hiram Standish, Junior?"

"Ah," said Hew, his eyes narrowing in a way that suddenly made Matthias aware that he could be capable of
nastiness. Hew settled back in his chair and crossed his
legs. Matthias was reminded of Bette Davis in a movie the
title of which he couldn't remember. "You haven't come
merely for my amusing conversation. Or even my father's
Armagnac—a cruel bastard, but at least he died young.
You've come for a purpose."

"That's right. But it doesn't negate the other."

Hew refilled his own glass, but offered none to Matthias.
He took a sip. "I never went for boys like you. D'you
know why?"

"I'm forty-four years old, for starters," Matthias said.
"And I'm not gay."

Hew snorted. A little glob of snot appeared on his upper
lip and stayed there. "You'd be surprised how many times
I've heard that," he said. "From lads I had between the
sheets two hours later. No, the reason is I don't like the
big strong type. I find it . . . alien."

"Wipe your lip, Hew," Matthias said.

Hew wiped his lip. "My God, how long has that been
there?" He went into the house. He came back with a
clean lip, a fresh shirt and a tray of Ritz crackers, which
he set on the table between their chairs. Hew didn't touch
the crackers. Neither did Matthias, when he saw the ants
crawling in them.

Hew filled Matthias's glass. "You certainly can drink,
though," he said. "I like that in a man."

"How old are you, Hew?"

"That's no concern of yours," Hew snapped. He took
another sip, started to put his snifter down, then drained
it in one swallow. "You want to know about Hiram Standish, Junior, is that correct?"

"Yes."

"The plaintiff."

"That's right."

"Comatose."

"Yes."

"In that event, who is actually the moving force behind the suit?"

"Lawyers."

"How true. But who is paying them?"

"His family, I suppose. But me, in the end."

"Inge," said Hew.

"Inge?"

"Hiram's wife."

"I didn't know he was married."

"I refer to Hiram Senior," Hew said. "A fellow pupil at one time. And we played together on Cable Beach as children. A brilliant sort, I suppose one might say. Although his career was cut short."

"Why?"

"Drowned, the poor man."

Matthias put down his glass. "Are you talking about the father or the son?"

Hew's eyebrows, plucked in neat arches, rose. "You are quick," he said. "A big man, and so bright. Goes against the grain of my experience. But in this case, I am speaking of the father. He drowned. Completely, I mean."

"Where?"

"In the blue hole."

"Which blue hole?"

"Why yours, of course. The one in the woods behind the shuffleboard court."

| 22 |

"They called him Happy," Sir Hew said. "Never Hiram—a dreadful name—and certainly not Junior or any such vulgarity."

"Did you know him?" Matthias asked.

"The boy?" Hew shrugged. "I saw him from time to time. The Standishes' house wasn't far from mine. I'm referring to the Nassau house. Lyford Cay. But the Standishes weren't really my type at all. I associated as seldom as possible with their set."

"What set?"

"You haven't had one too many, have you my boy?" asked Hew. "I'm talking about the Bay Street crew. My father was one of them, of course. My God. They ran Nassau like a private plantation. A rather inefficient one, I should add. And great bores, one and all."

"You said that Hiram Senior was brilliant."

"Did I?" Hew poured the last of the bottle into their snifters, then tossed it over the terrace. After what seemed like ten or fifteen seconds, they heard a faint crash. "Low tide," said Hew. "High tide—splash; low tide—smash." He sipped his Armagnac. "Hiram Standish. A very conventional sort, in taste, attitude, conversation, perceptions. His brilliance, perhaps that's too strong a word, expressed itself in a narrow field."

"What field was that?"

"Science. Biology, I believe, to be specific. He studied

in Europe before the war and worked with various brainy fellows over there."

"I thought the Bay Street Boys were all merchants and shippers, that kind of thing."

"Oh, his father was. And his father before that. The Standishes were rich, much richer than we ever were, even at the peak of my father's plundering. They owned half of New Providence at one time, I mean that quite literally. And that included the entire north side of Bay Street, from the British Colonial to Rawson Square. They also had big investments in Miami and other places. Plus this and that. I've forgotten the details, if I ever knew them. The getting of money bores me. Only the spending is remotely amusing, and the Standish habits in that regard were hopelessly dull. They never did anything interesting with their money."

"What about sending Hiram to Europe for his education?"

"Is that considered interesting?" asked Hew. "I was educated—if that's the word—in Europe myself. So was most everyone."

"Not me."

"I meant then. Now is different. Goes without saying. There is no education any longer, and no one knows anything."

"Why don't you sell the Gauguin?" Matthias asked, not knowing why: the question seemed to pop out on its own.

Hew's eyes misted over. "I'd rather die," he said. He got up and went into the house, returning with another bottle. He tapped the wax seal lightly against the balustrade, chipping it away, and drew the cork. "Well, maybe not *die*," he said, filling the glasses. "But I'd be upset for a day or two, and who wants that? 'Not I, said the pig.' " Hew slipped a little as he sat down, sitting heavily on his chaise longue. Amber liquid slopped over the rim of his snifter and stained the crotch of his pleated white trousers. "Damnation," said Hew. He rose and went back into the house. Matthias remained on the terrace, drinking Armagnac, listening to Edith Piaf and her lachrymose string section, and watching the moon, which had risen as high as it was going to, start sliding back down to the horizon.

Hew came back on the terrace, wearing a fresh pair of pleated white trousers, but now barefoot. He sat down, swinging his legs carefully onto the chaise like a woman in a tight skirt. His toes were long and gnarled and the nails needed cutting. Picking up his glass, he said: "Where was I?"

"Hiram Standish, Senior, in Europe."

"Right you are. Hiram studied in Europe. Medicine, and so on."

"Where in Europe?"

"Heidelberg, I believe. Berlin, perhaps. Not my kind of city at all, Berlin. One knew Isherwood in those days. Before the war, that is. I read his book. Rather over-flavored the pot, I thought. Still, that's the right of the artist. The duty, I daresay." Hew swished his drink around until he had a whirlpool going in his snifter. Staring into the vortex, he said: "Hiram came back before the war. Well before, if I remember. I was still in Paris. When I got back he had already established his practice in Nassau."

"What kind of practice?"

Hew looked up. The turbulence in his glass subsided. "Obstetrics? Does that sound right? He had a clinic on Shirley Street, and a little laboratory behind the Princess Margaret, if I'm not mistaken. For his research. Although he closed all that up after the war."

"Closed what up?"

"His practice. I have the sense you're not paying attention. Perhaps it's all that diving. Holding your breath, and what not. It can't be good for the brain cells."

"You're right about that," Matthias said. "Better take it one step at a time."

"Take what one step at a time?"

"Hiram Standish's story."

"Hiram. But I thought it was Happy you were interested in."

"Both."

"Both." Hew glanced up at the moon. Its white light illuminated his fine bones, slightly hooked nose, Cupid's bow mouth. "A beautiful night, I suppose. That's the trick of night. By day it's so obvious that the world is one vast slum." Hew's eyes closed. Edith Piaf sang on: Hew must have pushed the RESET button. After a song about a hood on a motorcycle and a mournful one about village bells, Matthias finished his drink and rose to leave. Without opening his eyes, Hew said: "The boy was afraid of the water, you know."

"What boy?"

"Happy Standish." Hew's eyes opened. "Where are you going?"

"It's late."

"But don't you want to hear the story?"

"You're tired."

"Rubbish. Here. Have some more. It's not bad brandy, although I've tasted better."

"You have?"

"Once. In the dressing room of Mistinguett, if memory serves. Cognac, it was. A *fine champagne*, must have dated from the middle of the last century, or even before. It was like drinking the sweetest breeze that ever blew."

Matthias sat down. "How do you know Happy was afraid of the water?"

"I saw his nanny with him at the beach once. Trying to get him to swim. He was quite wretched. This must have been after his father drowned, now that I think of it. So it's hardly surprising."

"What beach are you talking about?"

"Their beach."

"At Lyford Cay?"

"No, no. I already told you. Hiram closed up his practice. Gracious. It was only a few minutes ago. They sold the Lyford Cay place and moved here."

"Here?"

"There," said Hew, gesturing to the darkness.

"Two-Head Cay?"

"Precisely. You really don't hold up your end of the conversation very well, do you? Never mind. I've had a lifetime of that."

"So you saw Happy on the beach at Two-Head Cay?"

"Isn't that just what I said? A lovely beach, as beaches go. But I'm sure you've seen it."

"I've never been on the island."

"No? Well, it's unoccupied now. Except for old Albury and his wife." Hew paused, his eyes hooding in anticipation of another stupid question.

"The caretaker?"

Hew sighed, a sigh that would have carried to the back row of any theater Mistinguett ever played. "Just so," he said. "The house was quite magnificent, actually. She had it redone entirely by some Italian. All boarded up now, I expect."

"Are you talking about Mrs. Albury?"

"Mrs. Albury? She was a servant. The boy's nanny, now that I think of it. I meant Inge. Didn't I just get through telling you about Inge? Hiram went to Europe. He brought back Inge. Man and wife. Till death do them part. Do you know why you have such trouble following a simple narrative? Television."

"I don't have a television."

"It doesn't matter. Television beams are in the air." Hew waved at the night sky. "They've contaminated your brain."

"Bullshit."

Hew winced. "I detest that expression." He knocked back his glass. "Do you know what you need?"

"What?"

"Visual aids. I have some, in fact." He went into the house and stayed there for a long time. When he came back he brought a large leather-bound volume and a flashlight. "My filing system isn't what it could be, I'm afraid. This is all I could find. But there should be something here."

Hew laid the book on the table and opened it to the first page. It was a plain sheet of thick black paper with a photograph pasted on. Hew shone the flashlight on it. In the photograph two young men, one fair, one dark, both dressed in dinner jackets, sat at a banquette, raising champagne flutes to the camera. It took a while for Matthias to realize that the fair-haired man was Hew.

"Hew. You keep scrapbooks."

Hew's eyes hooded again. "You're a snob, Matthias, d'you know that?"

"It's the basis of our friendship."

Hew laughed, a little trill that sounded quite joyful. Then the photograph won his attention, and he leaned forward to study it. "That must have been Ledoyen," he said. "Overrated, even then."

He was starting to turn the page when Matthias asked: "Who's the other guy?"

Hew looked shocked. "Why, Nijinsky, of course."

Matthias examined the picture more closely. He noticed that Hew was looking right into the lens, while Nijinsky's gaze seemed to be focused on something off-camera.

"Quite insufferable, actually," Hew said, moving on through the book.

Matthias saw photographs of fair-haired Hew in a bathing suit, brandishing a lobster at two other men also in bathing suits, who shrank back laughing; in Venice, with his arm around a gondolier; sitting beside a picnic basket, with his eyes on a man in a beret; holding hands in a garden with a man who wore an Ascot. Hew began turning the pages faster: the fair-haired man flashed by like an animated cartoon character in a film that was doubly gay. Hew always had a nice smile for the camera; his teeth had been much better in those days.

"Here we go," said Hew, stopping at the end of the scrapbook. "Nassau society news of the day." Yellowed newspaper clippings covered every inch of the final two black pages: stories and pictures of engagements, weddings, charity balls, parties and important visitors to the islands, long ago. Hew aimed the flashlight beam at a clipping on the bottom of the last page. Taken from the *Nassau Tribune*, 27 March, 1934, it showed an imperfectly focused photograph of three men standing over a microscope. The man on the left was young, with a high forehead, intelligent face and slightly weak chin. The man in the middle was perhaps ten years older. He was tall, with an aristocratic face, and dominated the picture. The man on the right looked about the same age and was almost as tall, but much heavier, with a jowly face and a barrel chest. The caption read: "Dr. Hiram Standish of Lyford Cay (left) at the University of Heidelberg where he was recently awarded a doctorate in cellular biology, with colleagues Dr. W. von Trautschke (center) and Dr. G. Müller (right)."

Matthias found himself bending forward to look more closely at Dr. G. Müller. But the closer he looked the more the man's face disintegrated into monotonic dots on the cracked newsprint.

Hew laid his finger on the tall man in the middle. "This worthy became Hiram's father-in-law. Von Trautschke. He was Inge's father."

"Did you know him?"

"No. He didn't survive the war, if I recall. Rather a bad egg, in fact."

"What sort of bad egg?"

"I'm not sure I ever knew."

Matthias examined von Trautschke's face. It too disintegrated into dots. "He was Happy Standish's grandfather, then."

"You do function better with visual aids," said Hew.

"Have you got any more?"

"More what?"

"Articles or pictures about the Standishes."

"Possibly," said Hew. "Probably. I've got loads of scrapbooks around somewhere. But I'd have to dig them out. What exactly are you looking for?"

"Hiram Standish's obituary, for one thing."

"I told you. He died in that blue hole of yours."

"When?"

Hew thought. "Before I had to sell the Lyford Cay house. I was still in Nassau. So it must have been the early fifties. They didn't stay on Two-Head Cay very long after that."

"Who didn't?"

"Inge. Happy. The household."

"Where did they go?"

"Moved to the States. There really wasn't much here for a woman like Inge. A beauty, of course, and rather accomplished at this and that—a crack shot if I recall. They were always going after boar, right here in the interior. Plenty of it in those days."

Matthias put down his glass. "Have I got this right? The Standishes left Lyford Cay after the war and moved to Two-Head Cay. In the early fifties, Hiram drowned in the blue hole. Then you sold your place in Nassau and came here. You went to Two-Head Cay and saw Happy, already afraid of the water, which fits with his father being dead by that time. Then they moved to the States. Is that it?"

"My, my," said Hew. "You have been listening." He reached under the table and put his hand on Matthias's knee.

"Knock it off, Hew," Matthias said.

"Aren't I wicked?" said Hew, trilling again. But he removed his hand.

Matthias thought of some of the men he'd known on the Isle of Pines and said: "No."

"No?" said Hew, sounding disappointed.

Matthias studied the picture of the three doctors. "I don't understand why the owners of half of Bay Street would move out here."

"No one did," said Hew. "Though the Standishes didn't own so much by then. In fact, there were rumors."

"Rumors?"

"That they had made bad investments, were deeply in debt, the whole dreary tale. But there couldn't have been much to it. People who saw them after the war—in Connecticut or some such dreadful place—said they were richer than ever."

Matthias closed the scrapbook and laid it on the table between them. "I'd like to see the others."

"Others?"

"Scrapbooks."

"Tonight?" All at once Hew sounded very tired. The skin sagged on the fine bones of his face.

"How about tomorrow?"

"Tomorrow night. That will give me time to search. But I can't quite see what it is you're looking for."

Matthias had no reply. He swallowed the rest of his Armagnac.

"They both drowned, or in Happy's case, nearly so," said Hew. "Is that it?"

"Sort of," Matthias said. "About a quarter of a mile apart."

"But Happy's accident was at sea."

"Right."

"And the blue hole is on land."

"Right."

"Ergo?"

"I don't know," Matthias said. "When was the last time you saw Happy?"

"As a boy. Perhaps that time on Two-Head Cay. I don't believe I saw him or Inge after that. Certainly not much after."

"He didn't visit you when he came to the club?"

"What do you mean?"

"Last September. The day before the accident."

"No. Why would he?"

"I don't know," Matthias said. "What was Hiram Senior doing in the blue hole?"

"Swimming, I suppose."

"Alone?"

"I have no idea. Why don't you ask Gene Albury?"

Inside Hew's house, Edith Piaf went to work on "La Vie en Rose." Hew's eyes dampened. He got lost in the music. "Thanks for the booze," Matthias said, rising.

For a moment, he thought Hew hadn't heard him. Then Hew said: "I'll miss your company."

"It's not over yet. Eleven days left to file an appeal."

Hew gave him a look that said: "On what grounds?"

That was the question. "Good night," Matthias said. He climbed down the steps from Hew's terrace, found the path and walked toward home. Something rustled in the palms that grew between the path and the beach. A dog started barking, somewhere in the bushes, then another dog, and another. The moon had set and it would be an hour or so before the sun rose. Matthias couldn't see a thing; because of that, or what he'd drunk, he stumbled and almost fell. He reached down and felt something big and soft.

"Who it is?" said a deep voice. Nottage.

"For Christ's sake, Nottage, get up."

"Sea on fire, boss, sea on fire."

"Get up, Nottage. Don't sleep here. You can sleep on the deck."

But Nottage wouldn't get up. He would just say, "Sea on fire, boss, sea on fire." Matthias left him on the path and went to bed.

23

"Matt?"

Matthias felt a heavy hand on his shoulder.

"Wake up."

Matthias didn't want to wake up; he wanted to stay where he was, in his sandy sheets, and the way he was, unconscious, but he opened his eyes anyway. Brock was looking down at him. "What is it?" Matthias asked.

"Better come with me."

Matthias got up, pulled on shorts and a sweater and followed Brock outside. The wintry sun, low in the sky, shone with a white, glaring light that made his eyes water. His head ached too, and his mouth felt dry: overnight, his body had deconstructed the 1909 Armagnac, leveling it down to the status of the meanest hangover inducer on the shelves.

Brock led him along the crushed-shell path to the beach. They walked north, with the Bluff rising on their left. The wind, stronger than the day before, blew in stereo: on one side hissing over the wave tops, on the other whining in the sea-grapes. The sand ended abruptly at an outcrop of dead coral, covered in slippery moss. They climbed over and continued along the coral, a spiky and uneven beach that ran all the way to the tip of the island. Matthias had seen Blufftown children playing barefoot on sharp coral beaches, but his own feet, callused though they were, hurt with every step, and he was about to go back for shoes when he saw a dark buzzard circling the top of the Bluff. Below, on the rocks by the edge of the sea, stood Moxie, looking down at something twisted and white. It could have been an object tossed up by the waves, but it wasn't. Matthias knew that even before he started running.

It was Hew.

He lay on his side, one arm thrown up in a way that made Matthias think of the Nijinsky photograph, as did his long hair, swept back off his face, and his clean white trousers: he might have been posing for an avant-garde fashion photographer, except that his legs were in an impossible position and half a dozen red land crabs were scuttling back and forth in the shadow of the Bluff, biding their time. All around lay shards of dark green glass, 1909 Armagnac glass, not yet dulled by the sea.

High tide—splash, low tide—smash.

Matthias looked up. Hew's balustrade loomed directly above, thirty or forty feet overhead. From where he stood, Matthias could just make out the neck of an overturned bottle extending over the top like a toy cannon.

"Jesus Christ," he said.

"Yeah," said Brock.

Moxie said nothing. He wore only a threadbare Speedo; perhaps that explained the goose bumps on his skin and the ashy tint around his eyes and mouth.

"What time is it?" Matthias asked.

Brock checked his Rolex. "Eight-fifteen," he said.

Matthias had probably left Hew's less than three hours ago. "Who found him?" he asked.

Brock turned to Moxie. Moxie said: "Boys on the beach."

"What boys?"

"Fishing boys," said Moxie. "Down to Blufftown."

"Which boys?"

Moxie gazed over Matthias's shoulder. "Craig be one. And the short boy with that bad foot."

"Larry?"

Moxie nodded. "Larry, he be the one that tell me."

"When?"

"Morning time."

"An hour ago?"

"Yeah. An hour."

Matthias looked up again: at the cliff, the balustrade,

the bottle, the buzzard in its holding pattern. "And he was just like this?"

"Like this," Moxie said. "But the tide be out then."

Now it was rising. Waves foamed up the coral beach and slipped back down, not far from Hew's outstretched hand. Matthias knelt and patted Hew's pockets. They were empty.

"What's that for?" Brock asked.

Matthias wasn't sure. "Anyone seen Nottage?" he said.

"Nottage?"

"He was on the Bluff last night."

"Meaning?"

"Maybe he saw something. Or heard something."

"Like what?"

"Falling."

"Nottage?" said Brock. "He's bloody pickled twenty-four hours a day."

A ball of nausea quickly coalesced in Matthias's stomach and almost came up.

"What's wrong?" Brock asked.

"What's wrong?" Matthias, still kneeling, gently raised Hew's head and revealed the crushed side. The eye on the crushed side was open; the other closed. "That's what's wrong."

No one blanched. No one turned away. Moxie came from a world where curable birth defects like club feet went uncured; Brock had seen a diving partner taken by a great white off the Queensland coast; Matthias had encountered men with caved-in heads before, starting with a few of Cesarito's *compadres* on the Isle of Pines. The ball of nausea in his stomach dissipated. "We'd better call Conchtown," he said. "For Constable Welles."

"Why?" Brock asked.

"To examine the body."

"Welles?" Brock said. "He can't even write his name." Matthias glanced at Moxie. His eyes had gone blank. "Isn't it obvious what happened?" Brock asked.

They all looked up. "I guess so," Matthias said.

"He was a funny old ponce," Brock said, "but he was as big a lush as Nottage. He didn't have to get by with aftershave, that's all."

Matthias stood up. "I'll call Welles anyway. You stay here, Brock. And Moxie, see if you can find Nottage."

Moxie went off down the beach. Brock said: "What am I supposed to do here?"

"Keep the crabs off him." They watched the crabs, no longer scuttling: they had advanced a foot or two and waited in pools in the rock, claws folded neatly before them; each pair of wide-apart eyes formed the short base of an isosceles triangle with Hew's body at the apex.

"Better hurry," Brock said. The tips of the first waves lapped at Hew's bloodless fingers.

Matthias returned to the office. He called the one-room police station in Conchtown and counted thirty rings before hanging up. When he tried again he couldn't get a dial tone. Walking out, he saw that he had left red footprints on the office floor. He slid on a worn pair of boat shoes and went up the path to Hew's house.

Inside, everything looked the way it had a few hours before: the mildewing antiques, the shelves of paperbacks, the stacks of *Punch*, the Gauguin, all in their places. Matthias moved to the terrace. The tray of Ritz crackers still sat on the table between the chaise longues, but now a cockroach had joined the ants inside. One empty snifter stood beside the tray. The other, which he had not been able to see from below, was on the balustrade, not far from the overturned bottle. The second glass was one-third full. Matthias picked it up and sniffed. He smelled the smell of 1909 Armagnac. It had lost its magic.

Matthias glanced over the wall. Brock stood gazing out to sea, arms folded on his chest, Hew's body at his feet. The sea half-covered the graceful outstretched arm and was beginning to foam in the long white hair. In ten more minutes it would lift Hew off the rocks and carry him away. "You might as well bring him up here," Matthias called down.

Brock lifted Hew on his shoulders in one easy motion and brought him up to the terrace. He started to lower him on one of the chaises, but Matthias said: "Just lay him on the floor."

"On the floor?" Brock said. Matthias didn't reply. Brock laid Hew down on the white marble. A strand of seaweed had caught in his hair, curled like a limp garland.

Matthias sat on the balustrade, his back to the sea. Brock sat nearby, on the other side of the snifter and the over-

turned bottle. "How much did he have last night?" Brock
asked.

"Enough."

"Then you left and he had some more."

"Looks like it."

"Maybe he sat up here."

"Maybe."

"To watch the sun come up, say. With his feet on the
other side."

They swung around to look east. Brock's arm barely
brushed the overturned bottle, but it was enough to start
it rolling. He snatched at it, missed; the bottle rolled off
the edge and pinwheeled down, landing with a little splash
in the waves that now covered the spot where Hew had
lain. A red crab shot out of the water and sidestepped
quickly out of sight.

"Shit," Brock said. "That was evidence."

"Of what?"

"I don't know. Maybe it wasn't an accident. Maybe it
was suicide."

"Why would Hew commit suicide?" Matthias asked.

Brock shrugged. Overhead the buzzard had been joined
by another, slightly smaller and blacker. They flew in tan-
dem, banking into the stiff wind, beating their heavy wings,
then banking again and gliding swiftly on the breeze, round
and round.

"Ever been in the blue hole, Brock?"

"What blue hole?"

"Our blue hole."

"The sink hole by the shuffleboard?"

"Yeah."

Brock shook his head. "Can't really call that a blue hole,
can you? It's not even blue."

"All the inland ones are that way."

"You dove it?"

"Years ago."

"Yeah? I've never seen the point." He glanced at Matthias. "What's down there?"

"Nothing."

They fell silent. Small, quick brown flies appeared and
descended on Hew. Then came slow fat black ones. They
found his nostrils right away, then his lips, then his open

eye. "Maybe we should cover him up," Brock said. But then they saw Constable Welles making his way steadily up the path. News could still travel on Andros without electronic aid.

Constable Welles climbed the steps to the terrace. He paused at the top and took a deep breath. Constable Welles was a tall old man with tightly curled white hair, a long bony face and a big frame that suggested he had once been very strong. He wore his summer uniform all year long: black shorts with red stripes down the sides, black knee socks, black shoes cracked but highly polished, white shirt with red trim. He nodded to Matthias and Brock, then gazed down at the body. "That be Sir Hew?" he said. Constable Welles had a bass voice, not frayed and rumbling, like Nottage's, but smooth and musical, like Paul Robeson's. His knees cracked as he knelt to examine the body. The quick brown flies darted away; the fat black ones took to the air with more reluctance.

Matthias told him how Hew had been found and why they had moved him, about the night before and the overturned bottle. The constable acknowledged this explanation with a deep sound from his chest, longer than a grunt, shorter than a hum: it resisted interpretation. Then he picked the seaweed out of Hew's hair and rose. The flies descended.

The constable bent over the snifter and smelled its contents. "Anyone be touching this?"

"I did," Matthias said. "But that's where it was."

Constable Welles made his deep sound again. He gazed down where the Armagnac bottle had fallen. It had drifted away, or filled with water and sunk out of sight. The constable pulled a clean white handkerchief from the pocket of his shorts and carefully wrapped the snifter in it, spilling nothing.

"Do you want the bottle too?" Brock asked.

"It be gone," Constable Welles said.

"We could look for it," Matthias told him.

The constable shook his head. "Too late, mahn." He stood before Brock and Matthias, but looked between them rather than at either one. "Sir Hew has no kin," he said.

Was it a question? Matthias said: "I'm not sure."

"No kin," Constable Welles repeated, like a mournful theme sounded on the lowest string of the bass viol. He stared down at the seaweed in his hand. Time passed. The flies buzzed; waves began slapping the base of the cliff; a third buzzard rose out of the pine trees and went into an orbit of its own, not as high as the other two. Brock yawned.

At last Constable Welles looked up. "I don' like to dirty the name of a dead man," he said.

"What do you mean?" Matthias asked.

"If a man take his own life."

"Is there evidence of that?"

Constable Welles was watching the cockroach in the Ritz crackers. "That wall be plenty wide," he said quietly. Then there was a silence until Reverend Christie came on the terrace with a few men from Blufftown.

Reverend Christie was a fat man with a clerical collar, a stained white suit and a heavy gold watch which he consulted frequently. He gazed down on the body. "Poor sinner," he said. "What happened to him?"

"Death by accident," replied Constable Welles without hesitation. "Give him a Christian burial."

"May he rest in peace," said Reverend Christie. The men from Blufftown gazed at the objects in the constable's hands: seaweed and a crystal glass wrapped in a white handkerchief.

"No kin," said Constable Welles.

Reverend Christie frowned. "No kin anywhere?"

"No kin."

"Then, my good friend," said the reverend, "who shall pay for the Christian burial?"

Not I, said the pig. "I'm sure his estate will cover it," Matthias said. "In the meantime, I'll pay whatever's necessary."

"God bless you," said Reverend Christie.

The men from Blufftown carried Hew away. Reverend Christie poked his head through the open sliding glass door, glanced quickly into the house and followed. Constable Welles walked to the balustrade, poured the contents of the snifter into the sea and set the glass down where he had found it. Then he left, taking only the seaweed.

"What was that all about?" Brock asked.

"He liked him," Matthias said.

"Yeah?"

Half an hour later, Matthias was in his office, on the phone to a man named Willoughby at the trust department of Hew's branch of Barclay's Bank in the City of London.

"What did he die of?" asked Willoughby.

"A fall."

"I see. He lived a long time, considering." There was a silence. "Well then, Mr. Matthias, thanks so much for getting in touch."

"Will someone be coming over to handle his estate?"

"His estate?" said Willoughby.

"Yes. I don't know if he has a lawyer, or whether he left a will."

"May I ask what your relationship was to Sir Hew?"

"We were neighbors."

"Ah. Did you know him well?"

"I wouldn't say well."

"Not well," said Willoughby. "Then perhaps it will surprise you to learn that there is no estate."

"Hew told me he received monthly income payments from you."

"Not income, Mr. Matthias. He'd been encroaching on principal for the last decade. Encroaching heavily. The balance in his account is presently . . . two hundred forty-seven pounds, thirty-six pence."

"That's all he had left?"

"I'm afraid so."

"There's still the house to be sold."

"I don't think we need hurry about that," said Willoughby.

"Why not? There are bound to be some expenses now. The burial, for one."

"I gather you haven't been apprised of all the facts, Mr. Matthias. Sir Hew hasn't owned the house for a number of years now."

"Who owns the house?"

"We do. The bank, that is. Sir Hew mortgaged it heavily at one time. He proved unable to maintain the payments. We were forced to foreclose. Naturally we continued to allow him residency, at a very reasonable rent."

"Which you skimmed off the top of the trust account."

"I don't quite follow you."

"Never mind," Matthias said. The image of Hew subsisting on ant-infested crackers made him angry. "Do you own the contents of the house too?"

"Not me personally, of course. The bank. All contents and furnishings."

"Including the Gauguin? It must be worth hundreds of thousands all by itself."

Willoughby laughed, a laugh quickly masked by genteel coughing. "The Gauguin. Did Sir Hew never tell you the story of the Gauguin?"

"What story?"

"I'm taken aback. I would have thought he'd have dined out on it for years."

"What story?"

"Simply put, the Gauguin is a fake. Sir Hew must have known it all along—he bought it in Paris sometime in the twenties at a rather low price, too low, I'm afraid, for a Gauguin, even then. But it was thoroughly inauthenticated, if you'll pardon the coinage, in the appraisal conducted before he entered into the initial mortgage. He was quite a character, as I'm sure you're aware."

"What was going to happen when he couldn't pay the rent?"

"Fortunately we'll never have to face that decision."

"But it's in your interest to maximize your return."

"Without doubt. I'm glad you understand, and I'm sure Sir Hew would have as well. He was quite realistic, beneath his rather colorful . . . patina. I met him several times in the late fifties. A most amusing fellow. Thank you so much for your call. We'll be in touch with the local authority."

"What do you want done with the Armagnac?"

"The Armagnac, Mr. Matthias?"

"Do you want me to send it to you personally, or to the bank impersonally?"

"Armagnac? I'm afraid I don't follow quite."

"Goodbye, Willoughby."

Matthias hung up. He went outside. Brock was passing by, a tank on each shoulder.

"Something wrong, Matt?"

"He killed himself."

"Why d'you say that?"

"Just take my word for it."

Matthias returned to Hew's house. Piaf, the drinking, the scrapbooks, two hundred forty-seven pounds, thirty-six pence: it added up to suicide; and put a different slant on Hew's last words. *"I'll miss your company."*

Matthias stood before the painting with the Gauguin signature. "Gauguin," it said, "1897." It looked like a good painting to him, but he knew nothing about art. He was still gazing at it when he remembered the scrapbooks. Hew had promised to search for all his old scrapbooks. He walked out on the terrace to get the scrapbook Hew had shown him hours before, with the Nijinsky picture, and all the young men, and Dr. Hiram Standish at the University of Heidelberg. It had been on the table, beside the tray of Ritz crackers. The tray was still there, empty now, and so was the flashlight and Matthias's glass. But the scrapbook was gone.

Matthias searched the entire house. He found drawers full of old love letters, a collection of erotica from the twenties that seemed refined compared with what was available in any American city, and a copy of *Mr. Norris Changes Trains* with the inscription, "To Hew, who remembered the wine, gratefully, Christopher," but he didn't find the scrapbook, or any other scrapbooks.

Hew had three old suitcases. Matthias put the "Gauguin" in one, for reasons he couldn't explain. The other two he filled with all the bottles of Armagnac that were left because he didn't want Mr. Willoughby to get his hands on them and he didn't think Hew would have wanted that either.

| 24 |

Now he was sick.

It was Fritz's fault.

Fritz had let him get cold. He had caught a chill. It made him want to cough, but he couldn't cough. He felt his chest filling with liquid. It was, he thought, like drowning. That struck him as appropriate, somehow, but he couldn't think why. His memory was very bad.

The medical man appeared. "Hi, I'm Dr. Robert. Remember me?"

Certainly, doctor. I even remember when you said I might not remember. You were right.

Dr. Robert stuck a breathing tube in his nose and hooked him to a respirator. He became a component, one third of a device—IV, respirator, him—designed for a purpose he couldn't figure out. He left out the catheter, which for some reason bothered him most of all.

"This is merely temporary," said Dr. Robert, leaving. "Not to worry."

But temporary went on and on. Happy no longer saw the outside. He lost touch with the tingling electromagnetic force and the smell of the living planet. The IV forced nourishment into him, the respirator air. His body accepted them. He watched the white ceiling and the brown spider and longed for painkillers, even though he wasn't in pain. He had caught a chill. Now he was in the white room all the time. But he couldn't blame Fritz. Fritz had

always been nice to him and now he was a simple old man.
He had always been a simple old man.

There had been a song about a white room. And another
about a white rabbit. Or was it the same song? A song
about a white rabbit in a white room? He didn't think so,
but he wasn't sure. He slept. He woke. He slept. When
he woke again he knew they were two different songs. His
memory began to stir at last. After a few more sleeps, he
could remember all the words to the song about the white
rabbit, and soon he could sing the white room song too,
sing it in his mind. He spent time singing songs in his mind,
not scanning them and realizing he knew them and going
on to the next—there was no forgetfulness in that kind of
remembering—but singing them in real time. He sang and
sang: Rodgers and Hart, the Beatles, the Stones, Frank
Sinatra, Patsy Cline, children's songs, nursery rhymes,
spirituals, Gilbert and Sullivan, Elvis, Cole Porter, Leon
Redbone; sometimes in an organized, logical order, some-
times randomly. *Camptown Races, America the Beautiful,
Teen Angel, Positively Fourth Street, Fly Me to the Moon,
Jailhouse Rock, Bring It on Home to Me, When Irish Eyes
Are Smiling, The Little Old Lady from Pasadena, Big Rock
Candy Mountain, Your Cheatin' Heart, Isn't It Romantic?,
Two Sleepy People, The Locomotion, The Flying Purple
People Eater, Marie.*

Then one day he just stopped. He didn't want to sing.
He didn't even want to hear music, had it been provided
for him, which it never was. He just lay there, component
number three. But his memory was coming back. It was
very sharp. He decided to relive his life.

He began with his first memory.

He sat in the paneled compartment of a train. Outside
snow fell, slanting across the window and obscuring the
view of forested countryside. Inside his mother wore a
black hat with a long hat pin. She sat beside him, but not
touching. Opposite sat Fritz, also wearing a black hat.
Sometimes Mother and Fritz talked, but he couldn't understand a word they said. Sometimes his mother dabbed
at her eyes. He cried. Fritz gave him black licorice. He
ate it and stopped crying. The world was black and white,
black on the inside, white on the outside.

First memory. Happy took his time with it, going over
the details, sleeping, waking, sleeping. He knew it was

time to move on to the next memory, but he resisted it.
Not because he wasn't going to like it; he could see it
coming and knew he would: a piano, beams of sunlight
filled with dust motes, a buzzing fly, finger pressing the
lowest of the white keys. No: he resisted it because he felt
another memory beneath the first memory, waiting, like
the bottom layer of an archaeological dig, to be discovered,
or struggling, like a smothering creature, to be free. Archaeological dig. Smothering creature. He concentrated
on those two images, shifting them, rubbing them together,
superimposing them. But they wouldn't mate, wouldn't
conceive, wouldn't bring forth what he wanted.

"Hi, I'm Dr. Robert. Remember me?"

Dr. Robert bent over him, felt, measured, timed.
Mother stood behind him, wearing diamond earrings that
caught all the white light in the room and shone with it.
"I don't like this fever," said Dr. Robert.

Oh I do, I do, I like it a lot.

Dr. Robert and Mother moved out into the hall. The
room darkened. They lowered their voices. "I don't like
it at all," said Dr. Robert. "We may have to take more
aggressive steps."

"How much more aggressive can we be?" asked Mother.
Happy knew she was under stress because she said "we"
like "vee."

"We still have options," replied Dr. Robert.

"But to what end? And for how long? Where do we
draw the line?"

"It's one of those blurred lines, I'm sorry to say," answered Dr. Robert. "Perhaps you should consult your
priest or minister. I'll be in touch, Mrs. Standish."

Mother came back. Her diamonds caught the light. The
room brightened. She stood over him for a while. Once
she lowered her palm to his forehead. Her hand felt cold.

Someone knocked at the door. "Come in," said Mother.

Fritz entered. He had garden shears in one hand and a
letter in the other. "Madam?" he said, giving her the letter.
He always called her "Madam." Happy was thinking about
that when he noticed that the envelope had already been
torn open. His mother took out the single page inside,
unfolded and read it. He watched her face. It told him
nothing. Fritz was watching her face too. His mother refolded the letter and slipped it back into the envelope.

"Thank you," she said to Fritz, returning the letter.

Fritz bowed and left. Mother stood by the door, lost in thought. Then she too went away. But Happy wasn't really paying attention. He was thinking about the stamp on the envelope: a blue and yellow tropical fish hovering beside an orange sea fan. The tropical fish, the archaeological dig, the struggling creature. Just as he was the third component of a device with no purpose, the fish was the third component in his aide-mémoire. But when he tried to recall the memory that lay beneath his first memory, all he could see in his mind was a suitcase tumbling through the water, brass corners flashing like coins. And that wasn't the memory he wanted. It was close, in some way, to the memory he wanted, but it wasn't the one. He would get to that memory later. Chronologically, and in every way, it came at the end. For now, he had to concentrate on that memory beneath the memory, that primordial, that antediluvian memory.

The IV fed him.

The respirator filled him with air.

Happy had nothing to do but think.

He thought:

Antediluvian: Before the flood.

| 25 |

"Laura got stuck in the denial stage," said Hal Palmeteer. "As her therapist, I feel very, very badly about that. I can't tell you how badly."

"The denial stage?" said Nina.

"Sure. You know. Denial, anger, grieving, acceptance. The four stages."

Nina remembered skimming an article in a dentist's office. "I thought they had to do with facing death."

Hal Palmeteer smiled a kindly smile. Nina had only been in his Brookline office for a few minutes, but already he reminded her of an aging hippie she had often seen strumming a guitar in Washington Square; though cleaned up and prosperous, Palmeteer had that same serene yet slightly superior smile of the psychic voyager who has long ago learned the truth. " 'Facing,' " he quoted. "I'm very impressed by your choice of words, Nina. I can see you're no stranger to the quest for self-knowledge. Facing"—he put his feet—he wore red wool socks and Birkenstocks—on his desk—"the response that must be made, in the final end, to everything. And facing means opening the doors one after the other, the doors to denial, anger, grieving, acceptance, and then closing them, quietly but firmly, and moving on."

"What about slamming them?"

That brought the smile again. "Have you been in therapy, Nina?"

"Never," Nina said. "Are you telling me that Laura should have accepted that her baby was gone, that's that?"

Hal Palmeteer frowned slightly. Then he put his finger-tips together, shaping a church with his hands. He made a steeple, a pair of doors, opened them, gazed within. "Wouldn't that have been better than what happened? Overdosing on Seconal? But I'm not going to come out and say that. I'm only saying she was stuck in the first stage and I couldn't get her out." The church doors closed. "Do you know they found her in the room she'd set up for the baby? But by then it was too late, much, much too late." Hal Palmeteer's eyes filled with tears. One overflowed, then the other. He opened a file, turned pages, read to himself. "I was very involved in this case. Maybe more than I should have been."

"What do you mean?"

He sighed. "I don't suppose there's any harm now."

"What are you talking about?"

Hal Palmeteer looked up from the file. "Shortly after the disappearance of Laura's child, I got a call from the pediatrician. Some hospital test had indicated possible liver malfunction in the baby."

"Life-threatening?"

He nodded. "The pediatrician wanted my recommendation on whether Laura should be told."

"And you said?"

"No. She was frantic enough already."

"So the liver problem was never publicized."

Hal Palmeteer frowned again, more deeply this time. "That was something I had to face. We all make decisions we don't want to make, Nina." He took out the last page from the file and pushed it across the desk. It was a Xerox of a sheet of memo paper with a bouquet of flowers at the top, a printed letterhead—"from the desk of laura bain"— and a typewritten note. Nina read:

> I am so sorry it has come to this but I just can't
> go on. Please forgive me and try to understand.

Laura's signature followed. There was nothing more. Nina handed the note back. Hal Palmeteer replaced it in the file. His voice was husky when he said: "I'm seeing my own therapist about it this afternoon. That's how bummed out I am." He removed his feet from the desk and dabbed at his cheeks with the sleeve of his Vassar sweatshirt. "There are no easy answers, Nina."

"I'm sure he'll have you to the acceptance stage in no time," Nina said.

This remark brought forth no smile; it also signaled the end of the monsoon season in Hal Palmeteer's eyes and the onset of drought. "Who are you talking about?" he asked, sitting back in his chair and trying to sound more authoritative, although it was too late: his Birkenstocks and salt-and-pepper ponytail had already made their egalitarian statement.

"I'm talking about your therapist," Nina said.

"My therapist is a woman."

"That makes all the difference."

Hal Palmeteer looked puzzled. Nina was puzzled, too; she had come to Boston to find out what she could about Laura's suicide, not to spar with someone who had tried to help her. But the truth was that Nina didn't like men who cried. This was an indefensible position, she knew, wrong and retrograde, but she couldn't help thinking that a crying man had it both ways. She also didn't like the way Hal Palmeteer came close to blaming the victim while feeling sorry for himself at the same time.

Nina took a deep breath and started over. "Maybe you're right, Dr. Palmeteer. Maybe Laura was stuck in the denial stage. But when I last saw her, a day before she died, she didn't seem suicidal to me."

"Recognizing the suicidal mind-set is a tricky business. And call me Hal."

Calling him Hal was fine with Nina. His framed certificate on the wall testified to a doctorate in psychology. That didn't elevate him above the plane of Misters in Nina's eyes. "I'm no expert in recognizing suicidal mind-sets, Hal," she said, "but just meeting me—another woman in a similar situation—seemed to cheer her up. And it sparked a few ideas in her mind. She was going to call me after she had reached her obstetrician." In fact, Nina thought, Laura had called, and left a message on her machine.

Hal was drumming his fingers on his desk. To stop them, he raised his little church again, and stared at Nina over the steeple. "What sort of ideas did you spark in her mind, Nina?"

"They were still forming, I guess. She was going to try to track down the sperm bank she used, for instance, maybe through her obstetrician. The point is she was figuring out where to go from here. She was making plans."

"With what end product in mind?"

"What?"

"What was she trying to do?"

"Find her baby, of course."

Hal's church collapsed. He folded his arms across his chest. "May I speak frankly, Nina? Frankly and openly?"

"Why not?"

Hal smiled his guru smile. "Because you may not like what I'm about to say. But my job is all about taking risks. The truth shall make you free—Dylan."

"Dylan?"

"Bob, not Thomas."

Nina didn't recall Bob singing that line, but if he had he was only quoting Jesus—Christ, not Alou. She kept that to herself. "And what's the truth, Hal?"

"No one knows that with certainty. Einstein proved it and Freud—no matter what you may think of him from a feminist perspective, and believe me, I'm a feminist myself—showed how it applies to human life. But in this matter I'm only suggesting you think about whether these sparks you set off in Laura's mind only acted to reinforce her denial."

"Are you accusing me of helping cause her suicide?" Nina's voice rose and she did nothing to stop it.

Hal flinched. "I'm not accusing you of anything. I never accuse anyone of anything. I'm a trained therapist."

"Then what are you saying?"

He looked at her for a long moment. She looked right back. "You've never been in group, have you, Nina?"

"No. I told you that. Are you suggesting I should be?"

"That's up to you. A lot of people find it helpful, especially angry ones."

"I've got good reason to be angry."

"I know. And I empathize. Empathize and sympathize. But at the same time I see it as a good sign."

"In terms of your four stages?"

"*The* four stages, yes. Laura never got to anger." He sighed, leaned back in his swivel chair and swiveled it a bit. "Have you ever read the book about why bad things happen to good people, Nina?"

She recalled the cover, the book's long ride on the bestseller lists, a publication party with someone's agent vomiting in the women's room. "Just the flap copy," she said.

"What's inside may be worth your perusal."

"Why?"

"Because it may lead you toward acceptance."

"Why should I accept something so inexplicable?"

"Isn't the world sometimes inexplicable?"

"That's what the priests and rabbis say. I thought people like you represented the alternative."

A muscle jumped in one of Hal's cheeks. "Would you be able to come up here once a week, Nina?"

"What for?"

"I think I could help you. I sense that you have things to work through, more than just this difficulty."

"Difficulty?"

"Tragedy. Whatever."

Nina laughed out loud; she couldn't help it.

"Is something funny?"

She wiped her eyes. It was the kind of laughing that could turn to crying at any moment. "Nothing's funny," she said. "I guess I'm just working through it in my own stupid way."

"Good," said Hal, "good."

Nina was aware of his face, intent, waiting for more laughter, or crying, or any other fuel for his forge. She clamped off the supply. "I'll think about your offer," she said, rising. "May I have a copy of Laura's note?"

"You want a copy of the suicide note?"

"That's right."

"May I ask why?"

"It's part of the case."

"What case?"

"Kidnapping is a criminal matter, Hal."

"I know. But there are two cases here, aren't there?"

"Yes."

"Then why do you want the note?"

"Because Laura thought it was important to get in touch with me."

"I'm still not sure I understand you."

"I owe it to Laura to follow through."

"Follow through on what?"

By that time, Nina understood Hal well enough to know that no explanation was going to yield up Laura's note. Concession was required. "Maybe it doesn't make sense," she said, suddenly picturing herself as a color version of Gracie, or Our Miss Brooks, or Lucy. "But I'd like that note."

George, or Mr. Boynton, or Desi nodded. "I think you're beginning to come around. Not everything does make sense. Bad things do happen to good people. And if the note will help you with your grieving for Laura, by all means have it." He held out the note.

"Don't you want a copy?"

Hal made his little church again and gazed inside. "No, I don't think so, I really don't. This talk has helped me too, helped me work through my own feelings about Laura. Of course, I didn't know her long, in the sense of time. Only since her . . . loss. But, as I said, I was very bummed out by what's happened. Suicide is the worst possible end prod— the worst possible thing in this line of work." He looked up at Nina. "But this little session has helped me, it really has. I may even cancel my therapist this afternoon."

Nina took the note. "Goodbye," she said.

"Bye-bye," said Hal. "Be strong."

Nina drove her rental car to Dedham. For a while her mind was a blank. Then it began to occupy itself with Hal Palmeteer's suspicion that she had deep-down troubles having nothing to do with the kidnapping. Like what? Like the compulsion to have the baby in the first place? Because she felt incomplete, perhaps? And she couldn't get a man, so she settled on a baby? What did she really want? A man? A baby? A man and a baby? Something really bizarre like that?

"Fuck this shit," she said aloud, and switched on the radio. She found an oldies station. Aretha was singing "Natural Woman." Nina sang along, softly at first, at the top of her lungs by the end. Her mind was a blank again as she parked in front of Laura's house.

The house, set well back from the street, overlooked the Dedham Common. It was much grander than she had expected: an overgrown shingled Cape Cod, three stories high, with fresh white trim, white shutters and a turret room at the top left corner, nicely setting off a big maple on the right side of the lawn. A woman with a cigarette hanging out of her mouth was hammering a FOR SALE sign into the ground.

Nina got out of her car and approached the woman. "This looks like a nice house," she said.

The woman glanced up. "Can't beat the location," she said, ash drifting down on the lapel of her trench-coat.

"Can I see it?"

"Inside you mean?"

"Yes."

"Gee, I'm not sure," the woman said. "It's not really even listed yet. I haven't been inside myself. The owner was, uh, suddenly transferred or something." She whacked at the sign; it wasn't going in straight. Nina tugged at it while the woman hammered again. The sign sank into the hard ground, not too crookedly. "Thanks," said the woman. "Well, I don't see why not. You in the market?"

"Thinking about it."

"Where are you living now?"

"In the city."

"Whereabouts?"

"Downtown." It was all true; she just hadn't said what city.

"I used to live in the city," the woman said. "I'd never go back." She stubbed the cigarette out under her heel, straightened her hair and led Nina to the door. She tried several brass keys before finding the one that fit. They went inside.

"Very nice," said the woman, looking around. "Very, very nice."

Nina and the woman walked around the ground floor. It was nice: pine floors, a stone fireplace in the living room and another in the dining room, high ceilings, a big kitchen with up-to-date machinery, nice rugs, nice furniture, including a steel and glass coffee table with a vase of dead flowers on it and a book: *How To Survive the Coming Depression.*

"It really is a dream," said the woman. "This one's going to go quick, even in this lousy—" She stopped herself and picked up the hall phone. To Nina she said, "I don't even know the list price." Into the phone she said, "Hi, it's me. Is Mrs. G. around? . . . I'll wait."

While the woman waited, Nina walked up the carpeted stairs to the second floor. She saw the baby's room, where Laura's body had been found: crib, stuffed animals, books, some that she had chosen—*Go Dog Go, Madeline, Goodnight Moon*—and Laura's room: all drawers and closets neatly closed, bed neatly made, covered with a floral bedspread. It was a nice house that hadn't been lived in, not even when Laura was alive, except perhaps for the two days that Clea was there.

Nina went to the window and looked down at the backyard. It was a big backyard with a plastic chaise longue, covered with dead leaves, under an elm tree; perhaps the same chaise longue where Laura had fallen asleep with Clea in the carriage nearby.

Nina turned from the window. The bedside phone caught her eye. A pen and a notepad lay beside it. Nina riffled through the pages. They were all blank, but she noticed faint impressions on the top one, left by the pressure of the pen writing on the page that had been above it. She tore off the top page and held it to the light. She saw her own phone number traced on the paper. Laura must have called her from this room when she left her message.

I had a thought after you left.

And then what? Crumpled the page with the number and tossed it into the wastebasket? Nina checked the wastebasket. She found a Toblerone wrapper and an empty caffeine-free Diet Coke.

Nina left Laura's room and climbed the stairs to the third floor. At one end were two small rooms, bare and unfurnished; in the middle was a bathroom that looked unused: no towels, no shower curtain, no toilet paper; at the other end was the turret room. The door was closed. Nina opened it.

The turret room was equipped as an office. It had file cabinets, computer, printer, a desk. All that Nina took in on an unconscious level. What she was conscious of, first and solely, was the man sitting at the desk.

Nina made a startled noise. The man, whose back was to her, slowly turned in the chair. He was an old man, with soft white hair, a patrician face and clear blue eyes. He had some papers in his hand. He laid them on the desk, smiled at Nina and rose to his feet.

He was an old man, but tall, with broad shoulders and a big frame. Still smiling, he moved toward her. He had big hands, veiny and liver-spotted. Nina smelled pesticide, and thought at once of garden shears.

"Yoo-hoo!" called the real estate woman. "Are you up here? I've got to get go—" The real estate woman entered the room and saw the old man. "Yikes," she said. "Who are you?"

The old man stood still. "Who am I?" he said. He regarded them calmly, first the other woman, then Nina. "A duly constituted representative," he said.

"Huh?" said the real estate woman.

"Of whom?" Nina asked.

The old man laughed, briefly, but a laugh that sounded pleased, as though he would have expected a question like that from her. For a moment Nina wondered if he was senile. Then he said, "The attorneys acting for the estate. I am responsible for the inventory of all possessions, goods and chattels."

"Oh," said the real estate woman. She turned to Nina. "Sorry—I got a little mixed up about how the house came on the market and all. It seems there was a . . . passing away, or something like that." She looked to the old man for help and got none. Then she poked about in her bag, came up with a notebook, flipped the pages and said: "You're with Mullins, Smithson and O'Leary? That's who contacted us."

The old man nodded. "I am in the hire of those fine gentlemen," he said. He was answering the real estate woman, but his eyes were on Nina.

"In what capacity?" Nina asked.

The question sounded abrupt and a little rude. The real estate woman must have thought so: she looked at Nina closely, as though trying to see her for the first time. But the old man was unperturbed. "I am the appraiser," he answered.

The appraiser wore charcoal gray wool trousers and a heavy tweed jacket with shoulder patches. He might have been a gentleman farmer, or a model in some fashion magazine for the very old and well preserved. "But," he continued, "you have the advantage of me."

"Come again?" said the real estate woman.

He had chosen an expression Nina had encountered only in nineteenth-century novels. Somehow it made her aware of the slight accent in the man's speech, faint and indistinct rhythms which didn't quite match the English lyric.

"I'm asking," he explained, "who you might be."

"The real estate agent," said the real estate agent. "And this is . . . "

"A prospective client," said Nina.

"Ah," the appraiser said. "How quickly everyone moves these days."

"You can say that again," the real estate woman told him. "How soon do you think everything will be cleared out? So the house will be empty, and all."

"Soon," replied the old man. "Very soon." He slid his big hands into his pockets and looked out the window at the backyard. He seemed to be thinking. Nina and the real estate woman waited for him to say something. At last he did: "Please don't let me detain you, ladies."

The real estate woman checked her watch. "I am running late." She turned to Nina: "If you've seen enough for now?"

"Yes."

The old man kept gazing out the window. Nina and the real estate woman went downstairs. They were in the front hall, steps from the door, when Nina said: "One second. I just want another quick look at the backyard."

"Well, I'm really—"

Nina ran through the kitchen and the laundry room, into the little mud room leading to the back door. The door had a brass lock, a chain and a heavy sliding bolt. Nina unlocked the lock, unhooked the chain and slid the bolt open. Then she hurried back to the front hall. The real estate woman regarded her for a moment and then smiled.

"You like it, don't you?"

Nina realized her face was flushed. "It's very nice," she said.

"You've got good taste. And I haven't even gotten your name yet."

"Nina," said Nina. "I don't have my card on me. Why don't you give me yours and I'll get in touch?"

The real estate woman's mouth opened as if to raise an objection, but she just said, "I'll look forward to hearing from you," and handed over her card. "It's three-fifty, by the way." Outside, she got into her car and drove away. Nina got into hers and drove around the block. She parked a few hundred feet from Laura's house and sat in the car, not sure what she was doing or why.

In less than five minutes, a taxi pulled up in front of Laura's house. Laura's door opened and the appraiser came out. He strode down the walk—he moved vigorously, with spring in his calf muscles, like an actor playing an old man, after the director yells "Cut!"—and got into the taxi. It rolled away.

Nina got out of the car. She walked to Laura's house and around to the side. A picket fence enclosed the backyard. Nina glanced around, saw no one, hitched up her skirt and climbed the fence. She glanced around again, again saw no one and moved quickly to the back door. She turned the knob.

The door was locked.

Nina stood before it. Her heart pounded, as though it had suddenly developed the capacity to reason things out ahead of her brain, and had already comprehended what she was still groping toward. Once more, she looked around. She saw: the backs of other houses—decks, porches, balconies, all unpeopled on a working day in early December; other yards, some with scattered toys and sandboxes, some bare; and a fat crow perched on one of the top branches of Laura's elm. She heard a power saw, far away, distant traffic, an airliner high above.

Nina took off one shoe: a sensible loafer with a hard leather heel. She cocked it before one of the lowermost windowpanes in the door, ready to do something unsensible with it. Standing there at Laura's back door with the shoe in her hand, Nina felt a strange excitement, part fear but part power: the sense that she was taking action for the first time, was about to do something to get her baby back. Not talking to worn-out police detectives, or exposing herself to TV cameras, or paying ransom to pathetic scammers—but performing a forceful, violent, even criminal act. A criminal act had been performed on her; this somehow was an appropriate response. Nina banged the heel of her shoe against the windowpane.

It didn't break; it didn't even crack. Perhaps she didn't have the makings of a forceful, violent criminal; perhaps Laura had installed special glass. But Nina didn't consider walking away. Suddenly heedless of possible witnesses, she took a big windup and swung the shoe with all her might. The glass shattered, spraying the mud room with exploding shards. It made a deafening noise. The crow in Laura's elm took flight, cawing in panic.

Afraid to turn around, conscious now only of the wild beating of her heart and the unsteadiness of her hand, Nina reached through the hole, unlocked the brass lock, unhooked the chain, slid back the bolt and opened the door. Then she slipped on her shoe and stepped inside Laura's mud room, crunching glass beneath her feet.

Every sound she made seemed as loud and clear as if it had been digitally recorded and played back to her through earphones: the crunching glass, a creak on the stairs as she climbed them, a squeak of the drawer in Laura's desk in the turret room as she pulled it open.

Nina was thinking of the papers in the appraiser's hands, and she found plenty of papers in Laura's desk: spread-sheet printouts, memos she had prepared on cocoa production in Ghana, Brazil, the Ivory Coast, letters from cocoa exporters and cocoa importers, reports to clients, a notebook filled with nothing but dates and figures. What she didn't find was anything to do with the Cambridge Reproductive Research Center.

Laura's computer was an IBM clone, much like Nina's at the office. Nina switched it on, called up the main menu, checked the file directory: all cocoa, cocoa, cocoa. The drink that sitcom moms fix on cold days when Junior and Honeybun come home from school. Nina shut off the computer and searched the house.

She found things that interested her, like an old high school yearbook with a picture of Laura as Dorothy in *The Wizard of Oz*; things that upset her, like a four-year-old letter from a man named Philip, who had written: "Please try to understand that this doesn't mean I don't like you, because I do, and what we had together was great and will always mean a lot to me, but surely an intelligent woman such as yourself can see that people sometimes grow apart

and change. No one is at fault. I just want to try seeing
other people for a while and it's my fondest hope
that . . . " and gone on like that until he ran out of clichés
and signed himself, "respectfully and fondly, Philip"; and
things she would rather not have seen, like a collection of
auto-erotic gadgets neatly packed in a leather case in Laur-
a's bedside table. But she didn't find anything that would
help her.

Nina was standing in the front hall, unsure what to do
next, when the phone rang. It made her jump inside her
skin. At first she ignored it, but it rang and rang and didn't
stop. She decided to pick it up and listen, but say nothing.
And she did so, but whoever was on the other end was
silent too, and listening. Nina could hear breathing, not
deep, but regular and even; electronic puffs and sniffs that
came to her ear with that CD clarity that every sound
seemed to have since she had committed her criminal act.
Nothing was said.

Nina hung up. The plastic phone glistened with the sweat
of her palm.

Nina returned to the mud room, found a broom and a
dustpan, swept up the glass, dumped it in a bag under the
sink that contained a Toblerone wrapper and an empty
can of caffeine-free Diet Coke. Then she went to the hall
and called Hal Palmeteer's office.

"Dr. Palmeteer's office," answered the receptionist.

"There's a broken window at Laura Bain's house," Nina
said. "Tell Dr. Palmeteer to have it fixed."

"What?" said the receptionist. "Who is this?"

Nina hung up. She went out the front door, walked half
a block to her car, past a boy on a skateboard and two
girls carrying schoolbooks and cracking gum, all of whom
were probably anticipating cocoa, got into the car and
drove to the airport. No one clapped the cuffs on her, no
sirens tried to terrorize her, no one looked at her twice.
Crime was easy. It just didn't pay.

Nina caught a shuttle full of business people at the end
of their day. Some kept working, some had a few drinks,
some simply sat looking worried. Nina had a few drinks.
Too many, perhaps.

Jules the doorman had been drinking too. Nina found him
slouched on a chair in the lobby with an empty pint in his

lap. She banged at the door until his eyes flickered open; he pushed himself up and staggered over, letting her in. His jacket was stained and his breath smelled of vomit. He mumbled something she didn't understand.

"You'd better get it together, Jules," Nina said, "or the management's going to do something."

Jules's mouth opened and closed a few times, like a guppy gasping on the floor beside its aquarium. "I like you Mish Kishener," he said. "You're nishe to me. But manishmen can shove it upitsh ash."

Nina rode the elevator to her floor. She walked down the hall, turned the key, entered her apartment. She switched on the lights and went into the kitchen for a glass of water.

She had almost finished drinking it when she noticed her little electronic typewriter on the kitchen table. She didn't remember leaving it there. Moving closer, she saw there was a sheet of paper in it. She pulled it out, a sheet of Kitchener and Best letterhead, and read:

> I cannot live without my precious baby. Please,
> please don't think too badly of me.

At the bottom of the page was her signature, written in blue ink. "Nina Kitchener," it said, each letter shaped exactly as she always shaped it. Nina was still staring at the sheet of paper when she smelled pesticide. She turned in time to see a big liver-spotted hand right in front of her. Then her whole face was covered: eyes, nose, mouth. She started struggling, at the same time smelling another smell that drowned out the pesticide, a new smell that reminded her of high school chemistry classes.

Then all her senses shut down.

|MATT|

| 26 |

Did the inhabitants of North Andros like Hew Aikenfield, baronet? Matthias would have said so, but they didn't attend his funeral in great numbers: not Constable Welles, not Moxie, not people who had known him all their lives. Maybe it was just the weather: a raw December morning, with a northeast wind blowing dark clouds across the sky.

Reverend Christie's Church of Eternal Life stood on one side of the Conchtown road, a dirt track leading south out of Blufftown. On the other side was the Happy Times Bar. The bar was a small shack, made of tar paper and scavenged bits of lumber; the church, not much bigger, was a concrete block structure, painted turquoise. The bar was turquoise too: there had been a few cans of paint left over. Both buildings were owned by Reverend Christie.

Behind the church, and predating it, the bar and all the other buildings in Blufftown—only the well near the flame tree in the center of the village was older—lay the graveyard. There Reverend Christie supervised the lowering of Hew into a hole—shallow because the limestone foundation of the island reached close to the surface—dug between a grave marked BABY PINDER and another too eroded to read. Then Reverend Christie lifted his eyes to the clouds and addressed God. Perhaps taking a global view and realizing he had to compete with all the other funerals going on in the world at that moment, Reverend Christie spoke in a loud voice, almost a bellow.

"Thank you, Lord, for giving us the gift of death," he said. No one was shocked by this introduction: it was the reverend's standard oration. He went on to explain that death was the sweet release from the hardship of life and thus a sign of divine mercy; some in the little group of listeners appeared to agree, nodding and murmuring in the pauses he left for nodding and murmuring. But Hew himself served only as a starting point and Matthias soon found his attention weakening.

After the speech, a boy ran an extension cord into the church and returned with Reverend Christie's amp. The reverend plugged in his box-shaped Bo Diddley model and accompanied the singing of "Ain't Givin' Up, No Way." Reverend Christie played well, not as subtly and imaginatively as Krio, but well enough to incite a few restrained dance movements in the graveyard. Death, whether good or bad, slipped into the background. The mourners segued into "Can't Nobody Do Me Like Jesus" and went out on "Amazing Grace."

The reverend walked over to Matthias and shook his hand. "We should have sung 'La Vie en Rose,' " Matthias said.

"How does that one go?"

"It's not really a hymn."

"Then I'm afraid it's unsuitable. This is sacred ground." Reverend Christie reached into his pocket and produced a bill. "Reverend Thomas Christie, B.A., Enterprises," it said, "All-inclusive burial and service—$200.00."

Matthias, reading it, felt the reverend's eyes on him, perhaps calculating whether haggling would ensue. Matthias handed over the cash.

"Bless you," said Reverend Christie.

Matthias walked around the church to the road. Moxie, wearing a wool tuque with a Boston Bruins logo, was waiting for him. He nodded at the Happy Times Bar.

Matthias crossed the street, stepped over hunks of corroded car parts and peered through the glassless window of the Happy Times Bar. The bar had a dirt floor, a few barrels for sitting, and a big piece of plywood resting on two sawhorses for drinking. A chicken pecked at the dirt, a one-eyed cousin of Reverend Christie watched over the half-dozen bottles on a warped shelf, and Nottage sat on one of the barrels, his hand around a greasy glass and his head on the plywood. Matthias walked in.

Reverend Christie's cousin followed his progress with his good eye; there was no other eye, just an empty socket covered by a concave eyelid. Reverend Christie's cousin said nothing. White men didn't enter the Happy Times Bar; neither did Reverend Christie or any other respectable villager.

Matthias sat on a barrel next to Nottage. "I'll have a beer," he said.

"No beer," said the one-eyed man. "Rum."

"Rum, then," said Matthias.

Nottage spoke without lifting his head. "Rum," he said, in his deep, frayed voice. Matthias felt it vibrating in the plywood.

Reverend Christie's cousin reached for a bottle behind the bar. It had brown liquid on the inside and no label on the outside. He took a small, dusty glass off the shelf, dumped out the dead fly inside and set the glass before Matthias. He filled it to the brim and topped up Nottage's. Nottage made no attempt to drink, but his hand remained wrapped around the glass.

"They just buried Sir Hew," Matthias said.

No one said anything.

"Did you know he was dead, Nottage?"

Nottage didn't reply, but his hand tightened on the glass. Reverend Christie's cousin stood motionless behind the bar, looking at nothing.

"Let's go outside, Nottage," Matthias said.

Nottage didn't move. Matthias laid a hand on his shoulder. Nottage went rigid under his touch. Matthias removed his hand. Time passed, silent except for the sounds of the chicken scratching and pecking in the dirt. Then Nottage rose, quite abruptly, and walked outside without a misstep, leaving his glass on the bar. Matthias followed.

Nottage started down the Conchtown road. Matthias had never seen him move so fast—for a few seconds he came close to running. Soon he had passed the last mean dwelling; the road narrowed and jack pines closed in on both sides. Nottage, like an animal at the edge of its territory, slowed down and finally stopped. Matthias stopped a few feet behind him. It was quiet: just the wind in the sparse branches of the trees, the rustling of crabs in the brush and, almost inaudible, the sea.

"They're saying Hew fell," Matthias said, "but he jumped, didn't he?"

Nottage turned to him. His eyes were red; he needed a shave, a shower, a different personal history. He looked directly at Matthias for a moment; a red gaze that quickly shifted away.

"Did you see it happen?" Matthias asked.

Nottage didn't reply.

"You were on the Bluff. There was a moon."

Nottage, his eyes on the ground, said, "I don' know nothin'."

"I don't believe you."

Nottage's head came up. He took a wild swing at Matthias. Nottage's body, old and ruined, still possessed the raw power that came not from gyms but from a lifetime of hard outdoor labor. Matthias, too surprised to move, felt the blow land on his shoulder, heavy enough to hurt. Nottage seemed surprised too: he stared at his fist, as though unsure it had done what it had. Then he dropped it to his side, hung his head and spoke, but too quietly for Matthias to hear.

"I can't hear you, Nottage."

Nottage raised his voice. "Hit me, boss. Hit me."

"I'm not going to hit you. I just want to know what you saw on the Bluff."

Nottage shook his head.

"Look at me, Nottage." Nottage looked up, but his eyes had gone blank. Matthias had seen that blankness before: a protective blindness to white men's business. Nottage, a black citizen of a black nation, governed by black men and women freely elected by black men and women, still had that look. He had been born too soon.

"What are you hiding from me?" Matthias asked.

"Nothin'."

"Hew jumped, didn't he? But you don't want to speak badly of a dead man, is that it?"

Nottage said nothing.

"Did he say something before he died? Did you try to stop him, maybe, but too late?"

Nottage sighed, a sound that deepened into a moan. "Be a wicked place, mahn," he said.

"What do you mean?"

Nottage was silent for a long time. Then he said: "Sea on fire."

"I don't know what you're talking about."

Nottage stared down at his bare, dusty feet. His body sagged, once more incapable of punching, or any nonsubmissive movement at all.

"What sea?"

Nottage turned toward the east; shiny fragments of gray-blue, like puzzle pieces, quivered between the trees. "Where Happy sank down," Nottage answered quietly.

Matthias took a step closer. "You knew Happy Standish?"

Nottage backed away.

Matthias came no nearer. "Did you?"

Nottage nodded his head.

"When he was a boy?"

Another nod.

Matthias examined the red eyes, trying to see what hid behind them, without success. "But he wasn't in a fire, Nottage. It was a diving accident. He had bad air in his tank."

Nottage said nothing.

"Was there a fire near the compressor? Is that what you're saying?"

Nottage remained silent.

The sky darkened. A cold raindrop fell on Matthias's head, then another. "How did you know Happy Standish?" he asked.

Nottage sighed again. "I work for the family. On Two-Head."

"Doing what?"

"Garden work. Until the new man come."

"What new man?"

"Gardener man."

"What year was this?"

"I don' know. In the Duke's time."

"The Standishes let you go?"

" 'Sack Nottage,' he say."

"Who?"

"Gardener man."

Wind gusted down out of the sky, driving a fusillade of raindrops against Nottage's face. He didn't react.

"But Happy wasn't born then," Matthias said.

Nottage stared at his feet.

"How could you have known Happy if they sacked you before he was born?"

"I knows him. After." Nottage's head came up. "Where you think they get their fish, mahn?"

"You sold them fish?"

Nottage grunted.

"And that's when you saw Happy?"

"I be taking Happy in the boat. Mrs. Albury she be holding him and I row."

"You rowed from here to Two-Head?"

"No motor. Long time ago, boss."

"I'm not your boss, Nottage."

But Nottage stood still and slumping in the middle of the Conchtown road as though Matthias were indeed his boss and he was waiting to be dismissed.

"When was the last time you saw Happy Standish?"

"The night before he sank down."

"The night before he sank down? Do you mean just last year?"

"I don' know the years," Nottage said.

"Where did you see him? At the club?"

"No."

"Where?"

Nottage pointed in the direction they'd come from.

"At the Happy Times?"

"Yeah."

"He came there?"

"Yeah."

"Why?"

"To see me," Nottage replied, with something like pride in his voice.

"Why did he want to see you?"

Nottage shrugged.

"What did he say?"

"He say, 'I remember you Nottage. You teaches me to fish for grouper with a hand line and a bent nail.' "

"Is that all?"

"He shake my hand."

"And then?"

"He aks where is the fire at sea. And I tells him."

"What did you tell him?"

"Where is the fire."

"But there is no fire, Nottage."

Nottage stared at his feet; the dust on them was turning to mud.

"Did you see a real fire?" Matthias asked.

"I sees it."

"What do you mean? Now? You see it now?"

"Every night."

"Goddamn it," said Matthias, and before he knew it he had taken Nottage by the shoulders and shaken him. Nottage was a big man, but he shook. "Was this a real fire or a fire in your mind?"

Nottage didn't speak; he waited for the blow to fall. Matthias dropped his hands. "Shit, Nottage," he said. "Let's go home."

But Nottage didn't move. He opened his mouth, closed it, opened it again and said: "Real fire."

The rain fell heavily now, but Matthias hardly felt it. "When?" he asked.

"In the night."

"Every night?"

Nottage shook his head.

"What night?"

"In the Duke's time."

"Did you see it?"

He nodded.

"Where from?"

"The Bluff."

"What happened?"

"The sea got on fire. Then it be black."

"Do you mean a boat? Was there some boat on fire out there?"

Nottage shook his head.

"Did wreckage wash up?"

Nottage shook his head again.

"Did anyone else see it?"

"See what?"

"This fire."

"God."

"God?"

"The Lord He see. Send down a warning to Nottage."

"What warning?"

"Sea on fire."

"But why would God warn you? What did you do?"

Nottage hung his head and didn't reply.

Rain beat down, soaking them to the skin. Nottage kept his head down. The rain saturated his white curly hair and ran down his wrinkled brow. Then, without warning, he vomited. He didn't bend forward, he didn't move away, he simply vomited, and looked at Matthias like a sick and helpless child. Matthias put his hand on Nottage's shoulder. It went rigid again. Matthias took it away. "Let's go," he said.

They walked back into Blufftown. The rain cleaned Nottage's body. As they came to the Happy Times Bar, he slowed down, now like the territorial creature returning to home base.

"Come on," Matthias said. "Have something to eat."

But Nottage, without another look or another word, went inside. The chicken was on the bar now, headless and plucked. The two glasses of rum were still there too. Nottage downed them both. Matthias turned and headed for the dock at Zombie Bay.

The rain began falling more lightly, then not at all. Water ran down the stony roadside gullies, toward the sea. Matthias passed a boy rolling a hoop with a stick, a woman staring out the window of a concrete-block house that had been half-finished for as long as he had been at Zombie Bay, and a pregnant girl sitting in a doorway, looking at the pictures in a worn copy of *Mademoiselle*.

As Matthias came to the beach, *So What* was gliding into its slip. Brock tied up. A guest who might have been in shape long ago put down his beer and tried to help with the unloading. A tank fell in the water. Moxie, anticipating, plucked it out before the man finished saying, "Oops." A woman in a pink wet suit said: "Wrasse—is that spelled like 'Rastafarian'?"

"Aks Krio," Moxie told her.

"Is he the scary-looking one?"

Moxie busied himself with the equipment.

Matthias climbed on the deck and checked the fuel level.

"Going out?" Brock asked, heaving a tank on each shoulder.

"Yeah."

"It's lousy out there today," Brock said. "Water's all stirred up."

Matthias cranked the engines.

"Want me to come along?" Brock called out over the noise.

Matthias shook his head and cast off. He backed *So What* out of the slip, swung the bow around and hit the throttles. Arms folded across his chest, Brock watched him go.

So What cut across the chop on Zombie Bay, rounded the Angel Fingers and surged into open water. Big pointy-headed waves rolled in endless formations from the west. They bounced the little boat up and down, and hurled their torn-off tops at Matthias, soaking him. Seawater did what the rain had not: it awakened something in him— hope, purpose. And the speed of the boat and the roar of the engines gave birth to possibility. He had a week to file his appeal. He didn't have the money to pay a lawyer, but perhaps a lawyer could be found who would handle the case if the chance of winning was 100 percent, with a coun-tersuit in the future. For the first time since he walked out of Dicky Dumaurier's office, he sensed that it could be done. The two heads of Two-Head Cay appeared on the horizon. Matthias aimed the bow of *So What* at the blank space between them.

He skimmed over the top of the Tongue of the Ocean. Details appeared on Two-Head Cay, rapidly, like brush strokes on the canvas of a landscape-painting instructor on a half-hour TV show: two rocky bluffs, green and gray; a crescent beach between them, bracketed by royal palms and topped by wispy casurinas; and signs of man—a Whaler tied to a long wooden pier and glimpses of a large white façade behind the trees.

All at once, the sea changed from slate-gray to greenish-brown; the waves lost their aggression. He had reached the other side of the chasm.

Matthias pulled back the throttles and coasted toward the pier. The shield of noise fell away. He remembered that the sea had deluded him with feelings of power and possibility in the past, starting with the ride into the beach at the foot of the Sierra Maestra.

He was still thinking about that when Gene Albury came on the pier with a shotgun in his hand, barrel pointed down. There was a woman beside him, gray-haired and leather-skinned: Mrs. Albury. She was holding something. When Matthias drew nearer, he saw it was a Cabbage Patch Kid.

| 27 |

PRIVATE, said a sign posted at the end of the pier at Two-Head Cay. NO FUEL, WATER, FOOD OR PROVISIONS AVAILABLE. ABSOLUTELY NO TRESPASSING.

Matthias cut the engines and drifted in. He wound a few figure eights around a cleat at the end of the pier, tied off the line with a half-hitch and hopped up on the sun-bleached boards. Gene Albury and his wife hadn't moved. They watched him from the other end of the pier. Matthias had met them before, once at a fueling stopover in Chub Cay, once at the Conchtown regatta, where Albury raced his cigarette boat, but he didn't see any recognition in their eyes. He explained who he was.

"I know who you are," Albury said. He spoke softly, his speech slightly musical, slightly drawling, slightly burring: the white Bahamian accent, inherited from his United Empire Loyalist forebears. The physical type too had been preserved: Gene Albury was short, trim, pale-eyed. Mrs. Albury closely resembled him. Her skin, like his, had been roughened by a lifetime under the sun; her hair, like his, was gray, dried-out, wispy. They could have passed for siblings and probably were cousins of some sort, thought Matthias: the gene pool was small, and inhabitants of the old white Bahamian settlements on cays like Spanish Wells, Harbour Island and Man o' War seldom married outside it.

"I'd like to talk to you, Mr. Albury," Matthias said.

"What about?" asked Albury.

"Dr. Standish."

The woman shook her head, a movement so fleeting it was almost imperceptible. Albury was looking at Matthias, but he must have noticed it because he said: "Go on up, Betty. I'll not be long."

Mrs. Albury turned to her husband. They exchanged a glance that meant nothing to Matthias. Mrs. Albury walked away, dropping the doll in a trash barrel at the foot of the pier. Gene Albury stayed where he was. "I'm listening," he said. A man with a twelve gauge in his hands could take that risk.

"I'm trying to learn the circumstances of Dr. Standish's death," Matthias told him. "Hew Aikenfield said you could help me."

"I had no use for Hew Aikenfield."

"You've heard the news."

Albury licked his lips. "I heard."

"He said you knew Dr. Standish."

Albury nodded.

"He told me Standish drowned in the blue hole behind my place."

"It was not your place then," Albury replied in his soft voice.

"That changes everything."

Albury's brow furrowed. "What's that?"

"You're absolutely right, Mr. Albury. I suppose it belonged to Señor Perez in those days."

"No, sir," Albury said. "This was before the spic. There was nothing there, belonging to nobody."

"What year are you talking about, exactly?"

"I couldn't say," Albury answered, taking no time to think about it.

"But you can say it was before Señor Perez built the club."

"I told you that already."

"Where were you when it happened, Mr. Albury?"

"When what happened?"

"When Dr. Standish drowned in the blue hole. He did drown in the blue hole, didn't he?"

Albury squinted at him. "You the one with the bad air, right?"

"That was never proven. Not to my satisfaction."

Albury ignored him. "The one that got Happy Standish hurt. And now you're coming here to me that knew him from a boy and asking questions."

"I'm asking for your help, Mr. Albury. I take it you liked Happy Standish. Supposing what happened to him wasn't an accident. Wouldn't you want to find out what went on?"

Albury squinted a little more; his eyes narrowed to razor-edges of blue. "What are you getting at?"

The question forced him to put it into words: he couldn't believe that Hiram Standish's drowning in the blue hole and the near drowning of his son on the Andros drop-off was a coincidence. But Matthias didn't utter the words aloud. He had no facts, no explanatory theory, and no liking for the way Albury had spoken of Hew or of Cesarito's father. So he just said, "I'm not getting at anything specific. I'm just trying to find out about Dr. Standish's death."

Albury's index finger stroked the walnut stock of his twelve gauge. It was a fine old Parker side-by-side; Stepdaddy Number Two had liquidated entire flocks of ducks and geese with one just like it. "I can't help you on that, sir," Albury said.

"Weren't you around at the time?"

Albury's finger kept rubbing the gun. "I said I can't help you."

"What about Mrs. Albury?"

"Mrs. Albury?" The gun barrel came up a little, as if on its own. Albury pointed it back down.

"Maybe she remembers."

"No," said Albury. "She don't."

Matthias stood on the pier, silent. He saw the blue slits of Albury's eyes, heard waves slapping the pilings, smelled the sea, but could think of nothing useful to say to Gene Albury. Then he saw Albury's eyes focus on something in the distance. He turned.

A boat was approaching from the northwest. It was moving very fast, throwing up a rooster tail as tall as a waterspout. The boat grew, pushing forward a wave of engine noise, taking on shape and color: Albury's red and black cigarette. Matthias glanced at Albury. He was chewing his lip.

The driver came in over the reef, swung the boat in a

wide crescent, cut the engines and glided toward the side
of the pier, bow facing the sea. The cigarette stopped dead,
half a foot from the pilings and perfectly parallel to the
pier: a neat maneuver. The driver, who wore goggles, a
red jumpsuit and a red helmet, tossed a line to Albury and
stepped lightly onto the pier.

"Visitors, Mr. Albury?" she said, removing the helmet
and the goggles. She shook out her long, silvery hair.

It was beautiful hair, thick and almost glowing; it de-
stabilized the equation between old and gray. The woman's
age was impossible to guess: she had clear, pale, unlined
skin, delicate bones, and the body under the jumpsuit
seemed trim. Only her blue eyes, deep-set and watchful,
showed that she was no longer thirty-five; she might have
been twice that, Matthias thought, as she turned to him,
and he caught the full force of her look.

"The fellow from Zombie Bay," Albury explained.

The woman studied him for a moment more, then said:
"Mr. Matthias, isn't it?"

"That's right," Matthias said. "Have we met?"

The woman smiled, but not in a friendly way: a smile
at the least ironical, at most full of scorn. "Only through
legal representatives," the woman replied. "I am Inge
Standish," she said, and added: "Happy's—Hiram Junior's mother."

Matthias thought of saying he was sorry. But that might
have implied guilt, and he didn't feel guilty. So he said
nothing.

Inge Standish's deep-set eyes watched his face, as though
observing this thought process. "What is it you want, Mr.
Matthias?" she asked.

Before Matthias could reply, Albury said, "He's asking
questions."

"What questions, Mr. Matthias?"

"I've recently learned that your husband drowned on
what is now my property. I'd like to know the circumstances."

That brought the smile again: complex and unsettling,
like a cruel and elaborately designed assault weapon from
an earlier age. "How morbid," said Inge Standish. "Do
you have some special interest in our little family trage-
dies?"

"It's not like that, Mrs. Standish. I'm trying to piece

things together. There's a lot I still don't understand about your son's accident."

"I thought the court was rather clear on that subject," Inge Standish said.

"Hitler was clear," Matthias responded, to his own surprise: he didn't like when people used Hitler as a debating tool, but it was too late to stop. "That didn't make him right."

He waited for some sign of anger, but none came. Inge Standish looked puzzled instead. "Hitler?" she said.

"For example," Matthias said.

"Oh, of course," said Inge Standish. "Touché." She unzipped a pocket in her jumpsuit, took out three or four rings and placed them one by one on her fingers: diamonds, rubies and sapphires, mounted in settings too big for practical seamanship. "But I still fail to see how my husband's death concerns you. It was so long ago, Mr. Matthias. Perhaps you weren't even born then."

"That depends when it happened."

Inge Standish looked across the Tongue of the Ocean. Her eyes absorbed the light of the sea and the sky, became two deep-set pools of slate gray. "Nineteen fifty-three," she said.

"Then the answer's yes."

"But surely you had no interest in my family at that time? You're not from here, are you?"

"No."

"Then why now?"

Matthias considered several responses. "Hew Aikenfield gave me the idea."

"Are you a friend of his?" Her thin lips turned up like quotation marks around the word "friend."

"I was. Hew was buried this morning."

"I didn't know. I've just arrived, as you can see."

"From Florida?"

"Indirectly. I don't think I've seen Hew in thirty years."

"Longer than that, according to him."

"You've been discussing me with Hew Aikenfield?"

"Your name came up."

"I suppose I should be flattered. And was it then that he suggested you come here about my husband?"

"That's right. It was the night he died." There was a long silence. Inge Standish watched a gull swoop down from the sky, change its mind just before hitting the water and soar away. Albury fingered his shotgun.

"He fell off his terrace," Matthias added, when it appeared no one else was going to say anything.

"How dreadful," said Inge Standish. She looked at Albury, standing at the other end of the pier. "Do put down that gun, Mr. Albury. And please see to the unloading of the boat. I'll take Mr. Matthias up to the house."

"To the house, ma'am?"

"Certainly. I'll answer his questions. Hew Aikenfield was an old dear."

Albury left the pier and entered a nearby shed. A moment later, two men came down a path, carrying a wooden baby crib wrapped in plastic. They went into the shed too. Albury returned without the shotgun. The two men came with him. They were in their thirties, stocky, with hair worn in the style of Elvis, 1956, but blond.

"Do you know Mr. Albury's sons, Mr. Matthias?" said Inge Standish. "Billy and Bobby."

Matthias nodded. Billy and Bobby gave no sign of acknowledgment. The Alburys climbed down into the cigarette, began unloading suitcases, groceries, a knitting basket.

"Come along, Mr. Matthias," said Inge Standish.

Matthias followed her off the pier. They walked up a path bordered with pink and white hibiscus. Glancing into the shed as they went by, Matthias saw Albury's shotgun, locked in a rack with other guns, and the plastic-wrapped crib standing against the back wall, beside an old air compressor.

"Do you do much diving, Mrs. Standish?" he asked.

"Diving?" she replied, walking ahead of him.

"Scuba."

Inge Standish's back stiffened, but she kept moving. "I'm never here, Mr. Matthias. And the ocean has lost its appeal."

Matthias, judging from the way she handled the cigarette, didn't believe that, but he kept the thought to himself. The path went by a small house, past a couple of cottages, then bent inland, rounded a hill and cut through a formal garden. The garden had a pink marble pool in the center, three or four feet deep and filled with salt water. Matthias knew that from the fish swimming in it—sergeant

majors, blue tangs, royal grammas—and from the healthy
brain coral they never stopped worrying at. Topiary bushes
circled the pool, clipped in an alternating pattern of cylindrical and pear shapes; beyond them well-weeded plots of
oleander, red, white and pink, extended to a ring of fruit
trees, orange, soursop and lime.

"I haven't seen a garden like this anywhere in the out
islands," Matthias said. "Do the Alburys manage it all by
themselves?"

"It's not difficult. Everything was planted a long time
ago."

"By Nottage?" Matthias asked, trying to picture a young
Nottage somehow capable of that.

Inge Standish halted by the marble pool and looked at
him. "Mr. Nottage is still alive?" she said.

"Yes. You seem surprised."

"He drank, if I remember. I wouldn't have thought his
life expectancy very long, that's all." She watched Matthias's face for a moment, then turned and walked on.
"Mr. Nottage had nothing to do with the garden," she said
over her shoulder.

The main house loomed ahead. Matthias hadn't seen
anything like it either, in the out islands or anywhere else.
It was enormous, baroque: an overwrought mass of pe-
diments, columns, statuary and lots of features Matthias
couldn't name. Coming closer, he saw that the windows
were boarded up, the façade was crumbling at the edges
and marred by several long cracks, and some of the statues
had broken. Chunks of lost arms and heads lay in the
Bermuda grass like classical debris in a nineteenth-century
poem. Inge Standish seemed to notice none of this. She
mounted the broad marble stairs like a chateleine and
pushed open the heavy wooden door.

"Come in," she said.

Matthias followed her inside. It was dark; for a few
seconds he could see nothing at all. Then his pupils widened and he found himself standing in an entrance hall
that seemed as big as a hotel lobby. The only light came
through the half-open doorway, but it was enough for Matthias to see lots of furniture, all covered with white drop
cloths; a staircase rising into the shadows and a chandelier
dangling down; oil paintings on the walls. The shaft of
daylight cut across one of the paintings, illuminating the

bottom two-thirds, leaving the rest hidden. Matthias could make out two pale hands, a dark suit jacket, a weak chin. He remembered that chin from Hew's scrapbook.

"Sit down, Mr. Matthias."

There was a card table near the door, with two folding chairs. Inge Standish took one, Matthias the other. On the table rested a crystal glass with a fresh white rose inside, and a Horizon radiophone. Inge Standish pinched the bridge of her nose for a second; in that second she looked quite old. Then she shook her silver hair and the years fell away.

"I should hate you, Mr. Matthias. But for some reason, I don't."

"Maybe you realize I had nothing to do with what happened to your son."

"It's not that." She sighed. "Of course, I know you had nothing to do with it personally."

"Then why did you sue me?"

Her voice hardened. "You had everything to do with it legally."

Matthias looked at her, saying nothing. She looked back at him for a while, then turned away. "No," she said. "I don't hate you." There was a long pause. "I'm tired, Mr. Matthias. Tell me why you've come here."

"I already told you," Matthias said.

"To find out about my husband's death. But why?"

"Doesn't it strike you as odd that one drowned and the other almost drowned less than a quarter of a mile from each other?"

" 'Odd' wouldn't be the word I would choose, Mr. Matthias. I haven't your gift for detachment."

"Do you think I feel detached from all of this?"

"I wouldn't know, Mr. Matthias. I don't know you. And I'm not sure your feelings are what matter, in the circumstances."

A long-tailed rat ran through the shaft of light and disappeared in the darkness; Matthias could hear its clawed feet on the marble long after it was out of sight. Inge Standish appeared not to notice. Matthias waited for her to continue, waited for her to say that he had a lot of nerve to talk to her about his feelings while her son lay in a coma caused by his negligence. But that's not what Inge Standish said. She glanced for a moment in the direction of the oil

portrait, seemed about to smile and said: "Let me put your
mind at ease, Mr. Matthias. There is really nothing odd,
not in the sense that you mean. They both loved the sea,
loved this scuba diving you speak of. A dangerous sport,
even when the proper precautions are taken."

"Who are you talking about, Mrs. Standish?"

Her eyes narrowed. "My husband, of course. And my
son."

"Your son loved the sea?"

"Is it so surprising? He spent his boyhood here. He could
swim like a dolphin."

"And he loved scuba diving?"

"Very much. The coral reefs, the tropical fish. I'm sure
you know all about it. He was an expert."

"Your husband too?"

Inge Standish nodded. "He had one of the first Aqua-
lungs in the Bahamas."

"Do you mean he was wearing it when he drowned in
the blue hole?"

"That's correct. Is there anything strange about that?"

"What was he doing in there?"

"He was curious about the blue holes. Aren't they of
some scientific interest?"

"Yes. But nothing was known about them at that time."

"He wanted to find out. He was a scientist, after all."

"I thought he was a doctor."

"That's true. But research was his first love."

"What kind of research?"

"Human fertility."

"I don't see what that has to do with blue holes."

Inge Standish's voice rose: "I'm describing his mentality,
his character." More softly, she added, "He was a man of
science, as I said."

"What happened to him in the blue hole?"

"I believe he ran out of air, Mr. Matthias."

"What makes you think that?"

"His Aqualung was empty."

"Who brought him up?"

"Brought him up?"

"To the surface."

"No one. He—the body came up when the blue hole
. . . boiled. Is that what they do?"

"Some of them. Sometimes." No heat was involved; the

bubbles were caused by a tidal surge. But Matthias didn't get into that. Instead he asked: "Was he diving alone?"

"Yes."

"That doesn't sound very scientific."

"What do you mean?"

"Scientists are supposed to be careful. Careful people don't dive alone."

"It was a long time ago. Perhaps he had a partner."

"Who might that have been?"

"I have no idea."

"Was it Nottage?"

"Certainly not."

Matthias looked into her eyes. They had darkened in the dark room; he could see nothing in them. "So the body came to the surface?"

"The body did," Inge Standish said. "Is there anything else, Mr. Matthias?"

Matthias thought of asking her to withdraw the suit and rejected the idea with disgust. She smiled: maybe she had read his mind. "No," he said.

"Then perhaps I'll walk you—"

The radiophone crackled. There was something wrong with the speaker. A man's voice, obscured by crackling and a high-pitched whine, said: "Two-Head, calling Two-Head. Come in, Ge—"

Inge Standish switched it off. Her eyes shifted fleetingly toward him. Then she stood up. "If you're ready, Mr. Matthias."

He followed her out the door, through the garden, past the pool, down the path. Through a gap in the hibiscus, he saw a tiny graveyard, enclosed by a white picket fence. A few weathered gravestones were bunched together in the middle. In one corner stood another stone, all by itself: small, white and new, so new there was nothing engraved on it.

Matthias and Inge Standish walked side by side onto the dock. He could smell her perfume and, very faintly, her sweat. Everyone sweated, of course; he just hadn't expected it from her.

The cigarette had been unloaded and scrubbed down. Matthias climbed down on the deck of *So What*. The clouds were lower and darker than before; some trailed frayed sheets of vapor. "We're going to have nasty weather,"

Inge Standish said. She untied the line and held it until he started the engines. "Goodbye, Mr. Matthias." She tossed him the line with a gesture that made him think of someone flipping change to a beggar.

Matthias turned the boat toward Andros. Rain began falling again, hard and cold, but he didn't feel it. He had a lot to think about.

First, he knew Inge Standish had been telling him the truth when she said she didn't hate him. But why didn't she? She might have shown anger and bitterness; she might have talked much more about the lawsuit; she might even have ordered him off the island. But she had done none of those things.

Second, Inge Standish had told him that Happy swam like a dolphin and was an expert diver. But Wendell Minns and Hew had both said he was afraid of the water, and Minns had told him that he was a novice diver, whose experience totaled an hour and a half in a swimming pool.

Third, the voice on the radiophone, so quickly switched off, had been Brock McGillivray's.

|28|

Matthias came into the dock fast, tied up and ran along the crushed-shell path to the bar. Except for Chick on his perch, the room was empty. Lunch time. The bird's head swiveled as Matthias hurried behind the bar and through the door to the kitchen.

Krio was bent over a butcher block, slowly and carefully chopping onions, so slowly and carefully that he must be stoned, Matthias thought; a perception he had no time to deal with. It flashed quickly through his mind and out. "Where's Brock?" he said.

"Gone," Krio replied.

"Gone where?"

Krio looked up. Tears streamed down his face. "Employment interview."

"Where?"

"In the land of the free," Krio answered. "And the home of the brave." Then he looked more closely at Matthias and said: "What's happening?"

"When did he go?"

"Soon," said Krio, closing one eye like a surveyor and lining up an onion.

"Soon?"

Krio nodded. "Moxie be carrying him to the airport." He made a preliminary incision.

Matthias checked his watch: 12:25. There was one scheduled flight a day, leaving for Nassau at a quarter to one.

He ran out to the circular drive in front of the club. Zombie Bay had two Jeeps and a van. One of the Jeeps was still waiting for a carburetor to arrive from Nassau and the other was gone. Matthias jumped into the van. The key was in the ignition. Matthias turned it and sped off down the Conchtown road.

The airport—a wind sock, a fifteen-hundred-foot dirt strip and a one-room hut with a ticket counter and a baggage scale—was four miles away. Matthias put the pedal to the floor and kept it there the whole way. He skidded to a stop in front of the hut and beside his other Jeep at 12:33. He hurried inside.

There were two people in the hut, Moxie and the Bahamasair agent. They were kissing across the top of the ticket counter.

"Where's Brock?" Matthias said.

"Oh," said the ticket agent, stepping back in embarrassment.

"Where is Brock?"

The agent raised her finger to the sky. Matthias went out on the runway just in time to see the Hawker-Siddeley 748 vanishing into the rain clouds. 12:34. He did not see any other planes around, no rich island-hopping Americans, no charters in for the day, no one to take him to Nassau. He walked back inside. The ticket agent was alone now, straightening piles of forms behind the counter.

"I've got twelve thirty-five," Matthias said.

The agent frowned at her watch. "We took off a little bit early today, Mr. Matthias. Just a little teeny bit early."

It wasn't unusual. Sometimes the pilot got tired of waiting, sometimes he got hungry for a hot meal in Nassau, sometimes the agent told him she didn't think anyone else was coming. Sometimes the plane didn't arrive at all.

Matthias went outside. Moxie was standing by the van, kicking pebbles. "Where's his job interview?" Matthias asked.

"Florida," Moxie replied, looking at the dirt.

"That's it? Florida?"

"Florida, that's what he say."

"Did he say anything else?"

Moxie shook his head. "He was down on the boat, then he come up and say, 'Carry me to the airport, Mox.' "

"What boat?"

"*Two Drink.*"

Matthias thought: It's the only boat with a radiophone. "Did you go right to the airport?"

"No, mahn. We stop first by the fish camp for his things."

"What things?"

"Suitcase," said Moxie. "Stuff." He kicked at a pebble, then another.

"What is it, Mox?"

Moxie looked up and briefly met Matthias's gaze. In a low voice, perhaps in case the agent might hear, he said, "Brock say we all better be looking for a job now."

"Brock's wrong," Matthias told him. He got into the van and drove away. He regretted slamming the door almost at once.

Matthias drove north, back toward Blufftown. After three miles, he turned onto a rutted track and drove through woods of scrub pine that gave way to sea-grapes and ended at a rocky outcrop: Turtle Point, the southern tip of Zombie Bay. Four wooden cabins stood on the point, sheltered by a few small palms bent backwards by the prevailing wind. This was the fish camp, owned by the club, but much older than the rest of it. People said that long ago Hemingway had stayed at the fish camp, but no one recalled actually seeing him themselves. Neither did anyone know who had painted the signs, now badly faded, over the doors of each cabin: Nick Adams, Lady Brett, Robert Jordan, The Old Man. All were unoccupied now, except The Old Man. Brock lived there; it was the biggest, and the only one with running water.

The door to The Old Man was ajar. Matthias pushed it open with his foot and went inside. There were two rooms: a bedroom, with a bed, a chest of drawers, a poster of Ayer's Rock taped to the wall, a regulator hanging on a nail; and a bathroom, the size of a closet, with a toilet and a sink. The shower was outside.

Matthias pulled out all the drawers and dumped them on the floor. He found five T-shirts, three Speedos, five pairs of cotton shorts, a sweater, a rain jacket, a pair of jeans, a wet suit top. He looked under the unmade bed, saw nothing. Then he stripped off the sheets, gritty with sand, just like his. He lifted the mattress and toppled it onto the floor. Beneath it lay rusty springs on a rusty bed frame. A piece of paper was caught in the springs.

It was a bill from the Plaza Hotel in New York, marked "Paid." Someone named B. Muller had stayed there on the twenty-eighth, twenty-ninth and thirtieth of July of last year, spending $1366.02 including laundry, room service and tax. Matthias put it in his pocket.

He went into the bathroom. A damp towel with the ZB logo lay on the floor. He picked it up; there was nothing underneath. A can of shaving cream was set on the edge of the sink. Matthias pressed the button, releasing a hiss of aerosol. He saw a broken comb, a small cake of soap dissolving in its dish, a few long blond hairs in the sink and speckles of toothpaste on the mirror. The face in it was dark and brutal.

He got a machete from the van, sliced open the mattress and poked through the stuffing inside, yanked it out, dropped it all around him. The stuffing felt slightly moist and smelled of mildew, but concealed nothing.

Matthias stood motionless in the middle of the cabin for a while. Then he wheeled around and ripped the poster of Ayer's Rock off the wall. There was nothing behind it but the cheap pine boards, crudely finished, carelessly painted.

Matthias returned to the van and came back with a crowbar. He began prying up the floorboards. He was working quickly now, and roughly. The boards cracked and splintered; sweat dripped off his face and onto the two-by-fours of the foundation.

He went into the bathroom, jerked the sink off the wall, kicked the toilet to pieces, smashed the mirror with the crowbar. He broke up the chest of drawers, dismantled the bed frame, drove one of the iron bars at the walls like a battering ram, bashing holes in several places. The rain came in.

But he found nothing.

Matthias walked outside. The rain washed away his sweat and cooled him down. He became aware of the iron bar in his hand, and dropped it. Then he searched the other cabins. This time he didn't wreck anything, hardly touched anything, and found nothing.

He went outside, down to the end of Turtle Point, and

sat on a rise overlooking the rocks below. The tide was
ebbing, leaving behind strings of green and brown seaweed, a few slowly pulsing jellyfish, a bald truck tire, and
exposing glossy black sea urchins in tidal pools. And, in
a crevice at the edge of the receding wave, something else,
something black and square; a shingle, maybe, or a boat
cushion. Or a book.

Matthias scrambled down the rise and ran across the
mossy rocks. He squatted beside the crevice. What lay in
it wasn't a shingle or a boat cushion. It was a book, a black
leather-bound book, like the one he'd seen at Hew's, except that the leather was soaked, salt-stained, scratched.
He picked it up and opened it to the first page.

A small snapshot of the young Hew posing beside a
Greek column was stuck loosely to the black paper. Matthias didn't remember seeing it in the scrapbook Hew had
shown him, but he hadn't looked at it for more than a few
seconds before the wind blew it away, leaving a dark rec-
tangle on the page. There were other rectangles like it.
Matthias turned the page. It came apart in his hands.

He closed the book and carried it up the rise to the van.
Sitting on the front seat, out of the wind and rain, he reopened the book and examined it, separating the pages
slowly and carefully. On most of them he found only the
dark rectangles, or bumpy spots of hardened glue. But in
the middle pages, where the sea had done the least damage, there were a few pictures of Hew, all new to him:
Hew on a horse, Hew and a mustached man playing back-
gammon, Hew wearing a carabinieri helmet. He also found
yellowed newspaper clippings, cut from society pages of
long ago and describing the fun times of people he had
never heard of.

There was one exception: a picture taken from the *Nassau Tribune*, March 18, 1936. The photograph showed a
man and a woman standing at the foot of a gangplank.
The focus hadn't been sharp in the first place and was
further blurred by the sea; Matthias might not have been
able to identify the man or the woman without the help
of the caption: "Dr. Hiram Standish returned from his
studies in Europe last week with his new bride Inge, daughter of Herr Dr. and the late Frau Dr. Wilhelm von
Trautschke of Heidelberg."

Matthias remembered Dr. von Trautschke from the 1934

photograph in Hew's other scrapbook. He was the tall
aristocrat in the middle. Standish had stood on one side,
and a heavy-set man on the other. Dr. Miller?

Dr. Müller.

Matthias switched on the overhead light and stared at
the watery faces of the young couple. They both wore hats.
Inge's fair hair touched her shoulders. Standish seemed to
be smiling. Inge didn't. Was it his imagination or did this
old and damaged picture of her somehow still project an
image of beauty? Matthias peered more closely, until all
he saw was the newsprint on the other side of her face.

He closed the scrapbook and laid it on the seat beside
him. Then he started the van and drove up the rutted track
to the road to Zombie Bay.

An hour later, Matthias stood at the edge of the blue hole
in the woods behind the club. It was one of many blue
holes on Andros and in the sandy shallows just offshore.
In the ice age, when the sea level was much lower, they
formed as caves in the porous limestone; as the ice melted,
the sea rose and filled them. Some of the island fishermen
believed, or said they believed, that tentacled monsters
called luscas lurked in the holes, waiting to grab them.
Matthias didn't believe in luscas, but he didn't like diving
in the blue holes either. Blue hole diving meant equipment:
tanks, gauges, regulators, lights, buoyancy compensators,
weights—and safety lines, if you wanted to do it right.
And he didn't like diving with all that strapped to his body.
In fact, he didn't like scuba diving. The difference between
scuba diving and free diving was the difference between a
tourist and a traveler.

Matthias began donning the gear. He wasn't really doing
it right—he had no BC, no weights, no safety lines—but
he had been in the blue hole once or twice before and
remembered nothing unusual. The rain had stopped and
the surface of the water, sheltered by trees from the wind,
was smooth, and under the dark sky, black instead of blue.
The hole was almost perfectly round, and not very big:
Matthias could have skipped a stone across it. He spat in
his mask, swished it in the water, strapped it on. Then he
stuck the regulator in his mouth and stepped in.

Matthias sank quickly under the surface, feet first, not
moving his body at all. The inland blue holes often had a

layer of fresh water on top, less dense than the salt water
below. It was very clear water. Matthias could see gray
limestone walls all around, pocked, eroded, inset with
chambers, some as big as prayer chapels in a church. At
50 feet, he reached a layer of brine shrimp; all at once, as
though a lighting director had punched some buttons, the
water turned red and cloudy. It thickened too, slowing the
rate of his sinking, and smelled of sulphur. Matthias som-
ersaulted and kicked down. Two kicks sent him through
the red layer. He came out of it into the dense salt water
below; it resisted him. He kicked hard and swam down
into blackness.

The red layer blocked all light from above. Matthias,
holding his wrist up to his face, couldn't read the numbers
on his depth gauge, couldn't even see the depth gauge.
He switched on his torch: 65 feet. He shone the light
around him, saw the gray limestone walls; shone the light
straight down, saw nothing. Andros was like a sponge,
soaking up the sea on every flowing tide and squeezing it
out on every ebb, and the inland blue holes were deep
holes in the sponge.

Matthias swam down. He sucked in air, blew it out; the
bubbles rose up in the blackness. He descended slowly,
pointing his beam of light at the walls. In its yellow circle,
he saw nothing but the rock: no fish, no crabs, no eels,
no life of any kind.

At 90 feet, a cave appeared in the west wall. He thought
he remembered it. The opening was big enough to stand
in. Matthias swam into it and found it was as he recalled,
just a big hole, ending twenty or thirty feet away in a
concave wall. At 105 feet, he came upon a second opening,
not as big as the other. This one he didn't remember: he
had probably stopped at the first cave on his earlier dives.
Matthias shone the light inside: half the size of the first
cave, and equally empty. He checked his watch. He'd been
down for twelve minutes. He was an efficient breather,
but a man his size with a 71.2 cubic-foot capacity tank had
enough air for perhaps another fifteen at that depth, less
if he went deeper. And he wanted to avoid decompression.
He was considering those factors, hanging upside down at
105 feet, when his light illuminated a third cave mouth,
not much farther down. He descended to it, checked his
gauge: 122 feet.

Matthias stuck his head into the cave and shone his light inside. The cave mouth narrowed quickly, ending like the others in a solid, concave wall. He began to back away, getting ready for his ascent. Then he stopped, and pointed the light once more at the rear of the cave. Had the far wall really been solid?

Not quite. A pile of rock lay on the cave floor in front of the wall. Not a big pile, and Matthias couldn't think of any reason why it shouldn't be there, but he swam into the cave anyway.

The cave floor sloped slightly down and the walls and ceiling closed in until his fins struck rock with every kick. At the end, he was pulling himself along with one hand, shining the torch with the other. He felt his bubbles, squeezed by the narrow space, flowing over his skin.

Matthias reached the pile of rocks and picked one up. It was heavier than he had expected and had an odd, squared-off shape, as though it had broken off a column. Green organic matter covered the rock. He scratched some off with his fingernail and held it under the light. The rock was heavier than he had expected because it was a piece of marble. Pink marble.

Matthias picked up a few more rocks and examined them. They were all the same, squared-off chunks of pink marble. He began clearing them away, sliding them beneath his body, toward the mouth of the cave, careful not to cloud the water. But when he pulled a big one out from the bottom, the whole pile suddenly collapsed, falling toward him in a little avalanche.

Matthias jerked his torch out of the way, quickly backed up to the mouth of the cave. He felt a strong current in his face, and hung on to an outcrop in the wall to keep from being swept away. The water turned murky in the beam of the torch. Something hard struck his faceplate, almost knocking the mask off his head. Then the current slackened, although it didn't stop flowing completely, and the water cleared. Matthias swam back into the cave.

The rocks were spread out now on the cave floor. Where the pile had been, he saw a small hole in the limestone wall, about the size of a manhole cover, perhaps smaller. He moved closer to it and shone the light inside. In the yellow beam he saw a narrow tunnel, stretching to the end of the range of his torch, and beyond. He squeezed his shoulders into the entrance, pulled himself a few feet inside. His tank scraped against the rock and he halted. He gazed along the beam again, still without seeing the end of the tunnel. He began to reconsider his aversion to safety lines.

Then he noticed the debris. There was lots of it, scattered on the tunnel floor. He began picking it up and examining it under the light.

Green sea glass.

A rusty nail.

Steel-framed eyeglasses, the lenses still intact, although the frame was badly rusted. It crumbled in his hand.

Matthias checked his air. Only 550 p.s.i., and now he'd have to decompress. Time to go. Past time. He started backing out of the tunnel. At that moment, his hand brushed something, something round with a handle. He knew without looking that it was a cup or a mug, and he held on to it as he pushed himself out of the tunnel, out of the cave, and into the blue hole.

Matthias swam up out of the salt water, into the red layer, up into fresh water. He stopped at 10 feet to decompress. The water was clear and luminous. He didn't need the torch to see what he had brought up from the tunnel.

It was a ceramic coffee mug, thick and heavy. He cleaned it while breathing the rest of his air. The mug was white, with black trim around the lip. Except for a small chip on the inside of the handle, it was unmarred. The mug was a simple, cheap, utilitarian object. There was nothing interesting about it except for where he had found it and the black swastika etched on the outside.

29

Nothing.

Not blackness. Nothing.

Then her lips burned, and nothing became blackness. Her lips burned again, and black and white flashed on and off, like a balky slide projector. The slide projector flashed up an image of Jason. He was very upset, crying and shaking and saying, "Oh my God, oh my God," over and over. Nina felt sorry for him until he burned her lips again.

"No," she said, or tried to say, and turned her head away. She felt hot liquid flow down the side of her neck, onto her shoulder. First it was hot, then warm, then she couldn't feel it at all.

"Oh my God. Drink, Nina. Please, please, please."

Her eyelids closed instead, all by themselves. They weighed thousands of pounds, and no human power could keep them open. The smell of coffee came. And went.

She looked down a long tunnel and saw flashing at the end: black and white. White, black. Black, white.

Then just black again. Nothing came next. There was a big difference between blackness and nothing: the difference between life and death.

She slipped toward nothing. It was easy. It was acceptable.

But a finger forced its way into her mouth, scratched her palate, prodded the back of her throat. She tried to twist away from it, but couldn't. The finger prodded. She retched.

"Puke it up, Nina, puke it all up."

The finger prodded. She retched, and retched again.

"Good girl. Good good girl."

Hands pulled at her body. "Come on, Nina. Get up. We're going to walk."

"No," she said, or tried to say.

Thumbs, somehow strong enough to lift thousands of pounds, pushed open her eyelids. She saw Jason's eyes, wet and wide open with fright. "Come on."

"No."

"Can you talk?"

"No."

"Make a sound."

"No."

"Come on." Jason pulled her to her feet. "Walk." She slumped. He held her up. "Walk."

"No."

He dragged her across the room, back and forth.

"No, no, no."

"Open your eyes, goddamn it. Walk. Say something. Oh my God. Why, Nina, why?"

Nina vomited again, all over him.

The Birdman had gorgeous red plumage and horn-rimmed glasses. He soared over the forest primeval with a blue-wrapped bundle clutched in his talons. Nina strained to see what was in that bundle. All at once she was soaring too, until she made the mistake of taking a peek at the greenness far below and immediately began spinning down, down, down.

"Nurse. I think she's waking up."

Nina opened her eyes. She was in a hospital room: far from the forest primeval.

"Nurse. Her eyes are open."

A blinding light shone in one open eye, then the other. Nina blinked a few times. Two faces came into focus. She could see every pore, every hair, every mole on those faces. One face had coarse skin, rough and dry. That was the nurse's. The other had smooth, beautiful skin. That was Jason's.

"Nina," Jason said. "Can you hear me?"

"Yeah."

"How do you feel?"

Her mouth was dry, her tongue crusty. She tried to swallow. "Like shit," she said.

"But at least you're . . ." Jason stopped himself. He exchanged a glance with the nurse; a glance Nina didn't like.

"What is it? Is something wrong with me?" She tried to sit up, but couldn't. Her muscles were slack and feeble, that was part of the reason. The other part was that her arms and legs were strapped to the sides of the bed with leather restraints. "What the hell is going on?"

"It's just a precaution," Jason said. "In case no one was around when you woke up."

"A precaution against what?"

"Well," said Jason, not meeting her gaze, "not against, exactly, more like just to be extra-safe."

"What are you talking about, Jason?" Nina had started to raise her voice, but reined it in when she felt the rawness in her throat.

"You're on suicide watch," the nurse said. "Frankly."

Nina shouted, a wordless howl that ripped through her throat. The sound, even to her own ears, sprang from the margins of human emotion; from Bedlam and Bellevue and the mouths of those mad wanderers in the streets who sometimes had to be strapped down. That realization didn't prevent her from uttering it again. She struggled to sit up, jerking her body on the bed, to no effect.

"Oh God, Nina, please," Jason put a hand on her shoulder. She tried to writhe away from his touch. "Please," he said.

Nina stopped writhing, forced her body to be calm. She lay quietly for what seemed like a long time, but was probably no more than half a minute. Then she took a deep breath and spoke in an even tone. "Untie me."

Jason turned to the nurse. The nurse said: "I can't."

"Why not?" Nina said, starting at once to lose her even tone.

"Because, like I told you," said the nurse, perhaps tiring of her dramatics, "you're on suicide watch, that's why not. Or don't you remember downing a bottle of Seconal?"

"Seconal? I didn't take any fuck—" Nina froze in mid-sentence.

"We pumped it out of you downstairs," the nurse told her, a little more gently.

"I—I didn't . . ." It all began coming back: the note in her typewriter, her signature, the liver-spotted hand. "I didn't do it," she said.

"Denial, huh?" said the nurse.

"You must have gone to school with Hal Palmeteer."

"What's that suppose—" said the nurse.

"Nina," Jason interrupted, "what are you saying?"

"I'm saying someone must have done it to me."

"Who?"

Nina had no answer. Jason and the nurse looked at each other again. Nina could see that the nurse didn't believe her. A handy diagnosis stuck to people who made Bedlam sounds and blamed their problems on "someone": paranoia. That hurt, but nothing like seeing that Jason didn't believe her either. He was worried; he felt sorry for her; but he didn't believe her. Nina began to cry. She cried like never before in her life, a wail that accompanied bad emotions: rage, bitterness, self-pity. This wasn't weeping: there was nothing pretty about it, nothing sympathetic, nothing feminine. It was the sound of unrestrained and unmannered female pain.

"Nina, please. Please, Nina."

"Go away," Nina cried. "Just go away."

"Nina, I—"

"Go away."

"I can't stand seeing you like this."

"Go."

They went. Nina's crying became sobbing, slowly diminished to nothing except the occasional sudden and involuntary gasp, like a crying baby's.

Like a baby. That set her off again.

Later she slept.

It was a dreamless sleep until the end. Then bright red wings fluttered in her subconscious. The Birdman was coming with his little bundle. Nina opened her eyes before he arrived.

Jason was gone. So was the nurse. They had been replaced by a thickset woman with frosted hair and a fresh

suntan. The woman resembled someone Nina had seen in
the past, but seemed much more rested and relaxed than
before. It was only because they were occupying the same
positions as they had on their previous meeting—Nina
in a hospital bed, the woman on a chair beside it—that
she recognized her visitor: Detective Delgado of the
NYPD.

"You're back," Nina said.

"Yup."

"With a tan."

"Cancún."

Nina's mind began to clear. She uttered the first thought
that came to it. "You've found him?"

"Found who?"

"Who? The—my baby."

"Oh no. Nothing like that." Detective Delgado was
watching her closely. The whites of her eyes were white;
the blue bruises under them were gone. "You don't look
so good," Detective Delgado said.

"I feel fine." Nina started to sit up; the restraints held
her in place. "For Christ's sake. Why are they doing
this?"

"To protect you. And them, from liability."

"Who's going to sue them if I jump out the window?
My ghost?"

Detective Delgado didn't smile. Her face sagged a little.
Cancún was speeding away from her, like another galaxy
in an expanding universe. "It's just routine," she said.

"But I didn't try to kill myself."

"That's what your partner says you said. Which is why
I'm here."

"Jason called you?"

Detective Delgado pulled out her notebook and plucked
a ballpoint from behind her ear. "Yup," she replied, and
flipped through the pages. "He's your business partner,
right?"

"Right."

Detective Delgado's eyes moved back and forth across
the page. "Jason," she said. "Came up to your apartment
with some take-out. Got worried when you didn't answer.
Couldn't find the doorman to let him in so he broke down
the door. He found you on the floor, found the note and

the empty bottle of pills, and called nine-one-one. He also induced vomiting, which is probably why you're alive now."

"Jason broke down the door?"

Delgado turned the page. "Only knocked the lock loose, actually. But it was good enough." Delgado picked up a metal evidence case, opened it and approached the bed. She held up a sheet of Kitchener and Best stationery. Nina read: "*I cannot live without my precious baby. Please, please don't think too badly of me.*"

"Is that your letterhead?"

"Yes."

"Your signature?"

"Yes. But I didn't write that note and I didn't sign it."

"Who did?"

"I don't know."

Delgado reached into the case and took out an empty brown pharmaceutical bottle labeled "Seconal: 100 milligrams x 36." "This was on your kitchen table. Is it yours?"

"I don't know."

"Did you have a bottle of Seconal in the apartment?"

"Yes, but I only took one, and it wasn't last night."

"Then how did the other thirty-five get into your stomach?"

Nina didn't reply right away. From the hall came sounds: squeaking wheels, a man whistling "Memories." Then there was quiet, and Nina said: "Someone tried to kill me."

"Who?" asked Detective Delgado.

"I—I don't know who. I only saw his hand."

"Why do you say 'his'?"

"Because it was a big hand, old, with big veins."

"There are big women."

"Yes, but . . ."

"But what?"

"I think I saw that hand before. Earlier yesterday. He was a man, an old man. But powerful looking."

"What man?"

"The appraiser."

"What appraiser?"

"I don't remember his name. I'm not sure he even said it."

"Why do you call him an appraiser?"

"That's what he said he was."

Detective Delgado rubbed her forehead, on the spot between the eyes. When she stopped there were two vertical furrows in her forehead that hadn't been there when Nina opened her eyes, but which she remembered from their first meeting. "What was he appraising? Where was this?"

"In Dedham," Nina said.

"Dedham?"

"A suburb of Boston. It's about—"

"I know where Dedham is," Delgado interrupted. "What were you doing there?"

Nina told her about Laura Bain. She told her about Clea in her carriage in the backyard, and the Cambridge Reproductive Research Center that was now an electronics store; she told her about Laura's hopeful last conversation with her; she told her about Laura's suicide note and Laura's Seconal; she told her about the real estate agent and the appraiser in Laura's study.

Detective Delgado watched her the whole time. The whites of her eyes weren't quite so pure now. There was a long silence after Nina finished. Then she said: "Seconal?"

"Yes. That's suspicious, isn't it?"

"That's one way of putting it."

"What do you mean?"

"No one takes Seconal anymore. Not as a sleeping pill. Too easy to abuse. They've got safer drugs now."

"Therefore?"

"Your friend left a note, you left a note. She took Seconal, you took Seconal."

"I'm not sure I'm following you."

Delgado opened her mouth as though to speak, then stopped herself.

"Go on."

"I don't want to give you a hard time. You've already had a hard time." Delgado reached into her pocket and took out a pack of Marlboros. "Do you think it's all right to smoke in here?"

"I don't know. Where are we?"

Delgado laughed. "Shit," she said. "Mount Sinai." She lit a cigarette, sucked the smoke in deeply, blew it out slowly. "First smoke since I got on the plane at Kennedy. Except for some weed down there."

"You still haven't told me what you're getting at."

Delgado took another drag. "I'm just saying it would be understandable in your case."

"What would be?"

"Don't make me say it."

"Say it."

"Okay. Ever heard of copycat suicide? It happens all the time."

"But I told you," Nina said, her voice rising; she tried to rise with it, but the restraints kept her down. "I didn't take those pills. I didn't write that note."

"Nevertheless."

"Nevertheless? What is that supposed to mean?"

"It means this, Nina—you just had a baby. Your hormones are all messed up. Then this kidnapping happened, and that messed you up more. Then you had the bad luck to meet up with this woman in Boston. You fed each other's anxieties. You identified with each other. You said yourself she reminded you of you, although you sound a little more together to me. Then she did what she did and you . . . you did it too." Delgado paused, waiting for Nina to say something.

Nina said: "Have you got a penis under that trench-coat?"

Detective Delgado's face reddened. "You're in bad shape," she said. "And I feel sorry for you. But you're a bitch just the same."

"Maybe. But I don't need to hear the hormone theory from you."

Delgado took a last deep drag, then dropped her cigarette on the floor and ground it under her heel. "All right," she said. "We're a couple of assholes. Tell me about this appraiser."

"I told you," Nina said. "I don't know his name."

"Who was he working for?"

Nina thought. He had told her the name of a law firm. Or had the real estate woman mentioned the name of the firm? She tried to remember the name: Mullin, Somebody and Somebody? "I'm not sure. But there's a woman from a real estate company up there who will know. Her card's in my bag." Nina glanced around the room. "Where's my bag?"

"I don't know."

"Can you check my place?"

"Yeah," Detective Delgado said. She rose heavily: her thick legs stretched the seams of her trousers, the skin under her eyes sagged. She was her old self. "I can do that," she said.

"And can you get them to untie me? You know I'm not a suicide risk."

"How do I know that?"

"Because you know I haven't given up. And I'm not going to. Never."

Detective Delgado looked down at her. "I'll see what I can do," she said.

Delgado left. Nina thought: But what if I don't get him back, and what if I do give up? What kind of a suicide risk will I be then? Never was just a word. Nina was still thinking about that when an orderly walked in and freed her arms and legs. A man with a stethoscope around his neck watched from the doorway.

"You all right?" he said.

"I'm fine."

"Don't let me down, now."

"I'll make that my first priority," Nina told him.

He frowned, but his beeper sounded and he left within seconds, the orderly following. Nina got up. She discovered that her legs had forgotten how to walk. They still knew how to stagger. She staggered to the window and held on to the sill. Her view was a brick wall, pockmarked with environmental disease. She stared at it for a long time, unthinking, almost detached. Then it occurred to her that she was no longer following Laura Bain through the time machine. Laura's path had led to death, while she had escaped. That must mean she had a chance. No longer staggering, Nina went out into the hall, looking for food.

She was fed, dressed and sitting on the edge of the bed when Delgado returned. "Well, well," said the detective.

"You got it?" Nina said, rising.

"I got it," Delgado replied, tossing her the bag.

Nina looked inside. Something was missing. It wasn't the real estate woman's card; that was in the zippered pocket where Nina had left it. A moment or two passed before she realized what it was: Laura's suicide note.

"Something wrong?" said Delgado.

"No." Nina dialed the real estate woman. She answered on the first ring.

"Sure I remember you," the woman said when Nina began explaining who she was. "I don't want to alarm you, but if you're thinking of making an offer it better be soon. And significant. I've already got two highly interested parties. Not counting yourself."

"Before I make an offer," Nina replied, "I'd like to talk to someone at the law firm."

"What law firm?"

"The one you mentioned. Acting for the vendor's estate, I think you said."

"What do you want to talk to them about?"

"The appraiser's report."

"What about it?"

Nina was conscious of Delgado's gaze as she replied, "I'm a little concerned about that elm tree."

"Elm tree?"

"In the backyard. It didn't look too healthy to me. If it's got Dutch elm disease, I'd like to know beforehand. There's a possibility of liability, to say nothing of the expense of having it removed."

"Liability?"

"Vis-à-vis the neighbors. There have been a number of cases lately. It doesn't lessen my interest in the house. I'd just like to know."

There was a pause. "I see," the real estate woman said.

"So if you'll just give the number of the law firm—Mullin and something, wasn't it?"

"Mullins, Smithson and O'Leary," the woman said. "In Newton Center." Another pause. "I guess it's all right," the woman said, giving her the number. Nina wrote it down, again feeling Delgado's eyes on her. "But don't waste any time. This one's hot."

"I won't. Thanks."

"Wait," said the real estate woman. "How can I reach you?"

"I'm out of town," Nina said. "I'll get back to you."

"But—"

Nina hung up, turned to Detective Delgado, who was smiling slightly; something green was stuck between her incisors. "You're not a bad liar," Delgado said. "And that's my area of expertise."

"I'm an ordinary businesswoman," Nina replied.

Delgado laughed. Nina almost laughed too, but she was already dialing Mullins, Smithson and O'Leary. The receptionist put her through to Mr. O'Leary's secretary. Mr. O'Leary's secretary put her through to Mr. O'Leary's paralegal. Mr. O'Leary's paralegal got Mr. O'Leary.

"Appraiser?" he said. He had the kind of accent you might hear in Fenway Park, way down the right field line.

"For Laura Bain's house. She was a friend of mine. I thought you were handling her estate."

"That's right. But that house was totally redone last year and besides we do a lot of real estate work in that area."

"I don't understand."

"What's to appraise? We know Dedham values to the dime. Why waste the money?"

"You mean you didn't hire an appraiser?"

Silence. "Listen—what was your name again?" Nina told him. "Listen, Miss Kitchener. Are you questioning, maybe, our representation of the estate? Because if that's the case—"

"Not at all, Mr. O'Leary. I'm sure you're doing a fine job. I just want to know if you hired an appraiser, that's all."

"Why?"

"A friend of mine is thinking of selling her house. She wanted to know who I'd recommend."

"I don't give advice of that sort. And the answer to your question is no. We didn't hire an appraiser. Now if you'll excuse me . . ." He hung up.

Detective Delgado was no longer smiling. "No appraiser?"

"That's what he says. But there was a man in her house, a man with big hands, the same kind of . . ." Her voice trailed off. "You don't believe me?"

"You're a . . . businesswoman, remember?"

"There was a man in Laura's house," Nina said. "Get that straight. And I wasn't the only one who saw him." She called the real estate woman, and reached an answering machine that began by playing the first four notes of Beethoven's Fifth Symphony. Nina put the phone down, hard.

Nina and Delgado looked at each other. Nina knew what Delgado thought she was seeing: a woman knocked off the tracks who may have seen a man in Laura's house, someone who didn't belong there, a thief perhaps, and who later imagined his presence while she was trying to kill herself, or invented it to protect herself, when she woke up and saw she hadn't. She searched for something to say that would change Delgado's mind, and failing to find it, sat slowly on the bed.

"All right, all right," Delgado said. "Give me her number."

Nina handed her the real estate woman's card. Delgado copied the number. "I'll be in touch," she said, and went away.

Nina stayed where she was. She remembered a song about paranoia striking deep. It played itself over and over in her mind, until she became almost unaware of the clatter of food trays, the rolling wheelchairs, the passing conversations, rapid footsteps coming down the hall. Then Suze burst into the room.

"Oh, Nina, are you all right?"

She grabbed Nina, hugged her tight, sat on the bed beside her, rocking her back and forth. Nina didn't cry; she was all cried out. She let herself be rocked back and forth.

"I should never have gone to L.A.," Suze said.

"Don't be silly."

Suze rocked her some more. Then she said: "Can you talk about it?"

"I can talk, but no one believes me."

"Talk."

Nina talked. She told Suze all there was to tell. Suze's face registered many things, but disbelief wasn't one of them. "You believe me," Nina said at the end.

"Of course I believe you."

"Then what's the explanation?"

"I don't know. We'll have to go over everything, from

start to finish. But first let's get out of here."

Getting out of there involved a wait of several hours, the signing of many forms and three loud arguments, all won by Suze. She menaced the hospital bureaucracy with her spiked hair, clanked her heavy jewelry, used at least one "attorney," "liability," "court," or "lawsuit" in every sentence and finally marched in triumph to the elevator, poked the DOWN button as though it were the eye of the chief resident and rode with Nina to street level. They laughed all the way to Nina's, and were paying the driver when Nina's mood changed: "I can't stay here."

"Right," said Suze. "Come to my place."

"What's it going to be, ladies?" said the driver.

"Keep your shirt on," Suze said, whisking a ten-dollar bill out of his reach.

On their way inside to get some of Nina's things they met Jules, in street clothes, on his way out. "You were right, Miss Kitchener," he said.

"About what?"

"They canned me. For booze. It's not fair. I can hold my liquor." He was holding some already and his eyes were watery.

"You weren't in very good shape the other night."

"That's why they canned me. But they're wrong. It wasn't booze. I was sick." Nina said nothing. Jules came closer. His breath reeked. "I only had one drink. I swear. An old guy gave me a bottle. I had one little nip. That's all. Or two. It made me sick."

"What old guy?"

"A big old guy with white hair. Walked in off the street. Said it was an early Christmas present from one of the tenants."

"Did you let him in?"

"No. He didn't want to come in. He just gave me the bottle and went away."

"Then you drank it?"

"Just a nip, like I said."

"And it made you sick?"

"As a dog. I passed out behind the desk."

"For how long?"

"Not long. I don't think. I was up when you came back, wasn't I?"

"So anyone could have come in while you were passed out?"

Jules looked at Nina, looked at Suze, looked away. "Jeez. I thought you were on my side. On the side of the little guy." He walked out the door, took a few steps down the block, then slowly turned and went off the other way.

Upstairs in Nina's apartment, the cleaners had done their job. They'd wiped up the vomit, straightened the furniture, put the typewriter away. Nina threw some clothes in a suitcase and was on her way out when she found herself pausing to look in the nursery. The cleaners had piled all the stuffed animals in the crib. Nina began rearranging them. Her hands lingered on the lion, the polar bear, Winnie. She stayed there, bent over the crib, unaware of time.

"Let's go, Nina," Suze said quietly from the door.

She went.

In the lobby, Nina stopped to check her mailbox. It contained the latest copy of *Bicycling* magazine, two credit card applications, coupons from Gerber's and a letter from Laura Bain, postmarked on the day of her death. Nina opened it where she stood. Suze read over her shoulder.

Dear Nina,

  I called you last night, but I guess you weren't home yet. In case we miss each other in the next day or two—I've got a very heavy schedule before the Accra trip—I'll just send this off to make sure you know how glad I was to meet you. I really feel so much more hopeful since you came up here—you're such a strong person!

  I haven't been able to reach my obstetrician yet. He's on vacation. Meanwhile I'm trying to get hold of the doctor from the Reproductive Research Center. Dr. Crossman. A bit creepy. He kept asking if I was part Jewish and I had to draw my whole family tree to show I wasn't. Something about Tay-Sachs disease. I'd really like that printout. In the meantime, I have remembered one thing about the donor, at least I'm pretty sure I have—he was left-handed. I'm left-handed too, so it struck me at the time.

  I've also had a little thought. Did you ever find out

exactly what was wrong with the phone in your hospital room? I think it's worth looking into.

Must run. Three lines are blinking in my face at this very moment and there's talk of a coup in Nigeria, which we're nicely positioned for, actually. Speak to you soon.

Affectionately,
Laura

"And she committed suicide?" Suze asked. She had to repeat the question: Nina was staring at words on the middle of the page—*Dr. Crossman. A bit creepy*.

"Seconal, just like me," Nina replied. She looked at the envelope. "Probably before the stamp was canceled."

"Her mood must have changed awfully fast."

"Yeah."

They got into the taxi. "Where to now, ladies?" said the driver.

"My donor was left-handed too," Nina said.

"He was?" Suze replied.

"That makes Laura right about one thing."

"What's that?"

"We've got to find the father. Just as if this were a custody case."

"You think it was the same donor for both of you?"

"Why not? It was the same doctor."

"Tick tick goes the meter," the driver said.

"The Human Fertility Institute," Nina said, and told him where it was.

"Here?" said the driver, pulling in to the curb fifteen minutes later.

Nina glanced up from Laura's letter. They were on the Upper East Side, on the right street, in the right part of the block. "Here," she said. It was only when she got out of the cab that she noticed the Human Fertility Institute was gone. A rubble-filled hole in the ground had replaced the marble palace. A bulldozer was parked in the middle of it. At the controls sat a man in a checked lumberjacket, eating a sandwich. Nina ran to the chicken-wire fence at the edge of the hole.

"What's going on?" she shouted.

The man looked up. "Coffee break."

"With the Fertility Institute, I mean. What happened?"

"Dunno," said the man. "Trump? Zeckendorf? One of that crowd."

"But it was a national landmark."

"I guess it got de-landmarked," the bulldozer man replied. "That's what makes America great." He tossed the remains of his sandwich aside and shifted into gear. The bulldozer bumped away across the rubble.

30

"You look good, Suze," Nina said as they walked up the four flights of stairs to Suze's room.

"I do?"

"Yeah. Things going well with Le Boucher?"

"Mindy? She's a jerk."

"Le Boucher's name is Mindy?"

"Mindy Sue Lubke. She beat up a bouncer in Laguna Beach the other night. She's so pumped full of steroids she doesn't know what she's doing. But she's going to be a star."

"In barbarian movies?"

"That's just the beginning. She's up for the lead in the new Ma Barker bio."

"And you're her manager?"

"God, no," said Suze, unlocking the door. "She's a dangerous lunatic."

"But you look good anyway." This was a question, vague to anyone else, but clear to Suze. She smiled and said nothing. They entered her room.

Suze's room was the entire top floor of a converted warehouse a few blocks south of her gallery. Except for the cast-iron support pillars, it would have been a good place to play polo on rainy days, or hold joint sessions of the House and Senate. Their footsteps echoed on the bare pine floors.

"Home sweet home," Suze said.

Suze's home had a kitchen area, a table, a couch, a chair, a desk, a phone, a rug and, some distance away, a king-sized bed, a glass-walled shower stall and a toilet, half-hidden by a low steel wall scavenged from a superannuated Parisian pissoir.

"What's that?" Nina said, pointing to the far end of the room, where coils of barbed wire surrounded little metallic human figures.

"Auschwitz Cadillac," Suze replied. "In storage."

"It didn't sell?"

"We got a few offers, but not what we wanted."

"What did you want?"

"Seventy-five grand. But we'll get even more when they see the stuff he's working on now."

"What's that?"

"Tortured plants. It's going to rock the art world. He's on the cutting edge of the eco-installation movement."

Nina walked all the way to Auschwitz Cadillac. She didn't see how the barbed wire, despite being pink, could have come from a 1957 Eldorado. But the huts were made of pink bumpers and doors and the prisoners had hubcap bodies and direction signal eyes and striped uniforms made from two-tone leather upholstery.

"The eyes work, if you want me to plug it in," Suze said.

"That's okay," Nina said, lightly fingering the barbed wire. What was the artist saying? That we are all somehow implicated in Auschwitz? Or was Detroit the guilty party? Was living in a consumer culture a kind of Auschwitz? Or was it just a demonstration that scraps could be made into art, the way Picasso had turned bicycle parts into a bull?

"Nina."

"What?"

"You look tired."

"I'm not."

"Why don't you lie down?"

"I've got calls to make."

"What calls? I'll make them."

"Dr. Crossman. And I want to find out about that phone."

"Lie down. I'll take care of it."

"That's all right," Nina said. "I can—"

"Come on." Suze took her hand, led her to the bed,

not far from Auschwitz Cadillac, pushed her gently down. "Trust me." Suze pulled the comforter over her.

Nina heard Suze moving toward the other end of the room, heard her dialing the phone, heard her quietly talking. Outside darkness was falling. It sucked the color out of Auschwitz Cadillac and cast it in shadow. Lacking light, Auschwitz Cadillac floated closer to the line between art and reality. Nina's eyes closed.

Later she felt Suze slipping into bed beside her. "Suze?"

"You're awake."

"Yeah."

"Feel all right?"

"Fine. Did you find out anything?"

Suze sighed. "Dr. Crossman's office phone is the same number as the Human Fertility Institute. It's been disconnected. There's no home phone listed in any of the directories. I tried all the boroughs, Long Island, Jersey, Connecticut. I called the AMA but they wouldn't help me over the phone."

"They'll help Delgado. I'll call her in the morning."

"But I found out about your phone on the maternity ward."

"And?"

"The wall plug was crushed."

"How?"

"The maintenance man didn't know. He said someone could have stepped on it by accident."

"And the volunteer could have been a madwoman off the street. And Laura Bain's case could have nothing to do with mine. And I could have written that note, and signed it. And swallowed a bottle of Seconal. But I didn't."

"I know you didn't, Nina."

"Therefore?"

But Suze had no answer. Through the windows, Nina saw falling snow. She watched it for a while, then closed her eyes. Under Suze's warm comforter, with Suze beside her, she drifted toward sleep. Sleep was safe, as long as the Birdman stayed away.

When Nina awoke, Suze's hand was on her thigh and the phone was ringing. She pushed the hand away. "Suze."

"What is it?"

"The phone."

Suze jumped out of bed and ran to the desk. Nina felt

the imprint of Suze's hand on her thigh for a few moments; then the feeling went away.

Morning light streamed in through the many windows of Suze's room. It transmuted Auschwitz Cadillac back into art, and made Suze's body gleam like mother-of-pearl. Nina couldn't make out what Suze was saying on the telephone, but she could see that Suze was watching her while she said it. In a few minutes, Suze came back across the room, pulling on a sweater.

"Nina," she said.

"What?"

"There's something I should tell you."

"Tell."

"I've met someone."

"Someone other than Le Boucher?"

Suze's face wrinkled in an expression very close to wincing. "Forget her. She was just using me." Suze smiled. "And vice versa, I suppose. No. This is different. He's a man, for starters." Suze sat on the edge of the bed and began pulling on a pair of jeans.

"Continue," Nina said.

Suze's back tensed. "Maybe this isn't a good time to tell you."

"Why not? Is it Richard Nixon?"

Suze laughed and turned to face Nina. "Similar eyebrows, in fact. But nothing else. He's a film producer, potentially anyway."

"Potentially?"

"He was assistant to the producer on *Ten Tall Ducks*."

"I don't recall seeing it."

"It's not out yet. It won't be coming out either, except on video. There were problems. But Ernesto learned a lot on the shoot and now he's got a script he wants to do on his own."

"Ernesto?"

"Ernesto Cohen. Ernesto Che Cohen, actually. But everyone calls him Ernie."

"Except you."

Suze smiled, the same secretive smile she'd shown Nina the day before. "He's twenty-five. Almost."

"That's a relief. I was worried he might embarrass you by ordering Shirley Temples at Spago."

"I want you to look at the script, Nina."

"Sure. What's it about?"

"Dan Aykroyd and John Candy are seriously interested. And Ernesto has an uncle with a partner who knows Alec Guinness's agent. They're going to approach him for a cameo."

"Great. So the script's about putting together a movie deal."

Suze laughed again. "It's about giant rats from outer space. A spoof. But not like Mel Brooks. More like Jonathan Swift."

"Has Ernesto considered where the money for a Swiftian rat spoof is going to come from?"

"We're working on it."

"We?"

"I'm going to co-produce."

Nina had been afraid of that. Suze's father had money, lots of it. He owned the building Suze lived in, and the building the gallery was in too. But Nina didn't say, "Be careful," or "What do you know about producing movies?" or "You're out of control," although all three thoughts passed through her mind. Instead she said: "Have you got the script?"

"Not here. Ernesto's a little weird about letting it out of his sight. But I'll get you a copy." She bent forward and kissed Nina on the forehead. "Thanks," she said, and zipped up her jeans.

Nina sat up. "I don't understand why you were reluctant to tell me about this."

This time Suze couldn't quite face her. "There's a little more to it."

"Like what?"

"I'm pregnant."

Under the down comforter, Nina's hands closed into fists. "Ernesto's the father?"

Suze nodded.

"But you've only been gone for—" She tried to remember; time had grown disorderly since the kidnapping.

"I missed my period, Nina. And I'm Old Faithful when it comes to blood flow, you know that."

Nina got out of bed and started putting on her clothes as fast as she could.

"Say something," Suze said.

"About what?"

"About me having a baby."

"Congratulations."

"I knew this wasn't a good time."

Nina threw on her coat, buttoned it with quick, snapping movements of her fingers. "You said you never ever think about having a baby, not late at night, not when you see one going by in a stroller. Never fucking ever."

"So? Who am I betraying?"

"You're out of control, Suze."

Suze didn't move, didn't say another word. Nina crossed the huge room, went out the door and down the four flights to the street. There she stopped to catch her breath. The strength stored in her legs from all those hours on the bike seemed to have disappeared all at once. She was weak, weak from childbirth, weak from the loss of her baby, weak from the Seconal, weak from whatever had been done to bring her back to life. She stood in the doorway, just breathing in the cold air and breathing it out, until a ragged man went by talking to Jesus. Nina stepped out on the slushy sidewalk. She had things to do.

From a pay phone she called Detective Delgado to tell her about Dr. Crossman. Delgado was in court. Nina started telling someone else the Crossman story. After thirty seconds he said, "This sounds complicated. You better talk to Delgado."

"When will she be back?"

"Hard to say. It's the Ezekial trial. It might last forever, with the show his lawyers are putting on."

Nina hung up. The Human Fertility Institute was gone. Dr. Crossman was gone. That left the lawyer. Mr. Percival. Of Ablewhite, Godfrey, Percival & Glyde. The country squire in the black suit who had witnessed the signing of the papers.

Now sign here. And here. And here. And here. And once more. Good.

Half an hour later, Nina was riding an elevator to the top of a midtown steel and glass tower. A man carrying three briefcases whispered to a woman in red suspenders: "Point six, I can't remember point six."

"No escape clause, for Christ's sake," the woman hissed as the doors opened at the penultimate floor. "This is the most important meeting of your life, Bart," she added more loudly as they got off. "If you screw up on me . . ."

The doors closed before she got to the threat clause. Nina went up alone to the top floor.

Nina stepped out of the elevator and into a quiet reception room furnished with leather couches and chairs and decorated with oil paintings of English rural life that looked old enough to be early imitations of Constable. Except for the small brass plaque on the opposite wall—ABLEWHITE, GODFREY, PERCIVAL & GLYDE—and the woman typing at the desk beneath it, she might have wandered into a men's club. The woman resembled Alistair Cooke. She spoke like him too. "May I help you?" she said.

"I'd like to see Mr. Percival."

A pair of glasses hung around the woman's neck. She put them on and peered at Nina. "Have you an appointment?"

"No," Nina said. "But I've dealt with him in the past and I'm sure he'll see me. It's very important."

"Your name, please?"

"Nina Kitchener."

The woman pressed a button on her desk. "A Nina Kitchener is here to see Mr. Percival," she said, and to Nina: "Someone will be out momentarily." The woman took off her glasses and resumed typing.

Nina sat in a red leather chair with brass studs on the arms. It was a little less comfortable than the crosstown bus. She leafed through *Fortune, Barron's, Money, Inc.* Like pornography, they aroused an appetite, fed it and were interested in one thing and one thing only. Nina's head began to ache. She closed her eyes. Immediately she saw the face of her baby, clear and vivid. For days his image had been dimming at the center and blurring at the edges. Now his eyes, serious and blue, filled her vision: the eyes of the boy who had tried to show her from the very beginning that he would always hold up his end.

He didn't have a name.

"Ms. Kitchener?"

Nina opened her eyes. A woman in a gray flannel suit stood before her. "Yes?" Nina said.

"I'm Mr. Percival's assistant. Mr. Percival is fully booked today. Perhaps if you'd tell me what this is about I could arrange an appointment at a later date."

Nina's head ached. Her stomach hurt too, and her body

was weak. It would have been easy to arrange an appointment at a later date, to go somewhere and curl up. And maybe she would have done that, had it not been for the vision of the baby with the serious blue eyes. Nina didn't believe in the spirit world, or astral projection, or extrasensory perception, or even sensory perception sometimes, but she felt those eyes on her at that moment. And so, not raising her voice—she was too tired for that—Nina said, "That's not good enough. I want to see him now."

"That," said the woman, stepping back, "is impossible."

Nina didn't argue. "Tell him it's about the Human Fertility Institute. And the Cambridge Reproductive Research Center."

She felt the woman's cold stare, but didn't meet it. She was too tired to raise her voice, too tired to argue, too tired to get into a staring contest. Suddenly she understood the power generated by those silent mothers who had sat in protest for so long in some square in Argentina. She wasn't too tired to sit. She sat. Mr. Percival's assistant went away. The sounds of the receptionist's fingers tapping at her keyboard ceased, but Nina didn't look up. She reached for the *Wall Street Journal* and began reading an angry editorial about the money supply. She read it to the end, understanding nothing.

Mr. Percival's assistant returned. "Mr. Percival will see you now," she said in a businesslike tone, as though nothing impolite had ever flared between them. Typing sounds resumed. Nina rose and followed Mr. Percival's assistant across the reception room and down a thickly carpeted hall to a corner office. She led Nina inside, sat her at a gilded Louis Something chair opposite a gilded Louis Something desk, and left unobtrusively, like a minor courtier.

Mr. Percival had a fine view of Central Park. He was enjoying it now, swiveled sideways in his chair and talking on the phone, his well-fed profile to Nina. The France of the ancien regime didn't suit him; he would have been more at home in Fielding's England. "In the fullness of time," he was saying in his thick-cream voice, "never means tomorrow, Edgar. I believe you might consider other arrangements." While Edgar replied, Nina examined the photographs on the wall: Mr. Percival shaking hands with the Governor, both Senators, the President and John Wayne.

Mr. Percival said goodbye and turned to Nina, folding his plump hands on the desktop. "Now then, Ms. . . ." he began, glancing down at a memo pad, ". . . Kitchener, I gather you're anxious to see me."

He didn't seem to remember her at all. Perhaps it wasn't surprising—he had seen her for only a few minutes, ten months ago.

"We've met before," Nina said.

"Have we?"

"In February. At the Human Fertility Institute. You had me sign a lot of papers."

Mr. Percival didn't say he recalled the occasion. He didn't say he didn't recall it. He said: "And?"

"And?" *And I got pregnant and my baby was stolen and the institute's gone.* This was the hysterical, female answer that might stir the heart of John Wayne and make him hop on his Appaloosa and shoot up bad guys until things were straightened out, but it wasn't likely to get the same results in Mr. Percival's office. "And," Nina said, "I've got some questions about the institute."

"I'm afraid I'm not empowered to answer them."

"I don't understand. You were empowered to collect my signature."

"Your signature?"

"I told you. You had me sign a lot of papers."

"Perhaps," said Mr. Percival. "But I think any questions might be more properly directed to the institute itself."

"Where the hell is it, Mr. Percival? There's nothing but a bulldozer and a hole in the ground."

This outburst didn't seem to unsettle Mr. Percival. "Are they so far along already?" he said. "I never get out of the office these days."

"Then you know about it? What's going on?"

Mr. Percival unfolded his hands, rubbed them together, refolded them. "You haven't explained your interest in the institute, Ms. . . ." His eyes went to the memo pad.

"Kitchener," she said. "Nina Kitchener. And this is my interest—I was impregnated there, my baby was stolen and . . . and someone tried to kill me and make it look like suicide. And now there's a hole in the ground and I want to know why."

John Wayne remained where he was, up on the wall, but she had touched something in Mr. Percival. His lips moved, but for a moment, he said nothing; and when he did speak, his tone wasn't quite so creamy. "How . . . horrible," he said. "Have the police been informed?"

"Yes."

"And what action are they taking?"

"They're investigating."

"No one has contacted me," Mr. Percival said.

"I haven't really explained the connection to them."

"The connection?"

"Between the institute and the kidnapping."

"What connection would that be?"

"The father. He's the only possible connection. I want to find him."

"The father?"

"The donor. If this were a routine custody case, wouldn't the man be the first one they'd look for?"

"I don't practice matrimonial law, Ms. Kitchener," Mr. Percival said, no longer needing to consult the memo pad for her name. "Without regard to the merits of your idea, I think it's safe to say that there is no possibility of learning the name of the donor. First, the institute is defunct. It has been sold to Standard Foods."

For a moment, Nina felt that her fancy chair had vanished and she was starting to fall. She held on to the gilded arms. "Defunct?"

"No longer in business. The new owners have discontinued the donor program, which was the sole purpose of the institute."

"Then why did they buy it?"

He smiled. She had forgotten his teeth, yellow as old ivory. "You should be in business, Ms. Kitchener."

"I *am* in business. And I find it strange that the institute has suddenly been liquidated."

Mr. Percival stopped smiling. "Are you suggesting that a multibillion-dollar conglomerate like Standard Foods, owned by hundreds of thousands of shareholders, made this deal because of you?" Nina had no answer. "It was basically a real estate transaction, Ms. Kitchener, an exchange of shares for the land. There would be a question in my mind about the very existence of the institute's records at this point. But even if the records are extant, the name of the donor will not be available to you. You signed the anonymity form—'The donor shall remain anonymous and neither you nor any resulting issue shall make any attempt to learn the donor's identity.' "

"How do you know I signed that if you don't even remember me?"

That brought the yellow smile again. "Everyone signed it. I drew up the form myself. It was central to the whole concept."

"Why is that?"

"Because, Ms. Kitchener, what man would donate his sperm if there was a possibility it might lead to aggravation down the road?"

Nina had no response to that. She was thinking of Dr. Berry: *Are we simply manufacturers of sperm and egg, products like any other for trade on the open market*? She had bought some sperm, in a small-time way. Indemnified sperm. And Standard Foods had bought the sperm company, in a big-time way. Nina said: "Maybe the anonymity form no longer exists either."

Mr. Percival's voice was creamy again. "All the legal records remain in the care of this office. I think I can put your mind at rest on that issue." He buzzed for his assistant, scratched something on a memo sheet and handed it to her. The assistant left an expensive scent in the room.

Mr. Percival rose and went to the window. Slipping his thumbs into the pockets of his vest, he said, "Hypothesize for me, Ms. Kitchener."

"About what?"

"About what happened to you."

"I don't know what happened. That's what I'm trying to find out."

"But you think the donor is involved."

"I didn't say that."

"Then why do you want to know his name?"

Nina didn't answer.

Mr. Percival continued: "You think the donor is involved. Is it your contention, then, that the donor somehow learned your identity?"

Was that her contention? It was sounding thin already; perhaps that's why she had resisted putting it in a simple sentence. "Yes," she said. "That's my contention."

"What do the police think of it?"

"I told you. I haven't really expressed it to them."

"Then how do they explain the disappearance of your child?"

"They haven't explained it."

"But they must have a working theory. Who is in charge of the case?"

"A detective named Delgado. Her working theory is that some disturbed woman walked in off the street and just . . . grabbed him."

"But you don't believe that."

"No."

"Why not?" Mr. Percival asked.

Why not? There was the volunteer badge. The crushed telephone jack. The attempt on her life, but that itself was in dispute. And there was Laura Bain. "Have you ever heard of the Cambridge Reproductive Research Center?" Nina asked.

Mr. Percival turned from the window, pursed his full lips. "Not that I recall," he said.

"It is—it was—a sperm bank," Nina said. "Now it seems to be defunct too. A woman named Laura Bain went to it." Nina told him Laura's story. He listened silently, his eyes and face expressing nothing. Nina wondered whether he had somehow gained control of his involuntary muscle movements.

When she finished, he returned to his desk, sat in his chair, folded his hands. "Have you sought professional help, Ms. Kitchener?"

"Like a private detective?"

"No." Mr. Percival sighed. "I meant therapeutic help."

Nina banged her fist on the desk before she realized what she was doing. "I'm sick of hearing that."

Mr. Percival's eyes widened. "I didn't mean to cause offense. Dear, dear, dear. All I'm saying is that perhaps your meeting with this woman was somewhat unfortunate."

"Why do you say that?"

"This is a big country, Ms. Kitchener. I don't know if you appreciate how big. I'm like an air traffic controller. I'm in a position to know. It is teeming. And in any society this swollen, no one's experience can be unique. There are going to be coincidences. It's simple mathematics. If there are sperm banks and women who use them and people who kidnap babies, then these three factors are eventually going to appear in the same equation, and more than once. You've had the bad luck to stumble on an equation just like yours. It's a coincidence, Ms. Kitchener, in the basic meaning of the word. When a plane crashes in Chicago and another one crashes in Denver, we don't say there's a conspiracy behind it, do we?"

This was the rational explanation. It matched the experience of the experts, like Detective Delgado, and appealed to something basic in Nina. It would have been easy to nod her head, thank Mr. Percival for his time, and leave. But that wasn't going to get her baby back. So Nina said: "We do if Dr. Crossman planted bombs on both planes."

Mr. Percival's plump hands tightened their grip on each other. "I'm afraid I lost you," he said.

"Dr. Crossman. The director of the Human Fertility Institute. He handled my impregnation procedure. He also did Laura Bain's, in Cambridge."

"The name is new to me," Mr. Percival said. "I had no dealings with the medical staff."

"Are you telling me he wasn't director of the institute?"

"I'm telling you I don't know him," Mr. Percival said. "I'm not questioning his position."

"Good. Because I want you to help me find him."

"Is he lost?"

"I don't know. He doesn't have a home phone."

"I don't see how I could be useful, Ms. Kitchener."

"You could call the owners of the institute."

"The institute had no owners, as such. It operated as a nonprofit foundation."

"But someone must have been operating it. Someone must have put up the money. Someone must have hired Dr. Crossman. Some human being who might know how to get hold of him."

Mr. Percival rose and went to the window again. The view hadn't changed, but he didn't seem to be enjoying it as much. "I'll see what I can do," he said.

"You will?"

"Give me a few days. Where can I get in touch with you?" Nina gave him the office number. "Is that good all the time?" he asked.

"Days."

"What if I have to reach you at night?"

"Just leave a message on the office machine. I call in frequently."

"Fine," he said.

"Does your . . . helping me mean you've changed your mind about revealing the donor's identity?"

"It has nothing to do with me, Ms. Kitchener. It's a legal matter. The anonymity form protects all parties involved—the clients, their issue, the donors, the foundation. And, as I explained, there is no guarantee that the records still exist. But I think we should clear up the matter of Dr. Crossman's possible involvement with this other fertility clinic."

Was it his careful choice of words or his soothing tone that made Nina realize that the matter of Dr. Crossman would be cleared up in some benign way? She could sketch the outline already: Dr. Crossman specialized in artificial insemination. Why shouldn't he, like any other specialist, move from place to place? Nina sat in the gilded chair, foreseeing another dead end.

"Is there anything else, then, Ms. Kitchener?" Mr. Percival had returned to his desk and was writing on the memo pad.

Was there anything else? She found herself remembering the portrait of the weak-chinned man at the institute. It had been leaning against the wall on her last visit, and Dr. Crossman and his nurse had been packing things in boxes. The hole in the ground shouldn't have come as such a big surprise.

"If not . . ." Mr. Percival looked up from the memo pad.

"One more thing," Nina said. "What's the name of the foundation?"

"What foundation?"

"The foundation that sold the institute."

"It wasn't a sale, technically. It was a straight exchange of land for shares, as I mentioned."

"Shares in Standard Foods."

"Correct."

"And who got the shares?" He paused. "Come on, Mr. Percival. It must be a matter of public record. I could look it up in the *Wall Street Journal*."

Mr. Percival licked his lips. "The Standish Foundation," he said. "But I don't see how it matters."

"Who are they?"

He shrugged his round shoulders. "A nonprofit organization involved in scientific research."

"And they might know where Dr. Crossman is?"

"Perhaps." He stood up. "Don't worry. You'll know as soon as I do. Now, if there's nothing else at this time . . ."

He led Nina to the door. "Be patient," he said, shaking her hand. His was soft and warm, reassuring as his voice, his view of Central Park, his picture of John Wayne.

Mr. Percival's assistant was waiting in the reception room. She showed Nina the anonymity form. Nina sat down to read it. She had signed her name to everything Mr. Percival had said she had. There was her signature at the bottom. In blue ink. That was because the pen they had handed her at the institute had been blue. Not they: he. She remembered the two pens clipped to Percival's inside jacket pocket—a fat gold one and a cheap blue ballpoint. Nina herself always used black ink.

"Could you ask Mr. Percival if I could have a Xerox of this?" Nina asked.

"Certainly," said his assistant, starting down the hall.

As soon as she was out of sight, Nina rose and stepped into the elevator. She tucked the anonymity form under her shirt. She didn't want to lose it. Her signature on the suicide note was written in blue ink too.

|31|

Detective Delgado, sitting alone in a coffee-shop booth off Foley Square, looked terrible. The skin of her face sagged loosely on the bone structure. Her eyes, gazing into a steamy cup of black coffee, were red and puffy; has she been crying? thought Nina, sliding onto the opposite seat. Delgado glanced across the table at Nina, then stared down again into her cup. She didn't acknowledge Nina in any way.

"What's wrong?" Nina asked.

Delgado snorted. "Nothing. Things are peachy. Just peachy."

Nina sat silent, waiting for the right moment to begin. When it didn't come, she began anyway, unfolding two sheets of paper, the anonymity form and her suicide note, and laying them in front of Delgado. "I want you to look at the signatures."

Delgado's gaze shifted, slowly and without interest, to the papers. "I'm looking."

"What do you see?"

Delgado glanced up sharply. "I'm not in the mood for games. What is it you want?"

I want my baby back and it's your job to help me. This, her first response, Nina kept inside. She said: "They were both written with a blue ballpoint. The same shade of blue."

"So?"

"I signed this form at the Human Fertility Institute, but not with my own pen. I distinctly remember being handed a pen. But it couldn't have been mine anyway—I always use black pens."

"Why is that?"

Why did she use black pens? That was not the question Nina had expected. She recalled the reason only hazily— it had something to do with a girlhood rebellion against an art teacher. "It's just a habit," Nina said. "The point is I don't use blue pens. I'm sure there isn't even a single one in my apartment." Nina paused to let this sink in.

"So?" Delgado said.

"So? So it means I couldn't have signed this supposed suicide note at the apartment. But unless it's a perfect forgery, this is my signature. I'll accept that. Therefore I must have signed it in some other place, and at some other time—before, in other words. Like maybe before the suicide note was even typed on the page. When I was at the Human Fertility Institute, for example."

Saying it aloud awoke something in Nina, something hopeful, but nothing lit up in Delgado's eyes. "What the hell are you driving at?" She didn't get it. Did she even want to get it?

"Christ. I'm saying this proves I didn't try to kill myself. Somebody—"

Delgado reached across the table and grabbed Nina's jacket. "Don't curse at me, you neurotic bitch. I've got enough fucking trouble without you."

They stared at each other. Adrenaline coursed through Nina's limbs. She had a wild vision of throwing the coffee cup at Delgado's face, but it was followed closely by an overhead image of two women playing the roles of hot-headed little men. "Let go," she said.

Delgado let go. She stared at Nina a moment more, then sighed. "Shit."

"A crime was committed against me," Nina said quietly. "Even if I did try to kill myself, which I did not. Kidnapping is a crime. And these notes prove that there's much more to it than some random act of madness. They're evidence."

Delgado took a deep breath. "Evidence of what?"

"Of forethought. Of planning. Of a horrible, horrible . . . plan."

Delgado's hand inched toward the papers. "Just because they're written in blue ink?"

"Yeah. And not just that, but the same shade of blue."

"The same shade of blue?"

"Yes. Don't you see where this is leading?"

"No. I do not. Are you really telling me there isn't a blue pen at your apartment?"

"I am."

"Not in the back of some drawer, maybe? Or behind a pillow on the couch?"

"Not to my knowledge."

"Not to your knowledge. Did you look? Before you came to me with this theory?"

"No."

"Why not?"

Nina didn't reply.

"Why not?"

"You're going to make me say it."

"Say what?"

"I'm afraid to go in there alone," Nina said. "Wouldn't you be?"

"That's a tough one." Detective Delgado patted a bulge under her left armpit. "I've got this."

You'd be afraid, Nina thought. She said: "Then bring it."

"You want me to go to your apartment?"

"To get this blue pen question resolved in your mind."

"Now?"

"Why not?"

"Why not, she says. Shit." But Delgado got up, slowly and heavily, and walked outside. A cruiser sat by the curb with a uniformed man at the wheel. Delgado and Nina got in the back. They were pulling out when a man in a Mets jacket ran up and tapped on the window.

"Yeah?" said Delgado, rolling it down.

"Captain wants to see you after the shift change."

The skin around Delgado's lips went pale. "He walked?"

The man in the Mets jacket nodded.

"Surprise, huh?" Delgado said. The man moved away,

saying nothing. Delgado's eyes moistened with tears. Nina saw her fight them off. The cruiser started rolling. People flowed out of the courthouse, bobbed down the steps. The media closed in, wielding overhead booms like strange fishing gear. They caught a big silver-haired pinstripe. He didn't seem displeased about it: his smile was visible all the way across the square. Delgado watched, the same way players in the losing dugout can't take their eyes off the celebration on the mound at the end of the World Series. The cruiser rounded a corner and moved uptown.

"What's that all about?" Nina asked.

"No business of yours," Delgado replied.

They rode the whole way in silence. Delgado stared straight ahead. Once or twice she chewed on her fingernails. On the last block, Nina said: "Did you speak to the real estate woman in Dedham?"

"Yeah," Delgado said.

"And?"

"And she says there was a man in the house, calling himself an appraiser. Why do you think I'm here?"

They went up to Nina's apartment. Nina unlocked the door. Delgado entered first. There was nothing to fear. Everything looked the way it had when Nina and Suze had come to collect some of Nina's things. Delgado checked the hall, the nursery, the living room, and walked into the kitchen. "What's this?"

"What's what?" Nina said, following her in.

Delgado was standing at the kitchen table. The kitchen table where Nina had first laid eyes on the opening paragraph of *Living Without Men and Children . . . and Loving It*: "All happy families suck. Unhappy families suck too." The kitchen table on which her electronic typewriter had sat waiting with the suicide note. The manuscript was gone now, of course, and the typewriter put away. There was nothing on the table but an empty vase, a pepper mill and a ballpoint pen.

A blue ballpoint.

Delgado picked it up. She tore a sheet out of her notebook and wrote: *Nina Kitchener*. "Got those papers?" she said over her shoulder: a businesslike question, but the tone was venomous.

"That pen wasn't there before. I've never seen it in my life."

"Just give me the papers."

Nina handed her the anonymity form and the suicide note. Delgado placed them on the table, on either side of her notebook sheet: Exhibits A, B, C. Nina stared down at three representations of her name, two in the same hand, one different, but all penned in the identical shade of blue. Under her gaze, *Nina Kitchener* tore loose from its meaning, each character seeming to bear some coded message.

Delgado was watching her.

"It wasn't there when I left," Nina said. How feeble it sounded. She tried to make her voice strong. "Or ever," she added. "Someone must have—"

Delgado cut her off. "Did I miss something on the calendar?"

"What do you mean?"

"It's obvious, isn't it? Today must have been set aside for making me look like an asshole."

"I'm not—"

Delgado's voice began to rise. "First Ezekial walks because my witness, who I went to the fucking wall for, folds on the goddamned stand. Then comes you and your little mindgames."

"Mindgames?"

Delgado brandished the pen in Nina's face. "This is a Bic finepoint. There must be a million of them in the city, so it's no surprise that you've got one too."

"But I don't. I didn't."

"You have one, lady," Delgado said, holding it in front of Nina's eyes. "This is one, right here. A blue Bic finepoint. Maybe there are others under the pillows on the couch or at the back of the desk drawer. But we don't need to look for them. Because this is one. Get it?" Detective Delgado dropped the pen on the table and walked out of the apartment. The door closed. The lock clicked. Nina sat down at the table.

She folded the papers and put them in her pocket. *Nina Kitchener. Nina Kitchener. Nina Kitchener.* Then she had just the vase and the pepper mill to look at. The pepper mill made her think of chess. She felt as though she'd been playing chess with a faceless and vastly superior opponent. Winner keeps the baby. She laid her head on the table.

No tears came, not even tears of frustration. Did that mean she was beaten? She didn't know. Maybe she was one of those people who never knew when they were beaten. That didn't make them winners. It made them stupid. But Nina pushed herself up from the table anyway. *Keep punching, stupid. At least stay on your feet.*

Nina stood on her feet for a few minutes. Then she remembered the Standish Foundation. She checked the phone book. There was no listing. She tried information. Information didn't have it either. She called the reference room at the public library. Throwing punches. "I'm looking for a list of foundations," she said.

"Like the Ford Foundation?" The man at the other end sounded very young.

"Right."

"I've got one right here."

"You've got one right there?"

"People ask for it all the time. Free money. Then they see what the forms are like."

"Is there a listing for the Standish Foundation?"

"I don't know. You'd have to look."

"But I'm here. And you're there."

The young man laughed and looked it up. She'd landed one. "The Standish Foundation, P.O. Box 101, Washington, Connecticut, oh-six-seven-nine-three," he told her. There was no phone number.

Nina tried information for Washington, Connecticut. No number. She found the town on a map: a dot almost hidden in the folds of the Connecticut Berkshires. Nina estimated the mileage, called a rental-car company and reserved a compact. She was on her way out the door when the phone rang. Nina stood still in her doorway. For a few minutes, she had forgotten the fear of being alone in her apartment. It came back in waves, with each ring of the phone. She answered it.

"Nina Kitchener?" said a man; young, perhaps, although not as young as the man in the reference room at the library. And this man had an Australian accent.

"Who's calling?" Nina said.

"My name is Muller. Bernie Muller. I'm a producer for the Australian Broadcasting Corporation. Current affairs department. That's like your public affairs. I heard about the dreadful thing that happened to you, if you are Nina Kitchener, that is, and I'd like to meet if it's not too inconvenient."

"You came all the way from Australia to do a story on me?"

The man laughed. He had a loud, hearty laugh that made her think of beaches and beer and the fun life that the travel agencies were selling Down Under. "I was already here, love. I'm researching a documentary on missing children in America. I visited Channel Four the other day and they told me about you." He paused. "If you are Nina Kitchener."

"I am," Nina said.

"Great," Bernie Muller replied. "Then what d'you say?"

"I really don't see how an Australian documentary will help get my baby back."

"No argument there," said Bernie Muller. "More in it for me than for you. But I have gathered some material on child kidnappings that you're welcome to go over. I'm not suggesting a formal interview on tape, or anything like that. Just some preliminary chat. I won't take a lot of your time."

"What kind of material?"

"Case studies. Just a few, actually. We're still in the early stages."

"Case studies from New York?"

"None from New York. Philadelphia. San Francisco. Boston, if I remember. A few others."

"All right," Nina said.

"Great," said Bernie Muller. "Should we meet somewhere? My hotel? Your place?" Nina didn't like either suggestion. There was a silence. Then Bernie Muller said, "How about Grand Central Station?"

"Grand Central Station?"

"Down below. They've got a super oyster place."

"So I've heard."

Bernie Muller laughed his big laugh. "Have I said something horribly tourist, then?"

"No, no. The Oyster Bar will be fine."

"Great. I love seafood. How's tonight?"

"No. I'm . . . busy tonight."

"Tomorrow?"

"That should be all right."

"Six o'clock?"

"Fine."

"Great. See you then."

"Wait," Nina said. "How will I know you?"

Bernie Muller laughed. "Big lout," he said. "But not to worry—I'll know you."

"You'll know me?"

"I saw your tape. Don't take offense, but aside from all the personal tragedy, you're very good on the tube."

They said goodbye. *Aside from all the personal tragedy.* How authentically TV. Nina almost didn't bother calling "Live At Five." "Oh, sure," said the researcher who had come on the shoot at her apartment. "The Australian guy. He was in yesterday."

Nina picked up her rental car and stopped at Suze's. She didn't want to drive to Connecticut alone. But Suze was gone. The note said:

Never apologize, never explain, right? But the apology is I'm sorry and the explanation is there's a deal meeting tomorrow at Paramount and I've got to be there. Stay here. The fridge is full and there's wine in the top cupboard. See you soon. Love S.

Nina thought of Jason. But Jason was at the office. She couldn't ask Jason. He'd been handling the business for weeks. And that wasn't fair, no matter what; Nina decided at that moment to go back to work when she got back. She thought of asking the Australian man. Bernie Muller. But he hadn't mentioned the name of his hotel. So Nina drove alone to Connecticut.

Temporary went on and on.

Component number three, out of touch with the tingling electromagnetic force and the smell of the living planet, accepted what components number one and two had to give him: nourishment he could not taste and air he could not smell. Component number three was free, free of responsibility, free of distraction, free to pursue what it now knew to be its purpose—to think, to remember. Component number three: the living brain in the carcass.

Not quite true to say free of distraction. That would leave out Dr. Robert. "Pneumonia," he might be saying in a low voice, just outside the circle of vision. "I was afraid of this."

"What are you going to do?" asked Mother, also invisible.

"Let's not say afraid. Let's say cognizant of the possibility."

"But what are you going to do?"

"Be aggressive," spoke the voice of Dr. Robert. "We've got options." He listed three or four drugs, like a pagan priest invoking the gods.

O Hera, Poseidon, Anubis, Thor: heal me. Inject me with Venus and Mars, Herr Doktor Medicine Man. Lay the god pill on my tongue. Yes, the fever was good. It brought back the names of the gods, and much more. Fever made him hot, a hothouse where memory bloomed, and memory was his purpose. "What do you remember?" his strange little Latin-namesake had asked that very first night in Aix. "What do you remember?"

Not much, then. Just enough to get their feet wet: bad joke. Faint memories, like the stories the black fisherman had told him about fire on the water.

Now he remembered much more. He remembered all the words to "Mack the Knife." In German. Not that he, component number three, knew German. But he had known it long ago. He had understood, perhaps even spoken it. Mother knew German. Fritz knew German. And Daddy had spoken it too, with a funny accent.

Daddy. Daddy brought him to memory number one, the memory stirred by the sight of the gaudy tropical fish on the postage stamp, the antediluvian memory, hidden in the densest undergrowth in the farthest corner of the hothouse. The cast: Happy, Nurse Betty, Daddy, Fritz. The events: first, a boat ride on baby blue water; fingers trailing in its warmth, cutting tiny bubbling wakes of white froth, indescribably beautiful, until Nurse Betty slapped his hand, not hard, and said be careful or you'll fall out and drown. Second: a day at the beach with Nurse Betty. A hot day, with iced coconut milk in a paper cup, and later Nurse Betty asleep under a tree, and Daddy and Fritz gone.

Third event: A walk in the woods. Alone. Piney woods and mushy ground under his feet. Something gleamed through the trees. A pond. He stood on its rim. Things floated in the still water. Moldy things. A wooden crate. The brass-studded top of a trunk, the brass dull green. Something white as a slug in a rotting life jacket.

The little boy stood by the pond. He looked at the floating things. After a while he noticed two ropes, each tied around a tree near the pond. The ropes led to the water, disappeared under it. Bubbles rose up beside them, two sets of bubbles. It was so quiet the boy could hear them popping on the surface. Once he thought he heard Nurse Betty calling through the woods: "Happy? Happy?" He didn't answer. He wasn't fond of Nurse Betty. Her skin was leathery, not soft like Mama's, and although she had smacked him lightly on the boat ride, that was only because Daddy had been there. She smacked harder when they were alone.

The boy watched the bubbles rising, sometimes in long strings, sometimes in fat ones and twos that made miniature splashes when they popped. Two sets of bubbles. Then, quite suddenly, there was only one.

The remaining bubbles came faster. They zigzagged across the pond. One rope stiffened, the other slackened. The slack rope floated in loose spirals to the top. The other end hung a foot or so under the water, torn and frayed. Then the second rope slackened too and something big came surging up from the depths. It erupted through the surface in a tumult of white water, driving waves across the pond. The moldy things—the crate, the trunk lid, the white slug in the lifejacket—bobbed up and down.

It was a monster, a sea monster. Lusca was its name: the fisherman had told him. It had one eye, but huge, bigger than the boy's entire head. Glistening black coils wound up from its back. The monster held them in its mouth. It looked wildly around, saw the frayed rope, grabbed it, then let go and looked around again.

And saw the boy. The sun glared off its giant eye. The boy tried to run, couldn't move; tried to cry out, couldn't utter. He was mute. He was paralyzed. He could only see and hear. He saw the monster spit out its coils. He heard the monster speak.

"*Geh veg.*"

The monster had a loud and terrible voice, but the boy remained mute and paralyzed.

"*Um himmels Willen, geh veg Kind.*"

The boy stood rooted. The monster sucked in its coils, but spat them out again. The monster screamed. "*Du Lieber Gott! Keine Luft.*"

Now the boy screamed too. The monster churned the water white. Then it plunged head first under the surface. The monster had glistening black feet, webbed and enormous. The boy ran.

He ran through the woods, stumbling, panting, falling, crying. Far away Nurse Betty was calling. "Happy? Happy? Happy?" The boy tried to answer, but could form no words. He could only stumble, pant, fall, cry.

"Happy? Happy?"

Antediluvian memories.

|33|

Three days before the appeal deadline, the last guests—a hard-drinking couple from Atlanta and some divers from Montreal—left Zombie Bay. Matthias gave eight weeks' pay to everyone on the staff, leaving him with nine hundred and seventy dollars in the bank, and let all but Moxie go. A few went to Nassau, a few to Freeport, most just returned to their homes in Blufftown and Conchtown. Matthias understood what he should have known all along: they hadn't been counting on him.

Krio had job offers in Barbados and St. Vincent. He packed his knives. Matthias drove him to the airport.

"Smoke?" said Krio, offering him a joint as the Jeep bounced along.

Matthias shook his head. "Diving today."

Krio nodded, puffed away. He didn't speak again until they shook hands at the foot of the stairs leading to the plane. "Be all right," he said. "I and I." Krio had faith.

But Matthias didn't believe in Ras Tafari or any other benign superbeing. Three days left, no money for an appeal, and despite what Ravoukian had said, no grounds. Back at Zombie Bay, he locked and shuttered all the cottages. At the dock, Moxie scrubbed the boats. It was so quiet Matthias could hear the water gurgling from his garden hose. He looked into the near future, and saw new owners unlocking the cottages, hiring most of the same people, spending too much on brochures, welcoming the first guests with a little too much intensity. Fuck them, he thought, and started toward the equipment shed. He was almost running by the time he got there.

Matthias laid out what he would need: a backpack with new twin aluminum eighties, each topped up to 3300 p.s.i., each with a separate regulator; another set of eighties with a single regulator for decompression; BC; three-eighths-inch-thick full wet suit, jetfins, mask, snorkel, fifteen-pound weightbelt; two waterproof torches, guaranteed to a depth of 250 feet; plasticized decompression tables; five hundred feet of neutrally buoyant eighth-inch nylon line on a non-jamming reel; depth gauge, dive watch, compass. He was adhering to every rule of cave diving except the first: never dive alone. Moxie was a good diver, but he had no experience in caves and Matthias didn't have the right to make him start learning now. That was the morally defensible reason. The other reason was that Matthias preferred and had always preferred to dive alone.

He packed the equipment in the Jeep and drove along the narrow track that rounded the old weed-cracked shuffleboard court and ended in the woods near the blue hole. The sun shone, making the blue hole glow through the trees. Matthias carried in his gear and began donning it.

He made two dives. On the first, he descended to the top of the red layer at 50 feet and laid the spare tanks in a niche in the limestone wall. On the second, with the other tanks on his back but free diving to save air, he dove down to 122 feet, switching on a torch when he hit the blackness of the salt water, and glided into the sloping cave to the pile of marble blocks at the end. There, before the manhole-sized hole in the wall, he put one of the regulators in his mouth, purged it and started breathing. He clicked the red dot on the bezel of his watch into place over the minute hand. Then he tied the end of the nylon line around a cylindrical outcrop of limestone near the entrance to the tunnel and pulled himself inside. His tank scraped the rock as he went through, but after a few feet the tunnel widened and he began moving freely. Clipped to his weightbelt, the reel of line silently unwound. There was nothing to hear but his bubbles flowing out of the regulator. Holding the light, Matthias walked on the fingers of one hand until he was sure there was no silt to stir up on the tunnel floor, silt which could quickly reduce visibility to zero; then he shone his light at the ceiling. No silt lined it either, waiting to rain down at the slightest disturbance. All he saw were his own bubbles, clinging to the gray limestone ceiling like tiny flattened balloons. They weren't moving: slack tide. It would be flowing soon, at his back on the way out. On the floor Matthias noticed more debris—broken china, rusty nails, a three-tined fork—but he had no time to examine it. He flutter-kicked into the tunnel.

Cave divers like to say that caves don't kill divers, divers do. But Matthias had done enough of it, years ago in Florida sinks while assigned to the Navy Mine Defense Lab in Panama City, to know that wasn't true. Caves had killed even the most careful and best-prepared divers. The official explanation was always equipment failure, dropped equipment, not enough equipment, wrong equipment, getting tangled in equipment, or: nitrogen narcosis, vertigo, getting lost, or: staying down too long, failure to understand the decompression tables, the bends, or: going down while thinking one was going up, going in instead of going out, or: getting separated from one's buddy, searching too long for one's buddy, getting caught in buddy's death grip.

But unofficially everyone knew that caves do kill people. In open water a diver can easily kill himself too, but at least when trouble strikes he can usually manage to start going up before he dies. In a cave he has to get out first. Cave diving was the most dangerous sport Matthias knew—more dangerous than boxing, hang-gliding, bull-fighting, bear wrestling. The reward was the chance to experience the fun and esthetic pleasure of coal mining. Matthias kicked his way along the tunnel.

It began doing the things cave tunnels do: it widened, narrowed, divided in two. Matthias checked his compass. One tunnel led in a northern direction, at least as far as he could see with his torch. He paused before it, completely still, and felt no current on the skin of his face. The second tunnel led due east. That was the right direction; he also felt water flowing weakly around him, gentle as a summer breeze. The thought made him smile and he looked at his depth gauge: 155. Not deep enough for him to feel the effects of nitrogen narcosis; more accurately, he'd never been narced at that depth before. So why was he smiling? Matthias stopped smiling.

He tied off at the dividing point, looping his line around a limestone spur sticking out from the wall. He checked his air: 2400 p.s.i. No sweat, as his commander in Panama City had liked to say. One-third in, one-third out, one-third in reserve. Matthias caught a handhold inside the eastern tunnel, pulled himself in. He felt the line at his waist, made sure it was unreeling. The nylon line beat Hansel's bread crumbs, but not by much. His commander had used one too, but that hadn't stopped him from disappearing one day in the maze under Warm Mineral Spring.

Matthias swam along through the cone of yellow light. He found himself thinking about the day Danny was born. It was too Freudian, but he thought about it anyway. He was thinking about it so hard that he almost missed the cave that opened up on his left. He paused and shone his light inside. The beam touched the far wall, about thirty feet away. A few stalactites hung from the ceiling and dark silt covered the floor. Matthias fanned his free hand through it. The silt rose quickly, muddying the water. He stuck his hand in up to the shoulder without reaching the limestone floor. But his fingers brushed something. He grasped it and backed out into the tunnel.

It was a military boot, well preserved. The silt would have protected it from the decaying effects of oxygen: it could have been there for a month, a year, a generation. The boot was laced to the top, knotted and bowed. He scraped it clean with his fingernails, then turned it over to see if there was anything written on the sole. There wasn't, but little bones fell out of the boot top and drifted like feathers to the cave floor.

Matthias tied the boot to his line and checked his air pressure: 1650. Then he moved on. His compass pointed east. His depth gauge read 80 feet. That surprised him. He was going up. The tunnel inclined to 70 feet before it dipped back to 80, then beyond—90, 100, 110. At 130 feet it leveled out, but quickly narrowed. Rubble covered the floor. It grew thicker, driving Matthias up to the ceiling. He squeezed along until he could move no farther. Rubble filled the tunnel, except for an opening at the top, just big enough to stick his fist in. He stuck his fist in, felt nothing, withdrew it. Was it the end of the tunnel or a rock fall? And if a rock fall, how extensive? Matthias pointed his light at the small opening. A baby nurse shark came swimming through, the first living thing Matthias had seen in the cave. It turned away from the light and swam back into the hole. Matthias considered the implications of its presence, then began pulling quickly at the topmost rocks. They came away, rolled down the rubble pile. Matthias slipped over the top and down the other side.

There was no sign of the nurse shark. The tunnel stretched ahead, widening slightly in the beam of his light, continuing beyond. Matthias swam on, but less than a minute later he felt a slight tug at his waist, glanced down and saw that he had come to the end of his line. He checked the time: he'd been down for twenty-five minutes; pressure: 1100. Depth: 120. Air one-third gone, out of line, still going in. He found himself smiling again. This was cave diving. Nothing went right.

Matthias unclipped the reel and jammed it between a cut-off stalagmite and the left-hand wall. Then, lineless as the silliest amateur whose body had never been recovered, he kicked on.

He swam quickly now. The tunnel grew to the width of a suburban garage. Matthias kicked harder, not even taking the time to read his pressure gauge. Then all at once the walls, the ceiling, the floor all vanished. It was as though he had stepped off the edge of the Grand Canyon, except he wasn't falling. He shone his light: behind him, and saw the opening of the tunnel he had come out of; overhead, and saw a great rocky dome arching high above. He swung the beam down. It barely reached the opposite wall. His eyes followed the yellow circle along the wall's face. Down, down it went, at least one hundred feet, to the limit of the light's range, and beyond. Matthias aimed the torch straight between his fins. It illuminated a long yellow column of clear water and no sign of the bottom. He was in an enormous underwater chamber, somewhere beneath Andros, or possibly beneath the seabed of Zombie Bay. His heart beat a little faster. That was bad. He took a few even breaths to slow it. Then he checked the depth— 150—and started down.

He spiraled slowly all the way, shining his light around him. He saw black caves in the walls, bare ledges, white limestone columns. But he didn't see the bottom. He hit 200 feet, 220, 230. At that depth he was sucking up ten pounds of air with every breath. There was something he should be doing, but what was it? Something Freudian? Matthias smiled and almost lost his mouthpiece. He squeezed the rubber between his teeth, muttered, "Christ," and kicked harder.

Two hundred and eighty feet. Two ninety. Three hundred. He paused. Three-hundred feet under and seven or eight hundred feet in was a good place for pausing. He smiled again. He was very witty today, down in the cave. A witty caveman. All at once, he wished there was a woman waiting for him when he came out. The wish was so strong it brought tears to his eyes. He was thinking of wiping them away when he remembered he was wearing a mask.

Narced. Matthias grabbed his pressure gauge. That's what he'd been trying to think of. Check the air: 100 p.s.i. As soon as he saw the number his air started to pull hard. He breathed the last of it and switched to the second tank. Three hundred feet down. Seven or eight hundred from the blue hole. "Step one," his old commander had said, "get narced. Step two, get bent. Step three, get buried, if they ever find you."

Get out. Matthias swept his beam into the depths for one last look. And this time he saw the bottom: a cone-shaped pile of rubble, boulders and other objects he couldn't identify. "Christ," he said again, because he knew he should get out. But he went down instead.

Matthias had never dived deeper than 310. Few people did. Fewer returned. Three hundred feet was the theoretical limit for compressed air. After 300 there was more to worry about than nitrogen. Oxygen itself became poisonous. Matthias went down. He hit 320, 330, 340. He felt like a little bird flying in a big night sky, a hidden picture of grace. He did a long slow somersault, wishing that the woman who wasn't waiting by the edge of the blue hole could see it. He was thinking of doing another one for her when he noticed things on the rubble pile, metal things: twisted hunks of rent and rusting steel plate. He checked the depth several times, but the numbers wouldn't register in his mind. He went deeper, and could now make out the rivets. A little deeper, and he saw a big cylinder wedged between two boulders. Deeper still, and he realized it was a submarine conning tower. He hovered above the top of

the pile. He was about to check the depth when he saw
something white in a silty depression. He couldn't look at
two things at once, so he forgot about the depth gauge.
He picked up the white object. It was a human skull.

Time passed. Christ, did it really? Matthias found himself staring into the empty sockets of the skull. How long
had he been doing that? He dropped the skull. *Get going.*
But he didn't get going. He watched the skull waft down
on the pile, saw it roll past a few other skulls and some
bones and out of sight.

Get going.

Matthias took his first kick toward the surface. Then his
torch imploded. His retinas retained a lingering yellow
image of the rubble pile. It quickly faded to blackness. He
could see nothing: not his compass, not his depth gauge,
not his pressure gauge, not up, not down. *Don't panic.*
Panic equals death. Matthias didn't panic. He breathed
slowly, regularly. But that didn't mean he remembered his
second torch right away. And when he did remember it,
he wasn't sure where it was. He felt around his body, finally
locating it on the back of his weightbelt. He spent some
time unclipping it, finding the switch. He pressed it. The
light shone in his face, blinding him. He turned it around,
felt it slipping from his grasp, held on. He aimed the beam
above his head and saw the rubble pile, not far above him.
He was upside down. He reversed himself and kicked up.

At 320 feet he glanced at his pressure gauge: 1900. He
was on the last third, his reserve. He should have been
out by now, but he was in, deep in. "Going to die, pal,"
he said, or thought he said. Then he saw something in the
east wall of the chamber: a big black cave mouth with a
wide ledge sticking out in front. A suitcase lay on it, a few
yards from the edge. Matthias swam over, grabbed it and
started up, kicking, kicking. His heart was beating fast
again, but there was nothing he could do about it. 300,
280, 250, 200. He was coming up too fast, but he didn't
look at his gauges or his watch. His gaze was on the west
wall. Where was the opening? Hadn't it been at 200? He
rose above the 200-foot point. 175. Had he missed it?
Would he go all the way to the dome and end up as one
of those cave divers who tried to claw his way out? No
one would ever know.

Then he saw the opening, a little farther up. He swam

into it and kicked hard. His mind began to clear. What was ahead? The end of the reel, the rubble pile, the cave with the boot. It didn't matter. Once he reached the line he was home, if his air lasted. He glanced at the gauge: 950.

Ahead the tunnel narrowed, as he remembered. Then it divided. He didn't remember that at all. The tunnel divided, but at a sharp angle; the division had been at his back on the way in and he had missed it. Matthias stopped, flashed his light in both entrances. They looked the same. But one led back to the blue hole and the other led nowhere. Air pressure: 600. He had to be right the first time. He forced himself to be still, hoping to feel a current entering either tunnel. He felt nothing. Shouldn't the tide be flowing by now? Perhaps there was some other phenomenon at work in the cave. Was that it, or had he already made his mistake and entered the wrong tunnel coming out of the domed chamber?

Decide. Matthias shone his light into the two tunnels again, hoping to see anything that might differentiate them. There was nothing. He closed his eyes, trying to will the right answer into his consciousness. Because of that, he almost missed the baby nurse shark swimming out of the right-hand tunnel. Matthias turned into it and swam as fast as he could.

He went past the reel without noticing it, so wasn't sure he was right until his light picked out the line running along the right-hand wall. Was it his imagination or was his air just beginning to pull hard? He didn't check the gauge because there was no time and he didn't want to know. The suitcase slowed him down, but he wouldn't let it go. He dragged it over the rubble pile, passed the cave where he had found the boot, reached the second tie-off. He started skip breathing, sucking at his regulator, receiving a grudging breath of air and holding it in. Skip breathing meant risking death by embolism, if the tunnel was going up. Not skip breathing meant running out of air.

Matthias breathed out, breathed in, kicked. He went by the first tie-off. Ahead lay the manhole-sized opening. He shoved the suitcase through, squeezed past after it, swam up through the sloping cave entrance, letting out his breath, and into the blue hole.

Matthias stopped kicking and rose very slowly. Plenty of air left: three or four lungfuls. No sweat, commander. He went up through the red layer and into the light.

His spare tanks lay where he had left them, in the niche at 50 feet. He laid the suitcase on the ledge, doffed his backpack and put it beside the suitcase, opened the valve on the spare tanks and donned them. Then he stuck the regulator in his mouth, breathed out the last breath from the old tanks, sucked in the first one from the new. Air flowed smoothly through the regulator. Perfect. Plan your dive, as every beginner was told, and dive your plan.

Matthias hovered beside the ledge, breathing. For a while that was all he did. Later he looked up at the blue glow above. He breathed and gazed at the blue. That was nice.

Matthias took the decompression tables out of the pocket in his BC. He studied them for a few minutes but they weren't much help: they stopped at 300 feet. He tried to recall the deepest reading on the gauge. 320? 340? Then he recalled that he hadn't checked the gauge at the deepest point. Matthias dropped down to 70 feet. He decompressed there in the darkness for ten minutes, then moved up to 60 for ten more. After that, he returned to 50, and fifteen minutes later rose to 40. Then 30, then 20, then 10. His air began pulling harder. He wished he had brought another spare. But he hadn't, and all he could do was breathe the tank empty and go up.

A few minutes later, he sucked the last mouthful of air out of the tank and finned slowly toward the surface, breathing out all the way. His body didn't twist and bend, he didn't lose control of his legs, nothing stabbed his spine, his shoulders or his hips, his fingertips didn't prickle, his eyelids didn't itch. That meant no nitrogen bubbles were fizzing through his bloodstream: he wasn't bent. A lucky man.

Matthias broke the surface and took a deep breath. He felt the sun and the breeze and reveled in the feeling. Then he shoved the suitcase up on the bank of the blue hole and climbed out after it. He sat on dry land. The warmth of the sun was his; as a bonus, he had a whole skyful of air to breathe. All of a sudden he was a lucky man. A lucky, witty caveman. That thought reminded him of the wish he'd had while narced in the domed chamber, the wish for a woman waiting when he came up. His brain was a domed chamber too. He had penetrated it and found that some part of him hadn't given up on . . . what? Say it: love.

Matthias turned to the suitcase.

| 34 |

It was a small leather suitcase fitted with brass corners and two brass snap locks. The brass had turned green; the leather was coated with algae and felt no stronger than wet cardboard. A plasticized luggage tag hung from the grip. The writing on the tag was blurred, but Matthias could still read it:

NAME: Goldschmidt
ADDRESS: 216 East 33rd St. Apt. 234. New York N. Y.
PHONE: (212) 555-6127

Matthias pushed sideways on the buttons to unsnap the locks, but they broke off and the locks remained shut. He took his dive knife out of the sheath on his arm and sliced the suitcase open. Inside he found two pairs of pants, three shirts, underwear and socks, all decomposing; a plastic shaving kit containing a disposable razor, an exploded can of shaving foam, a toothbrush and a comb; the remains of a book, an airplane ticket, what might have been a passport and some other papers, all of which came apart in his hands and were unreadable.

At the back of the suitcase was a zippered pocket, rusted shut. Matthias tugged at it and the pocket tore open. Two plastic cards fell out. One looked like a Visa card, except it said: "Carte Bleu. Banque National de Paris." The other said: "Fédération Française des Sports Aquatiques." The holder of both cards was named Goldschmidt. Felix Goldschmidt. *But what kind of kike got a name like Felix, right?*

Matthias sat by the blue hole, tapping the cards together. Implications began taking shape in his mind, but none appeared clearly other than this: he would have to dive the blue hole one more time. Matthias pictured the ledge where he had found the suitcase and the black tunnel entrance looming behind it. No one had ever found a blue hole with two openings, but no one had ever explored all the blue holes. Caves with two openings existed. Blue holes were caves. And the baby nurse shark had come from somewhere. Therefore. But not today. No repetitive dive table had ever calculated the decompression stops required if he went back down now.

Something flashed between the pines. Moxie appeared, wearing his Boston Bruins tuque with its gold pompom. "All finish," he said.

"Finish?"

"Scrubbin' down."

Matthias imagined a cross-section with Moxie at the dock scrubbing the boats, ten or fifteen feet of ocean beneath him, then the sandy seabed, and below it the limestone core of the island, and himself tunneling through the rock. A lucky man.

Moxie's eyes roamed over the equipment scattered around the blue hole, came to rest on the suitcase. "What you got?"

"Felix Goldschmidt's suitcase."

"Felix Goldschmidt?"

"The man who went diving with Hiram Standish, Junior."

Moxie squatted beside the suitcase, ran his fingers lightly over one of the brass corners; his gaze moved to the blue hole. "You find it in there?" he said.

"Sort of. Ever been in the blue hole, Moxie?"

"No."

"Or any blue hole?"

"No, mahn."

"You're not curious?"

Moxie shook his head.

"You don't believe in luscas, do you?"

Moxie smiled shyly. "Nottage he say they be down there."

"There are no monsters in the blue holes," Matthias said. Not in the sense Moxie meant. But there must have been monsters of some kind; Matthias thought of the skulls in the domed chamber. He flipped Felix Goldschmidt's dive card to Moxie. "Seen that before?"

"The French one," Moxie said. "I took it down to Brock."

"And then what happened?"

"I tell you so many times, mahn. I tell the police, the judge, everybody."

"Tell me again."

"Brock say, 'Fill the tanks.' "

"Did he have any other reaction? Did he seem excited, or upset?"

"No."

"Did you show him the other card?"

"Other card?"

"Hiram Standish's card."

"The PADI card? No. I know PADI is okay."

"Did Brock meet Hiram Standish?"

"I don't know."

"Did you see them together?"

"No."

"So Brock might not even have heard the name 'Standish'?"

"Maybe not." Moxie picked at the raised letters on the dive card with his fingernail. "How come it be in the blue hole?"

"That's the question." Matthias drew a picture in the dirt: the blue hole, the tunnel, the domed chamber, the ledge, the tunnel in the east wall. He made an X on the ledge. "The suitcase was here."

Moxie stared at the X for a few moments. "All that be underneat'?"

"Underground and under Zombie Bay. It's at least seven hundred feet from here to here, maybe more. But from here to about here is five hundred. That's where I ran out of line."

"Under Zombie Bay?" Moxie said quietly. He touched the X. "How deep under?"

"Where I found it?"

Moxie nodded.

"Three twenty."

Moxie looked closely at Matthias. "You bullshitting me?" But he saw something in Matthias's expression that answered his question, and he looked away. Then he started to laugh. "You drop to three twenty, mahn? Three hundred and twenty feet?"

"More."

"More? Then why you alive, mahn? Why you still breathin'?"

"Luck."

"Luck?" Moxie laughed again, a harsh sound quite unlike his normal laugh. "You crazy, mahn. You want to die?"

"I want to find out who killed Felix Goldschmidt, who put Happy Standish in a coma, and why," Matthias said. Moxie stopped laughing.

"Killed?" he said.

"And tried to make it look like an accident," Matthias said. And thought: An accident blamed on me. He stood up. For an instant, he felt lightheaded and almost stumbled. His eyelids itched; his fingertips prickled. Skin bends.

"You okay?" Moxie said.

"I'm fine," Matthias replied, and began packing up. Moxie helped him. They carried everything to the Jeep and drove back to the club, Moxie at the wheel. Matthias glanced back once at the blue glow in the trees.

They sat in the bar. Matthias breathed pure oxygen from the tank he kept on the barge; the skin bends went away. "Beer?" Moxie said when Matthias laid the tank aside.

"Armagnac," Matthias replied, and sent Moxie up to the house for a bottle. It wasn't so much that he wanted Armagnac, but his body had started to shake a little and he didn't want Moxie there. He poured himself a glass of water, drank it down, then another and another. The shaking stopped. Chick said: "Mojo workin', mojo workin'."

Matthias carried Felix Goldschmidt's suitcase to the office. He placed the suitcase on the desk, beside the telephone. It was so quiet that he wondered whether he had damaged his ears. Then he heard the sea rustling against the shore, and Chick saying something in the bar. He picked up the phone and read the number on the luggage tag to the operator. He heard a clicking sound, like an electronic throat-clearing, followed by a long silence. He waited to hear that the number had been changed, or was no longer in service. Then it began to ring.

A woman answered. "Yes?" she said; one word, but enough for Matthias to know that she was old and that English was not her mother tongue.

He considered several openings.

"Hello?" said the woman. "Hello?"

Afraid she might hang up, Matthias settled on one arbitrarily. "Do you know Felix Goldschmidt?" he asked.

"Felix? Felix? Have you news of Felix?" All at once the woman sounded very near, as though her emotions had the power to shrink the distance between them.

"Not exactly. I found his suitcase. Your number was on it."

"Suitcase?"

"A small leather one."

"With brass corners?"

"Yes. You've seen it before?"

"It's mine. I lent it to him when . . . But you say you have no news of him?"

"I'm not sure. Are you a friend of his?"

"I am his mother, sir. And who are you? May I ask."

Matthias imagined her, hunched over the phone, cradling it with both hands. "My name's Matthias. I own a hotel in the Bahamas."

"The suitcase was at your hotel?"

"Nearby. I found it today. But . . ."

"But what, Mr. Matthias?"

"When was the last time you saw your son?"

"On the thirtieth of August last year. In this room. Why are you asking me?"

"Because I think your son drowned in the ocean here a few days later."

"It is not possible. Felix could swim—he can swim—like a dolphin."

So could Happy Standish—according to *his* mother, Matthias remembered. He said:

"I'm afraid it happened anyway, Mrs. Goldschmidt."

There was a long pause. "And just now you are finding the suitcase?"

"It was underwater, Mrs. Goldschmidt. And we had no way to identify your son. He—his body never surfaced."

"But then how can you say he is dead? He could be alive."

"I don't think so, Mrs. Goldschmidt. He went diving and never came—"

In the background a man said, "What is it, Hilda?" She said, "Shh." And to Matthias: "Sir. Are you there?"

"Yes. I'm sorry to have to tell you this."

"You're sorry."

Matthias said nothing. Tiny voices leaked into the line. Then he heard something that might have been a muffled sob.

"Mrs. Goldschmidt?"

Silence.

"Mrs. Goldschmidt?"

"What is it?" she replied, her voice quiet now, and toneless.

"Do you have any idea why your son came here?"

"I don't know what you mean."

"What was he looking for?"

"I know nothing about that. Nothing."

"But you said you saw him just before he came down. You gave him the suitcase."

"Yes. I said that."

"And he didn't tell you what he was doing?"

"No."

"Why did he have a French dive card? And a French credit card?"

"He was a citizen of France," she said, no longer able to fight off the past tense.

"Have you checked with people there?"

There was a long pause. Then Mrs. Goldschmidt said: "I called the school. He has not returned."

"What school?"

"The University of Aix-en-Provence. Felix taught there."

"What did he teach?"

"History. He specialized in Jewish history."

"How did he know Happy Standish?"

"Begging your pardon?"

"Hiram Standish, Junior. That's who he dove with when he—that's who he came here with."

"Hilda," said the man in the background, "why aren't—" Something muffled his voice. Then the line cleared. Mrs. Goldschmidt was saying, "Shh."

"I asked you about Happy Standish," Matthias said.

"The name is not familiar."

"Your son knew him. They spent time together in Florida."

"I am sorry. I cannot help you."

"You can't help me?"

"No. I— Thank you for troubling. And now I must go."

"Wait, Mrs. Goldschmidt. Don't you want to find out what happened to Felix?"

"Haven't you just told me?"

"I told you what happened, not why. Don't you want to find out why?"

"You said he drowned. I know why people drown, sir. It happens when they breathe water instead of air. Goodbye."

Matthias heard a click, then a faint hum. He hung up the phone, looked up and saw Moxie in the doorway, a bottle of Armagnac and two glasses in his hand.

"That was Felix Goldschmidt's mother," Matthias told him. "She doesn't want to know what happened to him."

"She in France?" Moxie said.

"New York."

"New York?" said Moxie, frowning.

"That's right. Why?"

Moxie looked away.

If you've got something to tell me, speak. Matthias kept that thought to himself; saying it out loud would guarantee Moxie's silence. Matthias waited.

Moxie backed out of the office, walked a little way across the lawn between it and the bar. He leaned against the flagpole. The flags—Bahamian, dive and Jolly Roger—snapped in the wind. Moxie heard them snapping, looked up, sighed. Matthias could hear the sigh from where he stood in the office.

Moxie turned to him. "You know Casey?" he asked.

"Casey?"

"The ticket girl."

Matthias went outside, leaned against the doorjamb. "Yeah."

"She have a friend in Nassau."

Matthias said nothing.

"The friend is a ticket girl too."

"Yeah?"

"At American." Moxie took a deep breath, sighed again. "That's true you found the suitcase at three twenty?" he asked.

"I'll show you the spot."

Moxie laughed, a delighted, open-mouthed laugh that slowly diminished to a giggle, a smile, a straight face. Matthias knew Moxie didn't consider him a friend, but there was something like friendship in his eyes when he said, "Brock he didn't go to Florida like he say. The ticket girl in Nassau be telling Casey. He got on the plane to New York."

Later that day, Matthias caught the Nassau-New York flight himself. He wore the warmest clothes he owned—corduroy pants, a flannel shirt, a plaid-lined windbreaker—but he wasn't prepared for winter in New York. He hadn't been north of Florida in a long time. He felt cold waiting in line for a taxi at Kennedy, cold inside the taxi, where he couldn't get the driver, separated from him by barriers of language and thick glass, to understand that he wanted the front windows rolled up and the heat turned on, cold as he got out of the cab, crossed Fifth Avenue and entered the Plaza Hotel.

He had forgotten how some people lived. He had forgotten about furs and diamonds and wrinkle-free faces on old people, and all the other things that had gnawed at Marilyn and eventually driven her away from him to a richer life with Howie Nero. Matthias, in his windbreaker, corduroys and flannel shirt, walked past a woman in a black silk dress who stood on a small dais playing Mozart on a violin, and stopped at the reception desk.

The clerk, who would not have looked out of place dancing with Katharine Hepburn in a thirties comedy, turned to him and in an accent not unlike Hew's said: "May I help you, sir?" Polite, professional, impersonal, but something in his eyes made Matthias think of Danny: *Mom says you're a dinosaur.*

"I'm trying to reach one of your guests. His name is Brock McGillivray."

"One moment," said the clerk, tapping at a keyboard.

He watched a screen for a few seconds, then said: "We have no guests of that name."

"He might have checked out," Matthias said.

"Checked out?"

"Leaving a forwarding address, for instance."

He tapped again at the keys, and didn't seem unhappy to say, "No McGillivrays in the past week, I'm afraid." Pause. Slight upturn of lips. "Is there anything more I can do for you?"

"Try under 'Muller.' "

"I beg your pardon."

"B. Muller."

The clerk's lips turned up a little more. He was formulating a response when a phone buzzed. He picked it up and started talking.

Matthias began to doubt himself. It was hard to picture Brock at the Plaza. He reached into his shirt pocket for the bill he had found caught in Brock's bedsprings. He turned his head slightly as he did, and so glimpsed an elevator opening on the other side of the lobby, and Brock stepping out.

Matthias almost didn't recognize him. His hair was short, his earring gone, the piece of eight which always hung around his neck not in evidence. Brock had a coat over his arm, wore a dark suit, a white shirt, a maroon tie and tortoiseshell glasses. Matthias had never seen him wear glasses. Except for his size, Brock fitted in perfectly at the Plaza. His size attracted one or two discreet looks. Brock didn't seem aware of them. He put on his coat—a long black coat with a split tail, the kind a gentleman rancher might wear—and walked quickly toward the Fifth Avenue door.

The dinosaur turned and followed.

|HAPPY|

A big Christmas tree lay across the northbound lanes of the Bruckner Expressway, damming thousands of cars in the Bronx. Nina's rented compact was one of them. It brought out the holiday spirit in the traffic reporter on her radio. "Never seen anything like it," he said, making no attempt to hide his glee. In the car next to Nina's, a red-faced man was shouting into a cellular phone. Nina switched to FM, found a classical station doing a Caruso retrospective. She stayed with it until the first two notes of "Salut Demeure." Then she turned off the radio.

Snow began to fall. Nina passed the accident spot. Workers had dragged the Christmas tree to the side of the road. They were cutting it up with chainsaws, as though making an example of it in case any other rebellious conifers were thinking of making a break for it. A policeman blew his whistle at Nina and furiously waved her on.

Traffic was heavy all the way to Danbury. The snow reduced visibility, closing Nina off from the outside world. There was nothing to do but keep the car at a safe speed, pointed in the right direction. With no distractions, her mind, prodded by "Salut Demeure," spun like a wheel and stopped at the night of the birth. Her memory had already edited the material. Struck from the record were the waiting, the pain, the nurses, most of Suze; what remained was the end: Dr. Berry's singing and the baby with

the serious blue eyes. A perfect baby, with all the right
numbers of fingers and toes.

*I trust you understand the importance of good nutrition
and health practices during pregnancy.*

Who had said that? Nina couldn't remember. Was it
important? Turning onto Route 7, she tried to concentrate.
But her mind didn't want to help her. It wanted to draw
up a list of boy names and linger over them one by one.
The names were already materializing, like photographs
in a darkroom bath. Nina forced herself not to see them,
to resist the pleasure, normally so domestic and maternal,
but in her case irrelevant and masochistic. She would get
no pleasure of any kind from what had been done to her.
She would never forget, never forgive, never allow herself
to heal, never accept. Until someone proved otherwise,
her baby was alive and therefore somewhere, and that
meant there was no excuse to stop looking for him. That
was her job.

Nina told herself that, and for a few miles felt strong
and purposeful. But in the darkroom, boy names kept
taking shape. She had to turn the radio on loud to make
them recede. Reggae vibrated through the car.

> *When it drops*
> *Oh you gotta feel it*
> *Know what you were doin' wrong*
> *It is you oh yeah yeah yeah*
> *I say pressure drop oh pressure oh yeah*
> *Pressure gonna drop on you.*

Nina drove up into the hills. For a while the snow fell hard
in thick, heavy flakes; Nina crept along on one narrow
road and then another. But as she entered Washington,
the snowfall stopped abruptly. After a few moments, it
began again, but very lightly, like the beginning of the
slow movement.

The town was a dream of long-ago America. White colonial mansions in perfect condition surrounded a small
green. There was no litter, no dirt, no advertising, no sign
of poverty or conflict or anything unpleasant, not even
evidence of how money was made. Pure white snow covered everything: the roofs of the white houses, the green,

the limbs of the huge old oaks and spruces. She might have been in a crystal paperweight that a giant had just shaken gently to keep the snow falling. Nina turned down the radio and drove past the green.

The post office was close by, opposite a Congregational church. Nina parked and went inside. Behind the counter stood the first human being she had seen in the town. He was a little man with protruding ears and a pointed tongue he was using to lick a FRAGILE—HANDLE WITH CARE sticker.

"Can you give me directions?" Nina said. "I'm looking for the Standish Foundation."

"Foundation?" the man said, slapping the sticker on a parcel and tossing it on a pile behind him.

"The Standish Foundation. Box one-oh-one."

"That's Mrs. Standish," the man said. "I don't know about any foundation." The word seemed to irritate him, as though it were some highfalutin import from a more sophisticated culture.

"Right," said Nina. "Can you tell me how to find her?"

"You already know."

"I already know?"

"Box one-oh-one."

A New York postal clerk might not have told her what she wanted either, but that would have been for his own enjoyment. This man was protecting Mrs. Standish's privacy like some old retainer. "But I want to talk to her," Nina said.

The clerk looked her up and down, not in a sexual way, but more like a movie butler searching for signs of social status. "Is she expecting you?"

"I don't know her," Nina replied. "But I'm passing through and an old friend of hers in Paris asked me to stop and say hello if I could." She spoke casually, as though the clerk probably had lots of friends in Paris too, and would understand the situation.

The man rubbed the day-old growth on his chin, perhaps imagining a scene in the future when Mrs. Standish discovered that the wishes of her Parisian friend had been thwarted in the village post office. Then he picked up a stack of letters and with his back to Nina began sorting them into post boxes with quick, jabbing movements. "One-oh-nine east," he said. "Take the third turning on the right. You'll see a gate."

"Thank you," Nina said. The clerk jammed *Architectural Digest* into someone's slot.

Nina found the third turning on the right about a mile past the last house in the town. It was an unplowed lane, densely lined on both sides with tall evergreens that darkened the sky and brushed the roof of the car. Deprived of traction, Nina's rear wheels whined in the snow, from time to time biting into something solid and making the car lurch sideways. Nina, who seldom drove and never in conditions like these, was so intent on the steering wheel and the pedals that she almost went by the gate without seeing it. She pulled to the side of the lane, got out and walked back.

The gate, mounted between two stone pillars in a narrow opening in the trees, was closed. It was made of narrowly separated wrought-iron bars topped high above with sharp-looking brass flourishes. Nina tried the handle and found it locked. She searched the pillars in vain for a bell or buzzer.

Nina peered through the bars. Whiteness extended for acres toward a house in the distance, a monotone broken only by a few bare trees, and occasional wooden stakes suggesting garden plots under the snow. It was the sort of house the editors of *Country Life* liked to put on the cover: four stories high, with a main section and two perpendicular wings, all solid stone that would probably glow if the sun were shining.

"Hello," Nina called. "Hello!" She waved her arms in case anyone was watching from the house. There was no response. Then she shook the gate in case the lock had frozen, and tried it unsuccessfully again. After that, she just stood there in the snow, which fell more heavily now, growing cold. She saw no footprints, no tire tracks, no parked cars, no sign of life.

People who lived in houses like this might not be around in December, Nina thought. She considered returning to the post office to ask if they were holding Mrs. Standish's mail. But she didn't want to go another round with the clerk. Instead she walked to the side of one of the stone pillars and tried to squeeze between it and the nearest tree. The tree was a spruce, so when Nina felt something prick her thigh she thought it was a needle and pushed on. Then something sharp dug into her, just below the cheekbone. She jerked back, hand on her face. When she re-moved it there was blood on her fingers. Nina carefully separated the branches and saw barbed wire. There were at least a dozen strands of it. Nina returned to the gate, again looked through and saw that the grounds were sur-rounded by an unbroken wall of evergreens. She walked twenty or thirty yards in one direction, then the other, parting the branches of the trees, finding barbed wire every time. She went back to the gate, stared at the snow, the garden stakes, the house. She got colder. Red dots ap-peared in the snow at her feet. Nina reached up and touched her cheek. This time there was more blood on her hand. She studied it for a few moments. Then she wedged her boots between the wrought iron bars and began climbing. First at Laura Bain's, now here: she was becoming a habitual trespasser.

Getting to the top of the gate was easy. The problems began after that. First, she had to somehow turn around and climb down the other side. Second, the brass flourishes at the tips of the wrought-iron bars proved to be as sharp as they looked. Third, the ground seemed much farther away than she had expected. With her hands on the cold bars, Nina raised one foot and placed it on top of a brass point. Then she released her hands, one by one, and gripped the bars from the other side, with her thumbs at the bottom. Now all that remained was a simple raising of the other foot, with a quick pivot and an equally quick change of grip so that her thumbs would once more be on top. It was neatly planned, like a big meeting at work. She could even picture herself doing it. Nina pictured herself doing it a few times. Then she tried it.

The foot raising was perfect, the pivot quick. But the grip change didn't happen. Instead Nina heard a ripping sound, felt pain on the back of her leg, saw the sky: solid gray clouds that tilted suddenly toward rising trees in the distance. Then she heard a thump, a thump that seemed to originate inside her chest. It knocked all the air out of her lungs. Nina tried to breathe some back in, and found she could not.

She lay on her back in the snow, gasping for air. Slowly her breathing returned to normal. She sat up, examined the long tear in the back of one of her pant legs and the deep scratch in the skin, shook snow out of her collar.

Except for the blood, the experience reminded her of a ski trip she had taken with one of The Boyfriends. Nina rose and walked toward the house.

The driveway had not been plowed, but snowbanks on either side made it easy to follow. As she neared the house she saw it was even bigger than she had thought, and luxurious in detail: leaded windows, stained glass, an open colonnade on the second floor. The entrance was a massive double door with a stained-glass rondelle of the head of a Gothic angel in each. Nina saw a button in the stone wall beside the door and pressed it.

Chimes rang in the house. Then there was silence. Nina pressed the button again. Chimes rang. Silence. Nina was reaching for the button once more when she heard a click and the door opened.

A silver-haired woman stood in the doorway. Beside her was the biggest, sleekest, blackest Doberman Nina had ever seen. Its eyes were on her. They didn't like what they saw. The muscles in the dog's back rose in rigid planes and it barked angrily.

"Quiet, Zulu," the woman said, not raising her voice, or touching or looking at the dog. Zulu stopped barking at once, but his muscles remained flexed. The woman was looking at Nina's cheek. "Yes?" she said.

"Mrs. Standish?" Nina said.

"Correct."

Nina had rehearsed a little opening, but it had lost its coherence in her fall. That, and Mrs. Standish's appearance, made her pause. She doubted that Mrs. Standish had ever wished that some feature of her face or body were different. She had perfect bones, perfect skin, perfect bearing. Except for the thick, silver hair hanging down past her shoulders and the deep-set eyes with irises so uniformly and brightly blue they might have been ceramic rather than human tissue, Mrs. Standish could have passed for someone Nina's age. In charcoal gray tweed with a diamond necklace and sapphire earrings she might have been expecting the photographer from *Country Life* at any moment. The only incongruity was the little blue sweater that hung from the knitting needles in her hand. She had one sleeve to finish.

"I'm Nina Kitchener," Nina said.

The deep-set eyes met hers. "Do I know you?" Mrs. Standish asked. "I don't think I do."

"You don't," Nina said. "But I've come from New York. I'm hoping you can help me."

"How is that?"

"It's about the Human Fertility Institute."

"The Human Fertility Institute?"

"It's owned by the Standish Foundation, isn't it?"

"Oh dear," said Mrs. Standish. "I'm afraid you're too late."

"What do you mean?"

"I believe we sold it recently. I can't remember quite to whom."

"Standard Foods. A straight swap for shares."

"My goodness," said Mrs. Standish. "You know more about my affairs than I do."

"I hope not," Nina told her.

Mrs. Standish smiled. Her teeth were small, white, perfect; the smile complex. "You've cut your face," she said.

"I know."

"Come in. I've got Band-Aids in the kitchen."

Nina stepped into the house. The dog growled and blocked her way.

"Zulu," said Mrs. Standish. "Be nice."

Zulu stopped growling. He let Nina pass, but rubbed his hard muzzle against her hip as she went by. She followed Mrs. Standish through a hall with a pink and white marble floor. A martyrdom of Saint Sebastian hung on the opposite wall. The saint, much larger than life, was suffering horribly, beseeching eyes on the heavens. Nina didn't need to read the signature to know it was an El Greco.

Many doors opened off the corridor. Nina glimpsed Persian rugs, plush furniture, paintings, tapestries, sculptures. The corridor made a ninety-degree turn into one of the wings of the house and they entered the kitchen. It had a freezer, two big refrigerators and a microwave, and a wall hung with copper pots and pans, but nothing was cooking. There was no smell of food, no bowl of fruit, no dishes in the sink, no sign that anything ever had been cooking. Mrs. Standish opened a cupboard and took out a brown bottle and a box of bandages.

"Come into the light," she said.

Nina moved to a window. It looked out on the hills at the back of the house. At their base stood a stone cottage. A wheelbarrow full of snow rested by the door and smoke rose from the chimney.

"Let's have a look," Mrs. Standish said, taking Nina's chin in one hand and peering at the cut on her cheek. Mrs. Standish's hand was cold; she smelled of some perfume that reminded Nina of roses, but mixed with the roses, faintly but unmistakably, was the smell of fresh sweat.

"Quite shallow," Mrs. Standish said. "I shouldn't think you'll need stitches." She let go of Nina's chin, uncapped the brown bottle and dipped a Q-tip into it. "This might sting a bit," she said, taking Nina's chin in one hand again and dabbing at her cheek with the Q-tip.

Perhaps because she was unprepared for more than a little sting, Nina was unable to stifle her cry of pain, or stop her head from snapping back: it felt as though Mrs. Standish had sunk a hot needle into her face. The deep-set eyes watched impassively.

"What the hell was that?" Nina said.

"Just some iodine," Mrs. Standish replied. "You don't want an infection, do you?"

"Iodine? No one uses iodine anymore."

"Really?" said Mrs. Standish. "My husband was a doctor and he swore by it."

"That must have been some time ago," Nina said, a remark she began to regret not long after it was voiced.

Mrs. Standish smiled. "Oh, it most certainly was." She took a small butterfly bandage from the box and stripped off the protective seal. "Shall we get this on?"

Nina moved forward. Mrs. Standish stuck the bandage on Nina's face in one efficient motion, not gentle, not rough, eyes intent on the task. Nina looked directly into them. They were like works of art, but from a culture Nina didn't know; she could interpret nothing. She smelled the roses and the sweat, but no longer just the sweat of Mrs. Standish. Now she was sweating too.

"All fixed," said Mrs. Standish, capping the brown bottle and returning it to the cupboard. "Now then, Miss—or is it Mrs.—?"

"I use Ms."

"Do you? Well, Ms. Kitchen, why don't we—"

"It's Kitchener."

"How inexcusable of me—first the honorific and now the name," said Mrs. Standish. "Not a descendant of Lord Kitchener, by any chance? My father met him on several occasions, if I'm not mistaken."

"No," Nina said. "The connection is one-sided."

"Connection?"

"We took his name, that's all."

Mrs. Standish blinked. "I don't quite follow."

"Some relative on my father's side. Before World War One, I think."

"Are you saying he changed his name?"

"Exactly. It's not that unusual, is it?"

Mrs. Standish's eyes shifted toward the window. "Of course not, Ms. Kitchener." She looked at Nina and smiled. The deep-set eyes didn't participate. "Shall we sit down?" Mrs. Standish picked up her knitting and led Nina out of the kitchen, along the corridor and into another corridor. "Let's try the little sitting room," Mrs. Standish said, opening a door. "It's quiet. We can talk."

The whole house is quiet as a tomb, Nina thought. And the little sitting room was bigger than her apartment. "Please sit," Mrs. Standish said, gesturing to a chair covered in gold silk. Nina sat, aware as she did of the tear in her pants and the scratch, possibly still bloody, on her leg.

The gold chair had a twin. Mrs. Standish sat in it. Both chairs faced a pink marble fireplace piled with unlit birch logs. Over the fireplace hung another El Greco, this one a crucifixion. It wasn't the only crucifixion in the room: another hung in a corner. It dated from an earlier period: Christ and one or two onlookers wore halos of beaten gold.

"It's real, I take it," said Nina, meaning the El Greco.

Mrs. Standish misinterpreted her. "Oh yes," she replied. "From a quarry near Siena. We had rather a lot of it after—at one point."

"I mean the painting."

"The crucifixion?"

"Yes."

"Real?"

"A real El Greco."

"I see. Why, yes, it is. Not one of his best, but not without its charms either." Nina gazed at the five bloody wounds, thought of the four on Saint Sebastian, and realized that Mrs. Standish hadn't asked how she had cut her face.

Mrs. Standish crossed her legs—long, elegant legs, still finely muscled, and reached for her knitting. "You wanted to talk to me about the foundation, I believe? I trust it's not about a grant. That's not my department at all."

All at once, there was something familiar about Mrs. Standish's voice. A memory stirred in Nina's brain, but didn't come into view. "It's not about a grant, Mrs. Standish."

"Good. It's nice to have visitors here in the country. If it's not about grants and getting money and that sort of thing."

"It's not about grants or money," Nina said. "It's about the Human Fertility Institute, as I mentioned."

"So you did," said Mrs. Standish, smiling. There was nothing simple about her smile: it had a language all its own.

"Do you know where Dr. Crossman is?" Nina asked.

"Dr. Crossman?" Mrs. Standish took up her knitting. She wore several big rings, but they didn't get in her way. The needles hooked and thrust with quick, sure movements and the sleeve began taking shape: it was a nice sweater with a white anchor on the chest.

"The director of the institute. At least he was."

"I'm not familiar with the name."

"But Mr. Percival said you hired him."

"Percival is misinformed," said Mrs. Standish, reacting not at all to the introduction of his name.

"The foundation, then. He said the foundation hired Dr. Crossman."

"That is not impossible. I had no dealings with the fertility people."

"Then who did?"

"May I ask what your interest is in this doctor?"

"I was a client of the institute. Dr. Crossman handled the impregnation procedure. My baby was kidnapped out of the hospital. And now Dr. Crossman has disappeared and the institute is defunct. Is that good enough?"

Mrs. Standish laid down her knitting. "How awful for you," she said. Her jeweled hands fell limply on the little sweater. "But I'm still not sure what it is you want with the doctor. Is he a suspect in the kidnapping?"

"No. But he probably knows the identity of the sperm donor, and I want that name."

"Is the sperm donor a suspect?"

"Yes."

"In that case, I'm surprised I haven't been contacted by the authorities."

"The authorities haven't been very helpful."

"Oh dear," said Mrs. Standish, taking up her knitting. The needles jabbed and darted their way past the elbow.

"The problem is that I can't find Crossman and no one seems to know where the institute's records are."

"That is a dilemma."

"It's more than that to me," Nina said.

"Of course it is," said Mrs. Standish, halfway to the wrist.

"Do you have the records, Mrs. Standish?"

"I?" she said, looking up.

"The foundation, then."

"I really have no idea. Is that what you want? My help in finding the records?"

"Yes." Nina said. "Someone at the foundation must know. Who handled dealings with the institute?"

Mrs. Standish sighed. "There is a board."

"And who's on it?"

"I am. Percival. And Happy."

"Happy?"

"My son."

"Can we talk to him, then?"

"Talk to Happy?"

"Since you and Mr. Percival don't know. That leaves your son, unless there are other members of the board."

"There are no other members," said Mrs. Standish. She hooked the last stitch, cut the yarn with scissors she took from her jacket pocket, held up the sweater and examined it. "We can talk to Happy," she said. "The problem is he can't talk back."

"I don't understand."

Mrs. Standish folded the sweater neatly and placed it in her lap. "Have you heard of the locked-in syndrome?"

"No."

Mrs. Standish looked into Nina's eyes. "It's a type of coma where the victim is totally paralyzed but aware of everything. The difficulty is finding a way to determine from the outside that awareness exists. In my son's case, we are fairly sure that this has been done. But not one hundred percent. That may be asking too much, I'm told."

"He's in a coma?"

"Has been for a year and a half. Will be for the rest of his life. Which may not be of normal duration. He's very susceptible to illness now."

Nina looked away. No words came to mind. The ground had tilted beneath them, raising her up, dragging Mrs. Standish down, changing the balance. Mrs. Standish felt it too. She glanced down at the sweater and said: "So you can see why I sympathize with you." She was quiet for half a minute, perhaps more, staring into space and stroking the sweater with her fingers. Then she said: "I'll do what I can to help."

"You will?"

"I'll talk to Percival in the morning. But you'll have to give me a day or two. Percival will get in touch with you." She rose.

Nina rose too. "Thank you, Mrs. Standish."

Mrs. Standish smiled.

Nina saw that she had left a red streak on the gold silk.

Mrs. Standish took her to the front door. Zulu was lying in front of it. He sprang up and flexed. "Be nice, Zulu," Mrs. Standish said. Zulu remained flexed. Mrs. Standish opened the door.

Clouds of snow blew into the hall. Outside the wind was blasting, hurling snow through the sky in sheets and twisters, piling it up on the threshold. The storm was playing the third movement in its score, and it was a wild one. "Gracious," said Mrs. Standish, raising her voice over the wind. "You can't go out in that." She slammed the door.

| 36 |

Night fell. Nature demonstrated its power, closing Route 7, then the Merritt, then 95, socking in all the little towns in the hills of western Connecticut.

"Call me Inge," said Mrs. Standish.

In the dining room, she and Nina ate tuna fish sandwiches on white bread and drank water. A birch-log fire burned in the grate, although Nina had seen no one light it. "Do you live here alone?" she asked.

Mrs. Standish finished chewing. "It's the servants' day off," she said. "And we're not as big as we look, especially since the south wing was closed."

They sat at one end of a long, dark table, Mrs. Standish at the head, Nina at the side, facing the fire. Candles burned in the center of the table, but they seemed far away and did little to lighten the room. It might have been a recreation of a medieval refectory; perhaps it was a real one, shipped across the ocean and reassembled. Dark wood encrusted with rosettes paneled the walls and ceiling; ornate, heavy buffets and armoires stood in the corners; over the fireplace hung an oil painting of a pale man in a dark suit. Nina had seen his weak chin before.

"Who is that?" she asked.

Mrs. Standish glanced up. The light from the candles and the fire flickered on her fine face but left her deep-set eyes in shadow. "Hiram Standish. My husband." She stared at the man in the portrait. "Long dead of course.

A lifetime, it seems." She looked away from the painting, picked up her glass, sipped. "I've had three lives, really, like so many women—before marriage, marriage, after marriage."

Times had changed. Nina, and a lot of women she knew, were still in life one, or had passed so quickly and unhappily through life two that it didn't count. "There's another portrait of him at the institute. Or there was."

Mrs. Standish nodded. "We founded the institute in his honor."

Nina waited for Mrs. Standish to continue. When she didn't, Nina said: "What kind of a doctor was he?"

"An obstetrician, by training. But research was his love. He spent most of his time in the lab."

"What sort of research?"

"He specialized in fertility. Like my father."

"Your father was an obstetrician too?"

"He never practiced. He taught and did his research." She turned to Nina. "My father developed the first fertility drug ever used." Nina heard the pride in her voice, and wondered if there were tears in her eyes, but all she could see were shadows. Mrs. Standish cleared her throat. "That was in 1922," she continued in her normal voice.

A normal voice, Nina thought, that she had heard before. And was it normal? It occurred to her that English, as perfectly, even stylishly as Mrs. Standish spoke it, might not be her first language. "Where was this?" Nina asked.

"Where was what?"

"Where your father did his research."

"Various universities and institutes," Mrs. Standish replied. "Whoever would pay."

"Was it marketed?" asked Nina, wondering where all the money had come from.

"Marketed?"

"The fertility drug."

"Not really 'marketed,' " Mrs. Standish said. "It was used experimentally and of course that led to the development of all the modern fertility drugs."

"That sounds important," Nina said. "What was his name?"

"Do you mean my father?"

"Yes. Is he still alive?"

Mrs. Standish pushed away the remains of her sandwich

and stood up. "My father died in the war," she said. "And his name would mean nothing to you. He never got the recognition he deserved." She walked to the window. "Look at that," she said.

Nina turned. There was nothing to see but driving snow. She checked her watch. Almost nine. She finished her water but left most of the sandwich Mrs. Standish had made for her. "Did any of your children go into obstetrics too?"

The skin of Mrs. Standish's forehead drew itself down into a V. "Happy is my only child," she answered. "And no, he did not. His inclinations were artistic. They are artistic, I should say. I don't suppose inclinations would change, even in his circumstances, do you?"

Mrs. Standish no longer gazed out the window. She was looking at Nina, and now the firelight shone on her eyes, hard and blue.

"I really don't know," Nina said.

Mrs. Standish snorted. It was unsettling, like seeing royalty do something vulgar. Perhaps Mrs. Standish saw this reaction on Nina's face. She returned to the table, sat down and sipped her water.

"Some wine?" she said.

"No thanks."

"I could get a bottle from the pantry."

"Not for me."

"I won't bother then," Mrs. Standish said, staring at the miniature flames dancing inside a diamond on her finger.

"Did your son end up pursuing an artistic career?"

"In a way. He studied music and became a critic. A published critic."

"Who did he write for?"

"Various newspapers and magazines."

"Freelance?"

"Is there anything unworthy about that?"

"Not at all. What sort of music did he cover?"

"Popular," said Mrs. Standish. The word seemed to displease her.

"Is the sweater for his child?"

"Sweater?"

"The one you're knitting. I thought it might be for your grandson."

"Grandson?"

"Because it's blue."

The V deepened in Mrs. Standish's forehead. "Happy never married." She was looking at Nina again, her eyes once more in shadow. "Not that he was homosexual or anything like that—he's had girlfriends. But none suitable." Her water glass was three-quarters full. She drank it down in one swallow. When she spoke again her voice was quiet. "There was no hurry, you see. A man can marry at any time. As opposed to a woman. Reproductively speaking, I mean." She paused, and her voice was stronger when she added: "But I probably don't need to tell you that."

"It's why I went to the institute."

Mrs. Standish nodded. Then she was silent. A log crackled in the fire. Mrs. Standish raised a hand and smoothed the V from her forehead. Nina tried to imagine her as a grandmother, and could: the kind of grandmother who might have tea at the Carlyle, and own a house in the South of . . . A strange idea began taking shape in Nina's mind, but before she could examine its implications, or even see it clearly, Mrs. Standish said:

"Tell me something about your family, then. We've exhausted the subject of mine."

"There's not much to tell. My father worked in a bank and my mother taught school. They're both dead and I don't have brothers or sisters."

"But you're still young. How did your parents die?"

"Cancer."

"Cancer?"

"There were other complications at the end. But basically it was cancer."

"My God," said Mrs. Standish. She seemed upset. "Is there a lot of cancer in your family? In the past, I mean."

"Not that I know of."

Mrs. Standish's shadowy eyes regarded Nina for a long moment. "Good," she said. Then she checked her watch. "Look at the time."

"I know."

They both faced the window, and saw what they had been seeing for hours. "I'm afraid I retire rather early," Mrs. Standish said. "You'll have to stay the night."

"I really couldn't."

Mrs. Standish smiled her complicated smile. Firelight

glowed on her even little teeth. "Is there an alternative?"

Nina pictured her rental car buried in snow, the local roads impassable, the route to the city closed. There was no alternative.

"We have a nice little guest room in the north wing," Mrs. Standish said. "It's all made up."

She led Nina along a long hall, up two flights of stairs and down another hall to a corner room with one set of windows facing the road and another overlooking the south wing. It was a pretty room, with floral-printed furniture and curtains and a four-poster bed. "The lavatory is through there," said Mrs. Standish. She folded down a corner of the eiderdown and patted the pillow. "Sleep well," she said, going out and closing the door.

Mrs. Standish's footsteps faded away. Nina went to the window that faced the road and watched a world that might have been created by Jackson Pollock, using only black and white. She sat on the bed, sinking into the soft feather mattress. It made her think of Europe. So did the prints on the wall—landscapes that were all dark skies, except for the occasional tiny rustic at the bottom. She opened all the drawers and closets and cabinets in the room, hoping to find a radio or television, something to connect her with the world outside the storm. All she found were wooden hangers, a book—*The Sorrows of Werther*, but in the original—two towels, a bar of soap from the Plaza Hotel and a business card. A scuba diver was on his way to the bottom of the card; bubbles outlined in blue floated toward the top. "*Zombie Bay Club*," read the card. "*N. H. Matthias, P.O. Box 9, Blufftown, Andros Island, the Bahamas. Tel. (809) 555-9865.*"

Nina went into the bathroom. Everything that could be gold-plated was, including the frame of the mirror over the sink. In the mirror Nina saw a purple bruise spreading beyond the borders of Mrs. Standish's butterfly bandage, and a streak of crusted blood that ran all the way to her jawbone. Why hadn't Mrs. Standish mentioned the blood, or even appeared to notice it? Nina splashed cold water on her face, washing the blood away. The bruise remained.

Nina took off her shoes and lay down on the bed, leaving her clothes on. She pulled the eiderdown over her body, but didn't get between the sheets. They were nice sheets, silk with a pattern of tulips and bluebells, but Nina didn't

want them around her. She switched off the bedside light
and closed her eyes. On the inside of her eyelids waited
a Jackson Pollock in black and white: the state of her mind.
It was too confusing to sort out. Clinging to one fact, Mrs.
Standish's promise to help, Nina tried to sleep.

She tried for a long time, lying in the soft bed in the
enormous house, listening to the little world of her own
breathing and the big world of the storm, firing snow pel-
lets at the windows. Then she stopped trying. That didn't
work either. Nina got up.

She stared out one of the windows facing the road. She
couldn't see it. All she could see was the storm. Then the
glass misted under her breath, blurring even that. It was
due to the mist that Nina wasn't sure whether she saw a
sudden yellow glow coming from the direction of the road.
By the time she rubbed the mist away, the glow, if it had
existed at all, was gone.

Nina stood by the window for a while, waiting for the
glow to reappear. Then she gave up. She lay down on the
bed again, pulled up the eiderdown. This time she couldn't
even keep her eyes closed. She got up, looked out the
window, saw nothing but the storm; then peered through
the curtains covering the other windows, those facing the
closed-off wing.

And Nina saw green light shining through a window on
the ground floor. Not bright, but steady: she closed her
eyes, looked again, and it was still there.

Nina watched the green light. Minutes passed. Nina
knew what she had to do long before she did it.

Nina opened the door of her room. She walked down
the hall. The lights had been switched off, but the faint
luminosity of night, even such a starless and moonless one,
came through the windows and lit her way. She reached
the stairs and started down, silent in her stocking feet.
Nina descended two flights and entered the long corridor.
It had no windows; she walked on in total darkness, feeling
her way with her hands. Many rooms opened off the corridor, great spaces full of shadows that seemed to move
under her gaze, although she knew they were only pieces
of furniture. She came to the dining room. Embers glowed
in the fireplace, bright enough to reveal Zulu, asleep on
the rug. Nina froze. Zulu shuddered, but he didn't wake

up. Perhaps he thought her smell was only part of a bad
dream. Nina tiptoed by.

At the end of the hall there were more windows. By
their light, Nina saw a closed door. She turned the knob;
the door swung open without a squeak: Mrs. Standish was
too rich to have squeaky doors. Ahead Nina saw a flight
of stairs leading up into darkness, and a corridor beside
it. She was in the south wing.

Nina walked along the corridor. Her feet felt thick carpet; would there still be rugs in the closed-off wing of a
house? She didn't know. She had never been in a house
with wings before, except as a tourist. Ahead she saw a
faint green glow.

It escaped through the crack under a door on her right,
not far away. Nina stopped before it, listening. She heard
nothing. She put her hand on the knob. Slowly, she turned
it, slowly pushed open the door.

On the other side was a room. Nina could see clearly:
a wall monitor lit everything green. A green line moved
across the monitor, rose to a peak, fell, moved, rose, fell,
moved to the end of the screen, reappeared at the beginning, rose, fell. In the center of the room stood a bed.
Wires ran to the bed from the monitor, and from other
machinery as well. On the bed lay a fair-haired man, with
an eiderdown, much like the one in her room, pulled up
to his chin. An IV feeding bag hung over him and he had
a breathing tube in his nose. The eyes of the fair-haired
man were open. They gazed at the ceiling. It was a white
ceiling, separated from the white walls by a gilded molding.
A spider web clung to the underside of the molding. A fat
spider, green in the light of the monitor, stood motionless
on the wall.

Nina stepped into the room, moved toward the bed. She
made no effort to be quiet now, but the fair-haired man
continued to gaze at the ceiling. Nina stood beside the bed
and looked down at him. His face was very thin, but it
was a fine face, with blue eyes as beautiful as Mrs. Standish's, but softer.

"Happy?"

The blue eyes gazed at the ceiling.

| 37 |

Dying was just like living, full of surprises. When he thought he finally had dying down to a system, a functioning arrangement made up of the in-crowd—components one, two and three—and the outsiders, the walking talkers—Mother, Fritz, Dr. Robert—who should appear but a stranger in the night, saying: "Happy?"

The stranger was in his sights. A green stranger, but he knew that that was because of the night. Nights were green when you were dying. Just another surprise.

The stranger had beautiful dark eyes. There was something familiar about those eyes, full of powerful, painful emotions, barely under control. Or was he reading too much in them? Probably. He had never been a good judge of things like that, and why would he be any better now, under the control of Dr. Robert and his drugs?

Lobsters? Did the green woman have something to do with lobsters? There was a scandal. PCBs. Had she poisoned the ocean with PCBs? He didn't think so. The woman was still looking down at him.

Say something.

"I'm Nina." The woman spoke, almost on cue. She had a lovely voice. "Can you hear me? Your mother says you can."

And then he remembered—not the lobster story, but the kidnapping story: *I want my baby back very much.*

How sharp his memory was! But why not? Memory was the sole task of component number three.

The dark eyes watched him. They were so different from the eyes of Mother, Fritz, Dr. Robert: they hid nothing. Or if they hid something, they did it so cleverly he didn't know, which was just as good. Or was it? Damn. His mind was wandering now, spinning uselessly like a motor when the gears were stripped. Don't spin. Look at the woman. A special woman, that was obvious. And one who had spoken to him at the very moment he was hoping she would. A suitable woman, Mother? That would depend on her background. He gazed into her dark eyes but could tell nothing about the woman's background.

Talk to me.

But now the woman didn't speak. She looked down on him for a few more moments: they were gazing into each other's eyes, weren't they, like lovers or something? And then she backed away, out of the circle of his sight, beyond his horizon. He heard her footsteps moving away, but he didn't hear the door opening or closing. Instead he heard paper rustling.

Nina crossed Happy Standish's room. She examined three framed photographs hanging over a desk. They were all of Happy Standish, so much healthier that he scarcely resembled the man on the bed. Photograph One: a young long-haired Happy Standish in a Dartmouth sweater, kneeling in the front row of a soccer team picture. Photograph Two: a slightly older Happy Standish, with slightly shorter hair, serving a tennis ball, the racquet in his left hand. Photograph Three: a still-older Happy Standish in evening dress, smiling at the camera, his hands on a piano keyboard.

Nina opened a closet. It was full of clothes: winter suits, summer suits, tweed jackets, shirts, ties. And shoes: tennis, jogging, hiking, climbing, boating, wingtips, penny loafers, tassel loafers, shoes still in their boxes. Nina picked up a box of Rockport walking shoes. Happy was an 11B.

On a shelf above the clothing lay a file folder. Nina looked inside. It contained clippings from newspapers and magazines—*Billboard, Melody Maker, The Boston Phoenix, Toronto Life, The Atlanta Constitution, The St. Louis*

Post-Dispatch, The Vancouver Sun, The Independent—all under the byline Hiram Standish, Jr. The last, a one-column report on a festival of North African music, had appeared in *The Village Voice,* datelined Aix-en-Provence, July 12 of the previous year, almost eighteen months before.

Happy had written about Sonny Rollins, Joe King Carrasco, Doc Watson, Etta James, Jay McShann, Dwight Yoakum, Linda Ronstadt, Lou Reed, Red Rodney, the McGarrigle Sisters, the Everly Brothers. There were about two dozen clippings in the folder. Nina wondered if that was Happy's entire output. She replaced the folder, closed the closet door, glanced at the monitor. The green line rose to a peak, fell, rose, fell, ran off the edge, reappeared on the other side. Nina returned to the bedside.

The dark-eyed woman came back inside his world. Nina. She glanced at the respirator machine, the IV bag, him.

Talk to me.

The woman spoke, but quietly, more to herself than to him. "I like Etta James too," she said. She was facing him but her eyes were on something far away, something that made her anxious.

Go on.

The woman focused her eyes on him. This time she raised her voice to normal conversational level. "I saw your clippings in the closet."

She had understood at once that his eyes couldn't follow her around the room! It had taken Mother weeks; sometimes she still forgot.

The woman bit her lip. It was a soft, finely shaped lip. Luscious. "I guess I shouldn't have opened it. It's your closet." She sighed. "God, I wish you could talk." She closed her eyes. "What a thing to say. But . . ." The faraway look returned to her eyes.

Go on.

The woman shook her head—she had thick dark hair, rich and healthy—as though trying to dislodge some troubling thought, and her eyes cleared. "But . . . if Percival didn't deal with the institute and your mother didn't either, then it must have been you. You're the third member of the board. Right?"

The board? Oh yes, I sign things, from time to time. But what was she talking about?

"Christ, listen to me—'Right.' I'm losing it." Tears rose in the woman's eyes.

Don't cry.

But she did cry. Tears spilled over her lower eyelids and ran down her face. He noticed for the first time a bandage on her cheek, and a bruise around it.

"But I need those records." The woman's voice broke. She dabbed at her face with the back of her sleeve. "I need to know who the donor was. It's all I can think of, don't you see? What other possibility is there?" She looked down on him with her wet dark eyes, as though waiting for an answer, treating him like an undamaged human being. She waited, waited for an answer.

And the answer came to Happy, all at once and awful. *God. God.* He wanted to scream. He needed to scream. He tried with all his might to scream. He commanded himself to raise an arm, to sit up, to speak, to scream. *Scream. Scream.* But he could do nothing. He was in a frenzy, more out of control than he had ever been in his life. But it didn't show.

The woman smiled a weak smile. "This isn't very fair to you," she said.

Don't go. Keep talking. She understood him. Happy had the wild thought that they were meant for each other, that everything was somehow right.

The woman, Nina, took a deep breath and let it out. Her gaze moved away from him, to the wall behind his head. He could just make out the spider, testing the air with one raised leg. Then she, Nina, did something that astonished him: she went to the head of the bed, stood on the edge of the frame, raised her hand high and smacked the spider. Just like that. And she, Nina, stepped down and wiped off the remains on her pants. It was that easy: a quick smack and the spider was gone, after so long.

"I don't like those fat ones," she said. "They bite." She leaned over him. "Well," she said, and brushed the hair off his forehead and laid her hand there for a moment, a soft warm hand: "goodbye." And then the soft warm hand was gone, and so was she.

Nina. He wished he could say it out loud.

                              *   *   *

Nina walked back to the pretty guest room in the north wing of Mrs. Standish's house and lay on the bed. But she didn't sleep. At first light she rose, put on her shoes and went downstairs to the kitchen. A man with a black bag was sitting at the table, drinking coffee and reading the comics.

"Hi," he said. "Are you the guest?"

"Yes."

"I'm Dr. Robert. Mrs. Standish has gone for the day, but she said to help yourself to breakfast." He turned the page. There were more comics on the other side.

"Are you Happy's doctor?" Nina asked.

"One of many," said Dr. Robert.

"What happened to him?"

Dr. Robert looked up. "Don't you know?"

"No."

"A scuba diving accident. Negligence, really, on the part of the resort. Down in the Bahamas. They gave him bad air. Caused an embolism in the brain stem."

"Is there any hope?"

"Hope?"

"Of improvement?"

"What sort of improvement?"

"That he'll be able to walk. Talk. Feed himself."

"Oh no," said Dr. Robert. "Nothing like that. We're just trying to keep him alive right now. He's got pneumonia." Dr. Robert sipped his coffee.

Nina put on her coat and went outside. The sky was blue, the air still and cold. Deep snow covered everything except the driveway, which had been plowed down to the pavement. In the distance she saw a tall white-haired man wrapping plastic around a fruit tree. Perhaps the servants had returned.

Nina followed the driveway to the gate. It was open. She went through and found her car still parked by the side of the lane. The lane had been plowed too, and someone had dug her out of the snowbank.

She got inside and drove back to New York. The roads were clear. Nina's mind had nothing to do but recall the feel of Happy Standish's fine, soft hair, and his unblinking gaze, blue and serious.

Nina parked close to Suze's loft. She let herself in,

called, "Suze," but no one was home, sat on Suze's bed. She phoned Delgado, who wasn't in. Nina left a message: "Tell her the Human Fertility Institute was owned by the Standish Foundation. Maybe she should find out who owned the Cambridge Reproductive Research Center." Then she lay down.

It was dark outside when Nina woke. She lay motionless on Suze's bed. Then she remembered her six o'clock appointment with Bernie Muller, the Australian TV producer. She glanced at her watch. 5:15. Nina got up, showered, dressed, went outside to her rental car and drove uptown.

Grand Central Station.

| 38 |

Brock McGillivray was a head taller than anyone else on Fifth Avenue. Following him was easy. He strode along briskly, keeping to the edge of the sidewalk, sometimes stepping into the street, his dramatic coattails flapping behind him. He never looked back.

Matthias followed.

It was cold and getting colder. Matthias zipped his windbreaker up to the top and stuck his hands in the pockets. Night had fallen, but it hadn't brought darkness. The sky glowed in dusty greens, yellows, oranges, pinks, like a colossal chemistry experiment gone wrong. Everyone—the shoppers with their Christmas parcels, the workers with their briefcases, the tourists with their cameras, the homeless with their cardboard domiciles—looked grim and ghastly. A ragged man with a bottle muttered, "Merry fucking Christmas," as Matthias went by.

"You said it," Matthias muttered right back.

The man was unused to this response, or perhaps to any. "*I* said it," he shouted after Matthias in fury. "*I* said it. And that makes you a thief and a robber."

Brock crossed Fifth Avenue and headed east on Forty-second Street. Matthias kept him in sight, but that didn't occupy his mind. His mind dealt with what he was seeing. There were homeless people in the Bahamas. Nottage, he supposed, was homeless. Somehow it wasn't the same. Then it occurred to him that he too would soon be homeless. The thought awoke something murderous inside him. He walked faster, closing the distance between himself and Brock. Brock strode on, never looking back.

Brock entered Grand Central Station, still moving quickly. Unseeing, he went through the dirty waiting room packed with ragged, defeated people. The sight of them huddled in such an imperial structure reminded Matthias of a guest in the bar at Zombie Bay saying that New York was now a Dickensian place. It didn't seem Dickensian to Matthias: Dickens, in his recollection, always opted for happy endings, or at least bittersweet, and how could that be a believable expectation here?

Brock crossed the main concourse and went down a broad staircase. There were few people on the stairs; Matthias hung back. He reached the bottom in time to see Brock avoid two medics who were trying to lift a bleeding man onto a stretcher, and enter the Oyster Bar. Matthias had been there once with Marilyn. She had sent back her oysters Rockefeller. He was trying to remember why when he saw that Brock had stopped inside the entrance and was turning around. Matthias stepped behind the ambulance men.

"Don' fuck with me," the bleeding man was saying.

"We're not fucking with you, pal," said one of the medics. "We're just trying to get you to the hospital."

"Don' want no fuckin' hospital," the man said. "I'm sick." Then he saw Matthias crouching by the wall. The sight displeased him. "What's your problem, chief?"

"Oysters Rockefeller," said Matthias.

"Oysters Rockefeller?" said the bleeding man with interest.

"Just get on the stretcher," said the other medic. "It's six o'clock. I want to go home."

The medics tried to lift the bleeding man. He resisted. Through a screen of arms and legs, Matthias saw Brock standing inside the entrance of the Oyster Bar, looking back down the hall. Brock checked his watch and frowned. He made a fist and smacked it lightly against his open palm. He checked his watch. He made another fist and smacked it a little harder. The medics shoved the bleeding man on the stretcher and hoisted him up. He rolled over, fell face down on the floor, lay still.

"God Almighty," said the medic who wanted to go home.

Then a woman came around the corner from the stairs, hesitated for a moment, and walked past the ambulance workers, the bleeding man and Matthias. Matthias didn't know her, had no reason to look at her twice, but he did. She had dark hair and dark eyes and something on her mind. Matthias glimpsed all of that, but it didn't take on significance until he looked at Brock and saw the frown vanishing from his face. Brock replaced it with a big, friendly smile, bigger and friendlier than any smile Matthias had seen him give before. He came forward, holding out his hand. "Nina?" he said.

The woman said something that Matthias didn't hear. She took Brock's hand, looked up at him. He smiled down, shook her hand, let go. He spoke. She spoke. They turned and went inside the Oyster Bar, Brock helping her turn with a hand on her back. His hand almost stretched across its entire width. A maître d' appeared. They followed him to the left, out of sight.

The bleeding man was unconscious. The medics got him on the stretcher with no further difficulty and carried him away. Matthias walked into the restaurant. To the left were booths and tables, as he remembered, with counters to the right. Brock and the woman were talking in a booth in the far corner. Matthias sat at a counter between two men hunched over the market quotation pages in their newspapers. A potted plant blocked his view of Brock and Brock's view of him, but he could see the woman in profile, and he had a clear line of sight to the door.

"What'll it be?" asked the barman.

"Oysters," Matthias said.

One of the market quotation readers ran his finger across a page of tiny type and groaned.

| 39 |

Big lout: Bernie Muller's self-description.

Big, yes, thought Nina, sitting opposite him at a booth in the Oyster Bar under Grand Central Station, but not a lout. Louts were stupid, Bernie Muller was not—Nina could see that in his eyes, quick and lively; louts were rude, Bernie Muller was not—he had escorted her to the booth and helped her with her coat; and louts didn't call themselves louts.

But big: men so tall and powerfully built, who pushed sexual dimorphism so far, almost seemed to belong to a different species. Everything about Bernie Muller was big—his head, his shoulders, his chest, his arms, his hands—everything except his quick eyes, which must have been normal size but appeared small in contrast to the rest of him. Despite his fine suit, his well-cut hair, bleached by the sun—he was tanned too; it was winter in Australia—this was not some puffed-up product of yuppie gyms. This was the dream they were selling.

Bernie Muller reached into a vest pocket and handed her a card. "*The Fifth Estate*," it said. "*Australian Broadcasting Corporation. Bernard Muller.*"

"I understand you're in the media business too, Nina," he said.

"In a way," Nina said. "What's 'The Fifth Estate'?"

"Like '60 Minutes,' but shorter pieces. Asian immigrants in Sydney. Dame Joan Sutherland. A man who eats

cactus. A scam involving old folks' homes and overpriced
Bibles. Pat Cash's father. That kind of thing."

"And you want to do something on child kidnapping?"

"It's on my possibles list," Bernie Muller replied. He
looked around the room. Nina saw a tiny hole in his left
earlobe. "But," he added, "so is the man who eats cactus,
and that sort of story is easy to sell. Child kidnapping needs
some focus before I can bounce it off the powers that be."

"And you're thinking that I might be the focus?"

Bernie Muller smiled. His smile was big too, showing
all his teeth to the molars. "I'd have known you were in
the media business even if they hadn't told me at Channel
Four."

A waiter appeared. "I hope you like oysters," Bernie
Muller said. "I should have asked."

"I do," Nina said.

"Super. I love any kind of seafood myself." He ordered
a dozen Belons and a Pauli Girl, Nina half a dozen and a
glass of water. "Half a dozen? I thought you liked oysters."

"I'm not very hungry."

Bernie Muller laid his hand on hers, covering it completely. "You should try to keep your strength up," he
said, "especially at a time like this." He removed his hand,
glanced around the room, smiled at her.

The oysters arrived. "Mind if I just slurp them?" Bernie
Muller asked.

"That's the best way," Nina said.

"A woman after my own heart," he replied, slurping a
couple and washing them down with beer.

"You mentioned a kidnapping in Boston, Mr. Muller."

"Call me Bernie. Everyone does." He raised another
oyster to his lips and sucked the soft body off the shell.

"I wondered whether it was the Laura Bain case."

Bernie frowned. "The name rings a bell," he said. "A
baby called Clara?"

"Clea."

"That's it." He gestured with the shell. A glob of liquid
flew onto Nina's face. "I beg your pardon," he said, reaching across the table with his napkin. Nina had hers there
first.

"It's nothing."

Bernie was looking at her face. "What happened there?"
he asked, indicating her bandage.

"I bumped into something."

"You'll have to be careful," Bernie said. "It's exactly at emotional times like this that accidents tend to happen. We did a piece on it."

"I'll bear that in mind."

Bernie smiled, but briefly this time, and squeezed lemon juice on his remaining oysters. "How do you happen to know about Laura Bain?" he asked.

"A Boston station ran the Channel Four tape and she got in touch with me."

"Why did she do that?"

"Because our cases are similar."

"In what way?"

"We both used a sperm bank, for one thing. And both sperm banks are defunct, for another. We found that out when we tried to trace the donors."

"Trace the donors?"

"They're anonymous."

"Why did you want to trace them?"

"It was Laura's idea. In child disappearance cases it's routine to account for the father."

"Isn't this a bit different?"

"I don't know," Nina said. "Suppose some man wanted to have a child without the bother of having the mother around."

"Who would want that?"

Nina had no reply.

Bernie finished his beer, patted the corners of his mouth with the napkin, a dainty gesture that didn't appear to suit him at all. "What's the status of the police investigation?"

"Nothing's happening. The detective in charge has bigger fish to fry."

"What's his name?" asked Bernie, taking out a notebook.

"Her name," said Nina, "is Delgado."

Bernie wrote it down. "Does she know about Laura Bain?"

"Yes."

"Is she working on this donor theory?"

"I don't think she buys it."

Bernie closed his notebook and put it away. There was a silence. Then he said: "You lied to me."

"Lied to you?"

"About liking oysters. You haven't touched them."

"I'm not hungry," Nina said.

"Mind if I scarf yours then?"

"Go ahead."

Bernie swept all the oysters but one off her plate and ordered another beer. "Join me?" he said. "Beer's full of protein."

"All right."

But when the beer came Nina took one sip and left the rest. "What have you found out about Laura Bain?" she asked.

"Not much so far. Committed suicide, didn't she?"

"So they say."

Bernie swished his beer around in the glass, stared into the swirling liquid. "But you don't believe it?" he asked.

"I don't know what to believe." The reply was true. It also allowed her to avoid the questions raised by her own Seconal overdose and the blue ballpoint on the kitchen table; to avoid looking like the kind of conspiracy theorist who might appear on a sleazy syndicated show but never on network TV. "But I'm convinced that Laura's case and mine are related."

"Just because you both used sperm banks?"

"There's much more to it than that."

"Like?"

"We were both impregnated by the same physician. Dr. Crossman. He's disappeared. And all the donor records may have too."

"What does your detective make of that?"

"She hasn't really absorbed it."

"And these sperm banks are defunct, you say?"

"Yes."

"What does that mean, exactly?"

"Laura's is an audio-video store. Mine is a hole in the ground."

Bernie raised his eyebrows, fair eyebrows bleached by the sun. She could easily imagine him riding a surfboard on weekends, or squeezing in a quick set of tennis after work. "Is it?" he said.

"Is it what?"

"A hole in the ground."

"Yes."

"That's interesting," Bernie said.

Nina wondered whether she had appealed to his pictorial sense. Had she given him the tool to pry a budget out of his home office? "It was a landmark building," she said. "Stills of it in the before state will be easy to find."

Bernie tipped the last oyster into his mouth. "Where is this hole?"

"On East Ninety-second Street."

Bernie scanned the room again, then rubbed his hands together. "I'd like to see it."

"Now?"

"Why not? This isn't a nine-to-five job."

"Okay," Nina said. "I've got a car."

"Great," Bernie said. "You're not eating that oyster?" Nina shook her head. Bernie slurped it down and swallowed the rest of the beer. He paid the bill in cash and rose to go.

"Don't you want the receipt?" Nina asked.

"The receipt?" Bernie said, looking puzzled. Then he smiled. "I'm on a set per diem." They went out to the street, walked around the corner to Nina's car. Getting in, Nina saw a man in a windbreaker hailing a taxi.

She drove Bernie Muller uptown. He seemed to fill the little car. "How long have you been in television?" she asked.

"Forever," Bernie answered. He turned up the heat.

Nina parked in front of the fenced-off rubble pile on Ninety-second Street. They got out of the car. "Here?" said Bernie. The word rose from his mouth in a cloud of vapor. It was a cold night.

"Here," Nina replied.

Bernie glanced up and down the street. No one was around. He walked to the fence and looked through. Nina followed him. The nearest streetlight was too far away to illuminate much, but Nina could see that work had progressed: the dark hole in the middle of the rubble had widened. The bulldozer sat at its edge.

"Looks good," Bernie said. "Very good."

"For pictures?"

"For pictures. Right." He moved to the gate, hefted the padlock that secured it. "You don't suppose they just buried all the records, do you?"

"I doubt it."

"But you never know," Bernie said, feeling in a pocket.

"The unexpected happens all the time, love. If I've learned nothing else, I've learned that." He took out something silver, stuck it in the lock, turned it. "Well, well," said Bernie. He shoved the gate open and smiled at Nina. "After you."

Nina stayed where she was. "How did you open that lock?"

Bernie held up a key. "I carry lots of masters. One of them usually does the job. You're not shocked, I hope? It's all part of the investigative reporter business."

Nina tried to imagine Mike Wallace carrying a pocketful of master keys, and couldn't. But she could picture one of his assistants carrying them for him. She walked through the gate. Bernie came after her, closing it behind him.

They moved through the rubble. Bernie kicked at a stone, a brick. He knelt and knocked a broken pipe aside, revealing more broken pipes underneath. He picked one up, patting it against his palm thoughtfully, like a cavalry general with a riding crop.

They came to the edge of the hole and gazed down. It was a deep hole. There was more rubble at the bottom. Nina looked up to find Bernie watching her. "You're a pretty girl," he said.

Nina took a step back, stumbling on the rocks.

"Careful," Bernie said. "You wouldn't want to fall in."

"I'd like to go now," Nina said. "Have you seen enough?"

Bernie tapped the pipe against his palm. "There's one more thing," he said.

"What's that?"

"This relative on your father's side. What was his name before he changed it to Kitchener?"

"How do you know about that?"

"I've talked to a few people."

"Who?"

"We'll get to that. But it would help if I knew the name."

"How?"

Bernie smiled. "This is more complicated than you imagine. And time might be a factor." He waited.

"I don't understand," Nina said. "It was Kapstein or Kupstein or something. How does it matter?"

"Jewish?"

"That's right."

Bernie shook his head. "It's too bad you didn't mention all this before."

"To whom? What are you talking about?"

Bernie didn't answer her question. He just said: "None of this would have happened."

"None of what?"

He came toward her. "This isn't personal," he said. "Believe me." Then he raised the pipe high over his head. Nina turned to run, but he caught her arm in one hand, so tightly she cried out. She looked up, far up, into his eyes. They were fixed on her, but didn't appear to be seeing anything at all.

"Don't," Nina said.

He shook his head again. "Sorry, love. There's no time to explain." Then he brought the pipe down.

Nina started to say "Don't" again but there wasn't time for that either. Many things happened, far too quickly for her to absorb. First a shadow came flying out of the darkness and collided with the backs of Bernie's legs. Bernie, the pipe still in his hand, still on its way down, rose above the ground, sailed over her head and landed hard on the other side. The pipe fell, making a metallic clatter on the rocks. The shadow danced by her, took the shape of a man in a windbreaker, stood over Bernie. All at once big men were abroad: this man, not as tall as Bernie, was just as thickly built, perhaps more. Had she seen him before? Nina was trying to remember when Bernie flipped over and looked up. He saw the man and recognized him: she could see the shock in his eyes. The man said: "Hi, Brock."

A slow smile spread across Bernie's face. At the same time, his hand reached for the pipe. The man in the windbreaker didn't appear to notice, yet he kicked the pipe away just before Bernie's hand closed on it.

"You've been careless, Brock," the man said. "Getting your prints on Hew's bottle. Calling Two-Head while I was there. This may not be your kind of work."

"Nobody's perfect," Bernie said, still smiling. Then he showed that he could kick too. His leg lashed up out of the darkness and caught the other man in the stomach. The man grunted and fell by the edge of the hole. Bernie scrambled on top of him, raised his fist, smashed it in the other man's face. But then Bernie cried out in pain, although Nina couldn't see why. The next moment both men were on their feet and there was blood on the face of the man in the windbreaker and Bernie was no longer smiling. He hooked a tremendous right-hand punch at the other man's head, but the other man was quicker. He ducked, sidestepped, cocked his own right. That was the last Nina saw clearly of the fight, because the other man's elbow clipped her under the chin and she went down.

Nina lay under a neon sky in the ruins of the Human Fertility Institute. Two enormous hominids fought over her: more thumps, more grunts, more blood, dripping off the face of the man in the windbreaker, and then off Bernie's face. Nina heard a crunching sound. Bernie cried out again. There was another crunch. Something fell on her, bringing blackness.

Nina opened her eyes. She sat up. The man in the windbreaker was squatting beside her. His face was bloody, his nose crooked. His dark eyes were full of concern. It seemed to be for her. "You all right?" he said.

"I think so. What happened?"

"He got away. I'm not much of a runner, after the first twenty yards or so."

"You mean he ran away?"

"I wouldn't put it like that. He would have beaten me in the end, but he just didn't realize it, that's all."

"Why not? Your face is a mess."

The man in the windbreaker laughed. It was a wonderful laugh, loud and free. The only disconcerting part was the blood flowing out of his nose. She had never met a man who laughed like that in any circumstances, and when it came to their own blood, she could remember a few Boyfriends who had ruined whole weekends because of shaving cuts. "It wasn't much to begin with," he said. He stopped laughing. "Think you can get up?"

"Yes," Nina said, thinking he was wrong about his face: it was a good face. "I can get up."

But she couldn't until he took her hand and pulled her gently to her feet. She looked up at him, but not as far up as she had had to for Bernie. "Bernie's bigger than you," she said. "Much bigger."

"Bernie?"

"The man you were fighting with."

"Bernie." He laughed his laugh again, then touched his nose. "The thing is I've had worse. Your friend Bernie hasn't. That's the difference, if it's analysis you want."

"He's not my friend."

"Good," said the man in the windbreaker. "And his name's not Bernie."

"It isn't?"

A woman walked by the fence, looked through, saw them, kept going. "We can talk about it later," said the man. "Right now we'd better change your tire." He walked her toward the gate.

"Why?" Nina said.

"It's flat."

"You can tell that from here?"

"Even with my eyes closed. I let the air out."

"You let the air out?"

"Just in case."

"In case of what?"

"I didn't think it out that far."

They went through the gate. The man in the windbreaker pulled it shut and closed the padlock. They approached Nina's car. The rear curbside tire was flat. "Got the keys?" he asked.

Nina paused. This man was big, like Bernie, had a tan, like Bernie, although he spoke without an Australian accent. Might he be a killer too? But if he had wanted to kill her, wouldn't he have done it inside the gate? Nina handed him the keys. He smiled, a smaller smile than Bernie's, but his eyes played a role in it as Bernie's had not.

The man in the windbreaker opened the trunk. "What's this?" he said.

Nina came forward and peered into the trunk. It was Dr. Crossman, curled in the fetal position. The handle of a knife stuck out of his chest. It looked a lot like the steak knives in her kitchen drawer.

The man in the windbreaker turned to her. He had a broken nose, a bloody face and a corpse in view, yet his eyes seemed amused. For one crazy moment, Nina thought he was having fun. "My name's Matthias," he said. "I don't believe we've met."

40

"N. H. Matthias?" said Nina, as the man in the wind-breaker jacked up her rental car. "From some hotel with a funny name in the Bahamas?"

"Zombie Bay," he replied, glancing up at her. She tried to read the expression on his face, but couldn't get past the blood. "Have we met, after all?" he asked.

"I saw your business card last night," Nina said. "In a drawer in someone's guest room."

"Whose?"

"Don't you know?"

"I'm waiting to find out."

"Are you saying you didn't leave it there?"

"This is shrewd interrogating," said N. H. Matthias, loosening the bolts and spinning them off with his hand. "But you're wasting it on the wrong guy."

"Am I?"

"Yeah. I'm the one who's not trying to hit you over the head with a lead pipe."

Nina almost laughed. The only reason she didn't was that she wondered at the same time how she could be in a laughing mood. "All right," she said. "I owe you that."

"You owe me nothing," he said, looking at her for a long moment. Nina looked away.

"The guest room is in a house in Connecticut," she said quietly. "It belongs to a woman named Inge Standish."

"A friend of yours?"

"No."

Matthias pulled off the flat, replaced it with the spare. "We seem to know some of the same people."

"Like who?" The traffic light at the corner changed, reddening the parts of his face not already bloody, rendering him demonic.

"Inge Standish, for one," he replied. "Brock McGillivray, for two."

"Brock McGillivray?"

"The man you call Bernie. He's a professional diver, working for me."

"In the Bahamas?"

"That's right."

Nina reached into her pocket. "Then what's this?" she asked, handing him Bernie's card: *The Fifth Estate. Australian Broadcasting Corporation. Bernard Muller. N. H.* Matthias moved under the nearest streetlight and studied it.

"Muller," he said. "How did he pronounce that?"

"Like duller."

"Was he at Inge Standish's too?"

"No," Nina said. Then she remembered the yellow glow near the road during the storm. "I don't think so."

"And this card was just sitting in a drawer?"

"With two towels and a bar of soap from the Plaza Hotel."

"That's interesting," he said, handing back the card and kneeling to tighten the bolts on the spare.

"What is?"

"The soap."

"Why?"

"It connects him to Inge Standish. And that means he committed two murders, not one."

"Dr. Crossman and who else?"

"Dr. Crossman?"

Nina gestured to the trunk.

"I wasn't counting him. Brock killed an old neighbor of mine. And a man who went diving near the hotel."

"Why?"

"I'm not sure. But the murders are related." N. H. Matthias paused. "Any idea why he wanted to kill you?"

"No," Nina said. "I thought he was going to help me."

"To do what?"

"Find my baby. My . . . son was stolen from the hospital the day after he was born."

Nina felt N. H. Matthias's eyes on her again. There was a silence, broken by an occasional squeak as he wound down the jack. "How long ago was this?" he said, picking up the jack and tossing it and the flat tire in the back seat.

"Almost six weeks."

"And how was Brock going to help?"

"He said he was working on a story about child kidnappings. I checked him out at Channel Four. They knew him. And he'd done some research already. He knew about . . ." Laura Bain. How had Bernie known about Laura Bain? Why hadn't she asked? "I guess I've been stupid," she said.

"I doubt that."

Nina looked at N. H. Matthias. The traffic light was red again. "Shouldn't you get to the hospital?"

"What for?" he said.

"Your face."

"My face is fine. You're the one who was out cold."

"I was not." He smiled at her; there was blood on his teeth. "I'm fine, really," she said.

N. H. Matthias kept smiling. "Me too," he told her. "So let's not bother with hospitals till the illusion passes."

It suddenly struck Nina that without sighs, grunts, swearing or difficulty, N. H. Matthias had just changed a flat tire; again separating himself, she thought, from The Boyfriends. Then she thought: Why should I be thinking that? and almost dropped the keys when he handed them to her.

"Do you think you can find Two-sixteen East Thirty-third Street?" he asked.

"Sure."

"Good," he said, getting in. "We might be in a bit of a hurry."

"Why?" asked Nina, climbing behind the wheel and starting the car.

"There's an old couple in apartment two-thirty-four. I wouldn't want them to end up like the fellow in back."

"I don't understand."

"It almost happened to you, didn't it?"

True, but Nina didn't understand that either. "Does this old couple have something to do with Dr. Crossman?"

"I don't know. Any idea how he ended up in there?"

Again Nina thought of the yellow glow in the storm. "No," she said. "But . . ."

"But what?"

"I think that's one of my steak knives."

"In his chest."

"Right."

"But?"

"I don't know how it got there."

"So," said N. H. Matthias, "assuming Brock was going to leave the car on the street, the police would have found you in that hole in the ground and Dr. Crossman and your steak knife in the trunk."

Nina considered that. "Do you think Bernie—Brock—could have made my death look accidental?"

"He did it with Hew."

"What do you mean?"

"I'll tell you later. First I'd like to know more about Dr. Crossman."

"No," Nina said, and suddenly her voice rose. Why now? Why at him? She didn't know. The sound came from somewhere deep inside, beyond control. "Why am I always fighting for every scrap of information? I want to know now." She heard the hysteria in her voice.

He must have heard it too, because his voice was soft when he said: "He was the neighbor I told you about. The police ruled he got drunk and fell off his terrace. But Brock interfered with the evidence."

"Thank you," Nina said. What did this information mean to her? Not much, but for some reason it calmed her; she even felt a rush of optimism, like a drug in her veins. Hysteria, optimism: what was happening to her? She focused her mind on Dr. Crossman, and was trying to organize a coherent speech about him when N. H. Matthias said:

"On second thought, pull over by that phone booth."

"Why?"

"It's morning in Australia."

Nina pulled over. N. H. Matthias took Bernie's card, got out, walked to the phone. Then he turned and came back. He tapped on her window. She rolled it down. "Have you got a telephone calling card?"

"Yes."

"Can I borrow it? I don't think I've got enough change for Australia."

"You own a hotel and you don't have a phone card?"

"It's not that kind of hotel," he said.

Nina gave him the card. He returned to the phone, dialed, spoke, listened, spoke again. Nina watched. A cold wind blew outside the car but N. H. Matthias didn't seem to notice. Now he was listening again, his feet planted shoulder-width apart, like an attentive helmsman in tricky water. Inside Nina's head a little ache came to life, threatened to grow into a prodigy. She closed her eyes; the illusion of painlessness was passing.

When she opened them, N. H. Matthias was sitting beside her. "Headache?" he said.

"I'm okay."

"Where's the nearest hospital?"

"I'm not going."

"That's what the guy in Grand Central Station said."

"You followed me from Grand Central?"

"I followed Brock. You were with him."

"Why were you following him?"

"Are you going to yell at me if I say there's no time to explain right now?"

Nina laughed. It made her head hurt more. "No. But it has something to do with Happy Standish, doesn't it?"

N. H. Matthias smiled. "You're like Clarence Darrow."

"How so?"

"Isn't he the one who never asked a question he didn't know the answer to?"

"I think it was someone else," Nina replied.

N. H. Matthias kept smiling. "You were right about Brock too. His real name seems to be Bernie Muller—that's how they know him at Australian Broadcasting. And probably at the Plaza Hotel too."

"Do you mean he's a legitimate TV producer?"

"No. 'The Fifth Estate' hasn't been on the air for two years. I talked to a production manager in their current affairs department. She remembered Bernie. He was never on staff. Five years ago they filmed a story about pollution on the Great Barrier Reef and hired Bernie as a guide, on a one-time basis. That's the extent of his TV experience."

"But he was so convincing."

"Yup," said N. H. Matthias. He handed her Bernie's business card. He had penciled another phone number at the bottom. "Bernie came back to Sydney and tried to land a job with them for a while. That's why she had this number for him—it's his father's house. I think we should call him."

"Bernie's father?"

"Yes."

"Why?"

"In case Bernie's using a disguise."

"What kind of disguise?"

"A dropped umlaut." N. H. Matthias looked at Nina. "It might be better if you made the call."

And say what, Nina thought; I don't understand a word you've spoken. But what came out of her mouth was this: "As a researcher from Channel Four?"

"That kind of thing."

They talked for a minute or two. Then Nina got out of the car and called Bernie Muller's father in Sydney. N. H. Matthias stood beside her. Was it by design, she wondered, that he had placed himself between her and the wind? The phone rang once. Then there was a click and a man said: "Yes?"

An old man, Nina thought, with a German accent: not a caricature, like Conrad Veidt's, more like the soft accent of Mr. Gruber, her childhood piano teacher. "Hello," Nina said. "Bernard Muller, please." It was a clear connection; the problem was the echo—her own words came back to her like radar signals bouncing off an unidentified object.

"Bernd?" said the man, and something else lost in the sound of her rebounding voice.

"Yes," Nina said. "This is Mary Good calling from Channel Four in New York." Out of the corner of her eye, Nina saw N. H. Matthias smile. "It's about that dub he wanted."

"Dub?"

"Can you hear me? There's an echo. Maybe I should—" She stopped herself—N. H. Matthias was shaking his head.

"I am hearing you."

"There's going to be a delay," Nina said. "Some mix-up in the tape library. I wanted to know if Bernie would like me to send the dub on to Sydney."

Silence, except for the echo of her voice, so obviously nervous, she thought, saying, ". . . dub on to Sydney."

"Hello?" she said. "Are you still there?"

A long pause. Then the man spoke. "Yes. But Bernd is not."

"He must be in transit then. He's checked out of his hotel."

Silence.

"Are you his father? Bernie said the best way to reach him was through you."

"He said that?"

"Yes, Mr. Muller. What I might do then—"

"Doctor."

"I didn't catch that."

"Doctor," he said. "Not Mister."

"What I'll do then, Dr. Muller, is—"

"Müller. It is Müller, Dr. Müller."

"Müller? Maybe I've got the wrong number."

"This is the correct number. I am Dr. Müller."

"Could you spell that? I'm going to send the tape on to Bernie care of you when it's ready."

"M-U-L-L-E-R. With an umlaut."

"Over the U?"

"Where else would it be, then?"

"Right. I'll just need your first name for the shipping department and we'll get this out next week."

"Gerd."

"G-E-R-D?"

"Yes, yes."

"All right. Dr. Gerd Müller, with umlaut. Tell Bernie he'll have the dub in two weeks and give him my best."

"One moment, please," said Dr. Müller.

"Yes?"

"What is this dub?"

"A story we did a while back on child kidnapping. Bernie's doing something similar."

"Something similar?"

"For Australian Broadcasting. Nice talking to you, Dr. Müller. I've got a call waiting."

"Your name was what, again?" he asked.

But Nina was already hanging up the phone. She turned to N. H. Matthias, saw admiration in his eyes. "You lie beautifully," he said.

"It's my job."

He held out his hand. "Mary Good?" he said.

"Nina Kitchener," she replied, taking his hand. It was big and warm; she thought of the expression "safe as houses."

"You were perfect, Ms. Kitchener."

"Call me Nina."

"Nina."

"Do I call you N. H.?"

"Matt would be better," he said.

"Well, Matt. You've flattened my tire. You've changed it. You've found out that Bernie Muller's father is Dr. Gerd Müller. Are you going to tell me what's going on?"

He laughed. "Gerd Müller was on the faculty of the University of Heidelberg with Inge Standish's father in the thirties. Happy Standish's father studied under them. How's that for a start?"

"Obstetrics?"

"Obstetrics."

"It's a start," Nina said. They got in the car. Nina drove south and parked in front of 216 East Thirty-third Street. "What was the name of Inge's father?"

"Von Trautschke," Matthias said. "Wilhelm von Trautschke."

"Is he still alive?"

"Not according to my friend Hew. Von Trautschke didn't survive the war."

They got out of the car and walked up the steps of 216. It was a brick apartment building, nine or ten stories high, shabby and unadorned. Inside there was no doorman, just a locked inner door with a row of buzzers and a list of residents. Matthias was running his eyes over it when a man in a yarmulke came out, lighting a cigar. Matthias caught the door before it closed. Nina followed him in. "He was a bad egg," Matthias said.

"Who?"

"Von Trautschke. That's what Hew said, although he didn't say why."

Apartment 234, on the second floor, had a plain wooden

door with a fisheye peephole and an empty nameplate frame. A mezuzah was nailed to the doorjamb. Matthias knocked.

A wide-angled eye appeared in the peephole, then vanished. Matthias knocked again. The door remained closed. Nina heard nothing on the other side.

"My name's Matthias," Matthias said in a normal tone. "I called you from the Bahamas. About Felix."

The wide-angled eye reappeared. A bolt slid. A lock clicked. Then another. The door opened three inches, held there by a brass chain. Through the gap, Nina saw a tiny white-haired woman clasping her hands.

"Mrs. Goldschmidt?" Matthias said.

The old woman looked up at him and didn't like what she saw.

"I've been in a minor accident," he said. "Nothing to be concerned about." He reached into the pocket of his windbreaker and handed her an envelope. "I think these belonged to Felix."

The old woman opened the envelope and took out two plastic cards. One looked like a Visa card, the other Nina didn't recognize. Eyeglasses hung on the woman's thin chest. She raised them to her face, examined the cards. Her lips moved slightly as she read. Somewhere behind her a man with a Yiddish accent said, "What is it, Hilda?" For a moment the old woman's eyes filled with tears, but they dried up so fast Nina wondered whether she had imagined them.

"What do you want from us?" the old woman asked.

"To talk," Matthias answered.

"About?"

"Felix."

"He drowned, you said."

"Yes."

"So what talk?"

"I don't think he drowned by accident, Mrs. Goldschmidt. I think someone did it to him." The old woman twisted the plastic cards in her hands, but said nothing. "Don't you want to find out who, and see that they're punished?"

"Don't I know already?" Mrs. Goldschmidt asked. "Doesn't the whole world know?"

"Tell me," Matthias said.

"Tell you? Why should I tell you? Read your school-books. They all died in 1945."

"What do you mean, Mrs. Goldschmidt?"

Behind her the man said: "Hilda, what is it?"

Mrs. Goldschmidt made an impatient noise with her tongue and unhooked the chain. Matthias and Nina stepped into the room.

A small room: a couch and chair along one wall, stove and refrigerator along the other. Framed photographs hung in one corner, all showing a man with dark hair and a dark mustache, thin and unsmiling. Beneath the photographs sat an old man in a wheelchair. He looked no bigger than Mrs. Goldschmidt, perhaps even smaller. He wore a blue shirt buttoned to the neck and a brown woolen tie; a blanket covered him from the waist down. He had soft white hair and soft dark eyes.

"This is Mr. Goldschmidt," the old woman said. "My husband."

"Matthias," Matthias said, crossing the room and shaking hands. Mr. Goldschmidt's pale hand disappeared in Matthias's tanned one, reappeared, slipped back under the blanket.

"Pleased to meet you," he said. He looked at Nina and smiled. He had a nice smile. "And this is your wife?" he said.

"No," Matthias replied. "Nina Kitchener. Mr. and Mrs. Goldschmidt."

Mr. Goldschmidt smiled at her. "A Jewish girl."

"No," Nina said.

"And so pretty," Mr. Goldschmidt continued, seeming not to have heard her. "Please sit."

Nina and Matthias sat on the couch. Mrs. Goldschmidt stood frowning by the door. Then she closed it, moved slowly to the chair and sat down: on the edge, upright and stiff.

"Did you know my son, Mr. Matthias?" the old man said.

"No. I was away when he . . ."

"Died?"

"Yes."

"Don't be afraid of saying the word, Mr. Matthias. If it's the truth." Nina saw how closely the old man was watching Matthias at that moment.

"It's the truth," Matthias said.

The old man tried to smile again, but it wouldn't come. He gestured to the photographs around him. "Then look," he said. "That is Felix."

They looked, and saw: Felix sitting on a bench with a stack of books beside him; Felix bent over a chessboard; Felix at the wheel of a Deux Chevaux; Felix writing on a blackboard—he had underlined the words "*avant le pogrom*"; Felix in cap and gown shaking hands with another man in cap and gown.

Mr. Goldschmidt had swung his wheelchair around and was gazing at the photographs too. "He was a professor. A full professor."

"Mr. Matthias knows already," said Mrs. Goldschmidt.

"A full professor at the University of Aix," the old man continued, as though he hadn't heard her.

"Aix-en-Provence?" Nina said.

Mr. Goldschmidt wheeled round to face her. "Is it so surprising?"

"No. It's just—"

"Felix was brilliant. He won fourth place in all of Paris in the *bac*. As a boy, he could add vast sums in his head." He licked his lips. "Three hundred and eighty two plus seven hundred and twenty seven plus two hundred and six plus one thousand nine hundred and eleven equals?"

"Couldn't tell you," Matthias said.

Mr. Goldschmidt turned to Nina. "Equals?"

"I don't know."

"Felix would know. Felix could tell you."

Mr. Goldschmidt's face had reddened and his blanket had slipped to the floor, revealing skinny legs, the color of bone; he was in his underwear. Mrs. Goldschmidt crossed the room and replaced the blanket, tucking it around his fleshless hips. "This gentleman and lady aren't interested in such stories, Pinchas."

"I'm interested," Matthias said. "I'm interested in Felix."

The old man smiled. "Good," he said. "It's good to talk about Felix."

"Then tell me what Felix was doing in the Bahamas."

Mr. Goldschmidt glanced at his wife. "We know nothing about that," she said.

"How did he know Happy Standish?"

"I told you before. The name is unknown to me."

"Hiram Standish, Junior."

"This is someone else?"

"The same man."

"And the same answer."

There was a silence. Nina saw Matthias looking first at the old woman, then at the old man. She didn't know anything about Felix Goldschmidt, didn't know what Matthias was aiming at. But she knew that the Standishes had controlled the Human Fertility Institute, and anything about them concerned her. So she turned to Matthias and asked: "When did the diving accident happen?"

"A year ago September," he said. "September third."

"Happy Standish was in Aix in July, covering a festival of North African music for *The Village Voice*," Nina said. "I've seen the clipping."

Something changed in Matthias's eyes; they fixed on her, expressing complexities there was no time to analyze. Then he spoke to Mrs. Goldschmidt: "Is that when they met?" Mrs. Goldschmidt said nothing, but she was twisting Felix's plastic cards in her hands again.

Matthias got up and approached her. He dwarfed the old woman. She backed away: backed away from his size, his bloody face, his questions. He stopped. "I wouldn't hurt you."

"Then go away, please."

"I can't do that."

"Why?" she said. "Why can you not do that?"

"You may not want to know what happened to your son, Mrs. Goldschmidt. That's your right. But he wasn't the only one who died. I want the people who did it to feel the consequences."

Mrs. Goldschmidt's eyes again filled with tears. "These people feel no consequences," she said. Again the tears dried up. Bitterness sharpened her tone. "You are an innocent."

Matthias's tone remained mild. "Give me the chance to prove you wrong," he said.

"Please, Hilda," said Mr. Goldschmidt, wheeling his chair toward her. The blanket caught under the wheels, slipped off him, revealing the skeletal legs. "Please."

"God in heaven," Mrs. Goldschmidt said. Her eyes

filled with tears once more. This time they overflowed.
The old woman covered her face with her hands and began
sobbing hoarse, ragged sobs. The plastic cards fell to the
floor. Nina rose and picked them up. She picked up the
blanket too, and covered Mr. Goldschmidt's legs.

"*Shayna maidel*," he whispered to her. "*Shayna maidel*."

"Yes," cried Mrs. Goldschmidt. "Yes, yes, that's when
they met. Horrid day." She ran from the room. Nina
thought of going after her. Mr. Goldschmidt laid his icy
hand on hers.

"No," he said. "It's good. She cries." He wheeled himself back to the corner. Matthias pulled back the curtain,
looked out. Nina sat on the couch and drew a calendar in
her mind. July: Happy meets Felix. September: Happy
falls into a coma, Felix dies. October: Laura is impregnated
in Boston. February: Nina impregnated in New York.
Like the calendar of an alien culture it resisted interpretation.

The walls of the Goldschmidts' apartment were thin.
Sounds came clearly to the living room: water running in
a sink, a drawer opening and closing, footsteps. Mrs. Goldschmidt returned with a Kleenex tucked inside the wrist
of her sweater and a worn briefcase in her hand. Without
a word, she gave the briefcase to Matthias. He sat beside
Nina, opened it and withdrew the contents.

Contents: a manuscript, not quite as thick as *Living
Without Men and Children . . . and Loving It*; a few loose
pages that appeared to be Xeroxes of official documents.
Nina read the title page of the manuscript. *Wilhelm von
Trautschke: Histoire d'un Homme de la Science Moderne*.
She looked at the copies of the documents. One had a
swastika at the top, all were in German, all had the name
Wilhelm von Trautschke displayed somewhere on the
page.

Matthias flipped through the pages of the manuscript.
"I don't read French," he said.

"I do," Nina said. She scanned a paragraph that seemed
to be a description of the structure of the department of
medicine at the University of Heidelberg after World War
I.

"Do you know of this man, von Trautschke?" asked Mr.
Goldschmidt.

"The obstetrician who invented the fertility drug?" said Nina.

Mrs. Goldschmidt snorted. "Obstetrician."

"What do you mean?" Nina said.

"The fertility drug. Such a blessing." Suddenly she reached down and snatched the manuscript out of Matthias's hands. "You do not understand. Perhaps you cannot understand. This is a masterpiece. Felix's masterpiece."

"A biography of von Trautschke?" Matthias said.

Mrs. Goldschmidt hugged it to her breast. "What better subject for biography in such a world?" she said. "Obstetrician," she repeated. "Even he did not so describe himself."

"What did he call himself?" Nina asked.

"A eugenicist," Mrs. Goldschmidt answered. "Do you know what that is?"

"I think so," Nina said.

"You think so. And do you also know that there are two kinds of eugenics, positive and negative?"

"No."

"No. No, she says. Well, young woman, Dr. von Trautschke knew. He was expert at both. Expert. Positive and negative. Breeding and weeding, he called them." Her voice rose, high and bitter.

"Hilda," said her husband. She took a deep breath, then went to him, put her hand on his shoulder, squeezed it. Mr. Goldschmidt looked at Nina. "We knew him, you see."

"Von Trautschke?"

"Yes. He worked on Block Ten."

"Block Ten?" Nina said.

"Where they did the medical experiments," Matthias told her quietly. "At Auschwitz."

"*Mazel tov*," said Mrs. Goldschmidt. "A goy who has heard of Block Ten."

"Hilda," said Mr. Goldschmidt.

"*Mazel tov*," she said. "I mean it."

"Hilda."

"It's all right, Mr. Goldschmidt," Matthias said. He rubbed the side of his face; Nina saw him feel something and look with surprise at the blood on his hand. "You were there," he said to Mrs. Goldschmidt.

"We were," she replied.

"And Felix?"

"Not Felix."

"He was born after the war?"

"No," said Mrs. Goldschmidt. "That would have been impossible. Felix was born in 1941. Mr. Goldschmidt and I were taken to the Vélodrome in 1942, but we were able to get Felix safely away to a friend in the country."

"Then you were sent to Auschwitz."

"That's what happened to the Vélodrome people."

"And . . ."

"And?"

"And von Trautschke was there?"

"Oh, yes. He was there." Mrs. Goldschmidt stood beside her husband, gently kneading his shoulders. He watched the conversation going back and forth.

Matthias rose, crossed the room, peered through the curtains. Then he walked back across the room, leaned against the wall. He was too big for the Goldschmidts' apartment, too heavy for their floor: it creaked under his weight. "I hate to drag you through this," he said.

"But you are planning to anyway," said Mrs. Goldschmidt.

"Hilda," said her husband.

"I am," Matthias told her. "I know how much you don't want to talk about it, don't want to remember. But I am."

Mrs. Goldschmidt's voice rose. "How do you know that? How can you know that?"

"I was in a prison camp myself once. Not a death camp. Nothing like Auschwitz. But people died there, and I don't like to talk about it either."

They all looked at him. He leaned against the door, nose crooked, face bloody. A good face, Nina thought.

"Very well," said Mrs. Goldschmidt. Her hands never stopped rubbing her husband's shoulders. "We were on Block Ten. Dr. von Trautschke . . . used us in his experiments."

Mr. Goldschmidt reached for his wife's hand, patted it. "But we were among the lucky ones, sir," he said. "We didn't die."

Mrs. Goldschmidt pulled her hand away. "We died," she said.

Mr. Goldschmidt stiffened in his wheelchair. Then his eyes glazed and he hung his head.

"What do you expect?" asked Mrs. Goldschmidt. "When a man who calls himself a doctor—an obstetrician, as you put it—injects caustic liquids into your fallopian tubes, and you are a young woman, full of life—and yes, sexual desire, Pinchas, why not say it?—you die, even if you walk out afterwards. And when this man who calls himself a doctor tapes your husband's scrotum to a plate and bombards it with X-rays, for five minutes, ten minutes, day after day; and when this doctor, for his important research, then collects your husband's sperm using a prod of his own invention to insert in the rectum and stimulate ejaculation, so he can take away this radiated sperm to study under a microscope for science—then you die."

Pinchas Goldschmidt smiled shyly.

No one spoke for a long time. Then Matthias said: "And after?"

"After?" Mrs. Goldschmidt shrugged. "The war ended. We went back to France, found Felix, went on. What else?"

"He was a wonderful boy," said Mr. Goldschmidt.

"Yes," said his wife. "And he made us happy. Didn't he?"

"Very happy."

"But then he grew up. And went away to university."

"And we came here," Mr. Goldschmidt said. "To America."

"Because we despised France," said his wife. "For what it let them do to us. *Liberté. Egalité. Fraternité.*"

Matthias pushed away from the door, returned to the couch. "I think you said Felix taught Jewish history."

"He taught all kinds of history," Mrs. Goldschmidt said. "He specialized in Jewish history."

"And he became interested in von Trautschke."

Mr. Goldschmidt looked at her over his shoulder. "This is a smart man, Hilda." His wife made no reply. The old man leaned forward in his wheelchair. "He became interested in von Trautschke, sir. Intellectually." Behind him, Mrs. Goldschmidt shook her head. The old man must have been aware of it because he added, "Maybe not just intellectually. But intellectually was part of it. He wanted to know how a man who invented the first fertility drug, who started as someone who appeared to be helping people, could finish as someone doing experiments on Block Ten."

"It was all part of eugenics," said Mrs. Goldschmidt. "Positive and negative."

"Yes," said her husband. He held out his hands. Mrs. Goldschmidt laid the manuscript in them. He leafed through it, stopped. "I translate—'Positive eugenics. Encouraging the propagation of desirable elements. Negative eugenics. Discouraging the propagation of undesirable elements.' Do you see Felix's point? Positive and negative came together in the same man. They were part of the same thing. It was like *Lebensborn*. Von Trautschke was involved with that too."

"*Lebensborn*?" said Nina.

The old man smiled at her. "She hasn't heard of *Lebensborn*," he said.

"Why are you smiling when she doesn't know?" asked Mrs. Goldschmidt.

"It makes life better," replied the old man. "Not knowing." He turned to the second page of the manuscript, showed it to Nina. On it was an epigraph from Heinrich Himmler, in German.

"I can't read that," Nina said.

"No? Himmler was the head of *Lebensborn*, you see. Well of Life. The idea was to set up a chain of houses where unmarried girls impregnated by SS men could have their babies without stigma. They wanted to encourage the making of lots of eugenically positive babies." He flipped through the manuscript. " 'In 1936, von Trautschke designed the questionnaire to establish the genetic heritage of the girls and women who wished to qualify for the *Lebensborn* program.' "

"But there was more to it than that," Mrs. Goldschmidt said.

"I know, Hilda. I am explaining to her. The rest is in the epigraph."

"What does it say?"

"Himmler," replied Mr. Goldschmidt, "speaking to the officers of the Deutschland Division, November 8, 1938. I translate—'I really intend to take German blood from wherever it is to be found in the world, to rob it and steal it wherever I can.' "

Nina's heart began to pound in her chest. "What does that mean?"

"Kidnapping, dear lady," answered Mr. Goldschmidt. "When the Nazis occupied conquered territories, SS men fathered illegitimate children by local women. If *Lebensborn* established their racial purity, they were kidnapped and sent to Germany."

"Oh God."

"Yes, it was horrible," Mr. Goldschmidt said. He reached over and patted her knee. "I didn't mean to disturb you."

"And von Trautschke was involved with this?" Matthias said.

"He helped plan it," Mr. Goldschmidt answered. "He wrote many learned papers for Himmler. He was an expert on fertility, you see. He even proposed artificial insemination of unmarried women, to expand the pool of—what does Felix call it?" He leafed through the manuscript, quickly found the place: " 'The biologically valuable.' But that was too much for Himmler. He believed in the conventional family."

Mrs. Goldschmidt snorted.

"Hilda."

"What? Are you going to tell me there was some good even in Himmler?"

"No, Hilda. I will not tell you that." She rubbed his shoulders.

"What happened to von Trautschke?" Matthias said.

Mr. Goldschmidt held up one of the Xerox document copies. "This," he said, "is his death certificate. It states that he died in a traffic accident on April 2, 1945."

"Just before the end of the war."

"Exactly."

Nina studied the death certificate. All she could read were two names: Wilhelm von Trautschke and Gerd Müller. She put her finger on "Müller." "Why is he here?"

"Dr. Müller," said Mr. Goldschmidt. "He signed the certificate. It has to be signed by a doctor."

"Is this the same Müller who worked with von Trautschke?" Matthias asked.

Mr. Goldschmidt looked over his shoulder. "This is a smart man, Hilda." He turned to Matthias. "Yes, Müller was on Block Ten too. He went to prison after the war."

"For two years and three months," said Mrs. Goldschmidt.

"But he went to prison, Hilda."

She rubbed his shoulders.

"Unlike von Trautschke," Matthias said.

"Who was saved by death," Mrs. Goldschmidt said.

Her husband sighed. "Except that—"

"Who was saved by death," Mrs. Goldschmidt repeated, a little louder.

Mr. Goldschmidt put his hand on hers, squeezed. "Let us be fair to Felix, Hilda. I think that this lady and gentleman want to continue his work, don't you see?"

"Except what, Mr. Goldschmidt?" Matthias said.

He looked back at his wife; her face was impassive. "Except that Felix could not find von Trautschke's grave," said Mr. Goldschmidt. "All he could find was the death certificate. He tried everything, official channels, unofficial. He even located von Trautschke's daughter, here in America, and Dr. Müller, in Australia, and wrote to them. They did not reply."

"He contacted them?"

"As a researcher. Not as the son of survivors."

"Victims," said Mrs. Goldschmidt. He squeezed her hand.

"When did he write those letters?" Matthias asked.

"About two years ago."

"Can you be more precise?"

"Why does it matter?" asked Mrs. Goldschmidt.

"Because Gerd Müller's son turned up at my hotel last August."

"Felix wrote his letters before that," said Mr. Goldschmidt. "In the spring."

No one spoke for a few moments. Then Matthias said: "And Bernie went to Andros and Happy Standish—von Trautschke's grandson—went to Aix."

"About this Bernie you must be right," said Mr. Goldschmidt. "But there was no connection between the grandson and the letters."

"Why do you say that?"

"Felix met him by accident, at a party. Felix knew the

name from his research. That's how it started. Felix made
the approach. Felix liked him. He was the grandson of a
monster, but he was not a monster. He knew nothing about
his grandfather."

"So he said," said Mrs. Goldschmidt.

"No, Hilda. Felix would not be mistaken about something like that. The boy knew his grandfather was German
and had died in the war, but that was all."

"Did they come here together?" Matthias asked.

"Pardon me?" said Mr. Goldschmidt.

"When your son borrowed the suitcase."

"Felix came alone."

"So they met later in Florida."

"We know nothing about that," said Mrs. Goldschmidt.
"Felix was here only for a few hours. He was in a great
hurry. He mentioned Happy Standish, but said nothing
about what they talked about or . . . anything."

"Sea on fire," said Matthias, so quietly that Nina thought
he was talking to himself.

Mrs. Goldschmidt heard him too. "What?" she said.

Matthias rose, walked across the room, leaned against
the door. Nina wondered if he could ever be comfortable
indoors. She had heard of men like that but never seen
one.

"I know what they talked about," Matthias said. "Von
Trautschke didn't die." Nina looked at the old couple.
Their faces were colorless; they scarcely seemed to be
breathing. "At least not on April 2, 1945. He escaped to
the Bahamas in a U-boat. I believe he blew it up with the
crew on board, so there would be no witnesses. Most of
the wreckage must have gone to the bottom. But, by an
accident of underwater geology, some of it didn't." He
told them what he had seen in the domed chamber under
Zombie Bay. "In 1953, bits of wreckage must have started
floating up in the blue hole. Maybe a storm stirred things
up, maybe it was just the result of normal tidal forces over
time. Hiram Standish, Senior, and a partner dove down
and plugged the leak, but something went wrong and
Hiram drowned. The partner survived to tell Inge Standish
about it."

Mr. Goldschmidt moistened his lips as though he wanted
to speak, but no words came. Mrs. Goldschmidt took a
deep breath and said: "Is this partner still alive?"

"I don't know," Matthias said. "He would be very old by now."

"We are very old," said Mrs. Goldschmidt. Her eyes filled with tears, quickly dried up. Mr. Goldschmidt turned to her and smiled his shy smile. She took her hands from his shoulders and dropped them to her sides. The smile remained on his face, stiff and meaningless, disconnected now from whatever was happening inside.

Nina and Matthias left the tiny apartment. "Are they safe?" Nina asked.

"Yes. Otherwise they'd be dead already."

Nina and Matthias walked toward the car. She knew it was a cold night, could see her breath; her skin burned anyway. She took out the car keys, but for some reason couldn't unlock the car. Then she felt Matthias's hand on hers, a cool hand, very big. He opened the car door.

"You'd better tell me everything," he said.

"I don't know where to start."

"Start with your baby."

Nina began to shake. "He's not biologically valuable," she said. "I have Jewish blood in me." She kept shaking. Slowly, hesitantly, Matthias reached out and put his arms around her. Safe as houses, she thought again, but the message didn't penetrate her body. Nina shook for a long time in the shadow of the building at 216 East Thirty-third Street.

41

Mother wore a black hat. Fritz wore a black hat. They were going on a trip.

Or was this simply memory? Memory number two? A train compartment, Mother dabbing her eyes, Fritz giving him black licorice, snow outside the window.

No: Mother was older now, Fritz was older, and he, Hiram Standish, Jr., was older. The older you were, the closer to death. Did it work the other way? If it did, he was the oldest, by far.

It was another trip. They were older, Mother's hat had no pin, she wore a black mink coat and had a bundle tucked inside the lapels. Fritz wheeled him out of the white room, down the long halls, to the front door. Mother opened it. Lying on his back, Happy felt the cold and saw falling snow.

Snow. Was this memory number two, after all?

No. He was on his back, hooked to the machines. And no train waited outside. At the extremity of his vision he could see a large van.

"Get him in," said Fritz.

He heard a car door open. Heavy footsteps sounded on the threshold. Then an enormous man stood over him. The man had a swollen lip and a black eye. That made Happy slow to recognize him. But a man of that size was hard to forget, even if his hair was shorter now, and his tan not so deep. Happy remembered. His memory was

sharp: he had seen this man once before, from a distance,
walking on the dock at the funny little club on Andros
Island.

What was he doing here?

The man was looking at him. "Christ," he said.

Then Mother came into view. "Spare me," she said to
the big man.

"It wasn't my fault," the man said. "How was I to
know?"

"You could have found out his name," said Mother.
"Simple curiosity—"

"Stop this at once," Fritz said, somewhere out of sight.
"It was bad luck, nothing more."

"Bad luck," said Mother.

"*Hör auf!*"

Mother was silent.

The big man pushed Happy toward the doorway. He
felt the cold. Snowflakes blew inside the house, fell on his
face, light as dust, without temperature. They melted and
slowly froze on his skin. Then, abruptly, he stopped rolling.

"Who's that?" said the big man.

Mother looked into the distance. Her eyes widened.
Happy heard a car approach. Fritz said: "Quick." And
Mother took the bundle from underneath her coat, raised
one corner of his blanket and tucked the bundle inside.

The bundle warmed him.

A car door closed. "Mrs. Standish," said a woman, outside Happy's sphere of vision.

"Yes?" said Mother.

"My name's Delgado," said the woman. "I'm a New
York City police detective."

Mother blinked. "And what can we do for you, Detective?"

The woman said: "It's about a child kidnapping case I'm
working on. There have been two, actually, one in Boston,
one in Manhattan. In both cases, the mothers went to
sperm banks for donor sperm. I've been digging around a
little and I found that the two sperm banks—the Cambridge Reproductive Research Center and the Human Fertility Institute—are or were supported by the Standish
Foundation. I'd like your cooperation in the investigation."

Mother smiled. "In what way, Detective?" Under the blanket, the warm bundle stirred. Happy felt tiny fingertips exploring the hair on his chest.

"It might help to give us access to your donor records," said the woman.

"I wish we could, Detective. And of course, we'll assist you in any way possible. But neither concern is part of the Standish Foundation anymore."

"I'm aware of that," said the woman. She had drawn closer now, still out of Happy's sight, but he could smell her: she smelled of cigarettes. Then he felt tiny lips rooting on his chest, and heard a tiny grunt. The woman continued: "But I don't see—"

"Excuse me," said Mother. "Fritz, I don't want him catching cold."

"Of course, madam," said Fritz, and snapped his fingers. The big man wheeled Happy back inside the house.

"Do go on," Mother said.

Fritz closed the door on the detective's reply.

"Jesus Christ," the big man said quietly.

"Shut up," said Fritz.

They wheeled Happy into the dining room. When was the last time he had been there? In another life. His bed came to rest under a portrait of his father. Happy gazed into his father's eyes. They looked worried; did he have a premonition that the lusca would grab him? Happy's mind was wandering back to his memories of the strange pond in the woods, when Fritz said: "Go wait in the kitchen."

The big man's footsteps padded away.

Then Fritz was gazing down at him. Happy looked into his pale blue eyes and saw nothing. Just pale blue circles with black holes in the center. They might have been manufactured from some high-tech material. Fritz sighed and shook his head.

"Grandson," he said.

Grandson. Had he known it all along? Maybe. Had he resisted the knowledge? Maybe. But Fritz had always been good to him. Hadn't he? Suddenly Happy remembered what Felix had told him. The memory bowled through his mind, making chaos of his inner world. At the same time, tiny moist lips rooted on his chest.

"Grandson," said Fritz. "Everything might have been

different." He winced and added: "If we had not attacked the Bolsheviks. Ach." And he waved that thought aside with his old, liver-spotted hand. Happy looked at that hand and understood: not everything, but at least what was under the blanket.

"Perhaps you have not developed as one would have wished," Fritz continued. "But that is not so surprising in a country like this." Happy looked into the black holes. "Still, you are my grandson. And I would not do this if it were not the humane and rational course, given your prognosis." Then Happy heard the flick of a switch. "Besides," said Fritz, "there is so little time."

Something was wrong. What was it? No air. That was it. *Keine Luft.* Like father like son. The pressure in his lungs had dropped to nothing. They were empty and the machine wasn't pumping the next breath into him. He listened for the sound of the machine and heard nothing. The room was quiet. Happy wanted to gasp for breath, but could not. He could only wait for it. He gazed into the black holes and waited. No air came.

Under the blanket, the tiny mouth finally found his nipple and began to suck.

| 42 |

They sat in the rented compact car, with the engine running, the heater turned up, the body of Dr. Crossman in the trunk; and they talked. Nina told Matthias everything. She told him about the papers she had signed at the Human Fertility Institute and Dr. Crossman's questions about her genealogy and intelligence; about Laura Bain and the appraiser in her house; about the blue Bic pen and the bottle of Seconal that Dr. Crossman had given her. She described the volunteer with the strange accent on the maternity ward; she described the appraiser. She described all she could remember of the donor, VT-3(h).

Matthias talked too. He told Nina about the diving accident and tank 27 containing carbon monoxide; about Hew Aikenfield's scrapbooks and his death; about the domed chamber and Nottage's drunken memories.

Hours passed. The windows of the car misted over. They might have been teenage lovers with no place to go. Maybe that's what the driver of the squad car thought as he slowed down, shone his flash on them, kept going. And after, like teenage lovers, they sat in silent thought. A band of gold appeared in the east. Nina, wiping the window, saw it reflected in the side mirror.

"How does it fit together?" she said.

"Like the blue hole," Matthias told her.

"What do you mean?"

Matthias drew a picture in the mist on the windshield.

"Blue hole. Tunnel. Chamber. And the ledge where I found the suitcase." He sketched another tunnel leading away from the ledge; it led to an opening in the wall. "The drop-off wall. There has to be a cave in it somewhere, a back door, probably with another ledge, big enough to catch pieces of the sub, and Felix's suitcase. Then tidal forces swept them inside. The point is there must be two entrances."

"So we're in a blue hole?"

"Exactly. You came in one end, I came in the other."

"And we bumped heads in the dark."

Matthias laughed. For the first time he glanced in the mirror, saw his crooked nose and bloody face. He stopped laughing and wiped away the diagram. "Let's see what Inge Standish has to say about the Goldschmidts."

Nina was tired. Her cheek hurt. Her head hurt. But she sensed something in the man beside her, something that seemed to fill the car and radiate through her, something that made her answer, "Sounds good."

"Drive or navigate?" asked Matthias.

"Navigate," said Nina.

"I was hoping you'd say that. I'm a lousy navigator."

They changed places. Nina navigated. Matthias drove. She got him onto the Hutchinson and leaned her head against the window. The cold glass took her headache away. She slept.

Nina awoke in a postcard: Kodachrome-blue skies, snow-covered evergreens and a little country store with an American Flyer leaning on the porch and a wreath on the door. Then the door opened and the man in the windbreaker came out, carrying a brown bag. N. H. Matthias. Matt. He had cleaned the blood off his face and combed his hair; it was still wet. She thought of schoolboys in the morning.

He saw she was awake and smiled. "Ham and cheese or tuna?"

"Ham and cheese. I had tuna at Mrs. Standish's."

That brought another smile.

Nina ate ham and cheese on rye. It was delicious. There was coffee. It was delicious too.

"Mustard okay?" he said.

"Yup."

"It was that or mayo."

"Mustard every time."

"Same here."

The car rolled through the hill towns of western Connecticut. They ate their sandwiches and drank their coffee. Nina could almost feel nourishment flowing through her body, carrying reinforcements to every cell. For a few minutes she even forgot about Dr. Crossman in the trunk.

"Were you really in a prison camp?"

Matthias nodded.

"In Vietnam?"

"Cuba." There was a long silence. "A long time ago. I was stupid."

"I doubt that."

They drove into Washington, past the green, the post office, the white church. "Do you have children?" Nina asked.

"A boy," Matthias replied. He turned onto 109 east. "He lives with his mother."

"Oh," said Nina.

They took the third right after the last house in town and drove between the tall trees to Mrs. Standish's gate. It was open. They went through.

An ambulance was parked in front of the house. Matthias stopped beside it. An attendant was closing the rear doors. Beside him stood a man with a stethoscope around his neck, beating his hands to stay warm. Dr. Robert.

Matthias and Nina got out of the car. Dr. Robert's eyes went to her, to him, back to her. "Dr. Robert," she said.

"That's me."

"I saw you yesterday morning."

"Oh, yes." He thumped his hands together. "It's really for the best," he said. "It always is, in these hopeless cases."

"What are you talking about?"

"Happy Standish." Dr. Robert nodded toward the ambulance. "He died this morning. Passed away."

"Of what?"

"Of what? You name it."

"That's your job, isn't it?" Matthias said.

Dr. Robert frowned. "The direct cause was pneumonia, I suppose."

Matthias went to the ambulance and looked through the

window. Dr. Robert's frown deepened. "Where's Mrs. Standish?" Matthias asked.

"Out of town," Dr. Robert said. "Old Fritz called me."

"Old Fritz?"

"The gardener. But he doesn't seem to be around either. I checked the cottage."

"All set, Doc," said the ambulance attendant.

"Okay. I'll be along in a while."

Matthias moved toward the house. The door was open. Nina went with him.

"Just a minute," said Dr. Robert. "Where are you going?"

"It's all right," Nina said. "I'm a relative."

"A relative?"

Nina closed the door behind her. She led Matthias through the house to Happy's room. The screen of the wall monitor was blank. Nothing lay on the bed but an IV bag, half-full. Matthias looked at the photographs on the wall. "Left-handed," he said.

Nina had noticed that before, but it hadn't hit her then. It hit her now, almost physically: she sucked in her breath. "And Laura's donor was left-handed too."

"VT-one," said Matthias, "Wilhelm von Trautschke. VT-two, Inge. VT-three, Happy."

Which is what (h) is for, Nina thought. She tried to bring to order the calendar in her mind. "Was the sperm taken after the accident?" she said.

"And because of it."

Nina thought about that. It made sense of many things, such as Dr. Crossman's questions about her background, and Inge Standish's reaction to the revelation that Nina's parents had both died of cancer. And she thought of Bernie, when he learned of the great-grandfather with the Jewish name: "*None of this would have happened.*" That memory turned her body cold, made her want to disbelieve. "But is it possible?" she said.

They went outside. The ambulance had gone. Dr. Robert was getting into his car.

"Dr. Robert?" said Nina.

"Yes?"

"Do you think Happy's normal production of sperm was affected by the accident?"

"That's a strange question. No reason it should have been."

"And his erectile tissue?"

Dr. Robert screwed up his face. "His erectile tissue?"

"I'm asking whether someone could have . . . collected Happy's sperm while he was in the coma."

Dr. Robert looked at her with disgust. "What a repulsive suggestion. Who would want to do a thing like that?" He got in the car, started to close the door. Matthias caught it with one hand. Dr. Robert kept pulling on the handle, but the door did not budge.

"The question is," said Matthias, "would it have been possible?"

"Yes. Now get your hands off my car." Matthias let go. The door slammed shut. Dr. Robert glared at them and sped away.

"He's going to call the police," said Nina.

"Probably."

"And we've got Dr. Crossman in the trunk."

"We'd better do something about that," Matthias said.

He opened the trunk, swung Dr. Crossman over his shoulder and carried him around the house to old Fritz's cottage. Smoke drifted up from the chimney but no one was home. The door was unlocked. They went inside. There was one big room, with a kitchen at one end and a living room at the other. An empty bottle of Rüdesheim stood on the wooden table in the kitchen. Books, most in German, lined the walls: medical books, scientific books, history books. The fire in the stone hearth was almost out. Zulu lay in front of it with a bullet in his head. Matthias put Dr. Crossman beside him, removed Nina's steak knife and cleaned it in the sink. He offered the knife to her, handle first. She made no move to take it.

"Aren't we tampering with evidence?"

"Think of it as putting the investigation on the right track," Matthias said.

Nina took the knife. "They couldn't trust him, is that it?"

"Could you?"

Matthias knelt by the fireplace, ran his hands through the ashes. "They've been burning paper," he said. "Lots of it."

"Where are they?" Nina asked.

"On the run," Matthias said.

"To where?" Nina asked. And thought: Bernie knows about my baby now. She felt herself beginning to tremble again. *No time for that. Move.* She hurried out of old Fritz's cottage and was running by the time she reached the car.

Matthias and Nina caught the last plane out of New York to Nassau. They sat side by side. The plane rose. The sun set. The plane droned through the night, warm, quiet, unreal: an escapism machine. Nina closed her eyes and began her escape. After a while she was aware of almost nothing; nothing at all, if she excluded the feeling of N. H. Matthias beside her. He was sitting straight up, not using the armrest, which he left for her, but still his body pressed against hers. As Nina fell asleep, she had a crazy thought, inappropriate and practical at the same time: *I'm going to need a bigger bed.*

| 43 |

That night Nina entered Matthias's world. Was it too much
to say it was the world of andros, in its Greek meaning?
A world where she sat for the first time in her life on the
back of a motorcycle, holding on to Matthias as they roared
along a narrow Nassau road by the sea; a world where she
boarded a little boat and skimmed over black water, with
not a light on the horizon; a world where she stepped onto
an island that smelled of pine, and walked under a sky full
of stars so bright they sparkled in the pearly insides of the
conch shells that lined the path, and into a deserted bar
where a gorgeous bird said: "Bugger off, bugger off."

"That's Chick," Matthias said. "Ignore him."

"*Amazona versicolor*," said Nina. "The St. Lucia parrot."

Pause. "How did you know that?"

Nina smiled and said nothing. A bowl of pretzels lay on
the bar. She offered one to Chick, aware of Matthias's
eyes on her. Chick pecked it from her fingers. She could
survive on Andros. She was still congratulating herself on
that when Matthias suddenly snapped off the lights. Nina
heard him moving across the room toward the patio, but
couldn't see anything. Then a voice whispered:

"Matt?"

And Matthias said, "Yeah," and switched on the lights.

A man appeared on the patio, entered the bar. He wore
a moth-eaten sweater and a woolen tuque bearing the Bos-

ton Bruins logo. He glanced once at Nina, then spoke to Matthias.

"Brock be here, mahn."

"On the island?"

The man nodded.

"You talked to him?"

The man shook his head. "He be coming to the dock in a Whaler. I hide in the bushes."

"Why?"

The man shrugged.

There was a silence. Nina heard waves breaking on the beach, like an orchestra of cymbals. "You have no reason to be afraid of Brock, do you, Moxie?" Matthias said.

Moxie looked at the floor.

Matthias watched him for a moment. "Who threw the suitcase over the side, Mox?"

Moxie took off the hockey tuque, wrung it in his hands. "Brock," he said. "He be taking it out after the accident. I say, 'What you doing, mahn?' He say, 'Best thing for Matt—he have no insurance.' " Moxie tried to meet Matthias's gaze and couldn't. "You be thinking it was me?" he said softly.

"No, Moxie. I never thought that." Moxie stopped wringing his hat, but still didn't look at Matthias. "Where is he now?" Matthias said.

"To the blue hole," Moxie replied.

"The blue hole? Did he have his gear?"

"A lot of gear," said Moxie. "And he have Danny too."

"Danny? What are you talking about?" Matthias didn't move, but Moxie stepped back anyway.

"Danny come yesterday. For a little break, he say."

Matthias ran outside. Nina followed. A crescent moon had risen above the trees, hard and white. It didn't provide much light, but enough for her to keep him in sight. Nina ran, hearing the wind rising in the trees, catching glimpses of her surroundings in the moonlight: a cracked shuffleboard court, an orange land crab frozen on a rock, the trunks of the pines, narrow and bare. Then a dog bounded into their path, barking wildly. The jolt of adrenaline that went through Nina almost lifted her off the ground, and she wasn't sure if she really had heard Matthias growl, but the dog's ears drooped and it turned away.

Little silver crescents glimmered through the woods. A few strides later, Nina saw that they were reflections of the moon in a round pool. Matthias was already kneeling by a tree at its edge. A boy was tied to the tree with nylon line. A broad-shouldered boy. Nina knew who he was right away. Matthias freed him.

"Dad," said the boy. He was shaking.

Matthias took him in his arms. The boy tried not to cry, but he did. Nina watched Matthias's hand on the boy's back. At first it was still; then it began patting him. "You all right?" Matthias said.

The boy nodded.

"Where is he?"

"In there," the boy replied. "He said he'd take care of me later."

A look crossed Matthias's face that Nina had no words to describe. He walked around the pond, stopped, picked up a cardboard box, the size a VCR might come in. There were scraps of wax paper inside. He sniffed at them. "Plastique," he said.

Matthias kept circling the pond, prowling now. He found more nylon line, tied to another tree. He began pulling on the free end. Two scuba tanks came to the surface of the water. Matthias gazed at them; Nina saw the hard moon reflected in his eyes. Then he released the line and the tanks sank from sight.

"I don't understand," Nina said.

"Those are his decompression tanks," Matthias told her. "I wouldn't kill a man like that."

But that wasn't what Nina had meant. "What is plastique?"

"Plastic explosive. He's going to try to blow the roof in."

"And cover the evidence?"

Matthias nodded. "Moxie," he said.

"Yeah," answered a voice in the darkness. Nina hadn't known he was there.

"I need my gear—two sets of eighties, three regs, compass, depth gauge, weight. Use the Jeep."

"I'll help," said the boy.

Matthias smiled.

Nina heard their running feet. Then it was quiet, except

for the wind, growing louder all around them. It ruffled the surface of the pond, making the white crescents flicker like lights on a marquee.

"You're going in there at night?" Nina said.

"That's the advantage of cave diving," Matthias replied. "Day or night—it makes no difference."

"Is your friend going with you?"

"Moxie? No."

Soon Nina heard the Jeep. She said: "I don't think you should do it alone." She couldn't stop herself. "Maybe I could go with you."

Matthias smiled: another white crescent in the night. "Done much diving?"

I've snorkled in Tahiti with Richard II, she thought. She said: "Never."

"This isn't the place to start. You'll be a big help just by staying right here."

"How so?"

He didn't answer.

Moxie and the boy appeared with the gear. Matthias stripped off his clothes. Naked in the moonlight, his body was every bit as powerful as Nina had thought, but now there was something vulnerable about it too. Unaccountable: except perhaps for the vastness of the night sky and the two white scars curving across his back. His son watched with an unreadable expression on his face.

Matthias put on a wet suit, fins, mask, a complicated-looking safety vest, tanks and a lot of other equipment Nina didn't even know the names for. "Lower the spares down to forty feet," he told Moxie. "Or so." Then he moved to the edge of the pond, pulled the mask over his face and checked his watch.

He stuck the breathing device in his mouth. "Ta-ta," he said around it, then stepped into the water and disappeared. The white crescents broke into madly blinking pieces, then slowly put themselves back together. Moxie tied tanks to a line, fastened the other end to a tree and lowered them into the water. His skin was the color of ashes.

"Luscas live down there," he said.

"Luscas?"

"Monsters. They be hiding in the blue holes."

He pulled his tuque down a little further on his head.

The wind blew a scrap of wax paper near Nina. She picked it up and held it to her nose. It smelled like burnt sugar. She stood by the side of the pond.

Well shit, Matthias thought as cold water found its way under his wet suit, caves don't kill divers, divers do. Switching on the torch he went down fast, through the fresh water layer, the brine shrimp, into salt water and down to the cave at 122 feet. He swam to the back, past the rock pile, to the tunnel entrance. There he shut off the light, peered inside—and saw blackness. He thought he felt a current flowing into the tunnel and remembered the rule about never entering an island cave on an ebbing tide. Then he kicked his way inside.

His light picked out the familiar details: broken china, rusty nails, gray limestone walls. But Matthias wasn't looking for any of that. He was looking for air bubbles flattened against the ceiling, and he saw them.

Matthias swam quickly along the tunnel to the first division. His old line was still tied off to the limestone spur. Again he cut his light, again saw nothing but the afterglow on his retinas, and then blackness.

He swam on, past the cave where he had found the military boot, past the rock fall where he had first seen the baby nurse shark, to the point where he had run out of line. His reel was there, still jammed between the stalagmite and the wall. That was the place where a diver should have tied off a new line, but Bernie Muller hadn't done so. It was a vote of confidence: Bernie Muller must have thought that the tricky part was over. But it hadn't been over, Matthias remembered: the tunnel had divided once more, but at his back, and he hadn't known until he was on the way out. He swam on.

The tunnel widened. Matthias played his beam along the walls, waiting for a glimpse of the edge. When he saw it, he switched off the light. He saw the after-image, blackness, and then a faint glowing cone of yellow in the distance. Leaving his light off, he kicked ahead, out of the tunnel and into the domed chamber.

The yellow cone trembled slightly against the far wall, near the ceiling. It illuminated a niche in the limestone and the bare hands of a diver working with a canvas haversack in the niche; the diver's body was lit in silhouette,

but it was Bernie Muller—Matthias recognized the long
spear gun that only he could load, dangling from his belt.
Matthias swam closer.

Long ago he had been trained for situations like this.
One: approach from above and behind. Two: rip off enemy
mask. Three: use knife on enemy or enemy regulator hose.
But Matthias didn't touch his knife. Here in the cave, it
was only necessary to knock Bernie Muller's torch from
his hand. It would fall to the bottom and he would be
helpless, with no choice but to follow Matthias out to
safety. If he came too close all Matthias had to do was
shut off his own light and swim away. Matthias rose until
he touched the ceiling, then swam along the curve of the
dome and came down on Bernie Muller from above.

It was a clear, logical plan, but clear logical plans for-
mulated in underwater caves at night didn't always work.
That was one flaw. Flaw number two: Bernie Muller was
a good diver and good divers have a sixth sense. It made
him glance up from his work just as Matthias swam down
at him. He saw Matthias coming out of the darkness and
terror filled his eyes, but it didn't stop him from reaching
for his spear gun. Matthias grabbed at Bernie Muller's
torch. There was no time for Bernie to load the gun; he
just swung it up and out with one hand.

Bernie Muller was a strong man. Even one-handed and
underwater, his blow had power. But it might not have
done any damage if it hadn't caught Matthias on his left
elbow. The barrel of the gun struck him. His hand went
numb. He dropped his own torch.

At the same time, his right hand closed on Bernie's
torch. He yanked at it. But Bernie held on. They wrestled
in an explosion of air bubbles. Something hit Matthias in
the throat. Then the only hand on the torch was Bernie's.
He backed away, trying to find Matthias in the dark. The
beam swept across the niche. Matthias reached out,
grabbed the strap of the haversack. He saw the tube sticking out, saw that its copper top hadn't been crushed. That
meant Bernie hadn't yet triggered the explosive. Until he
did, it was nothing but a bag full of nitrates. Matthias
ducked down between Bernie and the wall and let it go.

Bernie's beam stabbed at the empty niche, at Matthias,
at the haversack, falling fast. It sank to the end of the
beam and disappeared. Then the beam came up and shone

in Matthias's face, blinding him. Matthias didn't see the spear gun. It came out of darkness and glare and hit him in the side of the head.

Matthias opened his eyes. Or were they already open? He felt for his mask, his regulator: still in place. He looked around in all directions, or what he thought were all directions. Blackness surrounded him. No ceiling, no floor, no walls; no up, no down. He still had his depth gauge, his pressure gauge, his watch, but he couldn't read any of them. *Think. Don't panic.* But all he could think of was the woman waiting at the edge of the blue hole. His mind stuck on the image of her. Mental paralysis was a form of panic. *You're panicking. Think.* He thought: Is she real or did I will her into being, imagining her, imagining everything? Was this still his first dive in the domed chamber; and was he narced out, down so deep and in so long there was no hope?

No. Her name was Nina. He couldn't have imagined her. He blinked a few times to make sure his eyes were open. And then he saw a flicker of light, far away. The light disappeared and everything went black again. *Think.* The light must have been Bernie Muller, going back into the tunnel. Therefore Bernie was up and he was down. He had fallen after Bernie hit him, fallen deeper than Bernie cared to go. Or perhaps Bernie had thought that even if he regained consciousness he would never get out of the cave without a light; and even if he found the entrance to the tunnel, there was nothing to stop Bernie from waiting for him around some corner with his spear gun ready.

Good. He was having clear and logical underwater cave thoughts again. Bernie was up. He was down. The tunnel was in the west wall. Judging from the last position of Bernie's light, he himself must be near the east wall. There was a ledge on the east wall at 320, the ledge where he had found Felix's suitcase. He thought of the back door to the blue hole in the diagram he had drawn on Nina's windshield, and hoped it was a true picture.

Facing west, he thought, Matthias began backpedaling. His tank banged against rock. The east wall. Now the clear and logical question was this: had he already dropped below the ledge at 320, or was it still beneath him? If he was below it and had been there for more than a few minutes he would soon run out of air, or need so much decompression he would never survive anyway. Therefore he felt for his bubbles, and trying to hold a feet-first vertical position, slowly finned his way along the wall in the opposite direction: down.

Down, down, he went. He began to reconsider: perhaps it would be better to take his chances with Bernie in the tunnel. But he might not find it at all, and once in he had no chance. He thought of Nina and tears came to his eyes. Real tears for the second time in the domed chamber. There had been no other real tears since his last encounter with Stepdaddy Number Two. He was remembering Stepdaddy Number Two's Coupe de Ville when his fins touched down on solid rock.

The ledge. Matthias lowered himself onto it, ran his hands along the limestone. He found the edge of the outcrop, then turned what he hoped was one-hundred-and-eighty degrees and went the other way, keeping within touching distance of the bottom.

Matthias swam in blackness. He thought: what if this tunnel diverges? what if it leads nowhere? what if I'm going down? There was no point in thinking like that. He stopped doing it. He thought of Nina instead: *We bumped heads in the dark.* He thought of the way she ate her ham and cheese sandwich, the way she had said, "I'm a relative," to Dr. Robert, the way she had trembled in his arms outside 216 East Thirty-third Street. He was glad he had taken the chance of holding her then, but he wished he had more memories of her. Weren't there more? He was trying to recall some when he became aware of light all around him. Light, not strong, but real and natural. How long had he been in the light?

Or was he narced and imagining it? He checked his depth gauge and found he could read it clearly: 105 feet. That wasn't bad. He couldn't be narced at 105 feet. He swam on. He was in a tunnel and he wasn't alone. He had sponges, pink and yellow, for company. As he approached them, his air began to pull hard. Or had it been doing so for some time? He swam faster, but tried not to breathe faster. Each lungful came harder than the one before. Then they weren't full lungfuls anymore. And then there was nothing. Out of air, like a stupid college kid in a Florida sink.

Matthias held his breath and swam, watching his depth gauge at the same time, ready to exhale if he went up. Doing everything right. But why? Even if he got out and still had enough oxygen in his lungs to make a free ascent, he'd be bent to death.

Matthias swam on, kicking as hard as he could: beyond the point where his lungs were bursting, beyond the point where the cough reflex operated. The depth gauge remained at 105. His heartbeat pounded in his ears, louder and louder. Blackness began closing in. *Kick. Kick.* And then he saw something on the tunnel floor, just ahead.

A scuba tank.

With regulator attached. He could read the decal: ZB-27; and the pressure gauge: 2900. Matthias stuck the regulator in his mouth, gasped out the carbon dioxide in his chest, sucked in air.

Happy Standish's air. He breathed it in and out, in and out. And he saw it all: Bernie Muller had poisoned two tanks on the compressor at Two-Head Cay, stuck on Zombie Bay logos, painted them with the numbers of the tanks Moxie had already filled for Happy and Felix, switched them and dropped the originals over the side with Felix's suitcase. Matthias swam on with ZB-27 in his arms.

The light grew brighter. It seemed to come through cracks in a wall not far ahead. Matthias swam to it. It was not a wall, but a thick growth of staghorn coral. There was a big gap at the top. Matthias swam through and out into the open sea, endless and full of light. He looked at the staghorn formation; it was the formation on the ledge at 100 feet that he had seen before. It grew taller than the mouth of the cave, hiding it completely, and was perfectly placed to catch things falling from above.

Matthias rose to 50 feet with ZB-27 in his arms. Later, he rose to 40, then 30, 20, 10. He breathed Happy's air down to 50 p.s.i.: enough for laboratory analysis. Matthias already knew the air was good—he'd be dead if it weren't—but the court would want to know too. He still had time to file his appeal; almost a whole day.

Matthias kicked to the surface, unbent, and saw the sun, just risen over Two-Head Cay in the east. The sea was rough. Matthias turned: he was in Zombie Bay, no more than three hundred yards from the dock. Bernie would no longer be waiting for him in the tunnel. He would be decompressing in the blue hole, or on his way up. Matthias stuck his snorkel in his mouth and started swimming as fast as he could.

The stars faded away. Then the moon. The sky turned milky. The wind blew harder. Nina, Moxie and the boy stood by the blue hole. "How much air is in those tanks?" Nina said.

Moxie ground his sneaker in the dirt and said nothing.

"Eighty cubic feet in each one," Danny said.

"How long does it last?"

"It depends."

Before Nina could ask what it depended on, a bubble broke on the surface of the pond. More bubbles followed. They grew bigger. Nina peered into the water. Something was rising fast. Nina felt Moxie tugging at her hand.

"Get back," he said.

But she didn't move. The next moment a man came bursting through the surface, threw off his mask, swam frantically toward land. It was Bernie.

"Get back," said Moxie.

But Nina couldn't. Bernie reached the edge of the pond, pulled himself to his feet. He looked right at Nina, standing ten feet away. His eyes were bright red. He took the spear gun off his belt, jammed the butt in his abdomen and began pulling the thick rubber band toward the notch at the base of the spear. Muscles popped up inside his wet suit; cords stood out in his neck. The thick rubber band stretched taut; the clip at its end came to within an inch of the notch in the spear. At that moment, the boy took a step forward, his hands balled into fists. Bernie stared at him. No one moved. Then blood spurted out of Bernie's ears, his nose, his mouth. He gasped and fell at their feet.

Not long after, something came crashing through the woods: Matthias. He stopped, chest heaving, looked at Nina, Danny, Moxie, Bernie. He knelt beside Bernie, put his finger on Bernie's neck, checked his pressure gauge. "Still had air," he said, almost to himself. He pulled up the tanks that Bernie had lowered into the blue hole, checked the gauge. "Full."

"He scared, mahn," said Moxie. "He seen the lusca."

Matthias shook his head.

"No luscas down there?" Moxie said.

"He got lost, that's all," Matthias replied. "He must have taken a wrong turn on the way back and panicked."

"Brock?"

"It's easy, Mox." Matthias started to smile. "I get lost and panic every damn time I go in there." All at once, he was laughing. Nina thought that he might not be able to stop. But he did. The next thing she knew he was kissing her on the mouth. It seemed like the most natural thing in the world.

Matthias picked up Bernie Muller's spear gun. "Let's go," he said, and loaded it in one easy motion.

44

The wind rose. It blew a dark ceiling of rainclouds across the sky, whipped up a seascape of sharp gray peaks and white spume, cut the telephone link between Zombie Bay and Constable Welles's little station in Conchtown. Moxie jumped in the Jeep and drove toward the Conchtown road. Danny remained at the phone, trying to contact Sergeant Cuthbertson in Nassau. Matthias and Nina hurried to the dock.

As soon as he stepped on the deck of *So What*, Matthias thought of Cesarito and the nighttime crossing to the beach at the foot of the Sierra Maestra. Cesarito, singing to keep his courage up: *De ansair ma fren*. It had been the overture to so much that had gone wrong, beginning with the two years on Isla de Piños, ending with his marriage to Marilyn.

This crossing was going to be different. It was different already: day not night, with a strong wind to mask the engine noise and no deluded counter-revolutionaries on board. Instead he had Nina. He watched her freeing the bow line. He could tell she didn't have much experience in boats, but she glanced at the stern, saw what he had done and did the same. This was going to be easy: he had Nina, the wind, the day. And an older version of himself. He hoped he was smarter. Matthias cast off and hit the throttles.

So What surged forward. A cold gray wave broke over the bow and drenched Nina. "Better come aft a bit," Matthias called over the engine noise. "It might be bumpy when we get outside."

Clutching the gunwale, Nina made her way to the console, lurched toward it, grabbed, hung on. The boat shot over a wall of water. Were they airborne? Surely not, but the next moment they slammed back down with a force that buckled her knees. Then another wall appeared, much too big to be called a wave, and they did it all over again. Images spun by: walls of water, the air full of spray, and possibly rain too, Matthias's brown hands on the wheel. And was he whistling under his breath? Yes. He was a lousy whistler. It took a long time before Nina recognized the tune he was attempting: "Blowin' in the Wind." Was he trying to be funny? She glanced at his face and couldn't tell. The sea had soaked his hair, the wind had slicked it back: he looked like a seal in its natural element.

"We're out of the bay now," he said. "It could be worse."

Ahead waited the kind of sea Nina had only seen in news clips during hurricane season. The boat—so ludicrously tiny—rose up, slammed down, rose up, slammed down. Waves, not just their tips, but whole waves, broke over the boat and smacked against her. She hung on to the console with all her might, so intent on staying attached to the boat that at first she wasn't aware of her seasickness. Then she was aware of it. Then it was all she was aware of.

Matthias was saying something. She couldn't hear. The engines shrieked, the wind howled. "I can't hear a fucking thing," Nina shouted.

Matthias cupped a hand to her ear. She felt hard rough skin on her cheek, felt his breath on her earlobe. "This is perfect," he said. "We'll come in downwind. They won't hear a sound."

"What if they see us?"

He laughed. "Then it won't be perfect."

After a while a dark gray form separated itself from all the other grays. It was a small island, shaped like the top half of an H. Nina saw trees, a beach, a long pier. Matthias didn't head toward the pier. He swung around to the right-hand end of the island—the southern end, she thought—and pulled back on the throttles.

The sea was calmer in the lee of the island. Ahead lay

a narrow beach. They were still fifteen or twenty yards
from it when Matthias dropped anchor and cut the engines.
"Can't put it on the beach in this weather," he said, his
voice suddenly seeming loud. "We'll have to swim."

The sea was calmer, but not calm. Nina had never swum
in water like that. She heard herself say, "Let's go." Matthias picked up the spear gun. They jumped over the side.

Not so bad, Nina thought. The sea made her no colder
or wetter than she already was. And it took her nausea
away. She swam up one side of a wave and slid down the
other. She did that a few more times before her foot
touched bottom. Nina stood up. A wave knocked her
down. She stumbled to the beach.

Matthias was beside her. "Okay?" he said.

"Okay."

He moved toward a clump of sea-grapes, parted them
with the spear gun, disappeared. Nina hurried after him,
not seeing the narrow path through the vegetation until it
was a step away. She took it.

The path climbed to the top of a hill. Nina looked down.
She saw a small clapboard house, two cottages, sheds, and
in the distance a formal garden with a pink pool in the
center, and a big house beyond that. She saw no people,
no dogs, no living creatures.

"*Yo soy turisto*," Matthias said.

"That's not going to work."

He smiled and motioned her forward.

It was raining hard. The path down the bluff was slippery. They scrambled and slipped to the bottom. Ahead
lay a lawn of Bermuda grass and the small house Nina had
seen from the top. It was a tidy house, with white walls,
blue trim, lace curtains in the windows and a screened
verandah. At the end of the verandah sat a baby carriage.

"Run," Matthias said.

They ran: out of the bushes, across the Bermuda grass,
past the verandah, to the side of the house. They dropped
to their knees beneath a window, slowly raised their heads
and looked inside.

Nina saw a kitchen. Three men sat at a table, eating
scrambled eggs and drinking coffee. Two looked like blond
Elvis Presleys, thick-necked and stocky. The third was
older and trimmer. Nina had never seen any of them before, but she recognized the leathery-skinned woman

frying bacon at the stove: it was the hospital volunteer with the strange accent who had offered her candy, tricked Verna Rountree into leaving the nursery, taken her baby and left a Cabbage Patch Kid. Nina's heart beat wildly.

Matthias tugged her back down. He crawled around the corner of the house. Nina crawled after him. They stopped at a door. From its position, Nina knew it must open directly into the kitchen. Matthias rose. Nina rose too, conscious of nothing but her pounding heart: a scared creature trapped in her chest. Matthias looked at her. "Keep me out of trouble," he said in a normal tone. Then he rocked back and kicked the door in. It flew into the kitchen, hinges, screws and all.

And then they were standing side by side in the room. At the table, the two thick-necked men were looking up in surprise, one of them revealing a mouthful of yellow egg, but the older man was already rising from his chair, his eyes, Nina saw, on a shotgun in the corner. Matthias pointed the spear gun at him. "Let's do this right, Gene," he said. The man sat down. Matthias backed toward the corner and picked up the shotgun, as though he had known it was there from the start. "Hands off the frying pan, Mrs. Albury," he said to the woman, not looking at her. "Take a seat between Billy and Bobby." Wiping her hands on her apron, the woman moved toward the table and sat.

"Where is my baby?" Nina said to her.

Mrs. Albury's eyes narrowed. For a moment, Nina thought she was getting ready to spit. But Mrs. Albury didn't spit. She turned away and said nothing.

"That's not doing it right, Gene," Matthias said.

"I don't know what you talking about, fella."

Matthias opened the shotgun, knocked out the shells and tossed them through the doorway. Then he raised the gun and smashed it over the stove, breaking it in half. He approached the table, holding up the barrel. "Don't make me angry, Gene. I won't be able to stop."

Gene Albury opened his mouth, but before he could speak his wife said, "You keep your mouth shut."

Albury closed his mouth. The three men at the table looked at Matthias, then at Mrs. Albury. Nina understood why she had been chosen to kidnap her baby. The woman couldn't be scared. Matthias moved closer to the table. Nina realized he was capable of striking the first blow.

Everyone else knew it too. It was quiet in the kitchen; Nina heard nothing but the wind and the rain. And something else: a crying baby.

She ran from the kitchen, down a corridor, into a room at the end. A crib stood in the corner. And a fair-haired baby boy lay in it. He was on his stomach, raising his head and crying when he couldn't keep it up. He wore the blue sweater that Inge Standish had knit, and had blue eyes like Happy Standish's.

Her baby.

Nina reached for him, picked him up, held him. He stopped crying. Nina forgot everything; everything that had happened, everything that might happen. For a few moments she dwelt in a now of perfect peace, her arms wrapped around her baby and her baby wrapped within them. Her fingers stroked his fine hair, so long at the back. They had remembered the feel of it exactly. To feel his hair again was to be restored.

"Nina?"

She heard Matthias calling and carried the baby back to the kitchen. "Got him?" Matthias said.

"But not her," Nina replied. She faced Mrs. Albury. "Where is Clea?"

"Clea?"

"Laura Bain's baby. The one you stole from her backyard in Dedham."

Mrs. Albury started to speak, stopped, began again. She couldn't hold in her reply. "Six feet under," she said.

"You killed her?"

"Not hardly. She was defective right from the start."

"Did you get her treatment?"

Mrs. Albury met Nina's gaze but didn't speak.

"That's the same as killing her," Nina said. She heard hatred in her own voice. "And you're going to pay for it."

Mrs. Albury summoned up some hatred of her own. Nina realized the woman had vast reserves. "You're all talk," she said.

"Then how come I've got my baby back and you're going to jail?"

"I think not," said a voice behind Matthias. "I've made all the sacrifices I'm going to."

Inge Standish stood outside the door, with a rifle aimed at his back. Matthias didn't even turn to look. He sent the shotgun barrel spinning backwards through the doorway. It caught Inge Standish on the side of the head. She staggered but didn't fall, didn't drop the gun. Out of the corner of her eye, Nina saw Mrs. Albury move. The woman reached into her apron, pulled out a fish knife and darted toward her. Nina was turning her body to shield the baby when something silver flashed across the room and shot through Mrs. Albury's leg, pinning her to the wall.

"Ma," cried one of the younger men. Then the table tipped over and the Alburys were up and moving. Matthias threw the empty spear gun at them and started running toward the hall. He grabbed Nina as he went by.

The rifle cracked behind them. Wood splintered. They ran down the hall into the baby's room. There were no windows on the back wall. Matthias lowered his shoulder and ran through it. Nina followed him. With the baby in one arm, she ran as hard as she could, across the Bermuda grass, up the bluff, down the other side. The sea looked rougher than before, the boat smaller and farther from the beach.

"Here," Matthias said, reaching for the baby.

Nina wouldn't let him go.

"It'll be quicker," Matthias said.

Nina gave him the baby. They swam to the boat. Even with the baby he was there before her, holding him in one arm while he raised anchor with the other. Nina pulled herself over the transom and fell on the deck. Figures appeared on the hill. Something tore a chunk of fiberglass off the console.

"Stay down," Matthias said, handing her the baby and switching on the engines. He spun the boat around and shoved the throttles all the way down. The boat surged forward. Then something shattered the casing of one of the outboards. It stopped running and began to smoke. The boat slowed. Matthias glanced back at Two-Head Cay. "She's good," he said. He knelt on the deck, unclamped the ruined motor and pushed it into the sea. The boat went faster, but not like before, Nina thought.

They rounded the tip of Two-Head Cay and started back across the Tongue of the Ocean. "Take the wheel," Matthias said. "Aim for that bluff straight ahead."

Nina got up and took the wheel with one hand. She held the baby in the other. She looked for a bluff straight ahead.

She saw nothing but watery peaks on the move. They lifted the boat up and threw it down. She turned the wheel this way and that, but nothing she did made the ride any smoother. She glanced down at the baby. He was asleep.

Matthias had opened the bow storage compartment. He threw things overboard—scuba tanks, lead weights, the anchor. Then he returned to the console, took the wheel. He peered ahead. "Right on course," he said. He looked back. The expression in his eyes made Nina look back too. She saw a rooster tail rising off the water between the two heads of Inge Standish's island. "The cigarette," Matthias said. His hand moved to the throttle. It was already all the way down. He pushed at it anyway.

Nina wanted to say, "How much farther?" but she held her tongue, and from the top of the next wave glimpsed a long low smudge in the distance. It grew with every wave they passed, in size and detail. Nina distinguished a hill, a point, a bay. She hugged the baby. "Come on," she said softly. Then she looked back. At first she saw nothing but the sea, and thought they were safe. A moment later, the cigarette boat came flying over the crest of a wave, so close that Nina could see the eyes, all focused on her, of everyone on board: Gene Albury at the wheel, his sons in the stern, Inge Standish raising her rifle to firing position.

"Matt!"

Matthias jerked the wheel, flinging *So What* sideways, knocking Nina to the deck. She clung to the baby. He started to cry. She saw the dark sky, Matthias's face, the rooster tail rising behind him. Then Inge Standish's gun cracked and the compass ball exploded. Matthias swerved again. The cigarette went by, in a flash of black and red. Nina rose to her knees. Zombie Bay lay just ahead. The cigarette sliced a curving path through the water and roared back at them. Matthias cut to the right, steering *So What* not toward the dock, which Nina could now see, but toward the point at the northern end of the bay. He said something. Nina thought it was, "Hope it's low tide," but she wasn't sure. Then the cigarette was behind them again and Inge Standish was firing. Matthias angled to the left. The cigarette followed, swinging slightly wider because of its greater speed. The next moment it rose sharply into the air, high overhead, spun slowly stern over bow and crashed deck first on the sea. Matthias threw himself

on top of Nina and the baby. She heard a booming sound
and saw a ball of smoke and fire take shape in the air. Bits
of metal fell like rain. Then, despite the wind, the sea,
and their own motor, it was quiet.

They got up. Matthias circled back. Red and black
wreckage floated on the water, but there wasn't much of
it. Inge Standish, Gene Albury, his sons; they were all
gone. The sea hissed and bubbled.

Nina looked at Matthias.

"The Angel Fingers," he said. "It happens all the time."
He patted the baby's head.

When had she last slept? Nina couldn't remember. It didn't
matter anyway. It wasn't even lunchtime yet and the baby
didn't want to sleep. He wanted to lie in her lap. He wanted
to play pat-a-cake. He wanted a bottle. He wanted to stare
at his hands. He wanted to stare at her. He wanted to
stare at all the people who came into the bar at Zombie
Bay.

A constable named Welles.

A sergeant named Cuthbertson.

A lawyer named Ravoukian.

They all patted Nina's baby on the head, as though he
had done something remarkable. He batted his fists in the
air. Nina held him. After a while she tried rocking him.
He seemed to like it. She kept doing it.

The lawyer spoke to Matthias, used the phone, spoke
to Matthias again. Matthias nodded. The lawyer smiled a
congratulatory smile and held out his hand. Matthias
barely hesitated before shaking it. A bottle of Armagnac
appeared. It was wonderful.

The sergeant and the constable took a police launch and
searched Two-Head Cay. They overturned the little stone
in the graveyard and dug up the body of an infant girl.
They arrested Betty Albury and took her to the Conchtown
clinic. Later everyone looked at the pictures in water-
logged scrapbooks. Wilhelm von Trautschke had aged but
Nina recognized him. He was the appraiser she had seen
in Laura Bain's house. The sergeant and the constable
returned to Two-Head Cay, searched it again, found no
one.

The constable drove his Land Rover through Blufftown.
He came back with an old man named Nottage. Everyone

looked at the scrapbooks again. Nottage recognized Wilhelm von Trautschke too, but thought he was a gardener
named Fritz who had taken his job away a long time ago.

"Did you see the submarine?" Matthias asked.

"It be night."

"But you watched from the Bluff, didn't you?"

Nottage nodded.

"And you lent him your boat."

"He paid me fifty dollars. I didn't have no job."

"Did you help him load the explosives?"

"But I don' know what he be doing." Nottage hung his
head. "I was needing that fifty dollars bad," he said. "I
be a young man then, with ambitions."

Nottage went away. Matthias walked on the beach with
his son. Night fell. The baby slept. Nina wrapped him in
a blanket and put him on the couch in Matthias's living
room. She lay in Matthias's bed. The sheets were sandy.
Matthias returned, stood on the deck outside the open
sliding door of the bedroom. The wind blew the clouds
away, then died down. The stars came out. Nina turned
on her side and watched Matthias staring out to sea.

"You must be sleepy," Nina called to him.

"No."

"You don't want to lie down?"

"That's different."

He came in and lay beside her. The sea grew calm. Nina
heard it splashing lightly on the rocks. "I don't know what
to say to you," she said.

"Say, 'Give me a kiss.' "

"Only if it leads to something more."

He gave her a kiss.

|45|

"So this is the guy," said Detective Delgado the following afternoon. "What's his name?"

"I'm still working on that," Nina replied.

Detective Delgado drove Nina, Matthias and the baby into the city from Kennedy. Her car smelled of cigarettes and she glanced from time to time at the open pack tucked behind the visor, but she didn't light up. Nina wondered if that was her way of apologizing.

"We've turned the house in Connecticut upside down," Delgado said. "The FBI's involved and Interpol's been notified. Along with everything else, he'll probably stand trial as a war criminal for the Auschwitz stuff—they've got a huge file on him. Plus there's evidence he stole vast sums confiscated from Jewish prisoners. We're watching the airports, the train stations, the bus stations. It's a matter of time." They came out of the tunnel, into Manhattan. "Where to?"

Nina thought. There were things she should do. Stop at the office. Find a pediatrician. "Home," she said.

"Your place?"

"Why not?"

"No problem," Delgado said. "If that's your plan, we'll post a guard outside, that's all."

Nina didn't want that. She wanted normality. "I've got the key to a friend's. We'll stay there."

Delgado stopped at Nina's so she could pick up clothes for herself and the baby. Delgado came up with them and went in first. Nina packed two suitcases, one with clothes, the other with stuffed animals—the polar bear, the lion, Winnie-the-Pooh. She checked the answering machine. There was one message. Suze. "Are you still at my place? I've been trying to reach you. The Paramount project turned to shit. And Ernesto—never mind. I'll tell you all about it next week. I'm coming back."

They went downstairs, got in the car. Delgado drove downtown. Matthias showed the baby how Winnie-the-Pooh could fly. As they passed a bookstore, Nina said, "Could you stop here for a second?"

"Certainly," said Delgado, pulling over. She was on her best behavior.

Nina went into the store. They were advertising signed copies of *Living Without Men and Children . . . and Loving It*. Nina glanced at the jacket she and Jason had designed. It seemed like an unfamiliar object, strange and puzzling. The whole city seemed like that. She kept thinking of Zombie Bay.

Nina bought a book called *1001 Baby Names* and returned to the car. Delgado drove to the converted warehouse where Suze had her loft, parked, went up with them. "It's okay," Nina said. "This is where I was staying before."

Delgado went in first anyway. "Jesus Christ. Every goddamn Delgado who ever lived could fit in here." She pointed past the couch, the chair and the desk, past the king-sized bed, the glass-walled shower stall and the Parisian pissoir, to Auschwitz Cadillac in the distance. "What the hell is that?"

"Art," Nina told her.

Delgado left. Matthias had a closer look at the art. "I don't see the muffler," he said. "It would have made a nice chimney." Nina sat on the bed with the baby on her lap and opened the book of names.

"Lance?"

"Lance?"

"Ferguson?"

"Ferguson?"

"Rudy?"

"Rudy?"

"Then what?"

"Keep thinking."

Nina closed the book. The baby was giving her his serious blue look. "What's your name, baby?" she said.

He started to cry.

Nina rocked him. He kept crying. Matthias sat on the bed, showed him again how Winnie-the-Pooh could fly. He was no longer interested. He kept crying.

"Maybe he's hungry," Matthias said.

Nina opened her purse. She still had the bottle someone had given her at Zombie Bay, but there was no more formula.

"Where's the nearest store?" Matthias asked.

"Around the corner."

Matthias left, locking the door behind him. Nina rocked the baby. He stopped crying. Perhaps he wasn't hungry. Nina reopened *1001 Baby Names*. She tried some names on him. "Remi. Richard. Roone. Randolph. Ramesh. Ri—"

Nina stopped. Had something moved beneath her, under the mattress? The next moment Nina was leaping off the bed and onto the floor, the baby in her arms. It was too late. A hand reached from under the bed and grabbed her ankle. She fell. Nina tried to turn as she went down, to protect the baby; that made her land on her back and crack her head on the bare pine.

And then he was standing over her, with his patrician face and clear blue eyes. Wilhelm von Trautschke. He held the knife from Suze's carving set in one of his enormous, liver-spotted hands. The baby started to cry.

"You concealed information," von Trautschke said. His accent seemed stronger than she remembered. "The same as lying. That was a treacherous thing to do. Do you not understand?"

"I don't understand anything about you," Nina said. And thought: he heard Suze on my answering machine. She slowly shifted her weight on the floor.

"That does not surprise me—nothing done by you or your kind would. You mongrelized my legacy, Miss

Kapstein. My genetic legacy." A thought made him wince. "It might have been my own seed!—would have been—but for the risk of mutation." He looked down at her. "I suffered repeated exposure to radiation in my work, you see." A blue vein pulsed in his forehead. "Now I must do what I can, as a scientist, to purify, to cleanse."

"But it's not true," Nina said. "I made it all up."

"No!" The vein pulsed again. "It is all true. Yesterday municipal records were searched. I had to be certain, one hundred percent, having gone to so much trouble. Now give him to me, Miss Kapstein."

Nina shifted her weight a little more and held on to her baby.

"Very well," said von Trautschke. "Do not imagine I take the slightest pleasure in this." He raised the knife, bent forward and stabbed down, not at her, but at the baby. Nina rolled away, at the same time kicking out as hard as she could. Her foot caught him on the knee. It buckled enough to spoil his aim. The knife struck the floor hard, snapping the blade off the handle. It spun across the room. Nina sprang up with the baby crying in her arms. But von Trautschke was up too, standing between her and the door. He looked at her with a new expression on his face. It was close to pleasure. Then he came toward her, raising his hands. Nina backed away, backing, backing until she touched barbed wire.

Von Trautschke paused, regarded Auschwitz Cadillac and frowned, the way a person frowns when a thought is just out of reach. With one hand, Nina felt behind her and grasped a strand of wire, between the barbs. He didn't appear to notice. His eyes were on the baby now. The vein in his forehead jumped again: and he was on her. They fell in a tangle of pink barbed wire. Von Trautschke got one of his huge hands on her son's face. The baby howled. Nina was trapped under von Trautschke's shoulder. With all her might, she twisted her arm free, jerked the strand of barbed wire around his neck and pulled. A barb sank into her palm; she kept pulling. Von Trautschke's hand let go of the baby, went to his own neck, scratched at the wire. His other hand struck at her with blows she didn't feel. Nina clutched the wire and pulled. His face, inches from hers, turned red. He made choking sounds, then gagging sounds. His blood dripped down on her. Nina just pulled, and kept pulling even after his sounds had ceased and his face had gone from red to purple. She didn't stop until Matthias appeared and gently unclenched her fist.

|46|

"Friggin' bugger," said Chick.

The baby, strapped in a baby seat on the bar at Zombie Bay, gave the bird a serious blue look. Chick gave him a nasty yellow one in return.

Matthias came in. "Phone for you," he said.

Nina, in bare feet—she hadn't worn shoes for days—walked across to the office and took the call. It was Percival.

"Ms. Kitchener," he said in his thick-cream voice. "I'm so pleased everything has been resolved in such a satisfactory fashion." Nina was silent. He continued: "I have some good news. We were finally able to locate some of those records from the Human Fertility Institute."

"Were you?"

"Yes. Quite a job, I can tell you. And I'm happy to report that there is no doubt that Hiram Standish, Junior, was the father of your child." Pause. "No doubt at all." Longer pause. "Perhaps you don't appreciate the implications."

"What implications?" Nina said. Through the window she saw the sun sparkling on Zombie Bay. A fish leaped out of the water, splashed back down.

"Why, this legally makes your son the sole heir to the Standish fortune, Ms. Kitchener. We're talking about a great deal of money."

"What about the estate rider?" Nina said.

"The estate rider?"

"Neither I nor any resulting issue shall make any claim on the estate of the donor after his death."

"Ah," said Mr. Percival. "The estate rider. We have no record of you having signed it, Ms. Kitchener."

Nina was silent.

"Millions and millions," Percival went on, to make everything plainer. He cleared his throat. "It's this fortune, of course, that we at the firm have always worked so hard to serve, not so much its temporal controllers per se. As whatever sort of human beings they might have happened to be. Naturally we would have preferred that they had been different than they were, more like yourself, for example. If you take my meaning, Ms. Kitchener."

"I don't think I do."

Percival cleared his throat again, but he couldn't get rid of the creamy sound. "It's simply that we have always done our very best, using all the resources of what I think it fair to say is one of the most respected firms in the country, to preserve, protect and enhance the holdings which will now most probably come under your trusteeship," Percival said. "And it's my fondest hope that you will permit us to continue to serve in that capacity."

"How would I know I wasn't signing suicide notes?"

Pause. "I'm not sure I understand you, Ms. Kitchener."

Nina hung up.

She went into the bar. Matthias was holding the baby. Danny had Chick on his arm, to give the baby a good close look. The baby made a gurgling sound and started drooling.

"He's drooling because he's the sole heir to the Standish fortune," Nina said. It was all about breeding heirs. They couldn't let Happy be the end of the line. First they'd used Laura, then her; either because they wanted a boy, or wanted to increase the odds of a Standish surviving to propagating age.

"How much?" said Matthias.

"Millions and millions."

"He's going to need something to sign on all those deposit slips."

Nina sat at the bar. She stroked the baby's hair.

"What's wrong?" Matthias said.

"It's stolen money," Nina answered. "At least part of

it was. Maybe we should see about donating it. To a holocaust survivor fund or something. Certainly the Goldschmidts should get some."

"You're right," Matthias said. "Millions and millions. Who needs it?" He put his arm around her. The baby started to fuss. Nina held him, stroked his hair. For a while, she was aware of nothing but the feel of it. Then she remembered Dr. Berry's question: *How far are you prepared to go to have a baby?* Like him, she did not believe that human beings were merely manufacturers of sperm and eggs, but she had no precise answer. There was no rule of thumb. How far? Too far.

The baby's eyes closed. Nina looked up. Matthias was watching her. "How about 'Felix'?" she said.

"Terrible."

"Then what?"

"Give me a kiss," said Chick.

There's an epidemic with 27 million victims. And no visible symptoms.

It's an epidemic of people who can't read.

Believe it or not, 27 million Americans are functionally illiterate, about one adult in five.

The solution to this problem is you... when you join the fight against illiteracy. So call the Coalition for Literacy at toll-free **1-800-228-8813** and volunteer.

Volunteer Against Illiteracy. The only degree you need is a degree of caring.